THE BRYLCREEM BOY

Also by Bob Freeman
THE SOLDIER BOY
available from good bookshops or direct from the publisher

Bob Freeman

was

THE BRYLCREEM BOY

With a Foreword
by
Wing-Commander Patrick Barthropp
D.F.C. A.F.C. R.A.F. Ret'd

GEORGE MANN of MAIDSTONE

Bob Freeman

was

THE BRYLCREEM BOY

Copyright © Robert Bruce Freeman, 1992

Robert Bruce Freeman has asserted his right under Section 77
of the Copyright, Designs and Patents Act 1988 to be
identified as the author
of this book

First published 1996 by George Mann Books

ISBN 0 7041 0263 3

Printed and bound in
the United Kingdom by
Longdunn Press Ltd, Bristol
and published by
George Mann Books
in the English County of Kent

THE BRYLCREEM BOY

I owe my sincere gratitude to both Daphne Glazer and to Len Woodgate, the Keeper of the Aerospace Museum, Cosford, for their assistance and encouragement

Foreword

by

Wing Commander Patrick Barthropp, D.F.C., A.F.C. R.A.F. Ret'd.

As far as I am aware, I have never met Bob Freeman, either in or out of the Service. Had I been one of his Commanding Officers, I am sure I would have remembered for, in very many respects, his book shows him to be a man after my own heart.

We both are sworn enemies of o'erweening authority and stuffed shirts everywhere, which led to Bob's long-running battles with the dreaded Snowdrops, the R.A.F. Police, and in my own case, as a Squadron Leader, to being placed under arrest in the Sudan when I took a real live hippopotamus to a very toffee-nosed and upper-crust dance.

That was *after* the war, of course, round about the time that Bob joined the R.A.F. as a Boy Entrant. I had joined somewhat older, but hardly any wiser, almost ten years earlier, and I am sure I had the best of it—at least until I went in the bag. The wartime R.A.F. was mostly concerned with doing the business.

True, there were still some chairbound wonders of station commanders constipated with King's Regulations but, thank God, they were in the minority. The real enemy was the Luftwaffe, and the Nazi State which gave it its orders, not some poor sod of an erk who just happened to be improperly dressed.

And so, about 55 years ago, a small number of us were roaming around the skies of southern England in Spitfires and Hurricanes. Some of us in 1940 were under nineteen years of age and thus, at that time, were considered to be too young to vote, but not too young to die. Politicians pride themselves on being able to legislate such fine distinctions. Our pay was the modern equivalent of 68p a day. In 1996, there are about 390 of us left, half of whom will reach eighty this year and many of whom cannot afford to attend our annual re-union.

In my particular case, through a combination of over confidence and youthful bravado, I was blown out of the sky over France, at St. Omer, on May 17th 1942 by a gentleman called Karl Willius. When he visited me that evening he asked me if I had been treated properly. I told him that a somewhat itchy fingered German Army officer had relieved me of my silver cigarette case and gold half hunter watch—a 21st birthday present. The next day they were both returned with some lager beer, black bread and sausage. A note—*With the Compliments of the Luftwaffe*—was enclosed.

From St. Omer I was transferred to Stalag Luft III via Cologne and Frankfurt. In Cologne it was the night of the first 1000 bomber raid by the Royal Air Force and I was handcuffed, hand and foot, to a large iron seat in the main railway station whilst my guards took shelter. Perhaps they were protecting me from the civil population. Together with many others, this P.O.W. (Number 759) spent almost exactly three years behind barbed wire, where life was, to say the least, very boring, with a constant feeling of hunger and a total uncertainty as to the length of our sentence.

Towards the end of the war, more tons of bombs were being dropped on the Third Reich in one night than the British Isles received in the entire war. Prisoners of War had to be an expensive liability to the Germans. I am sure that the general concensus of opinion was that we would be disposed of before the end. 'Not to worry', we thought, 'because if we do get back our pockets will be bulging with our back pay.' But this, for us Britons, was not to be. Other nations treated their servicemen differently. Our Great

British Government made sure that a third of our pay was deducted at source because we were in enemy hands, and it has never to this day been returned. In spite of numerous attempts over the years to reverse this cruel and unjust decision, nothing at all has been done by the authorities and our small band does not have the financial resources to pursue this blatant theft through the courts.

I quote from a letter from Number 10 signed by Margaret Thatcher on September 13th 1984. 'Michael Heseltine, John Knott and Francis Pym have carried out an extensive inquiry into your case. I have concluded that there is no cause for the Government to re-open decisions by the wartime and post-war Governments. I believe we must concentrate our attention on the problems facing our present ex-servicemen rather than raking up the embers of the past.'

Sadly, there is no word in the entire Oxford Dictionary to adequately describe the treatment that all those horrendously ill-used wartime prisoners of the Japanese still receive from their representatives in the Mother of Parliaments. So far, all they can do is parade outside the House in their blazers and medals whilst the gentlemen within debate whether a tomato is a fruit or a vegetable.

It was fascinating to read in recent newspapers that an "artist" who arranged a pile of potatoes on a table received an Arts Grant of over £100,000, that the trials of the Maxwell brothers could cost the taxpayer over 23 millions, and that should next-of-kin of the Forgotten 14th Army who gave their lives for us in the Far East ever wish to have a photograph of their loved one's grave, they can have one—on prepayment of fifteen pounds

As has been remarked more than once recently,"'It's a funny old world."

And it was a funny old Air Force that Bob Freeman and I were part of after the Second World War, which gives me the best possible reason for recommending his book.

Virtually all of the events he describes *are* funny ... in one of two ways. Some are funny as in *very* peculiar. (If you'd never been in the Forces you could never conceive that grown men could really behave in this way.) Others are funny as in a great belly laugh. And it's all true!

I hope it has many thousands of readers. I am sure that it will.

Previously—

In 'The Soldier Boy' Bob Freeman told of growing up as a son of a cavalry trooper in India during those last golden years of the Raj before the outbreak of the Second World War.

Across the sub-continent, Britain was then at the pinnacle of its pomp, prestige and power. Life for the privileged hierarchy was one of luxury, leisure and pleasure. But it was not quite the same for the "lower orders", the ordinary British soldier in India or the cavalry trooper.

Through Bob Freeman's eyes another, and rarely glimpsed, view of British India unfolded. For 'The Soldier Boy' is a true story, not of palaces and princes, but of everyday life in Army cantonments and native bazaars. It is the story of one boy's life, different from most, because he possessed a truly independent spirit which his father could not tolerate. It simply had to be broken. Because a rebellious child was a father's disgrace in the eyes of his regiment, and the Regiment was his father's whole world.

When tragedy struck the family—back in England after the advent of war—"the uncontrollable" boy was packed off to Military Boarding School. There, not yet nine years of age, he was abandoned to loneliness, endless bullying and frequently harsh discipline as he fought his own battles with what he considered to be unjust authority: battles he could not possibly win.

This gripping, often funny and always unusual true story reached its conclusion when the shocking end to Bob Freeman's six years at Military School returned him, permanently scarred, to his family just after the end of war. A series of unsatisfactory short-lived jobs followed—until one day, on a recruiting poster in the Labour Exchange, he saw the picture of a Spitfire blazing a trail across the high blue bowl of the sky . . .

The story goes on—

CHAPTER 1

Pubic Hair

I should have known, the signs were there, but I was too blind to see. I should have walked straight out when the 'bolshy' officer had a go at me; I hadn't signed on, so I could have told him to go and get stuffed, but you don't think of these things until it's too late. I had two chances as well, that's the daft thing, but I just took his sarcasm and kept my mouth shut. I guess it was the influence of Mr and Mrs Bell, and the happy times spent working in their grocery shop; I'd nearly always been on best behaviour with them.

The first insult was at the interview with this pompous flying officer, who sat behind the table with the flight sergeant to his right. They had my exam paper in front of them.

'You call this an answer?' said the officer, 'or are you deliberately trying to be funny?'

'No, Sir,' I said, remembering my Dukies military school training.

'Then I'll ask you the question again, son.' The sergeant looked slightly amused, the officer annoyed.

'Right, son,' he said, 'if a ton of lead and a ton of feathers are dropped at the same time in a vacuum, which will hit the bottom first?'

A (long) pregnant pause ensued.

'Well, do you still think it's a daft question?' he said. That's what I had written on the paper, and it was a bloody daft question too.

'No, Sir,' I lied.

'Well, come on then, what's the answer?'

What bloody difference does it make? I thought, I just could not picture anything big enough to make a vacuum that could hold a ton of lead and a ton of feathers.

'Well, Sir,' I flannelled, putting on my innocent face, 'You can't get a ton of lead and a ton of feathers in a vacuum flask, not even the biggest.'

There is no answer to that, I remember thinking; he had to believe either in my innocence or my naïveté.

'All right son, we'll let it go for now, but in future explain yourself correctly; "daft question" is not an answer.'

So I missed the first chance of not going into the RAF.

In the afternoon, following my exam and the interview, it was mass medical inspection. About fifty hopeful boys were lined up in single file against the wall bars in the gymnasium.

'Right, drop your trousers, this line.' commanded a sergeant.

I was in the middle of the line, not a stitch on, and staring, like all the other boys, straight ahead. As the RAF medical officer drew nearer I could see out of the side of my eye what he was doing.

He had a leather-covered shiny swagger stick, about two feet long. He would stare a while at the boy's private parts and then poke at them with it. He would then say: 'TURN, BEND!' and look up their backsides. What the hell he expected to find up there, I don't know.

He got to me and I was ready for the poke. He took one long look and a step backwards. This surprise move had me worried.

Has it dropped off? I thought.

'You been shaving, son?'

Silly sod, I've never shaved in my life.

'No, Sir,' I said.

He bent down low and approached the forbidden area, concentrating hard. I could feel his breath on my 'dinga'.

'Amazing!' he exclaimed, 'Sergeant, come here,' whereupon the sergeant marched up.

'Sir?'

'What you think of that, Sergeant?'

By then I was getting a bit embarrassed and bored; I wasn't on bloody exhibition and my obstinate temper was rising. Dad was still outside with the other parents, they wouldn't leave until they knew whether we were accepted or not. I could pull up my trousers and say 'fuck you,' just like George, my best friend did, and walk out – but I didn't.

'His pubic hair hasn't started growing yet, sir,' said the sergeant, standing as stiff as a board.

'Most unusual,' commented the officer. 'Still – he's made up for it in other ways,' he said, putting his swagger stick under my dick and lifting it up. I could have hit him!

'Yes, Sir, he was first in the stores queue there,' quipped the sergeant.

Bastards, I thought, but it was too late, a quick look up my bum and he moved on.

Pubic hair, pubic hair, what the heck's he on about? I looked down at the boy's next to me. Good God, he had a mass of black curly hair but hardly anything else, just a little fisherman's hat buried in the jungle. I looked at mine: as bald as a badger but hanging like a sixpenny sausage. From that day on I knew I was different.

And so we were signed on, and I swore by almighty God that I would be faithful to His Majesty King George the Sixth. The oath concluded, '. . . and will observe and obey all orders of His Majesty, His Heirs and Successors, and of the AIR OFFICERS and OFFICERS set over me. So help me God.'

I didn't keep my promise for long, and God didn't help me either. Dad wished me well and left for home, no doubt somewhat relieved, and possibly hoping that eight years in the RAF would make something of me.

Victor, my elder brother, had joined the Army Physical Training Corps the previous week, so dear Mother had two fewer to feed and look after. Victor was to progress rapidly over the years, rising gradually through the ranks and becoming quite an athlete. He made his name and mark on the Army with innovative and advanced schemes at various stages in his career.

The first such scheme to put the Army spotlight on him was when he was in charge of Colchester Army Prison. The prison was built in a wooded area and two rows of double-stacked thick barbed wire made up the perimeter fences. Dogs patrolled between the two rows of wire. No prisoner, during his detention period, ever got outside that wire. That is, until Victor Freeman arrived.

He introduced a scheme that took prisoners outside the wire; they cut down trees and built a tough assault course. The prisoners could then vent their pent-up feelings of hatred and venom on the assault course under guard, and this reduced the tensions created by caging men up for hours on end. A television programme was made of this novel approach and Vic started to gain a reputation.

I could have done with his help at this time, as I was locked in my RAF prison cell.

Vic went on to greater things and some years later was in charge of the Army Physical Training Team at Olympia. That was the year he'd had all his men hanging from the roof at Olympia, one man in each square of a rope trellis as they completed their synchronised display.

There are certainly many more attainments that Vic achieved of which I am not fully aware, but I know he was Army champion at many sports, and I watched his muscles ripple many times as he threw the discus and javelin, or put the shot. Boxing and sword fencing, he did them all, and after travelling the world he retired from the army as Lieutenant Colonel V.K. Freeman.

My career was not to be as illustrious. How could two brothers be so different?

That first cold October night we bedded down in iron-framed beds in Nissen huts. The pale moonlight cut into the grey gloom of the room as I lay there, hands behind my head, listening to the sniffles and sobs of the homesick. I felt for the boys and their loneliness. I knew what they were going through; I'd been there – years before – while they were tucked up at home. It's one thing to get excited about the romance and glamour of joining the RAF when you're at home in familiar surroundings, with parents and security. At that age you can't see or recognise the realities of the life: cold Nissen huts, stone floors, twenty-four iron beds in a row, no privacy, impersonal and power-mad NCOs and no mother or father to run to. The shock to the system that first night soon dispels the romance and excitement, and the first six weeks is the testing time.

Oh, yes, I knew what these boys felt like as they sobbed away, and I felt sorry for them. Funny though, I thought, there's a chap over there, opposite side of the room to me, who isn't crying. Like me, he just lies there, hands behind his head, gazing at the curved roof.

Boys of fifteen and sixteen in 1947 had seen the romance, wonder and heroism of the 'boys in blue' during the war. Every Pathé newsreel showed their bravery and daring. It was no wonder this age group applied in droves to join up when it was decided to reinstate a programme of 'boy entrants'.

We were the second entry or batch since the scheme started. Our destination, the very next day, was to an RAF training establishment at Locking, Weston-super-Mare, two miles from Weston and the sea, along the A371 road. We were destined to spend eighteen months there, learning a trade and being trained to become disciplined and useful airmen.

I lay there, that first night, wondering what on earth I was doing there.

Everything was coming back now of my five years in the Duke of York's Royal Military School. The harsh discipline, the strict routines, the parades and inspections, the ridiculous orders: 'Blacken those boot soles again – they're filthy,' as some demented sod knocked over your beautifully polished and cared-for boots. I must be mad – must have had a brainstorm.

I wasn't homesick, not at nearly sixteen and what I'd been through, but I was frightened and apprehensive. The 'sobbers' of course had just left the nest for the first time, many of them from small families. For fifteen or sixteen years they had been kissed, cuddled and waited on hand and foot. They might be sobbing now, but 'Wait till we get started,' I thought. 'Tomorrow will be the first day of their great awakening.'

CHAPTER 2

You'll be Sorry

The train lurched and squealed to a stop, doors banged open against the carriages and bodies hurried in all directions as though it were the last day on earth. The station announcer's voice was echoing and vibrating in its own unintelligible language, making me wonder why they ever bothered. The fresh seaside air, sharp and cold on this late October evening, cleared our heads more quickly than a sniff of smelling salts. The waifs and strays of new recruits herded together for protection and for whatever feeling of security that could be squeezed from an unknown, slightly frightened and nervous bunch of mother's sons.

The sign said Weston-super-Mare and the young men's nervous eyes flicked in all directions trying to take in the focal point of their lives for the next eighteen months. The place where they would arrive sadly and leave happily.

'Right lads, are we all here?' asked the affable corporal who, with his sergeant, had the 'cushy' job of delivering us to our destiny at RAF Locking, some two miles out of town. No answer came; how were we to know if we were all there? There must have been nearly fifty of us that had made the train journey from RAF North Weald. Taking no answer as an affirmative, he continued.

'Follow me, keep close; there are two lorries in the car park waiting to take us to the camp,' and off the crocodile went, the nervous ones with hurried steps, eyes pinned to the corporal's back; a few others, ambling along, taking in the sights like veteran holiday makers. We packed into the back of the three-ton Bedford lorries and the diesel fumes transported me back to India, bazaars and sunshine.

So far everything had been very civilized. The corporal and the sergeant that had accompanied us on the train journey had been very laid back, even bringing us all tea and sandwiches, no doubt paid for by the RAF. No ridiculous shouting or bawling, no insults, and I was really looking forward to learning my trade and being in a crowd again.

The lorry lurched to a halt and brought me back from India and the bazaar. My first sight of the guardroom, but not my last.

The corporal of military police, erect in creaseless uniform, boot toecaps glinting like mirrors, white-topped peaked cap, and oozing officialdom and power, was attempting to talk on level terms with our sergeant, while glancing at us with threats in his eyes and promises of things to come.

'Take them to the canteen, Sergeant. You will be met there by the orderly sergeant, he'll take them off your hands,' he said with a grin, no doubt anticipating his future pleasure in 'assisting' us to become smart, obedient and efficient airmen.

The lorry moved off and I glanced at the traffic on the main road, and the woman pedalling her bicycle towards her family, her fire and her cosy home. I said goodbye to the world that I had only known for fourteen months and re-entered my military world as the barrier clanged down.

'Hut 6b, Corporal Jevons,' said the orderly sergeant in the first authoritative military voice we'd heard.

It came as a bit of a shock to the system, and eyes opened a bit wider with fear as we stood in half-light outside the canteen.

'The following must step forward and go over there to Corporal Jevons who will take you to your 'billet' and be in charge of you from now on.'

We looked towards Corporal Jevons, whom we could hardly make out in the gloom; his big frame was traced against the cookhouse wall but his face was a black blob.

'Rudolph, Harrison, Trotter, Kettley, Freeman,' and so it went on until twenty-four of us stood in front of Corporal Jevons.

We had already attempted to pick at an apology of a warmed-up meal, but the lumps, including the black eyes in the mashed potato and the 'bullet' peas, remained on the plate in their sea of greasy congealing gravy, as did the tough skins and gristly lumps of the two sausages. The tea had a funny taste: the taste we were going to have to get used to or starve. Bromide was supposed to suppress the sex urge, but I don't think it ever did.

'Form up in two files,' ordered the corporal.

Everybody then seemed to go for a walk – or were they dancing? The twenty-four seemed to be a hundred and four as they turned, talked, weaved, walked and generally attempted to do what they didn't know what they were doing.

'Two lines then, you silly buggers,' and still it went on. 'Stand still, stand still,' he commanded. 'I got a right bloody lot 'ere by the look of it, Sergeant.'

'You two, stand here, that's it, one behind the other; now, the rest of you stand shoulder to shoulder, in line with these two, and hurry up about it, else it'll be reveille before you get to bed.'

'At last,' breathed the corporal. 'Now we're going to turn to the left, that's that way,' he said sarcastically, pointing in the dark. 'Left turn,' whereupon we turned, over a period of a few seconds – 'Quick march!'

The crocodile ambled forward, across the camp road and along a path, skirting the drill square to the left, where pools of light were reflected on the shiny tarmac at ten-yard intervals. Rows of wooden huts stood on two-foot stilts just off the path to the right of the crocodile. Airmen were coming and going in ones and twos but stepped aside when they saw us. Much excellent advice was proffered from the dark to the attentive and sharp ears of the civilian crocodile. 'You'll be sorry,' was the common cry, but others were more specific. 'Poor bastards, I should fuck off now if I were you.'

We came to our hut, Hut 6b, our billet, our home, refuge from the cold October night and the worldly advice of 'those who know'.

The long cold interior was split down the middle by a line of naked silver light bulbs, hanging by their twisted threads below the timber cross-beams which supported the flattened wooden apex roof. The round black glistening coke stove in the centre of the hut looked at its twin, shining back at it from the mirror of brown linoleum. Two collapsible wooden-top tables, scrubbed ghostly white, were positioned either side of the stove, with two bottom-wrinkling slatted forms either side. Twelve brown blanketed oblongs, perfectly in line, and three feet apart, camouflaged the black iron frames and steel wire of the beds down each side of the billet. A six-foot-high locker stood to attention at the righthand side of each bed. Nothing was out of place. Everything was perfectly square and in line.

'Get on those felt pads; don't ever let me see your boots touch the floor,' said Jevons. We obeyed and took our first lessons at ice-skating on the holier than holy linoleum floor. Fate smiled on me for once as I was allocated a corner bed; at least, I thought, I'd get a little privacy.

'My room is at the end of the billet, through that bottom door,' said the corporal, 'I shall be back at ten o'clock for lights out, not nine fifty-nine or ten-o-one, ten o'clock sharp. That gives you one hour for 'ablutions' and getting your 'eads on them pillas. No talking after lights out, get to sleep, you'll need your energy tomorrow,' and he left.

The sheep sat in amazement, trying to absorb the newness and strangeness of it all. A few more mature sheep started to investigate their lockers and unpack their few belongings.

'What's "ablutions" mean?' asked a weedy kid on the bed next to mine.

'Lavatories and sinks, where you wash or have a pee,' I answered.

I waltzed the full length of the hut, towel and soap, packed by Mother, in my hand, and let myself out of the bottom door. Passing through, I noticed the corporal's door to the right and then stepped into a covered corridor. The corridor joined up, in a long dim-lit tunnel, all the other huts in the row. Vested airmen, with towels round their necks, some of them in blue and white striped pyjama bottoms, were going to and fro in the passage. Two others from my lot were behind me.

'Which way da ya think?' asked a true Scot behind me.

'Down there, I can see where they're coming out,' I said as I led the way.

A row of fifteen washbasins, mirrors above, lined the full length of the wall to the right. A communal urinal trough ran down the left wall. Cubicle toilets, doors ajar and with six-foot-high partitions between them were next to a ten-foot-square communal shower. Three cubicles held baths on legs, but the six-foot-high composite partition offered only limited privacy.

'Saw you on the train,' said the Scotsman, as he copied me in making a plug for the sink from toilet paper. Not a real plug in sight of the row of basins.

'Yeah, I saw you, and I saw you last night at North Weald. You weren't homesick like the rest, you were lying back staring at the ceiling.'

'So wuz you,' he said, and we clicked.

Jim Moore, shortly to be nicknamed 'Rudy' because of his handsomeness and facial resemblance to Rudolf Valentino, came from Glasgow's Gorbals. One of nine children, and with a father who liked more than a drop of the hard stuff, Rudy had seen the rough side of life. Barrel-chested, thick-set and compact, his body didn't seem to fit with his handsome face and his jet black long hair, greased and combed straight back. He had thick black eyebrows and round smiling brown eyes, and a squarish jaw. He stood five feet nine, an inch below me; he looked powerful but unthreatening. Rudy could smile, but there was still a hardness in his eyes, and a set to his jaw that warned he'd been on the wrong side of the track, he'd suffered and seen suffering; and that made him stand out in our crowd of softies.

At ten o'clock the lights went out and silence came in, each person wrapped in his own private thoughts. Silence within but not without, as the sound of 'Swannee River' drifted on the night air. White diagonals of light found their way from path-lighting through dirt-free window panes, and streaked onto floor and bed alike. Propped on my elbow I could see neighbouring huts lit up like Christmas trees, occupants still dressed and engaged in talk or horseplay. We, the new ones, had to go to bed early, it seemed.

The excitement of being back in a crowd, the opportunities of fellowship, sport, a trade, even the thrill of aeroplanes, had to be weighed against the military discipline, loss of identity, living by numbers, obedience without question and the hardest pill of all, subservience. I lay there letting my thoughts flow from happy to apprehensive, to scared, to happy; my brain was too active for sleep.

The sleepers are stirring, uneasy and restless. Some are moaning or talking to their dreams. They twist and turn, to the accompanying and twangling music of stretched wire across steel frames, as strange bodies mould strange thin, hard mattresses to new shapes. A half-asleep stumbling form, shirt-tail flapping, wobbles his way down the hut looking for relief of his weak nervous bladder, and forgetting to waltz on his pads. A plaintive cry here and passing of wind there, as the sheep huddle in their pen, apprehensive and unsure. The buffeting October wind, in sympathy with the mood, is clapped by the loose roof asphalt and, as I wonder 'why'? I join the sheep.

'Feet on the floor!' screams the voice, 'Move it, feet on the floor, parade outside the hut in fifteen minutes.'

I wake, startled as the rest. Has this man gone mad, is the world coming to an end? I look over my rough blankets and down the hut. The gibbering corporal, fully dressed and hatted, strides on our polished floor in his hobnailed boots, shouting and waving his arms like a demented demon. Bodies are not moving quickly enough for him, and feet are not touching the floor. Immediate response is what he wants and he is not getting it. He takes a handful of mattress and yanks upwards. A half-awake body flies through the air and slides on the ice; suddenly the body is fully awake. The peering sleepy eyes of those still in the warm pit suddenly come alive and warm feet kiss cold linoleum. The first race is on as we dash for a quick wash. Alas, all the basins are in use. I wash from a bath trap, others follow suit. Dressed, bed folded as per Dukies, bed space swept around, I'm ready to go outside.

'Who told you to do it that way?' said loudmouth Kettley from across the room.

'Nobody,' I said.

'Well, don't be fucking clever then,' he retorted.

A few others copied my example, most left their beds as they were.

Kettley had already made his presence known to most of the intake. He always had a lot to say and every other word was a four-letter swearword. Cocky, brash, big-headed and confident, Kettley was to become disliked by most of the hut for his sarcasm and nosey interference. He craved to be the centre of attention, the hard man, the knowall. He hailed from Brixton in London, was well-built but not as compact as Rudy. His problem in life was his pock-marked face with red blotches everywhere. Maybe his unfortunate appearance had given birth to his repulsive character, I thought.

After a passable breakfast and a few more well-chosen comments from the old sweats, we shuffled back to 6b and were instructed on hut rostering, bed make-up, kit layout and so on. The hut duty roster defined twenty tasks that were to be performed daily by individuals listed. These ranged from blacking the coke stove to changing the water in the two fire buckets. Cleaner water puts out a fire quicker, I thought. Communal tasks like floor polishing with great dollops of pink Mansion polish from five-gallon containers were carried out daily, although the floor looked virginal. Every man was responsible for his own space and had to move his bed and locker daily for polishing underneath.

Pushing brooms, whose heads were covered in rags from the stores, became a way of life as we sang like Paul Robeson 'I ee I oh-o-o,' and made a pleasure from a toil.

'Who taught you to make your bed like that?' asked the corporal of 'Weedy', my skinny neighbour.

'I copied 'im, Corporal,' replied the frightened Weedy.

'And who showed you, lad?' the corporal asked.

'My previous boarding school, Corporal.'

'What's your name?'

'Freeman, Corporal.'

'Well, you're nearly right,' he said, 'The mattress is folded into three equal lengths, then flattened, and then blankets and sheets folded neatly, to regulation size, and placed blanket, sheet, blanket, sheet, blanket, all edges perfectly square, like this one here,' he said, pointing at my bedding.

'Right, get to it.'

I felt a bit of a fool and wished I hadn't done it now. The last thing I wanted was to be noticed, picked out of the crowd.

Good news, the news we had been waiting for. Full kit would be issued to us after lunch. We were keen to discard the civvies that made us so obviously new recruits, and invited so much unsolicited comment from 'those who know'. We wanted to disappear in the sea of blue, we wanted to be airmen, we wanted to learn, we wanted to be proud, we wanted to belong.

'Form a single file and move down the counter when you're given your kit,' said Jevons.

The long counter seemed to stretch for half a mile. A row of bored stores assistants were equally spaced behind the counter and surveyed the motley crew with professional eyes, sizing us before we ever reached them. Behind the assistants were more assistants ready to pounce at the word of command and rob the ten-foot-high layered shelves of their livelihood.

We then 'walked the plank' as a hail of clothing was thrown, pushed or dropped on us by the uninterested assistants. At each barrage they sang out this biblical tune:

'Shirts, three of; socks, four pairs of; housewife, one of; plimsolls, one pair, size eight; shorts PT, two pairs; vests, three of,' and so it went on. An octopus would have had difficulty coping with the barrage. 'Boots – size eight, two pairs': at least the assistant had the sense to drape them round my neck, but still it went on. 'Webbing back pack, one of; water bottle, one of; mess tin, one of; webbing belt, one of; webbing harness, one set.'

By then things were being dropped, picked up and dropped again. Assistants began to smile, they were getting job satisfaction.

'Kitbags, one of; that's your lot, sign here, right – outside.' Kitbags last, I couldn't believe it, surely there was one brain somewhere in the stores fraternity but that was probably asking too much. Where would the job satisfaction be if the kitbag came first?

We staggered, steered and ached our way back to 6b with a few helpful comments *en route*. Never mind, we'd soon be part of it all. I was so excited as I dunked my lovely new possessions on my bed. I'd never had so many new clothes. Battledress for working and a smashing best blue jacket and trousers for ceremonials and walking out. Lovely blue shirts with six separate collars, and black ties.

To a man we all shed our skins and grew new ones. In five minutes of ribald comedy and comment we lost our identities and the embryo of a squad began to take shape.

Like most of the others, my uniform fitted where it touched. But for the canvas braces, my too-long trousers would have been on the floor, and at least five inches needed to come off the waist. The first impression was the sheer weight of the clothes on the body plus the itchiness. The stiff, bargelike boots with a thousand metal studs and steel heelcaps guaranteed the upright position in a force ten gale. We looked at each other in disbelief. Rudy was trying to perch his side hat on his mass of hair without success.

'Yon's too small,' he shouted across to me.

'I'll swop ya,' said Weedy, whose cap swallowed up most of his birdlike face.

'Don't stand there looking at your pimply faces in them mirrors, on parade, move!' said the genie corporal, appearing from nowhere, and we glided out of the hut.

'Tomorrow we become part of the camp routine,' announced Jevons. 'PT at seven o'clock on the square, seven o'clock, mind, anyone who lets my flight down will wish he had never been born. Seven thirty change into battledress and straight to breakfast. Eight thirty is what I am waiting for, on the square prompt, "square bashing", you've heard about square bashing, haven't you?' he hollered. 'Well, I'm your drill instructor, you've got me, you lucky lads, for six weeks, some of you might not last that long by the look of you. My job is to make men out of boys, got it?'

He was obviously enjoying himself and the power he held over us. I glanced at one or two of the others and could see fear and trepidation in their eyes. We'd thought we were going to learn a trade, not be soldiers.

'At eleven thirty, if you're still with us, back to your billet for daily roster and cleaning. Lunch twelve thirty, and back on the square, "my lucky lads" at two o'clock sharp.'

Jevons was really beginning to enjoy himself.

'When you come orf at four thirty – don't think for a minute you've finished, you've not back in Civvy Street, no nine to five 'ere. As junior flight you provide the legs and hands for essential work like fire picket, washer-uppers in the cookhouse and mess, and cleaners general. Now, I have to pick these fine fellows for extra duties, so watch your step.'

The discourse was over.

Corporal Jevons had seen war service and his one ribbon was worn with pride. At thirty-three years old with eight years service, he'd been about a bit, but the two years as a drill instructor had nurtured the worst side of human nature. He was a big man, broad of shoulder, and had a pear-shaped face. He shaved so close that his skin had a sheen on it as though he had coated it with clear varnish. He was smart to the nth degree and, like all the other drill instructors, he was determined to have the best 'flight' and make a name for himself, even if it meant putting the fear of God in the mothers' sons of Hut 6b.

'Left turn, quick march' and off we ambled in our ill-fitting uniforms and ton-heavy boots.

Sidecaps were falling off left and right, heavy stiff leather was chafing above the ankles, those behind were treading on the boot-backs of those in front, and Corporal Jevons was frothing at the mouth as he interpreted our birth certificates and we were informed that our mothers didn't know our fathers. I had to smile, it was funny, standard textbook stuff. I'd heard it all before.

'Flight – halt, you miserable bastards, thick as a ton of shit, you're a bloody disgrace to your uniforms,' he informed us.

'Get inside, the first four,' he shouted, pointing at a hut door with the word 'barber' on it. He followed us in, took a chair, and lit a cigarette.

''Nother batch, Jeff, twenty-four of 'em, sorry I'm late, can you do 'em by four-thirty?'

Jeff took a swift look at the ancient wall clock with no glass.

'No problem,' he replied. 'Get in the chair, lad,' he said to little Weedy.

Fifty-nine minutes to trim twenty-four people, never in your life, I thought.

At four twenty-four Jevons called us to attention and we marched back to Hut 6b. New white necks shivered in goose pimples and blinked at the cold light of an October dusk. The electric razor, in perfect rhythm of half a second a stroke, had travelled from neck to crown. Six to eight chops of the scissors to reduce the crown to an inch in length and 'next one'.

Twenty-four Stan Laurels proceeded to amble in shock, sidehats far too big and spread for warmth. We were dispirited, identical persons and fear could be felt through the silence as we trudged back to our new home.

'You, you and you,' said Jevons, tapping me, Weedy and Blondie Harrison on the shoulder, 'Cookhouse fatigues, report to the cookhouse at six o'clock.' He picked out more 'volunteers' for sergeants' mess and officers' mess duties. Fatigues became a regular extra until the next intake in six weeks time.

Fatigues are designed to dull the spirit, to prove one's unimportance, to imbue obedient subservience.

We reported as ordered, six o'clock sharp, to the back of the cookhouse.

The dingy bulbs, hanging on greasy flexes, threw dark patches around the vast stainless steel boiling coppers, ovens and sinks. The dull red stone-tiled floor was black with dirt and there were food morsels around the edges of tablelegs and equipment, exemplifying the slovenly incompetence and attitudes of those that cook and serve for their 'soldiering'.

We crept in against a wall of stale stench, the product of years of rotting food and uninterested fatigue cleaners. An obese, beer-bellied corporal in dirty vest, greasy blood-stained apron, and with a half-full beer bottle in his right hand, emerged from a lighted office and surveyed the three 'Laurels'.

'Christ, that the best they can do? You'll be here all night by the look of you,' he grunted. 'You two,' – Weedy and me – 'get washing up,' and he pointed to a Himalayan Mountain Range of haphazardly stacked crockery, cutlery and leftover food, all piled precariously around two kitchen walls. 'You,' he said to Blondie, 'sweep and wash the floor and counters!' He took a swig from his bottle and disappeared back into his den.

We dipped into a sink of tepid water, through a layer of floating grease and attempted to wash four hundred plates and mugs. Weedy attempted to dry some on greasy cold cloths. For three hours we scaled the mountain and, with Blondie's help, as he had by now finished the floor and servery, Everest and the Himalayas were reshaped, repositioned and a little cleaner. A stomach-turning, nauseating three hours was the prelude to repeat performances in the next few weeks. The corporal, now alcoholically happy, invited us to make ourselves a 'cuppa' and a bullybeef sandwich.

We returned to Hut 6b with shrivelled fingers, aching backs and my first wish anyway, that I hadn't joined, but maybe it was just a tired man's passing thought. With half an hour to lights-out we washed and fell into bed. Sleep came easily.

CHAPTER 3

Identical Men

A week later and I had wished again, more than once, that I hadn't joined. A week of daily PT, square bashing and then, completely drained of energy and willpower, fatigues, had taken its toll on Flight 6b. We were now five men short, all in the sickbay. Three had managed to walk there, two had been carried in. I'd had five years square-bashing in the Dukies, admittedly only an hour or maybe two a day; I'd watched soldiers being drilled all my young life, but at regular non-training bases. This was a different world. Of course a training centre for new recruits would naturally be more intense and severe than an active unit, but this was cruelty and debasement at its worst.

Paraded in our ill-fitting uniforms and new stiff boots, having already been put through our paces by muscled energetic PT instructors, our bodies and our minds were expected to perform to continuous and new (to the others, not to me) commands, until four thirty at night. While our bodies protested in every joint and our skin peeled off in various places, we were insulted, ridiculed and provoked, for the sole enjoyment and gratification of the drill instructors.

There is a glitter in their eyes as we pant for breath. Cold October it may be, but sweaty armpits, backs, crutches and feet are common to us all, as are pain and despair. I am desperate to try to help my mates, because Flight 6b are my mates. Comradeship and a sense of belonging is growing in Flight 6b. These mother's sons, with possibly three exceptions, are softies, and the pace of change will either make or break them. Five have already gone down the tube and may have to be put back to the next entry.

That first night after square-bashing the survivors collapsed on their beds, fully clothed and booted; most had no energy or willpower even to go to the cookhouse for tea. Kettley, Rudy and I stood the pace best. We fetched them tea and 'wads' from the NAAFI, took off their boots and tried to console them.

'Can't stand any bloody more,' said Weedy. 'I'll die tomorrow, I'm sure I will.'

'Bloody weakling, that's what you are,' said Kettley, with not a spark of compassion in him.

'Shut your mouth and leave him alone,' I said, annoyed at his selfish attitude.

'Are you going to shut it for me?' he asked, raising himself to full height in front of me. He was broader than me and was spoiling for a fight. His pockmarked face grinned down at me as I sat on Weedy's bed. He'd previously tried to provoke me and was out to impress his toughness on the rest of the flight.

'Fuck off and leave him alone,' said Rudy, equally as broad as the glaring Kettley.

'I don't need your help,' I said ungratefully, but Kettley had moved off. I continued to talk to Weedy as we sipped our tea and munched our Eccles cakes.

'Try to get in the rear rank,' I advised, 'Jevons can't see you so well there; and relax your body more, don't stay tense all day, think of nice things when we have to stand in set positions for a long time. Remember, it won't last forever. Trade training in a few weeks. Fight the bastard, don't give in,' and so my advice went on.

Poor Weedy, always full of cold and sniffles, with a permanent dewdrop on the end of his nose. Whenever he moved, a wave of eucalyptus was released on the air. He followed me around like a lost sheep, and from that first week I felt responsible for him.

If the first day was a nightmare, it was almost an unexpected one for the twenty-odd innocents, but the following days were anticipated nightmares which seemed even worse. Jevons was bad enough, but when on the Thursday we were handed over to Sergeant Thomas we knew we were in trouble.

Sergeant Thomas was a huge man. His six-foot two-inch frame was packed with muscle. He was immaculately turned out from his perfectly fitting battledress jacket and beautifully creased and 'weighed' trousers to his blancoed 'spats', and mirror-bright boots. Arrogance sparked from his butcher's eyes which were set wide apart in his flat, fryingpan face. His bulbous clown's nose gave the lie to his outlook on life. The black shiny peak of his cap was moulded to the curve of his forehead and accentuated the fierceness of his eyes. His wide cruel mouth sliced his face in two and turned upwards on one side, giving him a permanent sneer. With his swagger stick held under his right armpit he exuded authority, confidence and power, A frightening sight at a distance; a terrifying sight close to.

Thomas had been drilling the squad next to us for the previous three days and we had shuddered at his tormenting, as he picked on one after another to satisfy his inane pleasure. He had the ability to spot a weakling, and play with him, cat with a mouse, catching him, letting him go and, once the mouse breathed a sigh of relief, catching him again until the recruit was reduced to a slobbering heap.

We had marched in threes the length and breadth of the parade ground while Thomas warmed-up for his daily enjoyment.

'You apologies for bloody airmen, you sons of bitches, you're a bloody disgrace!' he yelled. 'Get those arms up, get in line shortarse, yes, you, shortarse! Get in bloody line I tell you. Fli-iht-hult!'

We stood breathless, waiting for the next insult.

'Flight, left-turn, Christ, that's like a sack of potatoes falling downstairs, I want to hear one crack as right heel hits left heel and the square, wake up you sleepy bastards, LE-EFT-TURN! You shower, you misfits, if I had my way I'd shoot the fucking lot of you. Flight, stand-dat-ease.'

We breathed easier but not for long. It was cabaret time.

'You, shortarse, what's your name?' he asked Weedy who, as advised, was hiding in the rear rank. Some advice, I thought, Thomas had spotted him within ten minutes.

'610 Trotter, Sergeant,' replied Weedy, coming to attention.

'When I speak to you, son, you come to attention, march to the front of the flight and then answer, got it?'

'Yes, Sergeant,' replied the nervous Weedy, staying put.

'Yes, Sergeant, yes Sergeant, you stupid little pillock, get out here.'

Weedy marched to the front of the flight and stood too rigidly to attention, his narrow shoulders hunched-up round his neck, and one could feel the fear in him. Thomas approached him slowly and deliberately, with a leering grin, easy little mouse, funtime is here.

We stood and watched, we had no choice; for this or a hundred other occasions we had to watch. Half of Thomas's pleasure was from making us watch as he debased his prisoner. Jevons had done the same daily; it was a way of life to drill instructors. My turn hadn't come yet, but half the others had been degraded and demoralised.

'Trotter, you're a scruffy bastard!' he barked into Weedy's ear. 'You're a runtarse, a shithouse, a bloody nothing!' he roared.

Weedy was squirming and hunched-up. Ten days ago he'd been in his mother's arms, now he was on another planet and part of an unbelievable nightmare.

'Look at me!' Thomas yelled, now oblivious to all the other flights drilling on the square; oblivious to all the other shouted commands, he was in a world of his own, doing what he liked to do best and savouring every minute. 'Look at me, look me in the eye you fucking midget of an airman!'

Weedy tried to look at him, and from the front rank I could see tears running down his hollow white cheeks. We stood pitying.

'Can't look me in the eye – gutless – weak as gnats' piss!' he roared. 'Trotter eh, Trotter, what a fucking moniker, from the PIG family are you? Ha, ha, ha!' and he looked at us. 'That's a joke, Trotter's a pig, now laugh!' he bawled at us.

Not a sound came from the pitying flight. Thomas was not amused.

'That was funny, Trotter's from the pig family, don't you think that was funny?' he bawled, taking a pace towards me and looking me straight in the eye.

I came smartly to attention. Paused, took two paces forward, halted with a high lift of my right knee, a foot from him and said sharply:

'No, Sergeant.'

He was dumbstruck. His bottom jaw dropped and his eyes expanded; there was a (long) pregnant pause while his brain struggled to comprehend the unexpected. I could feel the flight behind me rise up stiffly in solidarity. I kept looking at Sergeant Thomas, awaiting the explosion. He recovered himself and a slow smile crept over his face. He let his breath out slowly as he said:

'We always get one, one in every intake, I wondered where he was and now I've found you, hiding in Jevons's flight,' he grinned. 'So you don't think my joke is funny, eh?' he stated, pausing for effect, with veiled threat, in the hope I'd change my mind.

'No, Sergeant, I thought it was an insult,' I replied.

I had gone too far, I knew that as soon as I said it. His face went scarlet and his cheeks puffed out; his eyes stared at me in disbelief. A recruit answering back: unheard of.

'An insult, a fuckin' insult, who the hell asked you for an opinion?' he raved. 'Airmen don't 'ave opinions, airmen don't speak until they're spoken to, airmen are shit, when I say shit you jump on the shovel!'

He was now becoming demented and his tongue-lashing was not having the desired effect, I was not cringing and quaking in my boots but staring back at him, completely upright at attention.

'A hard case, a bolshie, I eat bastards like you for breakfast. What's your name, cheeky bastard?' he asked.

'683 Freeman, Sergeant.'

'Freeman eh, Freeman, a right fucking gem, well you've met your match, Freeman, I've got you for five more weeks and before then I'll break your fuckin' heart.'

He looked at the flight and noticed Weedy, still standing to attention out front.

'Get back in the ranks, shortarse,' he commanded. I stood where I was.

'Flight, atten-shon,' he ordered, 'Now smartarse Freeman will demonstrate the correct drill movements, watch carefully,' and he stood them at ease again.

'Freeman, left turn, quick march, about turn, right turn, left turn, about turn, halt, about turn, quick march, halt, quick march, about turn, halt!'

He kept this up for fully ten minutes and I enjoyed every minute as he got quicker and quicker in his commands, and more and more annoyed, as he couldn't fault my performance. I knew my mates would be enjoying the battle if, like Sergeant Thomas, somewhat amazed at my ability after only three days of square bashing. I was thinking of my friends in the Dukies and how proud they would be to see me now. Thomas was completely mystified and I, for one, wasn't going to help him.

'You done some marching before, cleverarse Freeman, haven't you?'

'A little bit, Sergeant.'

'A little bit, a little bit, you're a lying bastard, where did you learn to drill?' he wanted to know.

'My father's in the Army all his life; I followed the band.'

'Lies, all bloody lies, I'll find out about you, you smartarsed bastard, now get back in the ranks,' and so my first of many brushes with Sergeant Thomas began.

My hut mates now realised I'd had quite a different life so far to any of them, and as we flopped boneless on our beds there was some amusement and chuckling amongst the lads as David 'Taffy' Jones said:

'You showed him, boyo, he'll not forget you; we did enjoy that show, didn't we lads?'

We were now jelling together as a team, helping and depending on one another.

'You made an enemy there, Bob,' said Rudy, 'You'll have to watch your step, he's a hard bastard. Where did you learn to drill like that?'

'I'll tell you sometime, Rudy,' I replied. 'Let's get washed and go to tea early, I'm on fire picket tonight.'

That first week of PT, square bashing and fatigues left little time for anything else. The precious time that we did have was hardly sufficient to carry out the necessary tasks required of new recruits. Every minute was occupied trying to catch up. Each garment: socks, shirts, vest, pants, towels, and so on, required a regulation-sized tape to be neatly sewn in exactly the prescribed spot, displaying our RAF number. For socks, the tape had to be sewn on the inside of the back of the sock exactly one inch from top of sock to top of tape. When folded correctly and displayed on one's stretched out mattress for 'kit-inspection' the tapes, showing one's number, were clearly visible, in line and neat. All clothes had to be numbered and other items of equipment marked; for instance, the boot brushes, scraped pure white with a razor blade prior to the morning of inspection, had the RAF number of the owner black-inked along its rim. The 'housewife', the name given to a white cloth purse, contained needles and cottons for this task, and for altering our clothes, replacing buttons and darning our socks. We had to become quite proficient with needle and thread in a very short time.

This was only a small part of the 'bullshit' that pervaded military training camps in 1947. It continued with regular blancoing of all webbing equipment. This messy task, applying blue blanco to backpacks, sidepacks, harness, belt and so on, was usually carried out in the toilets, on lashings of newspaper spread on the floor. A toothbrush was the preferred instrument of application, and the technique was to keep blanco clear of the fitted-in brass buckles and attachments. Polishing the brass attachments required a patient technique or one ruined the blancoed surface. Polishing brand new buttons and badges presented problems of acceptance by the bullying corporals or sergeants.

'You haven't touched that, you lying bastard,' was the all too common retort, 'Report to me at eight o'clock tonight and I want to see your arse shine in it.'

Boots, two pairs, brand new, with pimply black leather all over, even the toecaps. From the first day, the NCO drill instructors expected toe caps to shine like deep mirrors. NCOs were so stupid, common sense and logic never entered their heads. No quarter was given, no understanding of the difficulties of time, naïveté or ignorance of their new chargelings. No encouragement, little guidance, no praise.

After the first few days, most of the flight had had 'bollockings' galore and would be working after lights out, in the dark, using the path light coming through the window panes to try to catch up on the bullshit requirement.

Blondie was the first to notice that my kit was smarter and my boot toes shinier than the rest.

'Show us how you did your boots,' he said, that first weekend we were off.

'Give me your best boots, Weedy,' I said, and he was overjoyed. His joy soon turned to fright when, having coated one toecap with a good layer of Cherry Blossom black, I struck a match and played the flame over the toecap surface whilst holding the boot upside down.

'Christ, don't burn 'em, you'll ruin 'em,' said fearful Weedy. Most of the others in the hut had now been drawn down out of curiosity, and were standing around watching.

'It won't burn them if you're careful; don't hold the flame in one place, move it around, and only for a few seconds.' Then using an old toothbrush handle and plenty of spit, I proceeded to 'bone' the toecap: short hard strokes up and down the toe cap. After a couple of minutes 'boning', I then reverted to forefinger in the cloth, plenty of polish and spit and pressing firmly, the finger rotated in layers of polish. Ten minutes of boning, spitting and rubbing in circles was enough for the demonstration. I then took the polishing cloth and, with the boot firmly gripped between my knees, proceed to see-saw the folded polishing cloth across the boot toe. Gasps of amazement from the audience and Weedy's face was a delight of excitement. When the polished toe-cap was placed against its partner the true differences could be seen.

'Smashing,' said Weedy, 'I bet you learnt to do that the same place as you learnt to march.'

'That's right, Weedy, now you do the other boot, but remember, careful with the match, and also one session's just a start; to get a real deep shine you need to do it for weeks. Don't use the match after the first time, just polish and toothbrush or spoon handle, else you'll crack the leather.'

Within minutes the hut was full of the smell of burning boot polish as Hut 6b bulled their toecaps.

As the days went by, other requests for 'bulling' brass and pressing uniforms were satisfied by demonstration. Trouser creases were soap-lined inside the trouser leg, pressed with a damp cloth on the outside and finished off with brown paper under the iron. Flight 6b amazed Jevons and other drill instructors in the next few weeks with their smart turn out. Team spirit grew tremendously, as did pride in appearance.

Saturday afternoon, a gruelling week of agony behind us, and at last we were free to do as we pleased, except of course to leave the camp. Rudy was all for a game of football.

'Let's go and play foota,' he said. Coming back from lunch we had seen five chaps kicking at goal on the playing field.

'I'll come,' said Kettley, whose ears heard everything in the hut.

'So will I,' said Blondie and Taffy in unison.

'I'll come and watch – I can't play, see,' piped up Weedy.

'Come on then, we'll challenge the buggers,' said Rudy, putting on his PT pumps. In the event, half the hut turned out. We played fifteen minutes each way. Taffy ended up referee and 6b provided the linesmen. Our supporters shouted their heads off and we won fifteen goals to two. We went back to the hut sweating and singing and Rudy was the hero, having scored eleven of the goals.

That evening, Hut 6b invaded the NAAFI, took up residence in one corner by the piano and, almost to a man, were drunk before eight o'clock. They were talking, singing, and telling stories and jokes and at last all barriers were removed and the nineteen survivors became one.

Greater heights of happiness can be achieved and appreciated much more when you have survived, come up from the bottom, gone through the fire, done it together. This is when the bonds start to grow, when friendships are formed, not for material gain, not for influence or favour, but purely out of suffering and survival and that sense of achievement. We belonged to one another, we depended on one another, we were proud to be Flight 6b.

I don't remember leaving the canteen or getting into bed that first Saturday night, I could never take alcohol; two pints and I start singing; and halfway through the third I go into a deep sleep with an inane grin on my face. Many photographs prove this point. When the story was told, it appeared Rudy had put me to bed; he was to prove a good drinker and could hold his beer. At least half a dozen of 6b had Rudy playing mother to them that Saturday night.

It must have been at one o'clock in the morning that I heard the shrieking noises, laughter, clanging of metal, swearing and hilarity. I lay on the floor, amazingly with my blankets still round me and looked up, through beery eyes, at the lightbulbs that were burning bright. I tried to focus toward the noise and noticed half the beds already tipped on their sides, the occupants sprawled in various positions across the floor. A gang of 'raiders', later identified as from a senior flight, were causing havoc in the hut. We should have expected something, being the junior flight, but we hadn't.

Jevons, like most of the NCOs, was away for the weekend, an ideal time for monkey business.

Unable to gather my senses, I lay there watching as they tipped everybody out of bed. It happened so quickly and with half the hut worse for drink, that no resistance was being put up as we were all in shock. They had chosen their moment well.

They got to the last bed, the one by the wall, next to Jevons' room but they didn't tip it up. They dragged the frightened occupant to the upright position and stripped off his pyjamas. Rudy was on his feet shouting, 'Bastards!' and charged towards them red-faced. There must have been fifteen of them and ten or so formed a line of defence facing us. I got up to join Rudy and fell down again. Kettley, Blondie and a few others, inspired by Rudy, raced barefoot up the hut. I stood up again and saw the chap in the end bed struggling and shouting as four invaders held him while the fifth was brushing a thick layer of Cherry Blossom black over his exposed private parts. They couldn't have expected any resistance from the new, shaven-headed recruits and it must have come as a shock to see the red-faced roaring Rudy charge and be backed up by others. Rudy's first furious blow knocked a surprised invader hard against the guy applying the black polish. He knocked into the pyramid on the bed and they all fell, releasing the prisoner. Panic set in as first two invaders made for the door by Jevons' room and others started to follow.

Most of our hut were now attacking and the invaders were fleeing like rats from a sinking ship. The whole episode had taken less than four minutes, and Rudy became the hero for the second time in twenty-four hours.

It was obvious to me and probably to the others, that Rudy had had a rough and hard upbringing. He was placid, helpful and caring most of the time, but when riled he changed into a ferocious force. He was frightened of no one and had learnt to fight the hard way, bare-knuckled in the hard school of the Gorbals. We were alike in many ways, both hardened off to life far beyond our years, both rebellious, both sportsman, both chance takers.

Blondie Harrison was fast becoming attached to the two of us. He had acquitted himself well on the night of the invaders, although his general demure bearing belied aggressiveness. A big chap in all ways, he stood five foot ten, the same as me, but he was broad and solid. His square head and square chin gave him a Germanic look but his blond hair, which had once been so long, could have meant he was of Dutch origin. His hair, or what was left of it, reminded me of a cornfield that had been hit by a gale. Inch long blond spikes that refused to lie down surrounded areas that had been flattened to his head by his sidecap. He was made square; his shoulders were a coat hanger still left in the battledress jacket. Yet for all his big square frame, his face wore a perpetual smile. He was always humming a tune and wanted to tag along or join in with what was going on. He was in fact somewhat naïve, unworldly and afraid of being left out. He was the only occupant of Hut 6b that had his parents regularly visit him and he was never short of money. He would never be a leader but he needed a leader, someone to look up to, someone to follow, and he tagged along and made a threesome whenever he could.

Blondie's one failing, which was the source of much amusement and contrived hilarity, was his telling of outrageous stories. He would always better any braggart's story even to ridiculous heights. This weakness first came to light on the Sunday after the invader episode. We were all sitting in the NAAFI, few drinkers, mostly tea, when Taffy was telling a plausible story about mushrooms on his father's farm.

'I've seen them twelve inches in diameter in the fields round our farmhouse, so big Ma couldn't get two in the fryingpan without cutting them up,' said Taffy, holding his two hands in a circle to indicate the size.

'That's nothing,' came the voice of Blondie.

All eyes turned in Blondie's direction and his smiling face put on another ten kilowatts of beaming; he loved and craved attention. We waited expectantly, for this was the first time of intervention.

'My father used to grow mushrooms in our old air-raid shelter,' he started. 'One day, a man was delivering dried blood and he dropped the sack accidently when passing over the front garden lawn and it burst open. A few days later Dad drew the bedroom curtains and the front lawn was covered in large mushrooms. He decided to pull them all up, except one, in the centre of the lawn.

We were all listening intently by now, taking in and believing every word.

'Well,' he continued, 'Father left just that one to see what would happen and next morning it was twice as big. Now, four days later he took the wooden sun bench from the back garden and placed it under the mushroom and Mother used to sit underneath it and do her knitting.'

The NAAFI roof nearly came off as hoots of laughter burst out from all the listeners.

It was a great story and everyone enjoyed it. Blondie sat there grinning at us all and enjoying the hilarity. As I looked at him I could see he didn't realize they were laughing at him in disbelief, he believed his own story and what's more, he believed that we believed it. It was amazing – what sort of guy was this?

From that night on, whenever we were socializing and the party was going a bit quiet, someone would say, 'Let's get another one out of Blondie,' and we would set a trap. We would send him for another round of tea and in his absence make up a quick story. Everyone was sworn to silence whenever Blondie was talking. For months he was led up the garden path and never did he know it was a put-up job. Of the fifty or so set-ups over the eighteen months together, the 'biggest box of chocolates' must take the Oscar. Blondie's final lines were: 'Father, Mother and I were ill with eating so many chocolates before they went bad. In the end Father put the remainder in sacks and we gave them to the dustbin men, but Father kept the beautiful boxes and we use them as wardrobes in two of our bedrooms.' Well, Blondie was quite a character and certainly accepted in the 'gang'.

Reality returned with Jevons on that cold Monday morning as he rattled our steel bed frames with someone's chipped enamel mug.

'Feet on the floor, feet on the floor, come on, my lucky lads, another glorious week begins, aren't you the lucky ones, have you missed me? Like bloody hell you've missed me,' he ranted as he banged away with his mug.

The wind was howling outside and light was only just creeping across the dark clouded sky. Lights could be seen in other huts, and bodies moving across windows in slow motion. Spots of rain were splattering on the window panes. Inside the hut was freezing cold, and its occupants, like cold blood in the veins, were moving sluggishly and monotonously about their tasks. Hardly a word was being spoken.

'Won't be any PT this weather, will there Corp?' queried Taffy hopefully.

All eyes and ears turned immediately and zoomed in expectantly on Corporal Jevons, who was now at my end of the hut and still talking to himself.

'No PT, don't be silly, lad, 'course there's PT, come shit, shine, rain or snow there's always PT, you're not made of bloody sugar, ha, ha, ha,' he laughed as we deflated with disappointment.

Soaked through and freezing cold we did our PT with all the other flights. The PT instructor, in sweater and tracksuit, stood on his table platform under the flagpole as nearly three hundred of us copied his exercise examples. The wind was so strong that we couldn't hear his words of command. By the time the flight PT instructor interpreted the instructions for us, the main sergeant instructor on the table was on the next exercise; we were always one exercise behind. If we weren't so cold and fed up it would have been funny because none of the eighteen or so flights were in time, and everyone seemed to be doing their own thing. The PT instructors, though, were a different breed from the drill instructors; they were tough and they made you work hard, but they treated you like human beings, and didn't go to the ridiculous lengths of debasement or ridicule which were the prerogative of drill instructors. Just fifteen minutes into our planned half-hour PT period we were dismissed and hurried away for a warm wash, then on with the nice thick clothes and uniform and to breakfast.

Normally we would have been happy to have Jevons back drilling us, anyone would be preferable to the dreaded Sergeant Thomas; but the icy wind and occasional cold rain shower made us withdraw into our shells.

For the first time we drilled in our new groundsheets, the RAF's idea of a raincoat: a square pyramid of blue canvas that slotted over the head and had three buttons done up to the chin. The cape hung to four points, one to the front, one to the rear, and one to the side of each leg about thigh height. This garment was designed to channel the rainwater to both outside thighs thus ensuring the trouser legs got an equal and fair amount of wetness. The rear points of the cape channelled the remainder of the catchment just beyond the back passage and the front point to the inside of the thighs. Within minutes of marching in the rain the various points directed the deluge which soaked the blue serge. As the water spread through the serge it joined up nicely with the wetness spreading from other points. It was a guarantee of the design of the groundsheet, that an even, soggy, cold, clinging wetness could be achieved within five minutes of rain, from crutch to corns.

Silence reigned in the ranks as we leaned into the wind; trying to keep in step, but Weedy and one or two others kept getting blown off-course. Jevons was bawling against the wind and was fighting a losing battle. His commands were not always audible as the wind gusted and I decided to liven things up.

We were marching towards the end of the parade ground. Where the gravel ended there was a ten-foot grass area around the ground, and the short black wooden posts set fifteen feet apart had thick white rope draped from post to post at the kerb edge. After the posts was the camp road and the other side of the road was the sports field.

I sent word down the ranks to 'keep going, pretend we don't hear the next command, keep going.'

The message was passed enthusiastically down the ranks. We closed our ears and marched. Off the parade ground we went, across the grass, over the ropes, over the road and reached the football pitch. Jevons, who had been shouting commands well behind and to the left of us, appeared at the run, face red with exertion and blaspheming for all he was worth.

'HALT, halt, you clever bastards, I'll 'ave you for this, think it's funny, eh?' he bawled, as a few of us couldn't help smiling.

'About turn, double march!' and we ran back onto the parade ground. 'Confined to your room tonight, you bastards, kit inspection at nine o'clock. You think you're fucking clever, do you? Well, I'll take the shit out of you,' he raved. 'Now, double march,' and we set off at a run.

He'd been running us up and down for a few minutes as the weather worsened and to his great disappointment drill was suspended. We breathed a sign of relief as we were marched off to the gymnasium for a lecture.

I was born a rebel, I'm sure of that, and a stubborn streak was part of my make up. I got a weird pleasure from going against authority in whatever form it presented itself. There were plenty of challenges here to pit my wits against and I had, unknown to them, an advantage, I'd been through it all before, not exactly the same but very similar. Going against authority seemed to me my way of life and the re-entry into military life brought back something that had been missing in 'Civvy Street'. I had a great sense of humour, which I was going to need in the future, but basically what spurred me on was the recognition, the mateyness, the essential feeling of belonging, the esteem, the friendships, the big-headedness. I needed to be in a crowd and I needed the crowd to like me.

CHAPTER 4

Sergeant Heckner's Guardroom

That evening, after tea, we started to prepare for our first kit inspection.

'Let's see how Bob does it,' said Taffy as we trooped back into the hut.

I had now become the guru of everything military, from kit to drill. Taking the fading diagram from the back of the entrance door I then folded and laid out my full kit on blanketed mattress. As each piece was correctly folded to size, number showing and laid in the correct position on the bed, I stressed the important points.

'Socks must be rolled up from the toe, to two and a half inches from the top. Then pull the two and a half inches back over the rolled portion. Make sure the tape with your number is uppermost, then flatten the sock. You must end up with a two and a half inch square sock with tape and number centre of the square and uppermost. Four socks only to be displayed, all identical in squareness, and positioned in a line, below your opened housewife, dead centre of mattress, OK?'

'Yeah, got that one, Bob,' said Taffy.

'Easy,' said Kettley 'what's next?'

'Best boots,' I said. 'First make sure your boots are highly polished, check welts carefully.' I demonstrated with the old toothbrush and Cherry Blossom.

'Now, check that when you blackened the soles you cleaned off any polish that got on to the steel studs or heelcap. Burnish them up with a side of a matchbox if they're dull. Now fold the leather of the boot inside, back first, then sides. If you've got some clothes pegs, peg it in until just before inspection time. The boots are new and you'll have difficulty holding the leather in for a while. Once you have folded the leather inside the body of the boot, place the boots, soles uppermost, at the foot of the mattress,' I paused.

Faces began to look rather anxiously at me.

I continued briefly and quickly through greatcoats, shirts, shorts, pants, pyjamas, plimsolls, best blue, peaked cap, buttonstick, brushes, comb, cutlery, towels and so on; until Kettley, in his best Bow banter said:

'Fuck a duck, that's not a kit inspection, it's a bleedin' work of art.'

'Come on,' I said, 'Let's get cracking, and shout if you need help.'

For the next three hours the hut was a hive of activity, laughter, frustration, jokes and skylarking.

'Help!' shouted a voice, 'How do you do the shirts again?'

'Just a tick,' I shouted back, as I struggled with Weedy's new overcoat that refused to stay in a square.

'I'll show him,' said Blondie, sliding across the billet on his pads. I looked up to the far end of the hut and saw Rudy rearranging Snowy's bed layout. A great communal spirit was being generated; everybody was mucking in helping one another. Even Kettley was scraping his neighbour's boot brushes with his Rolls cut-throat razor.

At ten to nine we checked the hut for general line up of beds, pushed the rag-covered brooms across the lino for the last time and then stood by our beds, at ease, chests puffed out, proud of the smart layout of our kit and feeling quite pleased with ourselves.

At nine o'clock on the dot the door nearest to me, and opposite to the one at the other end of the billet by Jevons's room, burst open. We were expecting the latter to open, so we were doubly surprised to see the grinning, bullying, Sergeant Thomas standing there. All eyes looked towards him and fear entered the hut.

His eyes slowly moved round from right to left. My bed was last on the left, next to the wall and behind the open door. When his eyes had gone full circle they suddenly brightened. He pushed the door fully back and entered the room, Jevons behind him. Suddenly I remembered seeing them both, in deep conversation, in the gymnasium that morning. So this is what they were talking about, I thought.

'Flight, atten-tion!' ordered Jevons.

'You call them 'Flight', Corporal, I call them a bloody shower, they can't drill and by Christ they can't lay out kit, look at this!' he bawled waving his arm generally down the row of beds. He then proceeded to inspect the layouts, starting opposite to me.

I surveyed his broad back, his thick bull neck and large head. A monster, a bigoted bully. How could a man like this have a mother, a wife, maybe children? I couldn't imagine him as a family man, talking softly, holding a baby, being human. I couldn't imagine him enjoying himself, laughing, talking, carrying on a normal conversation. Swear words were stock in trade to drill instructors. After a while one became immune to general four-letter words, so the poor instructor had to think up yet more insulting and provocative phrases to obtain from the recruit the facial reaction that gave him his pleasures and job satisfaction.

Sergeant Thomas was now halfway up the right hand side after bawling out most people for one thing or another. He had a full, well rehearsed repertoire.

'These boots haven't seen polish since they came out of the bloody stores,' he bawled 'Take his name, Corporal, extra fatigues.'

'Got it, Sergeant,' replied Jevons. Next bed was Snowy.

'You got two left 'ands, lad?'

'No. Sergeant.'

'Well, you fooled me – those socks are folded like a tart's fanny.'

'Take his name, Corporal.'

'Got it, Sergeant.'

The ritual continued and poor Weedy was shaking as they approached him.

'Ah, shortarse, the worst fucking airman in the Air Force,' said Thomas, sneering.

Whenever the drill instructor found weaklings, he was in his element. He would play with them while we all stood helplessly looking on. The power of authority, undisputed, took him to the heights of ridiculousness. He might feel the hate coming from the watchers but that just spurred him on. If he could only see himself, but he never would. With one blow of his hand Thomas knocked Weedy's greatcoat flying.

'Call that folded? Do it again.'

Weedy grabbed the bulky overcoat off the floor and attempted to fold it. He placed it back at the top of the bed.

'That's fucking worse, you stupid bastard. Look to your front, Freeman, I'll get to you in a minute,' and he knocked Weedy's overcoat to the floor again.

After the third attempt Thomas blasphemed Weedy into half his size.

'Take his name, Corporal, fatigues.'

'Got it, Sergeant.'

'Well,' drawled Thomas, 'It's smartarse Freeman, the one with all the answers, the hard case, the fucking barrackroom lawyer, I've shit better than you,

Freeman, shit 'em better than you,' he snarled, bringing his face within an inch of mine. I cringed back from his stale beer breath.

'Stand still, you clever bastard, when I'm talking to you.'

I was already tense from the battering he had given poor Weedy but I knew he would try to provoke me, so I was determined to stay calm.

'You don't think I'm funny, do you lad?' Pause, silence.

'I'm talking to you, shithead, answer when you're spoken to; am I funny?'

I knew if I said no he'd only explode; if I said yes it would be a retraction in front of my mates, so I remained silent.

'So you refuse to answer? Corporal, you're a witness – well, do you?'

He was dying to get me on a charge; I was determined to stay cool.

'No, Sergeant.'

'No, bloody what?' he screamed. 'I know about you, Duke of York's Royal Military School, eh, told you I would find out and by Christ, I bloody well have. No bloody good, chucked you out, didn't they, fuckin' misfit, and now you turn up here. Well, soldier boy, you're a misfit here, look at that kit, fucking disgrace, do it again and I'll be back in an hour!' he shouted as he played the conjuror, taking hold of the blanket, and pulling it straight off the bed. My lovingly cared-for kit shot in all directions, some right across Weedy's bed.

'Do it you blinkin' self, I'm not doing it.'

The words came before I could stop them. A hush descended on the whole room. Jevons went white, Thomas took a big breath.

'Arrest that man, Corporal, arrest him, quickly!' he screamed at the top of his voice.

I was marched off to the guardroom at the entrance to the camp. As I lay on the solid wood plank bed, bolster under my head and one blanket over my clothed body, I cursed my luck, my big mouth, my stupidity.

The bulb in the narrow cell was left on all through the night, the switch being on the outside. Every hour the corporal of the guard looked through the nine-inch barred peephole to see what I was up to. What could I have been up to? There was nothing in the cell: no window, no furniture, nothing. When I wanted a pee I had to bang the door and be cursed as I was escorted and watched every second.

No sleep came, that long first night. I relived a lot of my life in those few hours and could feel myself growing bitter again. When daylight came it was a blessing.

At six thirty I discovered a new breed of RAF personnel, the military police, or 'snowdrops', so called because they wore white cloth covers over their peaked caps.

The military police made drill instructors look like kindergarten teachers. They were not of this planet and must have been the lowest form of life ever hatched.

By six thirty I was sweeping, polishing floors and cleaning the toilets at the double. Supervised and tongue-lashed at every task, it was a nightmare.

At eight o'clock I was 'doubled' across the camp to the cookhouse with a snowdrop behind me and one in front. After a quick breakfast I was doubled back.

Sergeant Thomas had obviously put a word in the ear of the sergeant in charge of the guardroom and I knew that it was survival time again.

I was put on a fizzer, a two-five-two, a charge. Two-five-two was the number given to charge sheets and the exclamation 'put him on a two-five-two' was going to be heard quite a few more times before the RAF finished with me.

At ten o'clock I was marched to the administration block. Standing on a linoed floor corridor with two snowdrop corporals as escorts, I awaited my fate. A door opened and Sergeant Thomas came out, swagger stick under arm, leaving the door ajar.

'Prisoner – take your cap off.' he bawled. 'Prisoner and escort – attention!' All three of us came to attention. 'Prisoner and escort left turn, quick march, left wheel, left wheel, prisoner halt!' All this movement was done in exaggerated quick time. 'Prisoner and escort – right turn.' I was now facing a youngish flight lieutenant who was looking up at me studiously.

'Prisoner 1920683 Boy Entrant Freeman Sah, charged with insubordination and refusing to obey an order, SAH!' shouted loudmouth Thomas. My two escorts and I were standing rigidly to attention, staring straight ahead.

'This is a serious charge, Freeman, a very serious charge; you haven't taken long to get into trouble, have you?' he stated, 'And you compound the offence by refusing an order in front of other new recruits, tut, tut, this is a bad show, can't have discipline breaking down like this,' and he went on.

It was obvious from what the officer said that Thomas had given his version of the affair and I knew there was no way out.

'Have you anything to say for yourself?' he asked.
What's the use? I thought. It's cut and dried.
'No, Sir.'

'Nothing to say, eh, you're all the same, you get into trouble and have nothing to say; well, it is your first offence, and last I hope, but it must be taken seriously. Three days detention. Dismiss, Sergeant.'

'Sah. Prisoner and escort, right turn, quick march, right wheel, right wheel, halt.'

Grinning all over his face, Thomas leered towards me and gleefully said, 'You shouldn't tangle with me, laddie, now we'll see what colour your shit is. Take him away.'

First stop, at the double, was Hut 6b to collect all my kit. As we doubled along the path by the parade ground I knew my mates would be looking at me. Better there, though, than in the hut, I thought.

All my kit had then been neatly stowed in my locker, by Rudy or Weedy I presumed. Filling my kitbag quickly, I was doubled with my heavy load back to the guardroom.

The sergeant of the guard, Sergeant Heckner, stood in front of me as I was doubling 'on the spot' still holding my kit. It was his head I couldn't take my eyes off. A huge square block with half an inch of stubble-cut hair spiking up like a square-trimmed porcupine. With no visible neck, his head sat on the shoulders of his square five foot eight inch frame and gave the impression of a solid granite statue gone wrong. His short nose had a mind of its own and turned left at the end. Two sunken piercing black eyes glared from his white face, promising to avenge all those who came within its glare for the out-of-proportion body given to it.

Three snowdrop corporals stood watching, with their hard, uncompromising eyes. The bullhead, crew-cut sergeant snarled at me.

'Three days – three days – three days to change a hard man into a pound of shit. We should be able to do that, corporals, shouldn't we?' he screeched, as his voice went up in a crescendo.

'Yes, Sergeant,' they sang in reply.

'Your feet won't touch the ground, your body will ache in places you never knew you had, your brain – if you've got one – will turn to jelly, you won't know if your arsehole's been bored, countersunk or riveted. You're our meat, our bread and butter, we're going to eat you up, shit you out and sent you back to your mates a snivelling mess. Right, corporals?'

'Yes, Sergeant.'

'Well, get cracking on it then,' said Heckner.

I knew this was the big one, the next three days were going to test everything I'd ever learnt. I had to obey. I had to keep my mouth shut, I had to close my mind completely to everything except the task in hand. I had to forget my mates, my family, everything. Do as I was told, let the insults ride over me, keep going, never give in, force myself on. All these thoughts were going through my head. I had to believe I could make it, could climb out of this hole, could live again. One slip, one word, one excuse and I would be deeper in the hole, more charges and who knows where I might end up? I must survive and beat these bastards at their own game. This was the biggest challenge of my life to date, I was determined to get through whatever they threw at me, and they threw it all.

'Ten minutes, full kit inspection, get to it!' bawled my corporal jailer, and so we were off.

From that minute they hardly left me alone. My kit, neatly laid out on my wide plank of a bed was scattered at least three times a day to all four corners of the cell. The first day I set my kit up seven times. I scrubbed, polished and cleaned every inch of that guardroom from floor to ceiling and then repeated the process. I burnished fire buckets for sand and water until they shone like silver mirrors, then, with a laugh, I was handed a paintbrush and red paint and made to paint over three hours of paint-scraping and burnishing. I was becoming a punch-drunk robot, following orders blindly, just like they wanted me to.

RAF guardrooms are all built to the same basic design. Positioned by the main entrance to the camp, the building, constructed round the edge of the oblong, contains offices looking onto the main entrance road, cells off the main office, quarters for the duty guards, toilets, showers and so on. The centre of the oblong is the exercise yard, open to the elements, the punishment yard. There is one solid door leading from the general office and cells into this yard, and once in there the prisoner is surrounded by the four solid brick walls of the oblong. There are steel-barred windows looking out from the offices over the yard so that the prisoner can be supervised from within. All windows facing outwards are also barred. Regulations allowed for each 'prisoner' to be exercised for one hour per day.

My first breather was at lunch; I sat there in the cookhouse with two snowdrop guards watching me eating my ample meal in silence. The cooks and servers went out of their way to ensure I had plenty on my plate and gave me an encouraging wink, blind side of my escorts, as much as to say, keep your chin up, we're on your side. The same reaction was experienced as I was being 'doubled' across the camp for meals. Passing airmen would put their thumbs up, the brave ones would say, 'Stick at it, mate, soon be out,' and this unexpected encouragement was one helluva boost to my flagging spirits. It seemed everybody hated the MPs.

On my return from lunch I was put straight in the exercise yard and told to get doubling round the perimeter. The duty corporal then sat at his desk, feet up, lit a cigarette and watched me through the barred window.

'Get those bloody knees up, higher!' he bawled, but I'd settled to a steady trot. Every couple of circuits he would call me to the barred window and, lolling back in his chair, feet on the desk, would ask,

'Tired yet, prisoner? Would you like to walk?'

'Yes, please, Corporal.'

'Oh, we got a please, we are getting polite, now get running and get those knees up.'

He was obviously enjoying his undisputed power, but I now accepted the inevitable and each time I was stopped I replied politely. Lathered in sweat and decidedly tired, I was almost at a fast walk when a voice from another barred window bellowed out furiously across the exercise yard:

'Corporal of the guard!'

My lolling corporal came to life, quickly put his hat on and, standing to attention in front of his bars but facing into the yard, replied:

'Sergeant.'

They were only two barred windows apart and carried on their bawling without being able to see one another.

'Corporal of the guard, why is that prisoner strolling around the yard as if he's on a bloody picnic; do you want to join him?'

'No, Sergeant.'

'You bloody well will if you don't listen to orders. Class A I told you, Class A, that means full battle order; get to it.'

Sergeant Thomas's friend, for that was what I assumed Heckner was, had just come into his office, which I had previously noted to be empty. Within five minutes I was in full battle order; webbing harness, backpack, sidepack to hip, water bottle and canteen.

'Now, get doubling round that fucking yard if you know what's good for you.' Off I went, water bottle and sidepack leaping up and down around my waist. The backpack, empty, but squared with cardboard, was no problem. I hadn't completed one circuit when the 'voice' screamed out again.

'Corporal of the guard!'

'Yes, Sergeant.'

'Corporal of the guard, how the fucking hell can you go into battle without a rifle?' and on the word 'rifle' Heckner screamed to a new high pitch. Surely he will burst a blood vessel or have a heart attack in a minute. I thought; he sounded demented.

'The prisoner hasn't been issued with a rifle yet, Sergeant.'

'Well, bloody well give him yours.'

That first experience of the exercise yard left me a sweating, aching wreck, but, wonder of wonders, the corporal escorted me to the showers and I luxuriated for five minutes in its hot spray. I'm sure it was unofficial, and as the sergeant had left the guardroom, something, somehow, had touched the corporal into giving me this 'treat'.

I was locked in my cell at six o'clock, the first cell facing into the side of the main office. It was possible to hear most conversations that went on outside. Changing of the guard took place at six o'clock and the new corporal came into the office to take over.

'Just one prisoner?' asked the new corporal.

'Yes, and he's Class A, don't ask me why; he doesn't seem a hard case to me,' said the other corporal.

Those few words gave me hope and lifted my spirits a bit. Even these hardened MPs, used to all sorts of hard cases, recognised that I was being victimised and they probably knew why – sergeants.

At ten o'clock I was lying on my board, hands behind my head, and studying the pattern created by the single light bulb on the shiny ceiling when there was a helluva commotion in the main office. Three more airmen, poor buggers, were marched in and put in cells. I had company, attention would be taken off me a bit. My tired body drifted off into a deep sleep.

The other three prisoners weren't recruits but regulars; 'regulars' in more than one sense, as two of them had been 'inside' a few times. They took everything in their stride and knew exactly how much they could get away with. They wouldn't be rushed and they knew how to make a job last. All their answers stopped just short of being charged for insolence, they knew exactly where to draw the line and leave the questioner short of the satisfaction required for ego-boosting and total power control. I watched and learnt.

On Wednesday the three new prisoners returned at the double with their kit. The sergeant of the guard was giving them the usual pep-talk.

'Fourteen days, eh Gibbons? Never learn, lad, do ya; this visit we'll see if we can make life more interesting for you,' he grinned. 'Won't we, Corporal?'

'Yes, Sergeant.'

'Trying to work your ticket, aren't you, Gibbons, want a bloody cushy job in Civvy Street do ya, well you won't get no help here, and wipe that bloody smile off ya face,' he ranted. 'Kit inspection in half an hour, jump to it!'

We were standing outside our cell doors, in full battle order with kit laid neatly on our wooden beds. Sergeant Heckner had decided personally to carry out the inspection and started with Gibbons.

'Prisoners, ah-teh-shion!' ordered the duty corporal.

We came to attention, pulling our rifles smartly into our sides. I still had the rifle given to me the day before by one of the corporals. Heckner made straight for Gibbons.

'Rifle for inspection – present,' he bawled and Gibbons came up to correct position and released the firing bolt. Heckner took the rifle from him, held it up at an angle, butt furthest away and peered up the barrel.

'Filthy, fucking filthy, never seen a pull-through in years, bloody bird's nest up there, look lad, look,' he said, handing the .303 back to Gibbons.

Gibbons held the rifle up at the correct angle, butt towards window, and peered carefully up the barrel, his face a study of concentration.

'Yes, Sergeant, I see it, thrush's nest I think,' said Gibbons, casually proffering the rifle back to Heckner.

Heckner's face had blown up like a goldfish, he was puffing and spitting as his blood pressure rose. I stood there suppressing the laughter that was welling up inside me; this guy Gibbons was really something, as he stood there with a blank face, holding his rifle out to Heckner.

'Lies, lies, all bastard lies, taking the piss, are you? Right, clever bastard, into the exercise yard – move.'

Poor Gibbons, doubling round the yard whilst holding his rifle above his head, still in full battle order, and being cursed every five minutes. He had ten minutes on his own before we all joined him and ran for twenty-five minutes before lunch at one o'clock.

At lunch, Gibbons, tired and sweating like us all, still had the energy to laugh and joke about it; he had an indomitable spirit.

George Gibbons, a handsome-looking chap of twenty-five years was a 'stores GD', general duties. He'd served on active units of Bomber Command during the war but now was married and disillusioned with the peacetime RAF. He 'wanted out' but still had three years to go. A cheeky fun-loving chap, he had no fear of being inside: 'Only be filling bloody shelves and cleaning up if I weren't here,' he said. I noticed his layout for kit inspection was perfect and commented on it.

'Don't use that stuff,' he said, 'special for kit inspections, get yourself off to the army surplus stores and buy some specials, make up a set special for these silly buggers to look at, saves a lot of time, I can tell ya.'

'Thanks, I will,' I said and made a mental note to do so at the first opportunity.

Later that Wednesday afternoon, my second day inside, I had the red paint again and Gibbons had white. We'd been doing fire buckets for the admin. block and sergeant's mess, when the duty corporal went to refill his tea mug.

'Quick,' said Gibbons, 'let's paint the barrier, follow me.'

We nipped smartly off the front porch of the guardroom and Gibbons made straight for the large diameter weight that counter-balanced the steel arm that protruded over the road. I wasn't sure what he was up to but I went willingly along, anything to break the monotony. He quickly daubed plenty of white paint over the counterweight and then said, 'Come on, other end.' We crossed into the road and started to paint the red and white rings on the steel barrier.

'Who the fucking hell told you to paint that, get back in 'ere, you two.'

'We finished the buckets, Corp, what do you want next?' asked the innocent and helpful Gibbons.

'Corporal, how many times do I have to tell you, Corporal when you address me,' said the misery-guts of a corporal. 'Get rid of that paint and start on brasses, fire bell first.'

'But we did that this morning, Corporal.'

'Don't bloody argue, get on with it.'

Gibbons then found time to inform his two mates of what to expect shortly.

'Keep your eyes open for the next vehicle,' he said. 'As soon as that snowdrop bastard tries to lift the barrier, he'll be covered in white paint,' he grinned. 'Look away quick, and for Christsake don't laugh.'

We didn't wait long, as soon a three ton Bedford with 'L' plates drew slowly up to the barrier. The corporal left his desk, walked to the barrier, placed both hands on the counterweight and pushed down. He let go and jumped back quickly, turning his hands upwards like Al Jolson singing 'Mammy'. If the vehicle had been any other than a learner driver, it would have been halfway under the barrier when it came clanging down, and a double tragedy would have occurred.

'Fucking hell, who the hell's done that?' Freeman, Gibbons, come here, you two bastards!' he shouted, holding his hands out wide. 'OK, clever buggers, who had the white paint?'

'Oh, Christ, Corporal, I meant to warn you about that but you bawled us out so much when you came back with your tea, I quite forgot,' said the innocent and sorry-looking Gibbons. 'Stay there, Corporal, I'll go and get a rag and thinners,' and Gibbons shot off.

'He did that on purpose, didn't he, Freeman?'

'Oh no, Corporal, nobody would do anything like that on purpose, what would be the point? We couldn't get away with it.'

'You're a lying bastard too, Freeman, I'll have you for this.'

The story was recounted to the night shift corporal and all four of us were deemed to be in 'cahoots'. Our punishment was to continue working until late that night, and on hands and knees we scrubbed the wooden stage in the camp cinema after the last performance and were pleased to see our wooden beds just before midnight.

A particular 'hard' corporal was on duty on the Thursday morning. The eldest of the three new prisoners, Leading Aircraftsman (LAC) Gibbons asked, 'What about a mug of cha', Corp?'

'Corp, Corp,' bellowed the corporal, 'when you address me, stand to attention and say CORPORAL.'

Gibbons smiled, unabashed and unrepentant. 'Go on, Corporal, you can swing it, haven't had a drink since breakfast.'

'If you don't get on with those windows, now, I mean, this minute, I'll put you on another fizzer, move!' he shouted. Gibbons stood there smiling, not the slightest bit frightened by the threat.

'Finished them, Corporal, clean as a baby's arse.'

'Well, get those fire buckets emptied and put clean water in 'em – now move.'

Gibbons stepped the two paces from the corporal's desk in the main office to the three red buckets that sat on a tin tray just inside the door. Two buckets full of water either side of a bucket of sand. He picked up a bucket of water by the handle, looked at it closely and retreated into the room two paces to the seated and watching corporal.

'The water's as clean as a mountain stream, Corporal,' he said, pushing the bucket towards the corporal's face. The corporal, annoyed by Gibbon's constant queries, pushed himself upwards out of his chair as Gibbons proffered the bucket towards him and over his lap. It was beautifully time and executed. The bucket was tipped by the corporal's stomach and a wave of water hit him at chest level. Gibbons put the bucket on the floor quickly and was full of apologies, brushing off surplus water from the corporal's chest while his face showed abstract innocence and concern.

'You did that on purpose, you did that on purpose, I'll have you for this,' he squealed, but Gibbons kept up the pretence of innocence and apology. Once dried out with a towel, the corporal calmed down, but left dreadful threats of what was going to happen to hard man Gibbons.

On Friday morning at ten o'clock, I was standing in the front entrance porch of the guardroom. I'd made it, I'd got through. I was determined never to come back. The bullnecked Heckner stood in front of me. I stood to attention, eyes straight ahead, in full battle order, kitbag packed.

'Consider this your home,' he grinned, 'we'll be seeing you again, have no doubt. Now fuck off and don't look back, I've seen enough of your ugly face to last me a while. Dismiss!'

I was free, free to go back to 6b, back to my mates, back to life. I wasn't as happy as I thought I was going to be. The degrading treatment had left its mark, I felt ashamed. A black mark on my records to start my RAF career, a jailbird. What would my mates think of me?

I walked down the main road and came to the parade ground on my left. All the flights were drilling. I could see Flight 6b and Jevons towards the right of the square. They seemed to be moving very well, they were getting to be quite a smart flight. I wandered on, head down and walked two sides of the square to get to my hut. I went up the three wooden steps, through the door, onto my felt pads, dropped my kitbag on the floor, and lay out full length on my bed in full battle order, my backpack keeping me in the upright position against my folded bedding. Peace, perfect peace.

They came off the parade ground just after eleven-thirty. I'd stowed all my kit by then, rolled down my mattress and was fully stretched out on my bed as, like a gaggle of geese, they all tried to squeeze through the door at the same time.

'What was it like?' 'Was it tough?' the questions came thick and fast from all quarters as they gathered around my bed. Rudy pushed through the crowd, took one look at me and said, 'Not now, fellas, he'll tell us later; leave him alone.'

They all slid off to their beds as Jevons came through the door.

'How are you?' he asked.

I started to get up but he waved his hand. 'Don't get up, come to my room in a minute,' and he left.

Rudy lit two cigarettes together and pushed one towards me.

'Here,' he said, 'take a big drag.' I was full of emotion and holding back tears, confused, ashamed, fed up, but he seemed to understand.

'Taffy!' he called out. 'Get first in the NAAFI queue will ya, get some hot tea and wads.' The NAAFI opened at twelve o'clock and it was getting near to that now. We sat and smoked. 'You'd better go see what Jevons wants,' said Rudy. 'We'll talk later – stay calm.'

'Come in,' said Jevons, as I knocked on his door. 'Sit on the bed.' He was seated in the only chair, next to a small table. He looked at me, but I had difficulty in matching his gaze. There seemed to be a long silence, an embarrassing silence, as we both waited for each other to speak.

'Tough, was it?' he asked.

'Yes, Corporal, tough.'

He gazed at me as though mesmerized, seemingly lost in mixed emotions.

'You're excused all duties and fatigues for the rest of today and tomorrow morning,' the next day being a Saturday. 'With the weekend, that will give you three days to rest up,' he said quietly.

This unexpected statement completely surprised me.

'Thank you, Corporal.' I stood up to go and Jevons rose, too. He seemed to want to say something but was having difficulty. I paused. He cleared his throat:

'This thing went a bit further than I expected it to.' He seemed to stop abruptly, his face turning slightly red. 'Anyway, get rested up, it all starts again Monday,' he said, smiling nervously.

'Thank you, Corporal,' I replied as I left the room.

It took me a week to resurface, a week before the nightmare began to fade. My mates were wary for a while and left me to myself for hours as I tried to sort my confused mind. I gradually came to, but a régime or society rarely changes a prisoner or wrongdoer by punishment and depredation; all it achieves is a more resilient, more crafty, tougher wrongdoer. He still has the same attitudes, opinions and resentments. Sure, he doesn't want another dose of punishment, so he finds ways to reduce the risk.

I had grown up at the bottom of the pile; my father was at the bottom of the Army pile throughout my young years. He had been treated as an inferior by those fortunate enough to be born for higher things, their 'bought' commissions, their superior airs, their total lack of understanding and empathy towards those less fortunate, those that they should have led. No one was going to treat me like a piece of shit, not, that was, without some form of resistance. Sure, they might punish me but, in the end, I would hold my head high. Nobody, but nobody, was going to make a subservient 'yes man' of me for totally unreasonable egotistic reasons, for stupid inhuman and selfish personal aggrandisement. So I came out of my anti-detention coma determined to fight on, and I knew now what to expect if I got caught.

CHAPTER 5

Syphilis and Gonorrhoea

We were now half way through our square-bashing and the monotony had been relieved somewhat by changes to our programme. PT continued each morning but square-bashing was restricted to eleven thirty each day. The afternoons at that time were taken up with lectures, rifle range practice, learning about Bren guns – stripping and fitting together, removing blockages – and field training with ten in a section: eight riflemen, one on Bren guns and one on ammunition box. We were put through assault courses, which, although tough, were challenging to me, and great fun was had by most of us. Trade testing also took place during this period to determine in which direction each man would go.

Jevons became a little bit more human when he was off the parade ground. The change came after I'd been 'inside'; whether it was guilt on his part, or whether it was the normal change in corporal drill instructors, I don't know, but no longer did he rattle the beds at reveille, or shout like a madman in the hut. On parade was a different matter: he had to conform, keep up appearances, and he had reason to shout that first week we had our rifles.

Naturally, someone, this time Snowy, had to commit the cardinal sin by dropping his rifle on the first day. We were at the 'slope' when Jevons shouted, 'Order Arms!' and down went Snowy's rifle. He immediately bent forward to pick it up, and I think Jevons was going to let him do it, but a voice bellowed from the flight stood at ease next to us:

'STAND STILL, THAT MAN, STAND STILL I SAY!' and the mountainous Sergeant Thomas marched up.

We hadn't 'come together' since I had come out of detention. I stood there in the front rank thinking of my father. We were on the troopship and Dad, with a smile on his face, was reciting his favourite monologue. The words were going through my head; 'Sam, Sam pick up thy musket.' I was in dream land; 'Nah, tha' knocked it darn, tha' pick it up.'

'Freeman, do you think this is bloody funny?' bawled Thomas.

I returned to the parade ground. I was already at attention, so I sloped arms, paused, marched clear of the front rank, halted.

'No, Sergeant,' I said, staring straight ahead. I could kick myself. Why didn't I concentrate, I knew Rudy and the gang would be nervous. I waited.

'Well, what the fucking hell do you find to smile about?'

'I didn't know I was smiling, Sergeant.'

'I can believe that, you stupid sod, get back in the ranks.'

'Yes, Sergeant.'

This brief encounter put him out of his stride but he turned to Jevons.

'Corporal, are you going to put that man on a charge?'

'It's their first morning with rifles, Sergeant,' said Jevons, not committing himself.

'First morning or not, if it was my flight I would shoot any bastard that disgraced me. Carry on, Corporal,' and Thomas marched off to his own flight.

We all breathed a sigh of relief, including Jevons, who seemed not to be a bastard after all. When a flight starts to respect its drill instructor a change comes over it. Nothing is said, but suddenly everyone is trying harder, antagonism wanes, pride starts to come through.

Flight 6b suddenly came of age, no more messing about. We could be the best flight at the passing-out ceremony and the spirit rose. Flight 6b and Corporal Jevons were now as one.

'That was bloody close,' said Rudy, as we dismissed and made our way the short distance to the billet, 'What were you smiling for?'

'I'll tell you,' I said, 'when we get in the billet.'

So, during the hour of hut cleaning before lunch, I entertained, for the first time, the whole flight to Stanley Holloway's 'Sam'. I did all the actions, just like my father used to, and Weedy acted Sam, rifle on the floor in front of him. I even got off my pads and galloped, as the colonel did on his charger, and pleaded with Sam to pick up his musket, 'Just for me, Sam'. The flight was in hysterics at this pantomime and even Jevons, who'd come in halfway through, was smiling broadly.

'Well done, Fizz,' shouted Kettley, and the nickname stuck with me for the rest of my career.

'Why Fizz? asked Taffy.

'Well, he's the first bugger to go on a fizzer and he's always full of life, like a bottle of pop.'

So I was christened.

Flight 6b had started off like all new flights, a rag-tag batch of individuals, fearful, nervous, and untrained. Now, after five weeks, confidence in ourselves and team spirit had moulded us into a confident and fairly competent flight. We had pride in our ability to drill smartly as a squad and morale was high. At night time in the billet much friendly horseplay became the norm, and we spent evenings in the NAAFI as a flight all together, singing, joking and winding up Blondie Harrison for more exaggerated stories.

'PAY ATTENTION!' called Jevons, 'Parade at two o'clock outside the hut, you're all going to the pictures this afternoon,' he said, with a broad smile.

'Is it a cowboy, Corp?' asked Kettley.

'Nah, we don't want a cowboy, lovely women's what we want, with no clothes on,' rejoined Taffy.

'You'll find out when we get there, and no messing about when you're in the cinema, I'll be watching. I still need three of you for fatigue rota tonight, so watch out,' said the more human Jevons.

It appeared Jevons was respecting us more as a flight now and, at times, was almost 'matey'. We arrived at the cinema and took up the middle row, as many flights had beaten us to it. The cinema seemed to be purpose-built, with the normal upholstered tip-up chairs fixed to the floor. Film shows were restricted to Wednesday, Friday and Saturday evenings, the same film all three nights. Presently showing was *King Kong*, but because of fatigues we missed out that week. With about two hundred seating capacity, the building was used for lectures and demonstrations. Touring artists also appeared occasionally to entertain the troops.

The hubbub of noise ceased, slowly at first and then quickly, as eyes focused on a flight lieutenant and his entourage who had entered from the wings and were now standing centre stage.

'Right, chaps,' said a higher-than-expected voice coming from the officer on stage. 'You're now coming to the end of your initial training period and next week you're going to be let loose on the public.'

He looked round the auditorium, grinning all over his face and expecting a laugh, but silence reigned. He continued:

'Well, when you get out there, chaps, it's rather important that you know of the dangers lurking and waiting for the unwary.'

'What the fuckin' 'ell's 'e on about?' whispered the Cockney voice of Kettley.

'Women, I expect,' said Rudy.

'Quiet,' said Taffy.

'Now, there are many diseases prevalent today that are not discussed generally by people, but are taboo except in barrack room jokes. Our session here today is to make you aware of these dangers so that you will be in a position to avoid them,' he continued, in more serious tone.

'No shagging, no disease, that's what he means,' said Kettley.

'Shut up, for Christ's sake,' said Rudy.

'The diseases I'm referring to are gonorrhoea and syphilis' said the medic, as a lackey unveiled the words on the blackboard. 'Both diseases are transmitted through sexual intercourse with diseased women.'

A titter ran round the audience at the mention of sexual intercourse.

'It's no good standing on the seat, the crabs in 'ere can jump six feet,' recited Kettley.

'Fatigues for you tonight, Kettley,' came the voice of Jevons from the end of the row.

'I'm going to show you a film in a minute which explains these diseases and shows the results of the disease on infected parts.'

Titters from the audience.

'This is a very serious matter and not to be taken lightly,' admonished the officer to the unruly, amused audience. 'The film will also explain the treatments necessary for anyone unfortunate enough to catch these diseases, and I can assure you they're very painful.'

'Must 'ave ad 'um 'imself to know that,' whispered the unstoppable Kettley.

The lights went down and the fifteen-minute film commenced. Great amusement and comments from the security of the dark ensued for the first five minutes. Suddenly, there was a complete hush as a festering, bleeding, eaten-away penis appeared in full colour. Cries of 'fucking hell', intermingled with retching and two collapses through fainting. The stark reality of these diseases was punched home to the naïve audience. Vows were made to stay away from women for the rest of their lives, but the whole thing was forgotten within a fortnight or after the first date, whichever came first.

On the Wednesday of the final week we were practising for the passing out parade and the flight was unrecognisable from the rabble of a few weeks previously. Even Weedy had all his movements crisp and smart. We had practised the more difficult movements in the hut each evening, when Weedy could concentrate without fear, and now he was fully confident and proud. A wisp of a smile, and pride could be seen then in Jevon's face as he rapped out commands:

'Flight, ah-ten-shion!' bang, one movement, terrific.
'Flight, should-er-arms!' one, two, three, one, two, three, one.
'Flight, ri-aht, turn!' bang, as heel hit heel.
'Quick, march!' left, right, left right.
'Trailing arms on the march, trail, arms!' and so it went on.

Came the Friday, passing out day, and the boot toes and brasses hurt the eyes of the inspecting officers. We had stayed in all night, bulling our kit and helping one another. Six hard weeks had forged many friendships and created a flight with determination. Chest out, heads back, we performed as one and were awarded 'top flight' status. The pure joy and happiness of Flight 6b, the pride in achievement, meant more to us than anything else in the world.

That evening we took Jevons with us, pooled our money, and had a fantastic party in the NAAFI. We recounted stories from the past six weeks, we played 'sing, sing or show your ring', where everyone in turn has to sing or recite. If you couldn't do either it was 'show your ring' time. As most of us were drunk or well on the way, it caused no embarrassment at all to climb on the table in the centre of the ring of drunks and drop your trousers to ankles and bend over. In a drunken state it could take a couple of seconds to bring trousers up from the ankles to waist. That's when beer came from all directions aimed at the bent-over target. With noise, laughter, beer missing the target and hitting someone across the other side of the circle, it was a hilarious way to wind down and release the built-up tensions. Taffy had a lovely voice and gave a wonderful rendering of 'We'll keep a welcome in the hillside'. The whole hubbub of the NAAFI fell silent to listen to him and the applause was tremendous.

Rudy gave us one of his many Gorbals specials to a lively tune:

'I lifted her kilt and her arse was bare,
I could'ne see nothing for curly hair,
I took her behind a wall just then,
and gave her Geordie Lawry!'

Great laughter followed Rudy's risqué verses.

I gave them a rendering of Kipling's 'If', another of Father's party pieces.

Jevons, who by then had had more than a free skinful, put his arms round my shoulder and slurred into my ear, against the noise of the crowd:

'Take a fucking lead out of that Kipling's book, Fizz, keep your 'ead when they're all bloody losing theirs, the silly bastards,' and he fell off his chair laughing.

A fitting end to six hard weeks, as I looked down at Jevons, sitting on the stone floor in a sea of beer.

CHAPTER 6

Slow—Slow—Quick—Quick Slow

Hut 6b, our home, our font of baptism into the world of the Royal Air Force is abandoned, left to the world of square-bashing, spit and polish, to Jevons. We sally forth to pastures new, across the camp, away from the noisy, punishing square, to the quieter land of learning.

We're nearly all together thank goodness. Rudy, Taffy, Weedy and Blondie and unfortunately Kettley all end up in Hut 211, right next to the hangers. We lose Snowy and a few others but they're only a hut away. For the next sixteen months Hut 211 is to be our home. Blondie, Weedy, Rudy and myself have been designated trainee airframe mechanics, whereas Taffy and Kettley are trainee engine mechanics. We are not in a position to know who's better off but we are keen and excited and looking forward to starting our training.

'Right, you chaps, settled in all right?' asked a corporal, not too smart in appearance, upon entering the hut.

'Yes, thanks, Corporal,' said Weedy, standing up straight.

'You can forget that training bullshit here,' said the corporal. 'Call me Ted in the hut and on social occasions. If on parade or there's a senior NCO or officer about, it's Corporal, Got that, all of you?'

'Yes, Corporal Ted,' came the mixed reply and some laughter. Our spirits rose; this was better. I think I'm going to like this, I thought.

'I'm in charge of this hut but I'm not a soft touch; keep to the rules and there should be no problem,' he said. 'Any of you airframe mechs?' he asked.

'Five of us, Ted,' I replied.

'Good, I'm your carpentry instructor, so you'll be seeing more of me. My room's at the end of the billet, if you've got any problems,' and he left.

A buzz of excited talk filled the hut as realization dawned that the insults and degradation were left with Hut 6b. We all agreed that we didn't know what carpentry had to do with aeroplanes but we'd soon find out.

'Pity we're all broke,' said Rudy, 'just when we're allowed off camp, too.'

'I've got some money left,' said Blondie, whose parents visited him every Sunday.

'How much ya got?' asked Rudy.

'Five and tuppence,' replied Blondie.

It was Saturday lunchtime. We'd spent up the night before at Jevons' party and payday wasn't until Thursday. We were paid fortnightly during the first six weeks, twenty-eight shillings a week, but half was held back and paid to you when you went on leave. We therefore received twenty-eight shillings every fortnight and most of it went to the NAAFI for cigarettes, tea and wads, snacks on toast and, occasionally, beer.

'Not enough to go to Weston,' said Rudy, 'Let's go for a walk tonight and see what's nearby.'

It was pitch dark as we started out for a walk on that first Saturday in December 1947.

With some trepidation on my part, we made towards the guardroom and that awful red and white barrier. Five of us, dressed in our 'best blue' jackets and trousers. We stood out a mile from regular airmen as our peaked caps, just like our side hats, were ringed with an inch-wide brown detachable band to denote 'Boy Entrants – Trainee'. We came into the lighted area of the guardroom.

'And where do you think you're going?' shouted a voice from Heckner's office. He came striding out towards us. The others didn't know Heckner, so I took the lead.

'For a walk, Sergeant,'

'A walk, eh, top flight going for a walk; right, Freeman, my eyes are everywhere, my ears are everywhere and don't you ever forget it,' and he went back to his office with a grin.

We let out our breath and walked round the barrier, turned left up the main road and put distance between us and the camp.

The night was cold but we felt good as we strode along. Blondie started to sing. Before long, we all joined in and the sleeping cattle over the hedgerow were informed that 'eggs, eggs, growing hairy legs' were in the quarter-master's stores. We came to the village of Banwell, all lit-up and inviting. As we strolled through the village past a pub Blondie said;

'Let's have half a pint each, I've got enough.'

'Won't serve you,' Taffy said, 'they'll know we're under age by our "brown bands".'

'Could take 'em off, they're only clipped on,' said Rudy.

'OK, I'm for it, what about you?' Taffy asked Weedy.

'Well, I don't know, it could be risky,' he replied.

'I'll do a recce,' I said, and crept up to the window.

'It's OK,' I said, 'only three in there; if Weedy stays behind us, and we use the end of the room furthest from the bar, the landlord won't get a clear look at us, and Rudy and Blondie can get the drinks as they are the biggest.'

'OK,' said Rudy 'Hatbands off.'

We entered as nonchalantly as possible and all eyes turned on us. I was attempting to shield Weedy, who had the frame and stature of a fourteen-year-old. Taffy was also covering him. Blondie and Rudy made straight for the bar where a chalk board announced 'Scrumpy – eight pence a pint'. I heard Rudy boldly order 'Five pints of scrumpy, landlord, please,' The publican didn't bat an eyelid and was probably glad of the business.

'Err,' said Weedy, taking a sip, 'That's awful.' I tried it – by God, it was awful, but the others took big gollops.

'Gets better when you drink more, rough cider, see, made only from the apple, no sugar, no additives, puts lead in your pencil, boyos,' said the grinning Taffy.

We sat, enjoying the freedom of the big world, five friends together, telling yarns, puffing smoke, not a care in the world.

'Ted seems a decent chap; I wonder if all the NCO instructors are like him?' I said.

''Spect so, they're regulars, more interested in teaching than bullshit,' replied Taffy.

'I wonder what subject will come first?' mused Weedy. 'I still can't see where carpentry comes into it, though.'

'We'll know soon enough; what I want to know is if we're going to get home for Christmas,' said Blondie.

'Bugger Christmas, I want my leave for Hogmanay,' chipped in Rudy. 'It's a great way to start the New Year, pissed as a fart for a week, wandering up and down Shettleston Street, in and out of the neighbours', bottle of Johnnie Walker in ya hond, mon, it beats yon Sassenach Christmas.'

We talked and supped and made the pint last for nearly an hour.

'We'd better make a move, the place is filling up and we're sat with empty glasses,' said Taffy.

I was feeling decidedly wobbly and woolly-headed as we got into the fresh air but none of us expected Weedy to collapse in a heap, right outside the pub. Come to think of it, he had been quiet for the last ten minutes.

'He's surely not pissed on one pint,' said Rudy, as they lifted him upright, but sure enough he was, totally incapable; the fresh air seemed to have brought it on.

'Put his hat on, for Christsake and let's get out of this lighted area.'

Blondie and Rudy carried the comatose Weedy into the dark of a side street.

'We canny go thro' the guardroom entrance with him in this condition or we'll all get nicked for drinking,' said Rudy.

'He might sober up before then, let's walk him about a bit,' suggested Taffy.

'We canny take a chance on him sobering-up, we'll have to find another way inta camp,' said Rudy.

Taffy and I took the lead back to the camp. It was still only nine o'clock; traffic and pedestrians were still on the move. The pale, weak moon was throwing some light on our path and our plan was that we would stop and do up a bootlace if we spotted trouble (NCO, Officer or Police) approaching. Rudy and the gang were following twenty yards behind. If we stopped they would have to take avoiding action by pretending to stand talking. Weedy had come round and was mumbling away but couldn't stand unsupported. We could now see the lights of the camp, and cut through the roadside hedge and set off towards them.

Lady Luck was with us for once as we trudged across fields, through mud and cowshit and over a wire fence, and found Hut 211, to the great relief of one and all. We put Weedy to bed as he mumbled his poetry, completely oblivious to the problems he'd caused.

'Let's get rid of all this cowshit on our boots,' I said. 'Just in case Heckner sends someone to check whether we're in. I don't trust that devil and the cowshit's a dead giveaway.'

'OK,' said Blondie, 'I'll do Weedy's as well, then, when we've changed into our battledress we'll go to the NAAFI and blow the one and tenpence I've got left. I'll get some more tomorrow when my Dad comes.'

The forty-one survivors of our intake sat on chairs in a large lecture room on that first Monday morning of Technical Training. Seven new faces had joined our group from the previous entry. These seven had been put back through illness or other reasons. The chief instructor introduced himself and outlined the general technical programme we would be following.

'There are many subjects that are common to all trades and these you will do together,' he started, 'But most of the time you will be in specific groups according to your trade. There will be exams at various stages for all of you and, let me warn you now, the pass mark is 80% minimum. Standards are high. Aircraft are not like cars. If something goes wrong with a car it can stop safely and be put right. In an aircraft it's different. It you want to pass out as tradesmen you will have to work hard, very hard.'

'An airframe mechanic is basically responsible for, and capable of repairing, any and all of the aeroplane, other than the engines,' said the chief airframe instructor. 'The structure, be it metal or wood, mainplane or fuselage, has to be professionally inspected and repaired to set periods and routines. You will therefore learn all about metallurgy, heat treatments, salt baths, molecular structure, sheet metal work, nuts, bolts, rivets and so on. The systems that operate the undercarriages, brakes and controls will require a full and competent knowledge of hydraulic and pneumatic systems. You will learn how to repair tyres, how to spray an aircraft, how to repair a hydraulic and pneumatic component. But firstly you will learn the "theory of flight": what makes tons of metal lift off the ground and fly through the air.'

So he went on and the more the instructor outlined our job, the more excited I became. Here was a real challenge, something I really wanted to do, to become a qualified tradesman in the Royal Air Force, the cream of the services.

At ten o'clock we all stopped for NAAFI break. This was something new and was enthusiastically embraced. Each morning and afternoon the NAAFI wagon rolled up with smiling women serving lovely strong tea and wads. Ted had advised us to take our mugs with us, which we had, but as we were broke we just sat on the grass in the weak sunshine and enjoyed the new feelings of excitement, freedom and anticipation of things to come.

'Aren't you lot having a tea?' asked the Brummy voice with the red hair.

'We're broke,' replied Taffy.

'Here,' said the newcomer, handing us threepence each, 'Give us it back on payday.'

We got our pennyworth of tea and spent twopence on a lovely fresh Banbury cake and joined our benefactor on the grass.

'Thanks, mate,' I said, 'Pay you back Thursday. Seen you at the other end of our hut, how come you joined our intake?'

'I've had me appendix out so they put me back with your lot,' he said.

'What's your name, then?'

His small eyes twinkled amongst a million freckles, which made his pointed nose look even longer than it was, as he replied, 'Carrots, everybody calls me Carrots, it's me red hair you see,' he grinned.

'Well, cheers, Carrots,' I said, lifting my mug of scalding tea. 'This is Rudy, another airframe mech and my other mates: Weedy, Taffy and Blondie. What made you join up, Carrots?'

'Well, nothing much happening in Brum, chance to get a trade I s'pose, maybe see the world. Anyway, I always wanted to be a "Brylcreem Boy",' he replied, laughing.

'Not with that red hair,' I said laughing with him.

'Back in the lecture room, chaps,' said a strolling corporal.

I just couldn't believe the change in our lifestyle. Only that morning Ted had told us off for swinging our arms too high whilst marching to the lecture hut. Life was good; the only thing that could improve it would be a few shillings in our pockets.

The first two weeks of our new learning life were so interesting that they flew by. I was enthralled by the new subjects and found a great ally and study mate in Weedy. We would sit together at the table in the middle of the billet each evening and carefully re-write and redraw all the notes and sketches that we had done during the day's work. Most of the others were content with the notes they had taken during the day, but not Weedy and me. I found it an invaluable way of learning, to rewrite all my notes slowly, and in my best handwriting. I was determined to achieve the 80% minimum first time in every exam. After the first week of wisecracks my mates soon accepted my determined stand and I would not go out until I'd finished my day's notes. At practical exercises I was proving to be one of the best trainees. I got on really well with all the instructors, and life seemed to be on the up and up.

Blondie came rushing in the billet;

'Heard the news?' he shouted to all and sundry, 'The training school's closing down for Christmas, we're all going on leave for two weeks.'

The hut was in uproar as hats, towels and blankets, were thrown in the air and a great cheer went up.

CHAPTER 7

Kettley — Getting Out

Following our Christmas break there was a period of intense study, lectures, practical work and homework. Weedy had returned from leave with a set of mapping pens and coloured inks and we both sat, side by side, at the table in the centre of the billet, drawing our hydraulic and pneumatic systems in beautiful colours. When it came to the mathematics required for calculating bends, angles and stresses of our metal work, Weedy was tops. He seemed to get immense pleasure in teaching me how to calculate various formulae, and was now growing in stature and confidence. Rudy and Blondie now joined our evening homework group and it made for a greater effort from us all. Weedy was definitely the brains in the theory and mathematics but during the many practical sessions, be it repairing a leading edge of a mainplane, where the duralumin had to be perfectly formed, shaped and fitted flush with existing mainplane skin, then they all crowded around me to see how it was done. I thrived on the practical side and could recognise sizes of bolts and nuts, different threads from BSW to BA and BSF; I could size different types of metal rivets and loved the heat treatment and annealing sessions. I learnt quickly how to strip, repair and rebuild hydraulic and pneumatic components and how to repair cuts and tears in huge tyres.

In those early years after the war all items had to be repaired of necessity; there were insufficient stocks and equipment to renew items as they do today. An aircraft tyre that had a cut in the outside casing would be fully repaired by an airframe mechanic and be back in service within three hours. We would cut, at a prescribed angle, a two- to three-inch oblong hole in the outside rubber tread, with a special knife, blunted at the tip, to the depth of the cords. (If the cords were cut or damaged the tyre had to be scrapped.) Into the hole one would insert thin, one-sixteenth to one-eight of an inch thick pure rubber sheeting, cut to size, a layer of rubber solution, another layer of rubber, more solution, etcetera, until the new rubber was well proud of the tyre surface. All insertions had to be very carefully done and 'hammered' home to ensure no air pockets were left between the layers.

The next stage was to 'cook' the new rubber and fuse it into one with the tyre. A large electric iron, whose 'bottom-plate' fitted the contours of the tyres was now strapped over the repair with chains. The chains were tightened with screw toggles. Ten minutes for each layer of rubber, say eight layers, equals eighty minutes plus twenty minutes for the iron to reach maximum heat. The 'curing time' then would be one hour forty minutes. After removing the iron and letting the rubber cool, the airframe mechanic then had the great challenge and pleasure of re-cutting the tread and trimming off. Great job satisfaction was felt by the tradesmen looking at the finished job. It made me think of father mending our shoes when I was a boy.

'Why do we need to learn carpentry?' asked the pock-marked Kettley, that first morning with Ted the instructor.

'To repair wooden kites, what do you think it's for?' he answered.

'Didn't know there was wooden aeroplanes,' said Kettley.

'What do you think the Mosquito's made of, then, it's all wood, a balsa wood sandwich, that's the Mosquito, and there's plenty of them about.'

We were taught to recognise all the different types of joints there were; glues and gluing techniques; how to 'form' wood in hot water to various shapes; how to repair wooden leading edges of mainplanes. It was always leading edges that got damaged. When an aircraft takes off or lands, often a flock of birds, mostly starlings, will take off in its flight path. The impact of a bird on the leading edge of a wing has to be seen to be believed. Eighteen gauge duralumin can be indented far enough to put your fist in. These areas have to be neatly cut out and a flush repair inserted. Theory of flight teaches one to reduce the drag factor and these repairs are critical to the performance of the aircraft. Most aerodromes kept a hawk which was released daily at the end of the runways to chase away flocks of birds. With the advent of the jet engine the problem still remains and more modern methods are used to scare away the flocks of birds which are even more dangerous to today's high-speed aircraft.

As well as the many different trade subjects that were being studied, other subjects such as snow-clearing vehicles, crash recovery techniques and cranes were necessary for the operation of an aerodrome. It seemed the airframe mechanic had a lot to do besides maintaining aeroplanes.

We were now fully immersed in our studies but it wasn't all work. Wednesday afternoons were devoted to sport and while Rudy, Taffy and Blondie played football, I preferred cross-country running. Weedy preferred to be a spectator if he could get away with it, but occasionally he came on a run with me.

Time was flying by and we were all familiar now with Weston-super-Mare. Rudy and I joined ballroom dancing classes at the Wintergardens. The lady who took us seemed about sixty years old. Ruddy, bespectacled, owl-round face, silver-grey hair and massively built, it seemed the food rationing hadn't reached her household. When I first set eyes on Mrs Jenkins ('call me Jean'), I thought I could get three of me inside her tent of a dress and there would still be room for Rudy. For all her massive frame she was feather-like on her feet, and had a wonderful cheery personality.

'Robert, wasn't it?' she asked that first evening, as seventeen middle to oldish ladies, two middle-aged men, Rudy and I stood round the end of the ballroom floor. The room was cold, quiet and ghostly echoey. We had the building to ourselves. The full lights blazed overhead, which made the room colder and the learners more nervous.

'Yes, Mrs ... I mean, Jean,' I replied.

'Good, would you like to help me demonstrate the first steps. Tonight we're going to learn the waltz.'

Could I say no? I walked forward towards the massive treetrunks of her bare arms and was clamped into position. I looked at Rudy. He looked at me. His lips were compressed, holding in the laughter trying to get out; me as thin as a pipe-cleaner, she as big as St. Paul's.

'Now the steps are very simple, watch closely; the man leads off with his left foot taking one pace forward.'

I was carried forward and both feet followed.

'No, Robert, only move your left foot forward, your right foot stays where it is.' I wondered why I was inside her huge thigh. 'Take your right foot back to my left foot,' she said reluctantly, seeming to enjoy the contact. 'That's it, now, right foot forward and outward in line with your left foot.'

We stood, legs apart, facing one another. She smiled at me; was this some sexual ritual? I had my back to the others and couldn't see Rudy.

'Now we bring the left foot to the right foot, so,' she said, 'and that's all there is to it. Now, Robert, we're going to repeat that and we're all going to say, one, two, together, all right?'

We repeated the steps half a dozen times for the benefit of the watchers and I was returned to the safety of the group.

'Now pair up, some ladies will have to act as gentlemen, and we will all try the simple steps I've just demonstrated.

'Now, gentlemen, next week I want you to bring two nice clean folded handkerchiefs each. The correct way of holding a lady is with a clean handkerchief between the gent's left hand and the lady's right hand. The hands should be held outwards and above shoulder height. The second handkerchief should be held in the gent's right hand and placed gently between the hand and the middle of the lady's back, approximately just below the shoulder blades. The gentleman's skin should never touch the lady's skin, there's nothing worse than sweaty palms, is there? Ha, ha,' she laughed. 'There should be a clear eight inches of daylight between the two dancers.'

As she was talking, she moved round the floor adjusting the various couples' starting positions. We all stood there like Eros statues, in ungainly and uncomfortable positions.

'That's good, now all together: one, two, together, one, two, together.'

We continued to bruise one another for the next five minutes.

'That's good, you all seem to have got that, now let's try it to music.'

Jean moved to the oldfashioned gramophone where a record was already in place, and Victor Sylvester and his orchestra filled the ballroom.

We proceeded round the floor like robots, chanting our tune: 'One, two, together, one, two, together.' Everyone except Rudy and me seemed to be enjoying it immensely.

'That wasne dancing,' said Rudy as we left the Wintergardens and made our way along the front back to the bus-stop. 'More like bloody square-bashing with a smile,' he said. 'Dinny think I'll go again.'

'Oh come on, Rudy, that was only the first lesson; it will get better and more interesting as the weeks go on, you'll see.' So it did.

The next week we took our two clean handkerchiefs and danced eight inches apart. Within a few weeks we had learnt 'turns' and the quickstep, and as the weeks went by we became more and more enthusiastic. Rudy was a natural dancer, very graceful, and his handsome looks ensured he was never short of a partner, nor did he get a rest. We moved on to tangos and sambas, and just then all the rage was Danny Kaye and 'Ball in the Jack'. Jean taught us the dance and Rudy and I showed off our prowess in other dancehalls at weekends.

Harry James, the famous trumpeter, was at his peak, and his music and records filled the dancehalls in 1948. We kept up our dancing lessons all the time we were at Locking but I found that many of the intricate steps and sequences were no use in later life, for I rarely found a partner that could do them. I once asked a good dancer if she could do the seven point turn in a quickstep. 'Yes, I've done that before, many times.' We got on the floor first as the music started, glided around like Fred and Ginger; I swung my partner quickly into a turn, confident she would follow the steps, and ten seconds later she was minus a shoe and plus four bruises. She left the floor, never to be seen again and I gave up on the seven point fishtail.

It was Sunday morning, no church parade that particular day, and I lay in bed enjoying the comfort and warmth. Most of my mates were lying-in and we'd missed breakfast which started at eight o'clock. This was a day of leisure, not to be rushed. Weedy, Rudy and I would probably do a bit of swotting before going to the NAAFI for lunch, that is, if I could get Rudy out of bed; he'd lie there all day if he could, but hunger usually managed to get him moving. I looked down the billet at my lazy hut mates, most of whom were sitting up in bed, or leaning on their elbows carrying on conversations with a neighbour or across the billet. Rudy was snoring away, oblivious to the chatter that was going on around him. Carrots, the red-headed Brummy, entered the hut with three steaming mugs of tea he'd brought back from breakfast. The chorus went up from all the lazy bed-dwellers.

'Give us a swig, Carrots.'

He passed the mugs to the three owners who gulped the hot tea till it burnt their throats. Snowy and Taffy passed their half-empty mugs to the next beds, but not Kettley.

'Who wants a drop of mine?' he asked, with a gleam in his eye. 'What about you, Fizz?' he asked.

'Sure, thanks,' I said. He was out of bed coming my way, so I lay there, a little surprised at his generous gesture. When he reached my bed he held the mug at an angle above my head and, with the tea nearly spilling out, said for all the hut to hear:

'Fizz said he wanted a drop of tea, didn't he?'

The talking stopped and everybody looked in our direction. I still lay there, my head propped on my elbow. Kettley was waiting for a reaction or encouragement but none came, only silence.

'If one drop of that tea touches me or my bed you'll get a fire bucket full of water over yours,' I said calmly.

His hand steadied, he wasn't quite as confident, silence reigned; twenty pairs of eyes watched and waited.

'You wouldn't dare, it would muck up the whole floor,' he said with a nervous laugh but uncertainty was now there. He was in a predicament, trying to be big, trying to win over the crowd but nobody liked him.

'Try me,' I said.

He had no choice, a drop of tea hit me on the head. Like a shot, I was out of bed and bare-footed it to the fire buckets, lifted one up and carried it to Kettley's bed. I stood calmly at the bottom of his bed and slowly emptied the contents onto his bedding. Kettley hadn't moved in the few seconds it had taken me to carry out my promise; he probably thought I'd stop at the last moment. As the water hit his bedclothes, the cheers went up from the bedridden airmen and, at the same time, Kettley charged like a mad bull from the head of my bed, down the aisle towards me. He was mad with rage. His first wild swing hit me on the shoulder and the empty bucket shot out of my hand, making a hell of a noise as it hit the metal legs of a bed. We went into a clinch and fell onto the floor. He was trying to pin me to the floor by sitting on top of me but I was too slippery. Everyone was out of bed, crowding round and shouting advice. Then suddenly it was silent. We were being dragged apart.

I noticed for the first time it was Ted, our corporal, and Rudy that had parted us.

'I ought to put you two stupid sods on a charge, you're like a couple of kids,' he said, 'I'll not have fighting in my hut. Consider yourselves on fatigue detail, two nights, Monday and Tuesday; report to me at six o'clock for orders. Now, get this bloody mess cleaned up. Any more trouble and I'll throw the book at you,' and he stomped out.

I moved across to pick up the bucket when Kettley's voice cut across the billet.

'Good job Ted came in, saved you a bloody good 'iding, you bolshie bastard.'

'Shut your ugly mouth, you've caused enough trouble already,' I said over my shoulder.

'Ya both wanna calm down or yearl be in big trouble if Ted hears ya,' said Rudy, but Kettley wouldn't let go.

'I heard what Sergeant Thomas said,' Kettley baited, 'Thrown out of the army school, no bloody good, bloody misfit.'

I was passing Kettley with the empty bucket. His words bit home. I'd had to take them from Sergeant Thomas with all my mates listening, but I wasn't going to take them from Kettley. I saw red, instinctively dropped the bucket and brought up a vicious right hook to the unprotected and unsuspecting chin of Kettley. Dusty Miller would have been proud of the crisp contact and follow through. Kettley dropped straight backwards and hit the floor full length. Whether or not he caught his head on the stove surround I'm not sure, but he didn't move. Everyone crowded round the prostrate body and Rudy was slapping his face. I saw Ted pushing through the crowd of bodies. Kettley was sitting up and moaning.

'Right, you two stupid bastards, you're both on a two-five-two. If I hear another word from either of you I'll put you both in the guardroom until tomorrow. Now get dressed and sort this bloody billet out.'

Monday morning, ten o'clock and both Kettley and I were standing in the administration block corridor again. We were marched in together. The flight lieutenant glanced at my file and then looked up at me from behind his desk.

'You're soon back again, Freeman, are you going to make a habit of this?'

'No, Sir.'

'Fighting's for a boxing ring, not in a hut, what have you got to say for yourself?'

'We were having a bit of friendly horseplay, Sir, and it got out of hand.'

'That's not what I heard. What's your story, Kettley?'

'Same as Freeman's, Sir,'

'You're a pair of scoundrels if not liars, bad examples all round. Freeman, five days detention, Kettley four days detention, take them away.'

Five more days with Heckner, five days, Christ I could have died at the thought; and to add to the punishment, I would miss five important days of lectures and practical work just one month before midcourse exams. I knew I could catch up my notes with Weedy's help but the practical sessions would be lost. I could kill Kettley, I thought, as we picked up our kit from the hut. One consolation though, Kettley was in it with me, we'd see what he was made of.

We were doubled back to the guardroom, a much longer journey from our new billet, and this time with the addition of our rifles.

'Not tired already, are you Kettley?' said the snowdrop as Kettley was flagging halfway to the guardroom. 'You haven't started yet, 'asn't your mate Freeman told you what to expect – come on, pick those feet up.' We arrived to be welcomed by the smiling face of the sergeant of the guard, Heckner.

'Corporal, did you say halt?' shouted Heckner.

'No, Sergeant.'

'Well, why 'as that man stopped?' Poor Kettley was standing there puffing, his kitbag touching the floor along with his rifle; he was knackered.

'Prisoner, pick up your kit and double on the spot – now!' screamed the corporal. Kettley's legs attempted to move again and his kitbag and rifle lifted an inch clear of the floor. Poor sod, I thought. I was already feeling sorry for him. He never took part in any sports and was the worlds best 'skiver' when it came to doing anything energetic. His studies weren't going well either; his reports and homework were always poor. He had been stating quite often his desire to get out and he had lost any interest he had in learning. 'Back to the Smoke, that where I wanna be' was his boring tune, and in consequence he was friendless and shunned by everybody.

'Prisoners – halt.'

We stood in front of the grinning Heckner, trying to get our breath back. Three corporal snowdrops stood to his right. The July sun reflected back off the brass bell as another prisoner eyed us from the security of the main office, dusters in hand and one hand on the window pane.

'Welcome home, Freeman,' grinned Heckner, 'I told you you'd be back. Tough guy, eh? Fighting this time, we'll see if five days with us can take the spunk out of you, won't we, corporals?'

'Yes, Sergeant,' they chorused.

'Bad apple, that's you, cocky Freeman, you're fuckin' rotten to the core, and you, Kettley, should keep away from bastards like Freeman else you'll end up on the shit pile like 'im,' said Heckner. 'Four days, eh, Kettley, four days to remember, you'll wish you never set eyes on Freeman, that I can promise you. Now let's get moving, kit inspection in half an hour, move 'em, Corporal.'

We were put in adjacent cells and hurried to get our kit laid out. I knew what to expect, but Kettley didn't. The cell doors were always left open except when we were locked in at night. As the cells opened into the main office, and the corporal of the guard's desk was next to the only door, we couldn't go anywhere. Other corporals and the sergeant's office were fronting onto the entrance porch, so there were plenty of eyes to ensure we didn't abscond.

The corporal of the guard went outside to the barrier to check an incoming vehicle. I took the opportunity to poke my head around the corner of Kettley's cell door. 'How's it going?'

Kettley had shown no grudge or animosity towards me since the fight, quite the opposite, in fact. I think it was the fear of his first charge and the unknown of what to expect in the guardroom. He seemed a bit lost and needed something or someone to cling to in the strange and threatening environment.

'OK. Fizz, will that sergeant do the inspection?'

'Yes, he probably will, he usually takes the first one with new prisoners. Stay calm, he'll insult you, probably throw all your kit about and generally show off in front of his corporals. Just remember this, though, they can only shout, scream and insult you and that won't kill us, will it? They will probably put us in the – '

'Get back in your cell, what the bloody 'ell d'ya think this is – visiting time?' screamed the corporal.

Heckner started at cell one, the prisoner who was cleaning the windows when we arrived. He only looked about fourteen years old and his lack of hair and snow white neck were a dead give-away that he was a new intake.

'The runaway, five minutes in the RAF and he fucks off, wanted Mummy to change his nappy, didn't ya sonny? Only got to Weston station, poor bastard, no guts, no spine, just a little shithead aren't you son?' said loudmouth.

'I asked you a question, son, you fuckin' well answer me or I'll have you dancing round that exercise yard till midnight. You're a shithead – what are you?' screamed Heckner.

'I'm a shithead, Sergeant,' said a weak, trembling voice.

We stood and watched, helpless; there was nothing we could do to help the poor frightened lad. The duty corporal stood by the side of his sergeant, face expressionless. What made these beasts? I thought, they must have been human at one time; they must have mothers, brothers and sisters, but not a spark of compassion was in them. I glanced at Kettley, who looked pale and nervous, I gave him a wink, blind side of the Gestapo.

'Well, sonny, are you going to run away again? I hope so, it makes my life interesting, but use your fuckin' brains next time, don't make straight for the railway station, fuck-off across country, then we can have a few days out and pick you up from mummy's arms,' he grinned.

He stepped around the lad to look at his kit layout.

'What the hell is this supposed to be, a bloody jumble sale?' he shouted. 'Corporal, have you seen this?'

'He's only been at Locking ten days, Sergeant,' said the corporal.

'Ten days, ten days, what the hell's that got to do with it? No tapes with numbers, incorrect layout, kit folded by a one-armed blindman, fuckin' disgusting.'

With one movement of his arm he scattered the lot to the four corners of the cell.

'You have until tomorrow morning, Corporal, to lick this boy into shape, I don't care if he's up all night, I want a layout every hour on the hour, inspected by you. I will see the results tomorrow, got it?'

'Yes, Sergeant.'

Heckner came towards me.

'Rifle for inspection, present,' ordered Heckner.

I came to the 'present' position and released the firing bolt. Heckner took the rifle, turned to the window and looked up the barrel.

Here we go, I thought, more birds' nests. I used oil and pull-through two dozen times that morning; it didn't take long, and I knew the barrel was gleaming. Heckner studied it for quite a while, then slowly turned towards me, a half-inch smile at the corner of his mouth.

'Money spider, Freeman, that's what it is. You're going to come into money, have a look at your money spider sitting on his cobweb; you haven't cleaned your bloody rifle in weeks, go on, have a look.'

Oh Christ, more bloody stupid games. Should I agree? Should I act dumb? That's not my nature. If I say I see it I'm in trouble, if I don't see it then he's a liar and I'm in trouble. Hell, how stupid all this is. Kettley was staring straight ahead, no doubt fearing his turn.

'Go on – look, I said,' shouted Heckner. I took the rifle and looked up the shining barrel.

'I think I see it, Sergeant,' I replied. A big idiot smile spread across his flat pan face.

'So you admit you're a lazy bastard, Freeman?'

'Yes, Sergeant.'

'Right, Corporal, doubling round the yard, rifle uppermost, get to it.'

Off I went. Kettley couldn't have fared any better as ten minutes later he joined me. So my second spell of detention was under way.

I kept thinking of all the lessons I was missing and the futility of it all. Was it worth going on? Why had I joined? Was Kettley right to think of getting out? Wouldn't all camps have MPs? Would I always be in and out of guardrooms? Why me? Lots of guys had never been in trouble; it must be something wrong with me, my big mouth, my temper, or was it the 'flashbacks' I kept getting at certain times? Flashbacks always occurred when I was in a similar position to what I remember my father being in. He never got into trouble, he just took the injustice of it all, but I couldn't. Was I doing it for my father? Yes, that's it, I was making up for what Father had had to take, but where was it leading? What good was it doing? I was confused again, but sod them all, they wouldn't break me.

'Rest your rifle on your head till he shouts,' I advised Kettley, closing up behind him, 'And relax your body and legs. Take short steps, only lifting your boots just clear of the ground. That's it, they can shout and bawl. Don't listen to the loudness of the voice, think of something nice.'

I continued to encourage him, as the sweat marks spread round his armpits and over his shoulder blades.

The hot sun was now streaming into the exercise yard and half the time we were in the sun and the other half in the shade of the wall.

'Slow up in the shade, faster in the sun,' I whispered.

'How much longer?' he gasped.

'Not long, just keep moving.'

'Get those rifles up!' shouted the corporal.

'Tell him you're bursting for a piss,' I whispered, as Kettley stumbled, 'that will give you a minute's rest.'

Kettley stumbled to the barred window.

'Could I go to the toilet, Corporal? I'm bursting,' pleaded Kettley.

'Inside, both of you,' he replied. Pure relief as we entered the office.

'Wait there, Freeman, while I take Kettley for a piss.'

'Right, Corporal.' I was glad of the rest.

He returned, and I noticed Kettley was wringing with sweat, great globules all over his face and dripping off his nose and chin.

'Get your webbing off and put your rifles away, then you, Freeman, can help Pearson to get his kit into shape for Sergeant Heckner's inspection tomorrow morning, you heard what he said; but by Christ, not a word to Heckner that you've helped the boy, got it?'

'Yes, Corporal,' I said, pleased to get a 'cushy' job for an hour.

'Kettley, you get out the front there with a broom and sweep the road and round the outside of the guardroom. If you see Sergeant Heckner coming, you get in here quick and tell me, got it?'

'Yes, Corporal.'

'Right, you've got just an hour, then it's cookhouse; get moving.'

The three of us were doubled to the cookhouse at one o'clock and received worldly advice and encouragement from passing 'erks'. The MPs hated to hear this encouragement coming our way and would counter with,

'Watch it, airmen, else you'll be bloody joining 'em,' but often it was a crowd of 'erks' and the escort didn't know which one had spoken.

Kettley and Pearson were gobbling their food down as the escorts sat at the table behind us sipping mugs of tea and watching.

'I'm definitely getting out of the RAF now,' whispered Kettley, 'Why don't you get out with me, Fizz, we'd make a good team in the Smoke.'

'What will we have to do this afternoon?' asked Pearson.

I looked at the lad; he was a bit like Weedy; small frame but round innocent babyish face, completely at a loss, his nervous eyes flickering and his body seemingly ready to duck, as those expecting a blow from behind.

'Back in the exercise yard at two o'clock; have you been in there yet?' I asked.

'No, I only got caught last night.'

'Well, just learn to run easy, slow and relaxed. Some spells you run, some you walk, it's not too difficult if you relax and don't think about it, think of something else.'

'You been in before, then?'

'Yes, once, but – '

'Pack up talking and eat,' said the snowdrop.

Sure enough, we were back in our oblong of punishment at two o'clock but as we were not 'Class A' prisoners, no cumbersome webbing or rifle. Pearson seemed a natural runner and was doing better than Kettley.

'Corporal of the guard,' boomed Heckner's voice.

'Yes, Sergeant,' replied the erect snowdrop to the painted black steel bars four inches from his nose.

'Bring the prisoners in.'

'Yes, Sergeant.'

We stood in line in the main office getting our breath while we awaited the entry of Heckner. He entered with a broad grin on his face – we were in trouble – I could feel it. Two other corporal snowdrops were with him.

'Right, you two fighters, we're going to give you some fitness training so next time you 'ave a fight you'll bash each other's fuckin' 'eads in.'

His beer-laden breath filled the room. Been at the sergeants' mess bar all lunchtime, I thought.

'I want to help the ground staff, I like helping people, see. You're going to dig a drainage ditch – got it – and dig till you drop – got it – corporals – got it.'

'Yes, Sergeant.'

'Well, take them away, you know where to go, I'll be along at five o'clock and by Christ you'd better have something to show me.'

'Yes, Sergeant,' said the corporals. 'Prisoners, double march – not you, Pearson, stand still,' and off we trotted.

The ditch was three feet wide and four feet deep and had to be dug from virgin soil the whole length of the sports field. Between kit inspections, exercise yard, meals and insults, Kettley and I spent the rest of our four and five days digging, while our escorts sat in the shade of a tree watching and shouting. Every few yards dug had to be infilled by wheeling barrowloads of gravel two hundred yards from the stockpile. Kettley and I really got to know one another during this period. He'd been put in a home when he was young as his mother had died and his father couldn't look after him. He'd had no home life, like me to some extent, and maybe this had made him hate the world. We came to respect one another as we sweated and toiled in that ditch and the least expected happened: we became firm friends.

Kettley left on the Friday morning and his last words were, 'See you, mate, you've been a great help in 'ere, I won't forget it.'

He had previously apologised, in his way, for getting me in trouble, and it seemed uncharacteristic for him to show remorse, but the threatening régime of the MP's world overcame individual prejudices of prisoners and broke down normally unbreakable barriers. We had become mates, and his pock-marked face was no longer repugnant to me.

As I pretended to polish the glittering crystal windowpanes of the guardroom office, I watched Sergeant Heckner performing his well-rehearsed party piece with my departing friend Kettley. Over the period of four lonely, threatening days and nights, we had come to understand one another, see each other in a different light. We depended on each other for moral and physical support. Old prejudice was forgotten and friendship born of common suffering was forged with steel.

Kettley's ambition to 'get out', so often repeated and argued over the past four days had been like water dripping constantly on a stone. It had left its mark in my mind. His new belief that we should go together, become a team, travelled in my mind from ridiculous to possible. The more he talked about London and his haunts, the more enthused I became.

'We'll talk about it after you get out on Saturday,' he said.

I agreed.

That last evening I gazed up at the single bulb and sleep wouldn't come. Full of excitement at the picture painted by Kettley and enhanced by my imagination, I went over all he had said, and thrilled at the freedom and glamour of the life in prospect.

CHAPTER 8

The Little Red Car

'Come and see what I've got outside,' said Kettley, as I lay on my bed in a dingy basement flat in Chelsea Manor Street, just off King's Road.

I had been lying there all morning, surveying the flat that had been our home for nearly two years. The one bedroom, with its two dilapidated beds, left little room for any other furniture, other than the chest of drawers. My two conservative suits hung with Kettley's five loud suits from the picture-rail, and took up two complete walls. A cracked mirror hung on a nail over the chest of drawers and a pile of shoes filled the corner of the room. The one bedroom window, which was painted permanently shut, looked out at the base of a forty-foot-high warehouse wall not ten feet away. It was necessary to switch on the one sixty-watt bulb whatever time of day one entered the dingy bedroom.

The rest of the flat was no better. The nine foot by twelve foot living room resembled an upmarket pigsty with its grubby brown sofa bursting its horsehair contents from arms and back. One dark green, greased and torn armchair, a two-leafed oak dining table that took up the centre of the room, with four odd black metal chairs. The table was covered with half-eaten meals stuck to their plates, half a bottle of milk, sugar bag with spoon sticking out and a bottle of HP sauce with no top on it and a collar of congealed sauce around its neck. Half a loaf of crooked-cut bread, a pack of margarine with its guts torn out and now shaped like a saddle, cutlery and newspapers left where they dropped, all liberally sprinkled with bits of food, crumbs and sugar spilt from overflowing tea spoons. A veritable feast for the flies and silverfish that shared the flat with us.

The kitchen of six feet by five feet had a sink full of dirty crockery that had long given up hope of ever being washed. The gas cooker was straining under the weight of grime and boiled-over food. Pots and pans shared the three open shelves with the foodstuffs, such as they were. There was only room for one person at a time in the kitchen, not that we frequented the place unless it was absolutely necessary. A small bathroom and toilet completed the 'facilities'.

So this was what I've come to, I was thinking. How much longer we were going to 'enjoy' our home was in the lap of the gods and the landlord. We were under notice of eviction for non-payment of rent: six months rent, to be exact.

'Come on,' said Kettley excitedly, as I lay there showing little interest. I pulled on a jacket and padded along the corridor, up the basement steps and into the smog-laden air of London.

'What d'ya think?' he said, pointing to a lowslung red sportscar. 'A snip at forty-five quid.'

I was dumbfounded. We'd been broke for weeks and owed money to many friends.

'Yours?'

'Sure, bought it this morning,' he replied with pride, 'Sit in it, see what ya think, go on.'

'Where did you get the money?' I asked, ignoring his invitation.

'Borrowed a fiver off Sid in the market for the deposit, the rest's on the door knocker.'

'Where are we going to get money for the repayments, for Christsake? We'll have nowhere to live after next week and you go out and buy a bloody car, you must be fucking mad,' I said, as my temper rose.

Kettley had done many irresponsible things since we'd lived together but somehow we had struggled along, running a few dodges on the market back of Victoria, but of late our luck had run out and many of Kettley's contacts were no longer contactable.

'Now we've got wheels we'll be on the up and up, I needed wheels for our next trick,' he said, somewhat deflated after my unenthusiastic reaction.

'What trick are you on about?'

A crafty smile crept over his face.

'Well that's it, see, I've been keeping mum about it till I had wheels. Come on in and I'll tell ya.'

I looked at the bright red Flying Standard with its canvas top, long bonnet and black-painted wire spoke wheels.

'What year is it?'

'1936, and it's got twin carbs, it sure can motor.'

'And where do you think you're going to get petrol coupons?' I asked, annoyed.

'Got twenty gallons worth already, that 'ull do for starters till the money comes in,' he said confidently.

'You're crackers,' I said as I made my way indoors.

Kettley followed, his pock-marked face no longer looking so happy and confident. As he dropped his huge square frame onto the sofa, puffs of dust rose each side of him like a helicopter landing.

'The good times are coming,' he said, more to convince himself than me. 'I've been watching this filling station for weeks, that's why I've been coming in late. Saturday night is the best time, after they've got the weekend cash in. Only one old bloke and he walks out at ten thirty with his Gladstone bag full of the day's takings. It'ull be a cinch,' he said, his confidence returning as he gabbled out his plan. 'Now we've got the wheels it'ull be a doddle.'

'Are you mad?' I burst out. 'You must be completely doolally. I know we've done a few shady deals on the market but holdups is a whole new ball game, at least two to five years if we get nicked. It's not on and you know it. Whoever heard of doing a hold-up in a bright red car?' I laughed nervously, seeing the funny side of Kettley's ridiculous plan.

'All right, clever bugger,' he replied, annoyed at my laughing dismissal of his plan. 'You come up with an idea for a change instead of lying in ya pit all day stinking. I always make the running. How else are we going to pay the rent and the boys in the market?' he sneered. 'I've done all the thinking and made most of the deals, so come on, clever sod, what's your brainwave?' he raved as he got up from the sofa and started to pace around the table like a caged tiger.

It was true, he had come up with most of the contacts and ideas that had kept us solvent for the past year or so, but the last six months it had gradually got worse. I thought at first it was just a bad spell and we'd get through it, so we'd borrowed off our friends until things picked up.

Unfortunately, they hadn't picked up and now our friends avoided us. I'd give Kettley his due, he still kept going out looking for opportunities, whereas I'd hardly moved out of the flat for a month or more.

At last I realised where my rebellious and obstinate nature had led me, a good-for-nothing 'wide boy' on the very edge of the law and now really desperate, ready to do almost anything to earn a few bob. But robbery, actual pure crime, becoming a real criminal just like Heckner said I would, surely there must be an alternative; but what?

'Well then, what ya got to offer?' asked Kettley, stubbing out his half-smoked Woodbine in a plate of cold beans. 'We've got one week from today and then we're out on our arse.'

'I know that as well as you do, keeping on about it doesn't help none. If you had borrowed forty-five quid, instead of buying that motor, we could have paid off some rent and had a breathing space,' I said, really making things up, rather than admitting I'd no suggestions to offer to raise some quick cash.

'You're talking through your arse, you know as well as I do that our rating around the market is nix, nil, nuffin'. We owe every bugger. Who'd be mad enough to lend us that size of wad?'

I had to admit that what he said was true. We'd tapped every friend we had.

'Five minutes, just five bloody minutes, that's all it would take, snatch the bag, tie the old bugger up and away in the motor. We could pay off the debts, the rent, and maybe even the motor, just five bloody minutes' work and you're chicken,' he growled.

'Don't push it,' I said, 'You know I ain't afraid of nothing, so watch it.'

He could see my temper was rising at his insinuation and he had witnessed my explosive nature more than once recently.

'OK, OK, but what else are we going to do, tell me that?' he asked, cooling down a bit.

'Where is this garage, anyway?' I asked, really for something to say rather than out of any particular interest.

The unexpected question must have raised Kettley's hopes. He stopped pacing and drew up a black metal chair alongside my armchair. His face and eyes took on that excited look again.

'That's the best of it,' he said, his eyes brightening with his own thoughts. 'Right across town, through Edgware and Cricklewood to the A1 North, take us about an hour in the motor, I should think; so, when the alarm goes we'll be safe in our pad counting the money,' he grinned.

He'd taken my question as a sign of agreement to do the job and I knew I'd weakened my position.

'How do you know the money's in the bag he carried?' I asked, hoping he didn't know, so I could find fault and turn the tables on him.

''Cause I've seen 'im put it in, that's why. The silly sod thinks he can't be seen when he fills the bag on the floor behind the counter but there's this mirror, see, on the wall behind the counter, and I've watched him twice now.'

'Well, why didn't you nick it then?'

"'Cause I was on the bus, wasn't I, how'd the hell would I scarper – on shanksies?' he grumbled. 'Well, what about it, are you in?'

'I didn't say that, I was only asking,' I quickly replied.

'Look,' said Kettley 'one job, God's honest, that's all, one job, a new start and then strictly market business, I promise, so what about it?'

I could feel he was slowly wearing me down, bringing me round to his way of thinking; I was trapped.

'Let's think about it for a day or so, maybe something else will come up,' I said, trying to get out of the trap. Kettley exploded.

'Fuckin' 'ell, Fizz,' he shouted, jumping to his feet again and waving his arms like a trainee tick-tack man. 'Can't ya see we're fucking stoney,' he raved. 'You couldn't recognise an elephant's arse if you was stuck halfway up it.' He stomped round the table again.

A loud banging on the ceiling was a welcome interruption to Kettley's ranting. The old lady living in the flat above took regular and great delight in bringing down a shower of dust and dry plaster on our heads. It probably broke the boring monotony of her lonely days.

'Better keep our voices down a bit now,' I said 'She'll have her glass to the floor, nosy bitch.'

'Well – you'd make a mute shout; at least say you'll come and look at the place – that's all I ask – what about it?' he pleaded.

I could feel that if I said no it would be the parting of the ways, goodbye, the end of our relationship. I didn't want that, we'd been good friends and we'd had some good times together.

'All right, but just a look, no promises,' I said, hoping to find some way out.

'Agreed,' he said, beaming a smile as his hand shot out towards me. 'We'll go tonight.'

Bloody hell, I was in it up to my neck. Don't start arguing when to go, get it over with.

'OK,' I said, trying to look friendly.

It took us one and a quarter hours, through Edgware Road and Cricklewood and down the A1 North.

'Blimey, it's a bit isolated,' I said, as Kettley drove past the filling station. It lay well back off the main road, but seemed to be busy with three cars at one pump and two at the other.

A wooden ramshackle service bay was attached to the small brick-built office and shop. Old tyres and lorry wheel hubs were stacked along the outside wall of the service bay and the edge of the large gravelled and potholed car park. A bungalow, with lights blazing, lay slightly behind and to the right of the service bay. There was a great impression of neglect emphasized by a few rusty old bangers littering the sides of the car park. A pair of farm cottages lay a quarter of a mile from the garage and there were no other buildings for at least two miles.

'Sure, it's isolated, all the better; that's why I picked it,' said Kettley.

'What about the people in the bungalow?' I said, 'They will soon raise the alarm when the old man doesn't show up.'

'I've thought of that, all we need is about fifteen minutes to get into the built-up area of town and off the A1. If we tape his wrists, legs and lips he won't be able to do anything and they won't come looking for him for at least ten minutes or so, then they've got to raise the alarm. We'll be halfway home before the police are even on the scene.'

Kettley sounded so confident and I must admit it did seem easy. We turned the car and drove back again past the garage as Kettley said:

'Well, Saturday then, all right, all our money troubles will be over.'

As we drove home I felt definitely despondent. My heart was not in the job and yet I was committed to participate. The next few days of waiting and thinking made me quite miserable but Kettley kept up his confidence and bravado and was in high spirits, just waiting for Saturday to come.

We left the flat at eight thirty, just to be on the safe side, and drove out to the filling station. It was a miserable rainy night and there was more wind inside the car than outside. The one windscreen wiper rested after every stroke, which made driving difficult. I was cold, fed up and scared. It took us nearly one and half hours to get there.

We had previously picked a spot to hide the car from the passing traffic. Once parked off the road behind some young saplings, we made our way the hundred yards towards the lighted garage and watched the old man from a nearby shrubbery some thirty feet away. We could see lights on in the bungalow but there were no customers in the filling station. It's such a filthy night everyone's stayed indoors, I thought, as the wind lashed the rain into our freezing faces. My face was numb with cold. It was five past ten, twenty-five minutes to wait in appalling weather. We would both end up with pneumonia at this rate.

'Let's wait in the car,' I shouted in Kettley's ear but he would have none of it. His eyes shone with excitement.

'Won't be long, he might pack in early on a night like this,' he shouted back.

Sure enough he was right. The lights on the forecourt went off and we saw the old man lock the outside door from within. He then returned behind the counter, where the light was still on, and opened the cash till.

'Right,' shouted Kettley, 'Let's take up our position.'

I followed him with thumping heart around the back of the service station and along the side of the service bay. We kept close to the stacks of tyres and metal hubs and were now in a position which the old man would have to pass to get back to the bungalow. When the garage office light went out, Kettley gripped my arm. 'He's coming, don't forget the plan.'

I stood shaking with cold and fear. We couldn't go back now, the old man would be rounding the corner any second.

Suddenly, it happened. A dark shape ambled round the corner of the building. Kettley grabbed his arms, pinning them to his side. I attempted to put the wide tape across his mouth and round his head but the old boy broke loose from Kettley's grip. Panic ensued for some seconds as the two of us grappled with his writhing body. The old boy had spirit and was fighting back. Kettley was punching wildly now and suddenly the old man fell. He didn't move. He just lay there. An eerie silence followed the tussle, broken only by the wind and the rain. Kettley grabbed the bag.

'Come on,' he shouted, 'Let's scarper.'

I was on my knees by the old man's head. He lay in the supine position, head sharp to one side and motionless. I put my ear to his mouth, then my hand.

'He's not breathing,' I shouted. But Kettley had gone.

I moved his head straight and my hand came away sticky – blood, oh my God – he's dead. I panicked and ran for the car. Kettley was revving up impatiently as I shouted in at him.

'He's dead.'

'Get in, for Christ sake,' he bellowed.

I stumbled in, a shuddering wreck.

Kettley and I stood handcuffed together in the dock.

My mother and father had sat in the front row of the court for the past ten days. Mother's eyes were red with weeping.

'Has the jury reached a verdict?' asked the judge.

'We have, your honour,' replied the upright foreman of the jury.

'And what is the jury's verdict?'

I looked at Mother, she looked at me. Her face was creased in tension and anguish. Her eyes stood forward, full of fright and apprehension. They seemed to be asking a thousand questions. My heart went out to her, the one I loved most, and the one I'd brought more trouble to than all her other children. Why me? why? why? why?

'Guilty in the first degree,' said the foreman.

Mother's anguished scream ripped through the court as the judge put on his black cap.

'Prisoners at the bar – you have been found guilty of murder in the first degree. You shall be taken from this court and hanged by the neck – '

'WAKE-UP, WAKE-UP, noisy bastard, you've woken everybody in the bloody camp,' shouted the snowdrop.

I slowly focused on the RAF uniform. The duty corporal was standing above my cell bed. I was soaked in sweat. Fear must have still been in my eyes as he said:

'Must have been some bloody nightmare, you're screaming your head off. You look like you've seen a ghost.'

I lay there after he'd left and thanked God I was still in the RAF.

CHAPTER 9

Devon — Glorious Devon

Saturday morning, ten o'clock, dressed in full battle order, kitbag packed, I stood to attention as Heckner said his farewell.

'One of my regulars now, Freeman, leopards don't change their spots. Born to cause trouble and all you'll get is a life of trouble. Seen hundreds of stupid buggers like you, never learn, you'll be back 'ere again. If I was the powers that be I'd throw you out. Now fuck off and keep out of my sight – dismiss!'

Back to the hut, back to my friends, back to my studies. I vowed, as I strode through the camp, 'Never again', that was it. I was never going back inside that degrading guardroom. The effects of my five days, now that it was over, were nothing. I felt good, I wasn't depressed; in fact, I was excited. Happy to be out and keen to catch up with my studies. I'd taken this trip 'inside' in my stride. I think what helped was firstly that I knew what to expect, there were no surprises left, and secondly that I had two compatriots who were in a worse state and needed my help. Caring for them had lightened my load. Pearson had been released on Wednesday. I made a mental note to look him up sometime.

The hut was full when I walked through the door and a big cheer went up. Happy faces crowded round and one would have been forgiven for thinking I'd just climbed Everest. Weedy was beaming all over his face and quickly gathered his pile of exercise books with neatly written notes on every subject and tried, above the hubbub, to tell me what I'd missed.

'In a minute,' I said to Weedy, 'Give us a fag, Rudy, I'm dying for one.'

'Sure, here,' he said, producing a pack and some matches.

'What was it like this time?' asked Snowy.

'Same as before, hasn't Kettley told you?'

'No, he doesn't wanna talk,' said Carrots.

'Somebody see if the NAAFI waggon's about,' I asked, as it came by about ten thirty.

'How you feeling?' smiled Rudy.

'Fine, mate, just fine, can't wait to catch up with the lectures, though, what about this afternoon, Weedy?'

'OK,' said Weedy.

'What about foota?' asked Rudy.

'Christ, Rudy, I've had enough exercise this week.'

'You're certainly more lively than the first time; was it easier?' asked Weedy.

'No, not really, I just knew what to expect, that's all.'

'Well, it's certainly quietened Kettley down, haven't heard hardly a squeak out of him since he got back,' said Rudy.

'Where is he?' I asked, noticing his absence for the first time.

'He's away in the toilet, we've just got in from field training, we've finished now for the weekend. That's a vicious right hook you've got there, I dinny want ta get on the end of that 'un. You'll have to be watching your temper from now on. By the way, I made a good excuse for you at dancing on Wednesday, we did the tango again.'

Taffy returned with thick brown tea, scalding hot, and Eccles cakes. We sat and talked and it was good to be back.

I soon caught up with my studies and successfully passed the first exams at the end of July. Most passed that first exam except poor Kettley, Carrots and three other chaps in the next billet. We all felt sorry for them as they were put back to the following intake, Carrots for the second time.

All the intake were assembled in the hangar on the second Monday in August following the exams. We knew it was something special as the chief course instructor was going to address us. He entered the lecture room and conversation quickly dried up.

'You have all done very well so far, your technical training is going along very well,' he said, sweeping the excited faces with his eyes. 'Your military training, your field craft knowledge, your ability to defend an aerodrome under attack, is now going to be put to the test. Tomorrow morning you will be taken in lorries to a tented camp where you will live, under canvas, for two weeks. Special instructors are being brought in to put you through your paces in realistic conditions. Flight Lieutenant Osborne will be going with you and will be your CO for the two weeks. It's a toughening-up course and I'm sure you'll all do well. Your studies will recommence as soon as you get back. Good luck, chaps.'

The audience erupted into excited conversations as we considered the prospect of a 'holiday' under canvas.

'Don't like the sound of that, Fizz,' said Weedy, who was never far away from me.

'Don't worry, Weedy, it will be like a holiday,' I said, wondering myself what was in store for us.

We left in the lorries straight after breakfast and sang rude songs as we made through the lanes and along the roads. I sat inside the canvas-covered lorry surrounded by my friends. Now and again we shouted, 'Where are we now?' and those near the tailboard would call back the name of the village or town the convoy was passing through.

We had not been told our destination and this added to the excitement of the mystery trip we were now on. 'Bridgewater,' chorused the tailboard look-outs, the first big town we had come to.

'Let's swop an hae a look oot,' said Rudy and we replaced the protesters at the tailboard. The lorries meandered on through the summer sunshine as we wolf-whistled at anything resembling a female form. We eventually stopped at Minehead.

'All out for an hour's break,' said the corporal, and packs of sandwiches were handed round and an insulated urn of vile warm, sweet tea was produced.

'Don't wander off, any of you,' commanded the corporal. 'We leave at two o'clock prompt.'

All aboard at two o'clock and off we rolled. My mates and I bagged the tailboard end again and shortly we passed through Lynton. I was now realizing I was in Dukie country and I became quite excited when I saw Barnstaple on the next signpost. My excitement grew to fever pitch when we passed through Braunton. I couldn't contain myself.

'Crikey, Rudy, this is where I was in the Dukies Army School,' I said, all excited.

'Where's the camp then?'

'Well, if we keep going on this road we should pass the hotel soon.'

'A hotel, Christ, you must have had an easy time; whoever heard of living in a hotel without living in luxury?'

Of course that would be the impression everybody held. I didn't expect any of my friends had ever been in one so I let the remark pass.

'Was this where you learnt squarebashing and kit layout?' asked Weedy, who'd been fairly quiet up to then and was probably wondering if he was going to get through the next two weeks of the open-air life.

''Course he did,' Taffy answered for me, 'but a boarding school's a boarding school whatever building it's in. You don't have a waitress and lackies like a real hotel,' said the wise Welshman.

'There it is,' I shouted, pointing to the brilliant white Saunton Sands Hotel as the lorry drove on.

I was completely surprised to see it painted white instead of the dark green camouflage of the war years. It looked bigger now. The sloping car park was half full of smart-looking cars, and a shiny coach stood where the dustbins used to be. The memory of stealing the 'Lyons' pies and the birching came vividly back to me. I shuddered at the horrible thought.

We rounded the coastline to Croyde Bay and the lorries drew off the road through a five-barred gate into a field. I jumped down without waiting for the tailboard to be opened and gazed with happy excitement at the scene before me. It seemed stranger than fiction that I should end up back here, in the countryside that held so many memories of growing up. I had never thought for a moment that I'd ever see it again.

The large field was covered in khaki-coloured ridge tents, all in neat rows with duck-board paths up the centre. The field was mostly flat but the grass hill to the rear rose steeply and I realized that over that hill, not twenty minutes away, was the field where my Dukie friends, Alf, Joe and I had found the blind horse only four short years before.

The tented field looked out across Croyde Sands to the sea. I was right slap-bang in the middle of my part of Devon. We were soon allocated our tents, six bodies in each. Rudy, Weedy and I kept together and shared the same tent. Blondie and Taffy were next door. The large mess tent was positioned just inside the five-bar gate and we all trooped over for a hot meal cooked on open mobile stoves.

Our new instructors were introduced to us by Flight Lieutenant Osbourne and they looked a really tough bunch. Not a smile came our way from the hard-looking group as their searching eyes surveyed the raw material that they hoped to mould into a defence force.

We were rudely awakened at six forty-five by kicking and bawling drill sergeants, and rushed, half awake, through the early morning mist to the ablutions tent for a cold wash and shave.

A quick open-air breakfast thrown together in our mess tins and we split into groups to commence our outdoor field training.

Our permanent mode of dress for all training sessions was decreed as underclothes, thick overalls, and full webbing equipment. As the August sun grew warmer most of us appreciated the lightness of our garb, but within two days poor Weedy kept his pullover on underneath his overalls.

Our drill sergeant's name was Pepper, Hotstuff Pepper we called him. He was about forty-six years old, six feet tall, and broad-shouldered with a short thick neck. He would have been handsome but for the two black moles on the left side of his chin bone. His large mouth had a pencil-thin moustache to stop his upper lip from fraying at the edge. He was the senior drill instructor and, of course, I got him.

The first two days of mapreading to six-figure reference points, open air lectures and practical exercises went off without a hitch, but when we divided into 'sections of ten', complete with Bren guns, the fun started. One section had to take strategic hill positions occupied and defended by enemy sections. The frustrated drill sergeants ran out of adjectives to describe our hilarious and catastrophic performances.

Towards the end of the first week my section was in hand grenade throwing exercises. The ten of us were all in a deep slit trench at the bottom of a steep incline. Some seventy feet up the incline was a three foot high fence. Sergeant Pepper demonstrated throwing the red-painted dummy hand grenades up the hill and over the three-foot fence into 'enemy lines'.

'Once again, then, clasp the grenade in the right hand,' he commanded. I had to hold back the temptation to interrupt with 'What about if someone's left handed?' I was enjoying myself so much the last few days that these silly thoughts kept appearing in my head.

'Pull the pin with your left hand,' he continued. 'With this grenade you have fifteen seconds, some grenades have only five second fuses. Plenty of time to throw the grenade into enemy territory and get down in the trench – got it?'

He threw the dummy clear over the fence with no effort.

'Right, you, lad,' he said, throwing a dummy grenade to the first man. 'Let's see you kill the enemy bastards.'

We watched the first lad calmly pull the pin and, as instructed, on the word 'grenade', we crouched down low in our slit trench, counting to fifteen and then we all shouted 'bang'. It was hilarious. The drill instructor was not amused at our light-hearted approach to this serious matter of war.

'You won't find it so funny with a tracer bullet up your arse, you silly buggers,' he bawled from on top of the trench.

'Next man.'

We all had to have a go and I'd been enjoying myself so much that I hadn't been aware of my shadow's frightened face.

'You're next,' said Sergeant Pepper, throwing a dummy to Weedy which he immediately dropped. This caused more laughter but obviously made Weedy more nervous.

'Right, lad, get on with it.'

'Grenade,' squeaked Weedy as he pulled the pin and threw the dummy.

We crouched down in the slit trench at the word 'Grenade', and started our count. One-two-three-four. We had got to eleven when there was a clang and a plop as the grenade rolled back over the side of the slit trench, hit my next colleague on his tin hat and then settled between us on the muddy floor of the trench. Weedy's throw had not made the fence and the grenade had rolled back into our own trench.

'Ya dead, you're all bloody dead, stop that laughing, you silly buggers, think it funny, do ya? Out, out, out.'

We all got out of the trench.

'Right. Doubling up to the fence and back, go,' he screamed.

We ran up and down the hill until we were all knackered.

'You, son,' said the sergeant to Weedy, 'Come 'ere.'

Weedy then had private tuition on how to hold his arm at full length behind him and throw the grenade correctly using centrifugal force, shoulder and hip.

'Right, back in the trench.'

Weedy was then given another dummy.

'Throw it, lad, and throw it correctly this time, or we'll get you a fuckin' German hat.'

Weedy looked at me with a blank, deadpan Stan Laurel, look, defeat was in his eyes, his confidence gone. I smiled at him and gave him a wink.

'Grenade,' he squeaked again as he drew the pin and threw the hated missile.

We ducked down and counted. One, two, three, four, and at thirteen, the dull plop sounded as the grenade returned to the trench like a well-thrown boomerang.

'You puny apology for a human being, you bloody weakling, too much blanket drill, pulling your plonker, that's your trouble, lad,' screamed Pepper at poor Weedy. 'Here lad,' he said, handing Weedy a grey metallic hand grenade which he took from his pocket. 'This is a real one, now bloody throw it and blow the lot of your laughing mates to hell.'

We had all become serious, the trench had suddenly gone quiet. Weedy was trembling next to me, his watery eyes looking at me in terror.

'Come on, lad, throw it.'

Weedy hesitated as the sergeant stood above us glaring down at him in the trench.

'Throw it!' screamed the sergeant, nearly blowing a blood vessel in the red-flushed and demented face.

'Grenade!' shrieked the higher pitched voice of Weedy.

We dropped flat to the bottom of the trench without waiting for Weedy to draw the pin.

Silence reigned. No counting, just silence. How long we stayed down I don't know. We'd have probably been there all day if the voice hadn't spoken.

'Where's the laughter now, then; heads up, cowards.'

We all walked up the hill at the end of the exercise to collect the red dummy grenades. The sergeant, now smiling, walked forward along the fence and picked up the one grey metallic hand grenade that had travelled third furthest of all the grenades thrown that day. He tossed it up and caught it lovingly.

'Always works wonders, a live grenade,' he said, putting it back in his pocket and grinning at Weedy.

My antics during the first few days had focused attention on me and I'd earned three hours of fatigues scrubbing cooking pots and tables in the mess tent. Silly things had been my downfall, sometimes it was just seeing the funny side of a particular situation, like Weedy's hand grenade throwing, or, at other times, asking questions that just popped out of my mouth before I could stop them. A good example was the lecture on 'Advancing Through Enemy Territory'.

The lecturer sergeant stood in front of forty of us in a field adjacent to the camp. The day was overcast and dreary and the grass was damp. We were sitting on the grass, cross-legged and Indian style, preparing our backsides for piles in future life.

'Right, lads, your section comes to a hedge, there's no way you can know if Jerry's waiting for you on the other side. The section take up a position facing the hedge, the Bren gun in the centre ensuring a wide arc. The section leader then details one rifleman to go over the hedge,' he said as we all sat there quiet and attentive, nursing our rifles.

'The correct procedure for crossing a hedge is to run straight at it pulling your rifle hard into your right side, arm fully extended down the rifle,' he said, demonstrating with his own rifle.

As I pictured this my insides bubbled with laughter. How one could run full belt at a hedge with a .303 Enfield, a heavy rifle, pulled into your side, beats me, I thought, but more was to come.

'When you get to the hedge you throw your body ninety degrees to the left, horizontal to the ground, and roll over the hedge holding your rifle into your side,' he said in all seriousness.

Ninety degrees, horizontal, with a tin hat on, Christ, I thought, this must be a joke.

'When you drop on the other side of the hedge you immediately take up the prone position and scan the area for Jerry – have you got that?' asked the sergeant.

'What about if there's stinging nettles the other side?' said my voice before I could stop it.

Gales of laughter from the forty-odd airmen as the sergeant realized that his serious and important lecture had been turned into a music hall joke.

'You again, you stupid bastard, would you rather be stung by bloody nettles or Jerry's bullets? Come out 'ere, comic Freeman, the village idiot.'

It was no wonder that when Flight Lieutenant Osbourne asked Drill Sergeant Pepper to find three 'volunteers' to represent the RAF at an athletics meeting in Barnstaple on that first Saturday that I was one of the 'volunteers'.

A young pilot officer drove the three volunteers to Barnstaple on that fine sunny morning and eventually found where the athletics were being staged. We weren't very happy at having to give up our own time for this jaunt, although we had got out of Saturday morning drill. The officer parked the car and then issued us with our instructions.

'Freeman, you're in the obstacle race, programmed for two o'clock, Jenkins the one mile at two twenty-five and you, Robinson, the long jump that's programmed to start about two-fifteen,' he said looking at his typewritten programme. 'Remember, chaps, you're here to represent the RAF, wear those blue vests with pride.'

We had been given light blue vests with the RAF badge on the left chest and we did feel proud and important.

'We meet back here at three o'clock sharp; any questions? No? Well, good luck, chaps,' he beamed as he strode away.

We later saw him in deep conversation with the Mayoress and he seemed to be enjoying his day in the limelight.

I had plenty of time to look round the so-called obstacle course set out around the edge of the grounds. Forty yards from the start was a tarpaulin sheet pegged to the ground; under that, I supposed. Another forty yards to a series of spaced-out telegraph poles laid horizontally at two different heights, the first pole eighteen inches from the ground, the second two feet, then eighteen inches again and so on for twelve poles, I should think they called it the 'snake weave'. Forty yards to the water jump, forty to a ten-foot high net and so on. There were nine obstacles in all, if you can call rolling a barrel an obstacle. I was a bit disappointed, it was more like a kid's race.

I went to the start in my shorts and vest but barefoot. I had always preferred bare feet since my days in India. I felt I could get a better grip and I felt lighter.

Fifteen competitors in various coloured vests and shorts were limbering up. A few superior looks and smirks came my way. Sod you lot, I thought.

'On your marks.' shouted the white-coated official.

'Get set – bang,' went the cap gun.

I got off to a good start and reached the canvas at the same time as three other competitors. I was out from underneath first and through the poles way ahead of anybody. I bored on against the Civvy Street softies and finished the race embarrassingly quickly as the second man hadn't reached the last obstacle as I breasted the tape. My name was taken and I went to change.

My two colleagues, whom I'd never seen before we met in camp, didn't make the first three in their races and all three of us stood by the officer's car at three o'clock. He came striding up, serious faced.

'Looks like we'll have to wait, chaps, now Freeman's won his race,' he said, without any congratulations whatsoever. 'Prize giving's not until five thirty. I was with the Mayoress watching Freeman's race so we can't slope off, I'm afraid,' he said apologetically to the other two. I felt rotten about this and wished I hadn't run.

Obviously he didn't expect any of us to win and I'd upset the officer's plans. We kicked our heels until prize giving and eventually my name was called. I marched up in my uniform to cheers and applause from the crowd. The Mayoress congratulated me on my easy win and presented me with my prize, a pair of maroon elastic braces and a sealed envelope.

I was rushed straight back to the car as the officer seemed to be in a hurry and we set off for camp. As we drove away I excitedly opened the envelope which contained a handwritten piece of paper. 'This voucher entitles the holder to seven shillings and sixpence worth of fresh fish,' and signed Tindall's Fisheries, Barnstaple. Disappointment wasn't the word, I was deflated. The officer smiled for the first time; he thought it was really amusing. My colleagues sympathized and we forgot about the matter.

On arriving back at camp I was standing in my tent, absolutely starkers, having just come in from a cold shower, when the tent flap parted and Flight Lieutenant Osbourne stood there beaming at me. I quickly whipped a wet towel round my waist.

'Congratulations on winning your race, Freeman, bloody good show,' he said, half in and half out of the tent. 'I've had a whipround from the drill instructors – don't think all of them were that keen though -- ' he laughed, 'Take this, it will make up for that silly prize they gave you,' and he presented me with a bulky envelope. There were eight shillings and fourpence in the envelope. I was over the moon, not just with the money but with the recognition.

'Dinny go thankin' Sergeant Pepper for his contribution,' said Rudy. The thought of Sergeant Pepper putting his hand in his pocket for me, especially after he'd 'volunteered' me, seemed tremendously funny and we laughed our heads off.

Sunday was an absolute joy. I remember waking to the warmth of the early morning sun on the canvas tent. The air was peaceful and we could see the frothy white-topped waves breaking on Croyde beach. It was a day of rest and I desperately wanted to visit the farmer and his wife that had been so kind to me and my friends when I was a boy. My Dukie friend Alf had worked at the farm during the school holidays as he had no parents or home to go to.

Rudy and Weedy came with me. We ambled over green hills enjoying the splendid scenery of the countryside. The blind horse that I had befriended some four years earlier, had gone from his field and I had mixed feelings about that. I would have liked to have seen him again but all I could show my friends was the post that still stood there to substantiate my story. Duke, as we had named him, was probably in those lovely stables in the sky where no posts would make him a prisoner any more.

'There's the farm,' I said as we breasted the next hill.

We looked down on the neat little farm that appeared to be deserted. We dropped down the hill and as we crossed the farmyard, music greeted us from an open upstairs window. I knocked on the back door, no answer. I knocked harder.

Suddenly the door opened and there stood Alf, my friend and soulmate. Now he was six feet tall, still with the sharp features and locks of long unruly hair hanging in all directions.

'Blimey, Bob, where did you come from?' he gasped with surprise as we hugged one another. 'You must be a glutton for punishment, when did you get out of the Dukies?' he asked, looking at my RAF uniform.

'Come in, all of ya. Ma!' he shouted, 'Look what's turned up.' He was so excited there was no way I could get a word in.

A most glorious three hours were spent in the genuine warmth and love of that family. Alf and I swopped many stories, to the amusement and wonder of Rudy and Weedy, and the delight of Mr and Mrs Appleyard who had taken Alf in as their son. Mrs Appleyard put on a mouth-watering roast beef dinner and Mr Appleyard produced a jug of frothing beer as the babble of questions, answers and stories continued unabated. Mrs Appleyard, much to Alf's embarrassment, informed us he was courting a homely girl on the next farm and we came away with a general picture of happiness and contentment. I was so pleased that life had worked out well for my friend Alf and regret that I've never been back to see them since that day.

Monday afternoon, the second week, and we were all sitting cross-legged in the field, like a Hindu convention, getting a little more pile treatment and waiting to be addressed by the CO.

Sergeant Pepper had glared at me once or twice and I was tempted to thank him for the whip-round but Rudy's warning still rang in my ears: 'Don't provoke the bugger,' he had said when I had mentioned my itching desire to him.

Flight Lieutenant Osbourne strode across the field followed by his number two, the young miserable pilot officer.

'Good afternoon, chaps,' he smiled. 'Now, tonight the main exercise of the fortnight's training will take place and I thought I'd explain it to you. You will be taken in lorries at midnight and dropped off between ten and fifteen miles from this camp. You will be in battle fatigues; that is, overalls and underclothes only. You will be dropped off in pairs and your task will be to get through enemy lines back to this camp without being caught.' He paused and smiled, looking for reaction but blank stares was all he got. 'The local police and military police will be out looking for you and will arrest you on sight. You're escaping prisoners and you will not be allowed to use roads, transport or thumb lifts. Each pair of escapees will have a map and a compass. No money or food.'

Again he paused for the information to sink in, but we stared at him in disbelief, like mesmerized ferrets.

'The objective is to get through enemy lines undetected and if you manage that and make camp safely, you then have to write a brief report and hand it in immediately. Any questions?' Shock, fear, uncertainty, or whatever was going through our minds stunned us into silence.

'Right, chaps, good luck,' and away he strode.

We were inspected by the drill sergeants at eleven fifteen and emptied our overall pockets of everything including our cigarettes and matches.

'How am I going to read my map without my matches, Sergeant?' I asked as he pocketed my cigarettes.

'You won't have time to unfold it, Freeman, you'll be picked up before you know it,' he grinned.

The lorries set off to both left and right of the camp entrance gate. I squeezed towards the tailboard to see which way we were going. As we came out of the field gate we turned left on the Saunton and Braunton Road. Good, I thought, as the lorry engine disturbed the stillness of the night. The sky was overcast and it was very dark and quite chilly for an August night. We motored round the headland and past the Saunton Sands Hotel on the right. Sergeant Pepper and two other NCOs were by the tailboard talking, but Pepper's eyes were everywhere.

'Get back there, Freeman, you cheating bastard,' he shouted as I pushed between two seated airmen. I returned to my bench. We were motoring through Braunton, that much I could make out through the gloom, and still we went on. I was hoping to be paired with one of my friends but Pepper had other ideas.

The lorry made its first stop. 'Harrison and Gibbs,' called out Pepper and Blondie and a stranger went over the tailboard. The lorry moved on, took a sharp right down a narrow lane and two more were dropped off. The procedure continued for the next twenty minutes until there was only one other airman and myself left. The lorry stopped.

'Freeman and Duncan, the runner and the sickman, what a team, come on, move it,' said Pepper. I jumped from the lorry onto the tarmac lane.

I stood there waiting as Duncan gingerly climbed over the tailboard and slowly felt his way down to the ground. My God, Pepper had really lumbered me, I thought.

'Don't forget to write your report when you get back, Freeman, if you get back,' Pepper chuckled as the lorry moved off.

'Which way do you think we should set off?' asked the refined voice of Duncan as the lorry noise subsided.

'Follow me,' I said, 'and keep your voice down, you can be heard for miles on a still night like this.'

'Sorry,' whispered Duncan.

I had no idea where we were but just wanted to get off the road and away from our start point. Somehow I didn't trust Pepper. He could have told the military patrols where we had all started, or at least where I had started.

'Get on the grass verge, for Christ's sake,' I hissed at dopey Duncan who was following me but thumbing his boots on the tarmac lane. We climbed a gate into a field and traversed along the hedgerow until I made out a secluded gap where I crouched down. Duncan did the same.

'What now?' he whispered.

'We keep quiet for five minutes and see if there's anybody out there,' I whispered.

We sat on our heels, listening to our breathing in the still cold night. Thank goodness there was no moon that night; at least Pepper couldn't arrange that. We were just about to move on when a vehicle engine was heard in the distance.

'Stay still,' I hissed, 'Wait for the vehicle to pass.' It didn't pass, however, but drew up to the gate we had climbed over only five minutes before. Two dark shapes got out and stood by the gate talking in low whispers. They got back in their vehicle and moved on.

'That was close,' said Duncan 'What now?

'We'll follow the direction of the vehicle,' I said, 'It must be making inwards in the general direction of home. Keep behind me and don't talk. If I stop, you stop, but don't ask questions. We'll keep to the hedgerows until I can find a signpost and get our bearings, OK?' I asked.

'OK.'

Duncan didn't question my taking the leadership role and I never gave it a second thought. To me it was an exciting challenge but to him it was a hopeless quest. Although Pepper referred to Duncan as the sickman he showed no symptoms that night and his big frame moved well. I reckoned the military patrols would be concentrated nearer camp, probably within five miles or less, rather than right out where we were. No doubt the main roads, though, would be well covered by civilian police.

We stalked along hedgerows for fifteen minutes before I spotted a finger sign post. Duncan had kept up well.

'Rest for a few minutes,' I whispered. 'If it's all clear I'll nip out and read that signpost.'

After a few confidence-building minutes I crept across the road and was rewarded with the words Braunton – 2 miles. We had been going in the right direction, but more by luck than judgement. Up till then we hadn't looked at our map.

'Two miles to Braunton in that direction,' I whispered, panting. 'The danger starts there, but once I've got my bearings we won't need maps or anything as I was brought up around here. We will have to skirt Braunton as it will be well covered with patrols. Ready? Come on, then.'

Keeping the road in sight we trotted along hedgerows in the direction of Braunton, and in the clear cool night we heard a clock chime the half hour.

'Half past one,' whispered Duncan.

'How do you know?' I asked.

'I've got my watch,' he replied.

'Crafty bugger, they should have been handed in at inspection.'

'They didn't search me,' he said. 'I've got my cigarettes and matches too.'

'Great,' I said. 'We might find a place to have a smoke later.'

We trotted on until the panting breath of Duncan became too much to bear in the still night.

'Rest here,' I said as we approached the beginning of a built-up area. 'I'll go and have a looksee, see if I can recognize anything. Don't make a noise and don't smoke.' I trotted forward and crept behind a row of houses backing onto the fields. There was a goalpost and I crept nearer. As I reached the edge of the football pitch I made out a low stone wall on the other side and beyond that a row of buildings, which I knew to be shops interspersed with houses. I'd played on that football pitch when I was in the Dukies and at last I knew where I was. I returned excitedly to Duncan.

'I know where we are now,' I said, 'Just a matter of keeping our heads and being very careful. Follow me.'

We made our way round the outskirts of Braunton, having to stop only once for a vehicle, whose headlights actually swept the hedge we were crouched behind. We cleared Braunton within an hour and I was getting confident we could make it.

Duncan was starting to lag behind a bit and was puffing like a winded horse. I spotted a cowshed and while Duncan rested in the bushes, I crept forward in Indian tracker fashion, taking advantage of all the cover I could, and stopping and listening every now and then. I hunched down trying to breathe quietly some thirty feet from the cowshed when a sudden momentary lighting of the interior came and went. Someone was in there and that someone had struck a match. I waited nervously; it could be escapees or it could be a patrol. I crept back to Duncan.

'Someone's in the cowshed, come on, let's give it a wide berth.'

We jogged on, field after field and it became hilly. 'I used to scrump apples round here,' I whispered to the tiring Duncan, 'Know it like the back of my hand,' I said encouragingly.

'Let's have a rest,' pleaded the tired Duncan. 'Look, a copse over there, how about half an hour's rest?' he panted.

'A copse is the riskiest place,' I whispered, 'We'll rest here, where we get open views in all directions.'

We hunched up in a hollow as Duncan's puffing abated. He lay on the ground full length and had just about had it. My ears were tuned and listening for any sound. We must have stayed like that for ten minutes. Something caught my eye way across the fields towards the copse. I stared in that direction but could see nothing. There it was again and gone. It was the red end of a cigarette; someone was out there. I leant low to Duncan's ear.

'Someone's in the copse but we don't have to go near it,' I whispered. 'Buck up, we've only just over a mile to go but it will be the hardest mile. No running or jogging, just creeping. Keep below the hedge line. The camp's over that hill but there will be plenty of eyes looking for us. Are you ready?' I asked.

'Yes, OK, do you think we really could make it?' he asked, for the first time realizing it was possible.

''Course we can, if you keep up, keep quiet, watch where you put your feet and keep your eyes and ears open, follow me.'

We crept on and up, stopping every now and then like ghostly statues, slithered like snakes over the skyline and to the safety of a group of bushes.

'Rest,' I whispered. We could see the dark outlines of the tents below and hear the sea breaking on the beach.

'We can run the last four hundred yards,' said the excited voice of Duncan.

'Don't be daft,' I whispered, annoyed at the suggestion and the fact that the exercise was nearly over before he had made a contribution.

'Stay quiet.' Although I was impatient to finish, I was still cautious and we crouched there for some minutes.

'See that?' I whispered, pointing below. Two dark shapes moved along a dry stone wall. I pinpointed their position although I didn't know whether it was a patrol or not. I'd been watching another mass of bushes for five minutes but no sign of inhabitants there.

'See those bushes?' I whispered, 'I am going to creep towards them, you follow me in two minutes.'

I slithered, stopped and listened, slithered, stared and stopped and eventually made the bushes safely. Duncan followed. We were now clear of the two shapes by the dry stone wall and had seen no sign of any other movement in the past ten minutes.

'If there's other patrols down there, they'll expect us to come into the camp through one of the gates,' I said.

We were only forty yards from the camp field wall.

'Instead we'll go over the highest part of the wall. Just in case they're waiting for us, I'll go first, you follow in five minutes,' I whispered. 'I'll see you in 'K' tent, third up from the cook tent.'

'Right-O,' said Duncan.

I slithered up to the wall and lay a minute, listening. No sound at all. I tried the stones at the top of the wall to make sure they were firm, and peeped over. All clear. I quietly went over, crawled between the guy ropes and made 'K' tent, absolutely elated. I lay on my bed and relaxed for the first time; it felt terrific. Duncan arrived and he was over the moon.

'That was fantastic, Fizz,' he said, forgetting his tiredness. 'I never thought I'd get back when the CO announced the exercise. I'll really have a tale to tell when I write home tomorrow,' he said, full of excitement.

'Have you got your fags? I could do with one now.'

I lay full length on my bed, Duncan on Rudy's, as we smoked our fags. No one seemed to be about and I was wondering how Rudy was getting on and poor Weedy.

'What time is it?' I asked. 'Here – have my torch.'

'Four fifty-five, taken us about five hours, what about the report?' said Duncan.

'I'll do it now,' I said. 'You hold the torch.'

With a sheet of Basildon Bond I wrote:

To the Commanding Officer – Flight Lieutenant S.T. Osbourne

Sir,
I am pleased to report that 1920683 Bob Freeman and 1920713 H.R. Duncan successfully crossed enemy lines without incident and arrived back in camp at 0455 on this the 21st August, 1948.

Signed: *R.B. Freeman.*
H.R. Duncan.

'That will do,' I said, 'Now to hand it in.'
'Shouldn't one wait until morning?' asked the polite Duncan.
'No,' I said, 'The orders were, immediately.'
'But where do you hand it in? All the drill sergeants are out on patrols,' said Duncan.
'Leave it to me, I'm going to enjoy this,' I said, placing the report in an envelope and addressing it to the CO.
I left Duncan lying on Rudy's bed and made my way to the tent marked 'Officers'. I pushed back the flap and with my torch, saw two steel and canvas beds and the miserable flying officer lying on his back with his mouth open.
'Excuse me, Sir,' I said, touching his shoulder gently but no response.
'Excuse me, Sir,' I said again, giving him a little squeeze on the shoulder.
He moved so quickly he frightened the life out of me as his body shot into the upright sitting position.
'Who's that, who's that?' he said in a loud voice.
'What's going on?' said another voice as the CO was woken up.
They were now both sitting up in bed and I realized that neither of them could see me in the darkened tent, although my eyes were used to the gloom and I could make them out. I switched my torch on again and shone it on myself.
'It's only me, Sir,' I said, trying to keep a straight face.
'What do you think you're doing in an officer's tent?' shouted the flying officer. 'You'll be on a charge for this, Freeman, out of bounds, that's what you are.'
'Oh no, Sir, I'm following orders, here's my report, Sir,' I said, shining my torch on the proferred envelope.
'What report, for Christsake,' said the Pilot Officer, still muddled and half asleep.
'Successfully getting through enemy lines, sir.'

The penny dropped and a pregnant silence ensued. The quieter voice of the CO then said:

'We didn't mean in the middle of the night, Freeman, be a good chap and hand it in at reveille; now please go away.'

'Yes, Sir, sorry to disturb you, Sir,' and I left.

We couldn't sleep for the excitement as we waited to see who else got through. Only Rudy of all my mates got through plus two other couples. The lorries went out next morning to collect those in police stations. The CO addressed us all the following evening.

'Well, chaps, I'm afraid the whole exercise last night was a great disappointment. Only eight of you got back to base out of fifty-two starters, not very good, eh?' he said. 'Some of you didn't make the first five miles and two couples got completely lost and went in the wrong direction. I can't say I'm very impressed but I hope you've all gained valuable experience. The worst performers will repeat the exercise this Thursday night but this time only a five mile radius and no police, only our own military patrols. I've asked Sergeant Pepper to arrange for the successful ones to address you all and tell you how they did it and what to look out for. Over to you, Sergeant.'

'Sir,' said Sergeant Pepper as the CO strode away. One by one, Pepper called the names of the successful escapees and ordered them to step forward.

'Three minutes, lad, to educate the hignorant,' said Pepper.

Most of them were tongue-tied and little good came out of their three minutes.

'He's leaving me until last, I thought, as number five, then six and Rudy number seven did their three minutes.

'Times up, that's all we've time for,' he said as Rudy returned to his place, 'There's only Freeman left and he was led by the hand of Duncan, dismiss,' he said and we all made our way back to the tents.

'Dinny know what ya did to upset yon un,' said Rudy, 'but he does nee like you.'

'I can live with it,' I replied. 'Three days to go and then back to Locking.'

The sun shone brightly on the Wednesday morning as we assembled after breakfast in front of the piercing eyes of Sergeant Pepper.

'Squad, 'shun!' he barked. 'Right turn. Rifles at the trail, double march,' and off we jogged, through the five-bar gate and down the road towards Braunton. We had travelled for half a mile at a jog when he brought us to a halt.

'When you hear the whistle it means enemy aircraft attacking. You immediately dive into ditches or hedgerows and fire at the aircraft above, got that?'
'Yes, Sergeant,' chorused the happy and healthy bunch of airmen.
'Squad – quick march,' and off we went again.
No whistle as we swung along the lanes and quiet talking took place. We had almost forgotten about the whistle when it screeched out upon us. The squad quickly broke up as everyone looked for cover and a nice place to lie down. A few clicks were heard as firing pins searched the empty barrels.
'Get up, back in line,' screamed Sergeant Pepper. 'That was a bloody disgrace, you're not an old people's outing, you'd all be dead before you found cover, I'll say it again. When I blow the whistle you disappear like bloody smoke, got it, don't look round for a picnic spot, now quick march!'
We set forth again, all smiles, this was a good exercise, all but Weedy would be enjoying it.
'OK, Weedy?' I said.
'Yes,' he smiled weakly.
'Not long now, Weedy, back to our books on Friday.' That made him smile.
'Double march at the trail, double march,' came Pepper's command.
We jogged easily into another lane with hedgerows one side and dry stone wall the other. The whistle screeched out again. I ran towards the dry stone wall, put my left hand on the top stone and hurdled over. As I came up into the air I noticed for the first time there was nothing on the other side of the wall. I couldn't do anything as I was airborne and there, twelve feet below, was a flock of chickens contentedly pecking the hard dry mud. I thumped into the middle of them and my rifle landed a few feet away. I lay there winded as pain crept up my leg and arm. The ground was cut away this side of the wall to a flat plain and a bungalow stood just outside the chicken run. I lay there, panting and bewildered. I heard my name being called.
'Here, Sergeant,' I shouted, but I couldn't move.
I looked up at the wall and the light blue sky. Suddenly Sergeant Pepper's head appeared above the wall and the eyes dropped and focused on me sprawled out amongst the clucking chickens. Sergeant Pepper had an expression of incredulity on his otherwise serious face. Other heads appeared, all with different amused expressions and odd chuckles of laughter that couldn't be held back. The row of faces hung there, like wall plaques hanging from the sky.
'Now I've seen it all. You stupid sod, Freeman, what are you doing down there?' he barked.

What a stupid question. 'Collecting eggs, Sergeant,' was the answer that rose in my mind but I managed to hold my tongue for a change. The increasing pain in my leg assuaged the funny side of my normal reaction to such stupid questions. The other airmen were now seeing the amusing side of the scene below them and the sergeant's questions, and laughter was breaking out. This only annoyed Pepper more.

'Get your arse up here on the double,' he screamed, feeling the situation was getting out of hand.

'I can't move my leg, Sergeant,' I replied. It only then dawned on him that I might be hurt.

'Two of you get down there and bring him up,' barked Pepper.

Rudy and Blondie were quick off the mark. There was a sloping car track from the lane down to the bungalow only thirty feet further down the lane and my mates came running down this slope and made their way to the chicken run. No one had appeared from the bungalow so Rudy and Blondie hoisted me on my one good leg, collected my rifle, and with chickens clucking farewell, I hopped back up to the road.

An airman had been despatched back to camp for transport and within the hour I was whisked off to Barnstaple Infirmary.

I returned with my foot in plaster and my wrist heavily strapped. My leg still aches whenever I hear chickens clucking.

CHAPTER 10

Weedy's Parents

It was a pleasure to get back to Locking, the familiar surroundings, the NAAFI, our hut and a routine we had come to know and accept. No one was happier to be back than Weedy, back to his beloved books, lectures and non-physical life.

We soon settled down to our studies and I hobbled from lecture to lecture with Weedy, ensuring a seat next to him was always reserved for me as I peg-legged in to a little cheer from the class.

As the winter rolled by, our brains became accustomed to absorbing the vast amount of new knowledge being thrown at us. I felt sure that parts of my brain that had never been used before were unwrapped and came into use for the first time. I was keen and enthusiastic on all subjects to do with my trade. I found no trouble in rewriting my notes every night and discussing queries with Weedy and the others in our study group.

The training school closed down for the Christmas period and I went home and enjoyed the festive season with my family at Brentwood.

The last three months of study leading up to final exams commenced after the Christmas break. Only two things of note happened in that period, one good and one bad.

I visited my friend Sergeant Heckner, for a week's stay in his guardroom hotel. I came to take these visits in my stride. So much bad happened to me that no fear was felt on these occasions, just frustration at missing my lessons. Unfortunately Rudy, Blondie and Kettley were all in the 'can' with me. We had been to Weston celebrating Blondie's eighteenth birthday and we got paralytic. The local police arrested us and delivered us back to the camp guardroom. I was deemed the ringleader and got seven days. Rudy and Blondie got three days for their first offence and Kettley five days. The one saving grace was that Weedy wasn't with us, so my lecture notes would be assured.

The other memorable occasion was that Weedy's parents booked into a hotel in Weston for a weekend and he invited me to meet them.

We went on the bus to Weston and made our way to the sea-front hotel. I was surprised to see the fragile frame of the grey-haired and bespectacled gentleman who was Weedy's father.

He spoke very softly and had kind eyes. Weedy's mother was small and thin and her hair was nearly white. She appeared to be nervous and shy but obviously doted on her only child and beamed love towards him all during our visit. After tea, Weedy's father took me aside, out of earshot of his wife and son.

'I want to thank you,' he said nervously, 'for taking care of my son, he's always, talking about you. I'm sure he wouldn't have got through the last eighteen months without your help and guidance. I want you to know that my wife and I will be eternally grateful to you. We came here this weekend just to tell you that, and to give you our grateful thanks,' he said, proferring me a bundle of bank notes.

I was completely taken aback at his remarks. I liked little helpless Weedy; to me he was the underdog and I'd always supported his kind. I didn't know what to reply, but I certainly wasn't going to take any money.

He took my refusal of his money with surprise and embarrassment.

'Our house is your house, do come and stay with us some time, won't you?' he muttered.

'Yes, thank you, I'd love to,' I said as the heat went out of the situation.

They walked us back to our bus stop and Weedy's face was bright red as his Mother slobbered a kiss on his cheek with all the bus passengers watching.

'Good luck in your exams and thank you once again,' said Weedy's father as we boarded the bus for Locking.

'Thank you and goodbye,' I said politely. I'm sure Weedy had no idea why his parents had invited me for tea and the subject was never mentioned again.

We took our exams in March, written papers, practical metalwork tests, woodwork and oral exams. Two hectic weeks with plenty of late night swotting. When it was over, the waiting-on-results period of anxiety began. I felt fairly confident but one was never sure. We relaxed for some days and spent hours in the NAAFI or on the football field.

The exam results were put on the noticeboard the following week and all my close friends had passed; so had I – top of the practical exams with ninety-two percent marks. Our hut was full of happy faces and noise as everyone talked, banged each other's backs or lay on the bed kicking their legs in the air; everyone, that is, except Weedy. He was sitting on his bed staring at the happy throng. I sat down beside him.

'Well, Weedy, you've done it, you're now a qualified AC2 Airframe Mechanic,' I said, smiling at his bird-like face.

'Yes, thanks, Fizz,' he said sadly.

'What's the matter?' I asked, 'Aren't you happy?'

'Oh yes,' he replied in a flat voice, 'But now we'll all be splitting up and have to find new friends.'

I hadn't thought of that; he was right, we would all be split up.

'You'll soon make new friends, Weedy, wherever you go, so don't go worrying,' I said. 'Come on, we're off to the NAAFI to celebrate.'

Weedy was right. The next day the lists went up and I was posted to RAF Topcliffe in Yorkshire. None of my mates were coming with me. This was the parting of the ways. We all lay quietly in our beds that last night together; no one slept much, no one talked much, we all lay with our own thoughts. After eighteen months together we were like brothers but from the next day onwards each one of us would be on his own again. Weedy had recognised it first, then it dawned on all of us. Apprehension replaced the comforting blanket of security and togetherness. It was time to start again.

CHAPTER 11

The Berlin Airlift

As the train whistled through the countryside, I sat in the corner window seat of the carriage gazing out sadly at the dashing landscape. Whiffs of warm, smoke-smelling air entered the carriage through the two-inch gap at the top of the window, which was held by the leather belt adjuster on its first hole. The rhythm of wheel on track relaxed the body and mind and transported me into a world of my own. The trees in the apple orchard were just bursting their first buds, hedgerows were greening and fields, precisely laid out with a twelve inch ruler by a proud farmer, were lining up their spring crops in various shades of green. A brave family of rabbits nibbled at the new shoots, ignoring completely the train and its passing audience. Armies of daffodils were whizzing past my window; bright yellow bells, proud, upright and resplendent for ten days, were now turning to light brown, their bells shrinking and many of them lying down in surrender after their brief but glorious heralding of spring. The advance party of the first reserves, a few red and some yellow tulips, now nodded and smiled sadly on the dying daffodils. It was spring 1949 and the next stop was Thirsk in Yorkshire where, once again, I would search for friends, comfort and security.

We had said our last farewells that morning, promising to write to one another, and had taken off into the RAF world with mixed feelings of sadness, apprehension, and excitement. Whether we would ever see each other again was doubtful; we could but hope.

I came out of my reverie as the train started to slow down. I had a slight panic, as I'd left it a bit late. It took some minutes to get your webbing equipment on, and your kitbag on top of your backpack. A certain amount of space and technique was required to throw your webbing harness, with attached sidepack and water bottle, in a wide arc, whilst propelling your body in the opposite direction and then locating your right arm through the harness. When travelling on trains, which I did for many years, one became immune to the amused gaze of other travellers at one's gyrations when taking the equipment off or putting it on. In this instance I dragged my equipment down the corridor of the train and out through the door onto the platform, and performed my gyrations to the seated audience in the stationary train.

Two other airmen appeared and the three of us were met by a scruffy-looking lorry driver in greasy battledress top and sidehat. We boarded his lorry and soon covered the few miles from Thirsk to Topcliffe.

RAF Topcliffe was a well-laid-out aerodrome, quite isolated from the world, the nearest town being Thirsk. We passed through the guardroom barrier entrance and proceeded up the neat camp road, passed the medical centre and some more buildings and then the lorry stopped.

We jumped down from the lorry and I looked about me. A great oblong patch of grass was the centrepiece of the camp, with the tarmac road running round all four sides. Brick-built, one storey, flatroofed barrack blocks lined both the long sides of the oblong. A larger brick-built structure took up one end and I soon found out it was the canteen, NAAFI and recreation rooms. The other short side of the oblong was open, and in the distance I could see the huge hangars with a few aeroplanes dotted about. It all looked grand to me, no more Nissen huts or wooden huts and no looking at a parade ground every day.

The orderly sergeant appeared from nowhere.

'ACII Freeman?' he asked of the three of us. We were all 'erks', that is, airmen; the other two, I found out on the lorry, were national servicemen.

'Block H, room three, over there,' he pointed. 'Get sorted out, and the corporal of your billet will give you further instructions tonight.'

'Yes, Sergeant,' I replied, and made my way to H block.

As I climbed the stairs to room three on the first floor, I wondered what reception I'd get from the 'old sweats'. It was very quiet and had a hospital feeling about it.

I approached the door, took a deep breath, put on my best worldly expression and turned the door knob. The room was empty. I hadn't thought of that; they must all be at work. Then I noticed the floor: Oh God, not here, the lino was mirror bright, just like training camp and there was a great collection of thick felt pads just inside the door. What a let down; I thought I'd finished with all that bullshit.

I slid down the billet, found three beds and lockers in the middle of the row empty and selected one as my new home. There were ten beds with upright and flimsy lockers on each side of the room. The inevitable two trestle tables and collapsible forms occupied the centre of the room. All bedding was folded up fairly neatly and stacked at the head of each bed. I don't know what I really expected to find on an operational 'drome' but I certainly didn't think it would be shiny floors. I unpacked and stacked my gear and was pleasantly surprised to find a reasonable ablutions room on the first floor that boasted private bathrooms, showers and scalding hot water; we even had real plugs in the washbasins. I heard, for the first time, aircraft landing and taking off, and the sound that was to become part of my everyday life excited me.

Within a week of arriving at Topcliffe I felt comfortable and secure. I'd made a few friends in the billet, picked up the routine of a working aerodrome and was absolutely fascinated with my daily work, servicing and repair of the Hastings.

The Hastings was a large, four-propeller transport aircraft, much like a bigger version, plus two engines, of the reliable and faithful old Dakotas. My 'Chiefy', Flight Sergeant Richardson, was a great guy, not only technically but also he had a sense of humour and knew how to get the best out of his men. That first day he gave me a manual and a service sheet and told me to get on with it. To be thrown in at the deep end was certainly the quick way to learn to swim, but every job was checked and signed for by the Airframe Fitter Corporal in Form 700, and often inspected by the Chiefy as well, so there was no risk involved.

'If you get stuck, Fizzy, you know where my office is,' he said, grinning through his dirty lenses.

'It's Fizz, Chief, not Fizzy,' I said smiling.

'Well, let's see you sparkle, then,' he said, as he walked away laughing.

A great guy was Chiefy Richardson. I really was lucky getting such a good bloke as my boss and I was determined to do well.

The other mechanics were very friendly and helpful and with their help and guidance I soon knew my way around Hastings.

The Berlin Airlift period was still on. The British and Americans had been flying in, down the infamous Berlin Corridor, all essential supplies needed to keep their section of Berlin going since June 1948.

Hastings had been utilized for carrying cargoes of coal and flour in the last few months. They operated from our sister aerodrome of Dishforth just two miles away, but a lot of the servicing and repairs were carried out at Topcliffe owing to the overloading of the maintenance departments of Dishforth.

I was settling in quite nicely after the first week or so when the talk in the crew room was that two of our 'kites' had crashed. We didn't know whether they were Topcliffe's or Dishforth's. A day later the Chief came in the crew room to tell us that all Hastings had been grounded until essential repairs had been carried out. The accident investigation inspectors had pin-pointed the cause of the two crashes and it was the same in both cases: the aileron control tubes had parted owing to coal dust getting into the bearing and forming a grinding paste. We were to go on a seven-day working week until all aircraft had their control tubes replaced and were back flying. A hushed and disappointed maintenance team sat stunned as the Chief gave out the work patterns.

The control tubes that worked the ailerons on the Hastings were made of duralumin, a light aluminium mixture material. They were just larger in diameter than a broom handle and hollow, of course. They ran through a series of 'Tuffnal' bearings, much like a napkin ring. The tubes ran the full length of the Hastings' mainplane. The huge wings had various sizes of inspection panels on the underskin for general servicing entry.

Without ailerons the aircraft couldn't turn, bank, or indeed, fly. The first two aircraft were brought into the hangar and were jacked up for undercarriage tests. Scaffold trestles were arranged under the wings and we set to work removing the various tube lengths starting from the fuselage and working out towards the wingtips. Some of the bearings were very difficult to get at through the service panels, and the airframe mechanic and fitter had to use great ingenuity to reach some of the bearings. We had lead lamps inside the huge wings and sweated away with Chiefy nervously pacing around and shouting up questions. He'd been given a schedule of timescales to get the aircraft back in the air, as the British part of the Berlin airlift now relied heavily on the Hastings squadrons.

Two aircraft were being worked on together and, as I sweated in my dark hole with my head and one arm through the service panel attempting to unscrew a stubborn bolt, I felt a tap on my backside. I extracted myself from the hole and Spud, a fellow mechanic, shouted above the banging and noise:

'Chiefy wants you.'

I climbed down the scaffolding to where the Chief was waiting. He looked worried.

'Come with me, Fizz,' he said. Fred, the corporal airframe fitter, strode along with us across the hangar.

I was worried for the first time since I'd left Locking; had I done something wrong? I racked my brains as the three of us made our way through the din of compressors revving away, the scraping of moving trestles, clanking hammers, chatter, and an aircraft on engine test outside. We stopped under the wingtip of the second Hastings. Chiefy shouted in my ear:

'Fizz, you're the slimmest airframe mech we've got, do you think you could squeeze your arms and shoulders through that hole?'

I looked up at a small rectangular hole eight feet from the wing tip. We hadn't got that far yet on our aircraft.

'Don't know, Chief, I'll try.'

I climbed the scaffolding in my RAF issue rope sandals and looked at the small inspection hole. No way, I thought, but I put my right arm in and attempted to squeeze in my shoulders but I got jammed and slightly panicked and roughly extracted myself. There was a lead lamp that had been placed in the larger panel about six feet away and from its light I could see the Chief's problem.

The last Tuffnel bearing housing was about three feet down the wing and almost unapproachable. I climbed down the scaffolding.

'It's too small, Chief, I can't get in,' I said, feeling sorry for letting him down.

'What about if you were stripped to the waist, you've got a lot of clothes on, will you give it a try, Fizz? Our only alternative is to strip the metal skin off below the bearing and that will put us back at least six hours on each wing tip. Give it a try, lad.'

'All right, Chief,' I said, feeling important.

'Go and get Splitpin,' said the Chief to the corporal, 'And tell her to bring a pound tin of grease from the store.'

Splitpin was one of the WAAF contingent. We had quite a few WAAFS on camp and I found it very strange working in close proximity to females. I didn't think of them as women really, because they were always in trousers and battle dress top, were usually loud-mouthed and could swear with the best of the men.

Splitpin, so called because she was long and skinny, just like a splitpin, arrived from her stores job with the grease.

'Right, Fizz, strip off to the waist, Splitpin will give you a light greasing and we'll try again. If you manage it and you get the bloody bearing out, the beer's on me.'

I stripped off my overall, jacket, shirt, tie and vest and presented my snow-white body to Splitpin, who gently oiled my arms and ribs with thick brown grease.

'Lift your arms up,' she said and the words and her touch roused dormant feeling in the volcano below. The same words as Mrs Bell had said some hundred years ago, or so it seemed. Thank God I haven't got to climb right through the hole, I thought, as I awkwardly climbed the scaffold.

I put my right arm and head through and by pushing my right rib cage into the side skin of the inspection hole I managed to get my left shoulder in. I stopped for breath, then bowed my head a little and attempted to draw up into the wing my left arm. My ribcage was hurting and the grease was being scraped back off my arm as I drew it upwards and inside the wing. I let out my breath, I'd made it, but immediately I panicked; what would happen if I couldn't get out? I was just getting worked up when Fred's face appeared in the inspection hole further down the wing.

'Great stuff, Fizz, the Chief's over the moon. Come on now, get that bloody bearing out for us, where do you want the light held?' As soon as I could reach the bearing housing with both hands it was easy. Fred threw me the two spanners and once the bearing was removed the jubilant Fred drew out the last section of the aileron tube. He then threw me a new bearing and we fitted a new section of tube. I was pouring with sweat after the exertion and then came the last test. In desperation I forced my left hand down my body pushing my right rib cage into the metal skin. The skin burnt with pushing and suddenly my left shoulder dropped below the wing and I was out. Chiefy looked at my body.

'That was a near thing,' he said, 'You nearly skinned yourself. Come to the office, and you, Fred.'

We ambled over to the office, as amused glances came from my mates, and a few wise-cracks. Chiefy was smiling again, which pleased me no end. He phoned the medical officer and explained what was going on and the MO sent up his secret potion that had to be rubbed onto my rib cage and left arm before each wingtip job. 'Guaranteed to harden and protect the skin,' said the male nurse.

'Fred,' said the Chief, 'I want Fizz to work with you for the duration of the grounding job. Between the two of you, I want all the wingtips done. Fizz is excused all other work, just wingtips for him until the job's finished. Well done, Fizz, we're glad you were posted here.'

'Thanks, Chief, what now?' I asked.

'You've more wingtips to do out there but you've got until tomorrow morning, ten o'clock, to finish them,' he smiled. 'Then we accept two more aircraft and so on until they're all done. It's up to you and Fred how you space your work out, now go and get a cuppa.'

Fred and I worked just over fifteen days, sometimes late into the night, to replace all the wingtip bearings. No extra pay, no extra time off, but to me it was a labour of love, and Chiefy kept his promise and our morale up, by providing crates of half pints for everybody at regular intervals during the two weeks.

I'd made a couple of good friends in Spud and Geordie. Spud was from Ireland, a big bow-legged, innocent, earthy chap who never had a bad word for anybody. His large fat, red-cheeked face was typical of farming stock as was his big slow ambling gait. His tousled, thick, light-coloured hair, neither blonde nor brown, always fell in lumps over his forehead. His huge frame threatened power but he wouldn't harm a fly. Geordie, on the other hand, was slim like me. His black hair was wavy like mine had grown, but his half-moon bespectacled face often reminded me of Arthur Askey, although of course he was much taller. Geordie loved his Newcastle Brown Ale in the clear bottle.

The Berlin Airlift ended in mid-May 1949, and work in the hangar settled down to normal. I was surprised to find that some bullshit still continued in operational 'dromes but then, I suppose that was part of military life. Monthly kit inspections took place every fourth Saturday but an officer conducted them and common sense prevailed. Only if something was missing or genuinely badly done was the airman pulled up, which was fair enough in my book. We were detailed for church parades every few weeks, and had irregular square-bashing sessions on the tarmac aprons. The week prior to the AOC's (Air Officer Commanding) inspections little work was done on the aircraft. We spent the week whitewashing 'anything the doesn't move' and scrubbing the hangar floor with new bass brooms while the petrol tanker pumped two hundred gallons of high octane all over the place. The fumes nearly killed us off and the military police surrounded the hangars while this was going on to ensure nobody smoked.

A number of parade rehearsals took place during the boring week and the smell of new paint was everywhere.

It was said in those days that the CO of the smartest aerodrome always got an OBE in the Honours list in the following year. Some wit had stated that OBE was for 'Other Buggers' Efforts', which was a fair reflection of what went on, I think.

CHAPTER 12

The Flying Machine

It was sacrilege to stay in camp on a Saturday night. Just about everybody took off to the village and towns.

Spud and Geordie had a favourite pub in the cobbled market place at Thirsk, where they were well-known, Geordie for the quantity of Newcastle Brown he could put away and Spud for his delightful tenor voice.

Every Saturday night two lorries were laid on by the RAF, one for Thirsk and one for Ripon. They left camp at six o'clock full of happy-go-lucky smiling airmen, mostly dressed in civvies, and returned from the town, leaving promptly at midnight, with not so smart and worse for drink airmen. These Saturday night 'gharries' were the only mode of transport available to the poorer-off erks who had no motorbikes or cars for travel from the isolated aerodromes.

I joined Spud and Geordie on their weekly safaris and soon got used to the routine. The gharry would drop us off in the cobbled square at about six fifteen and we would get the choice of seats in the pub. The landlord knew my friends and greeted them with enthusiasm. I soon realized why.

The pubs were used quite a lot in 1949. I had not seen or heard of television, nor had most folk; the pub was the place to be on a Saturday night, or the dancehall. Our pub was full by eight o'clock and not a seat to be had anywhere. All the regulars knew Spud and Geordie and by nine o'clock shouts were heard calling for Spud to sing. He didn't need any encouragement and was on his feet by the piano in a flash.

I can picture Spud now, standing by the upright piano, his beautiful Irish voice singing the sad ballads of his native land. The audience were hushed and attentive and even the landlord stopped serving and was watching, pint beer glass in his hand as Spud rendered 'If you ever go across the sea to Ireland' – or

– 'I'll take you home again, Kathleen' – or my, favourite, 'Smiling Through.' I always thought of my mother when he sang 'Smiling Through' and of course, my eyes were wet with tears before he finished. That penultimate verse was a killer:

> There's a grey lock or two in the brown of her hair,
> There's some silver in mine too I see,
> Yet in all the long yer-ers, through our laughter and tear-ers,
> Those two eyes of blue, come smiling through, at ME.

Spud could really thrill his audience with his tear-jerkers and I'm sure half the customers came specially to hear him. He didn't need to buy his beer, it was free practically all evening.

Within a couple of weeks I was joining Spud at the piano. My idol in those days was Al Jolson; I'd seen his picture so often and imitated him in bathrooms and showers at every opportunity. With a pint of Newcastle Brown inside me I was anybody's so when the call came, 'What about a song from your new mate, Spud?' I didn't need much pushing.

I gave them 'Sonny Boy' with all the actions; a bit of Father's extrovert personality came out in me that night, and the applause and shouting went to my head. I became a regular with Spud for the next few months.

When the pub turned out we were last to leave. The landlord didn't mind as he knew we had to wait until midnight for the gharry to pick us up. We would then meander, well-oiled and often daft, to the fish and chip shop, that was a real treat, and then stand in the shop doorway waiting for the transport to arrive.

An airman in our billet was being posted overseas. I didn't get on very well with the fella as he was the billet moaner. Every billet had a moaner, a guy whom nothing suited, always jealous of others enjoying themselves but who would never join in with them. He always wanted the lights out an hour before anyone else, or there was too much noise so he couldn't write his letters. Born to be miserable, that was Jonesy.

'Fizz, have you heard? Jonesy has been posted overseas and wants to sell his motorbike, are you interested?' asked Spud.

'What about you, why don't you have it?'

'Not interested in bikes myself, but I know Jonesy's desperate, he goes the day after tomorrow.'

'What's he want for it?'

'He reckons twenty-five quid. It's an old AJS and half the rocker box casting is missing so he hasn't used it for months; reckon you could knock him down a bit.'

'No, I don't think so, I haven't got much money anyway,' I said, and the subject was dropped.

I'd been home for a long weekend, a seventy-two hour pass, and surprised my parents as usual. Although I wrote letters regularly to Mother I never did tell her in advance that I was coming home as I always thought it better just to turn up; she wouldn't worry then. A lot of my travelling was done hitch-hiking down the A1. Lifts were easy to get then if you were in uniform and it saved my poor pay for more important things. Mother would only worry if she knew I was on the road somewhere, and I used to arrive home at all times of the day and night.

The back door was never locked. I never thought it unusual, nor did anybody else. Of course we didn't have much to steal anyway but people in our social order just didn't lock their doors. I remember arriving home in Larchwood Gardens once at two o'clock on a Saturday morning. I can't remember where brother Ernie was sleeping that night but as I tiptoed into the back bedroom both single beds were unoccupied. I quietly closed the door and went to bed. I woke next morning with the sun streaming in and could hear the wireless on downstairs. Pulling on my trousers I walked barefoot down the stairs, along the passage and into the kitchen. Mother was slicing a loaf.

'Good God, Bob, you're enough to frighten the life out of anybody, where on earth have you come from?'

It was midday and all the family were sitting around the table having their lunch. Nobody knew that a body had been sleeping all morning in the back bedroom. No, we never locked the doors in our house.

That weekend I brought back with me my B flat cornet. The camp had a little group of musicians who used to play in the NAAFI on Thursday nights, and as they hadn't a cornet player I agreed to join them.

They were great musicians, most of them self-taught, and they could bash out tunes without a note of music in front of them, whereas I couldn't play anything without music. Our marriage was brief and embarrassing as, without one practice session together, I joined them that Thursday evening in the corner of the NAAFI. As they played a few tunes I kept a low profile and soft tone; only when I was sure of a note, usually at the end of a tune, did I blast out a bit.

It wasn't a dance or anything but that didn't stop the WAAFs from jigging about in front of us on the brown-coloured stone floor.

Laurel and Hardy were there, making fools of themselves as usual, dancing as partners. Hardy, at five foot eight and massive with it, had a huge backside. It resembled half of an over-ripe pumpkin and had a mind of its own. When Hardy's knees bent to the music beat her bum floated upwards in its retaining skin of blue serge, and when she straightened up the mass went down. But that was not all. At the front of this mountainous protein run riot of heaving flesh, a balcony of bursting breasts competed with her pumpkin backside for sheer size and agility. Even through her straining battle dress top her two cannons threw shadows a foot wide on the floor, and threatened to poke the eyes out of her poor little dancing partner Laurel.

Laurel, Hardy's best friend, was only five foot two inches tall and probably didn't weigh more than two pumpkin bums, say six stone. Skinny didn't really describe her matchstick frame. What a strange thing that these two total opposites should be attracted to one another. Melt them both down and remould two more and you could possibly get two acceptably sized females, but these two were neither 'nowt nor summit' as my friend Ted used to say.

I came back from my dreaming as the drummer shouted to me.

'Fizz, next one's "Momma don't want no jazz band playing here", d'ya know it?'

'Carry on, I'll follow,' I said, never having heard of the tune before.

The group started to play and sing what was then a completely new tune to me and as soon as the first musician was called upon to play his solo I started to panic. I looked towards the drummer who was the leader of the band but his eyes were on the audience and his flashing drumsticks, so I couldn't indicate 'not me!' They went on singing and playing as the dancing WAAFs gyrated round and in front of us. Then I heard it: 'Momma don't want no trumpet playing here – Momma don't want no trumpet playing here – we don't care what Momma don't want...' and then – silence – I couldn't blow a note.

Everybody was looking at me, the band didn't know what to do, I didn't know what to do. The dancers continued dancing for a few seconds and then got slower and slower as though their springs or batteries had run down.

The drummer came to first, mumbled something to the musicians that I didn't catch, then I heard 'one, two, three,' and the music started again.

I sat motionless and embarrassed as the dancing and talking got going again and at the end of the next tune I made excuses to the drummer about needing music to play properly, which I could see by his face he didn't believe, and I left. That was my first and worst experience in dance bands but things got better later on.

Jonesy approached me the next day, did I want his motorbike? He was desperate as he was leaving early next morning.

'No, not me, Jonesy, I'm nearly skint,' I said.

'How much you got?' he said.

'I'm not sure, hang on,' and I fished out my Post Office savings book. I opened the book on the first page.

'There it is, six pounds, twelve shillings and sixpence,' I said.

'That's not much, what else have you got?' he moaned.

'Hang on, I didn't say I wanted your bloody old bike,' I said, annoyed. 'I haven't seen the thing yet.'

'It's out the back of the billet, come on, I'll show you it.'

I went with him more out of idle curiosity than from any desire to buy it but once he took the dirty tarpaulin off the machine I could feel the excitement rise inside me. My imagination ran riot with pictures of me flashing along roads and lanes, scarf flying round my neck and wind blowing through my hair. I could feel the power beneath me as I sat on the stationary bike and revved the engine. I was sold on having it but I was determined not to show it.

'Sounds all right,' I said, 'but I've no more money, no licence or insurance and I can only draw three pounds out of the Post Office in one day anyway.'

'Well, you could borrow the six pounds or so off your mates and pay them back in a couple of days,' said the crafty moaner. 'But what else have you got, how about that cornet of yours?'

'You can forget that straight away,' I said, getting huffy at the suggestion.

We went back to the billet and twenty minutes later I had my AJS and Jonesy had seven pounds and my cheap watch. This was the beginning of my love affairs with a series of motorbikes over the next six years.

I obtained my learner licence and had my bike in working order within three weeks, practising my driving skills on the camp roads most evenings and, but for road tax, which I couldn't afford yet, I was ready for the open road.

I was letting my mates have a go one Sunday afternoon when Geordie said:

'Let's go for a drive off camp, Fizz.'

'We can't,' I said, 'I haven't got a tax disc.'

'That's no problem, let's make one,' said Geordie.

I didn't object when Geordie dashed off to another billet, where he knew a chap who had a motorbike. Geordie returned with a light green tax disc. It was Spud who said it looked like a Guiness Label.

'Let's go round the back of the NAAFI and look at the empties,' he said.

Like three excited kids we inspected the crates of empties and, sure enough, there was quite a resemblance. We steamed off the label and dried it out. With coloured crayons, black ink and scissors, we produced a poor reflection of the genuine tax disc we'd borrowed.

'Good enough for a quick glance, especially if we dirty up the glass in the disc holder,' said Geordie. 'Right then, let's have a ride out.'

I didn't think we would get to this, but I could hardly refuse now.

We took off the 'L' plates and set off through the camp entrance, Geordie on the pillion, and roared down the long drive to the main road. We turned towards Ripon and I opened the throttle. It was one of the most thrilling experiences I can remember.

They say that the first time's always the best. I remember hurtling down that road with Geordie trying to shout something in my ear but I was too excited to listen. Hearing the roar of the engine, feeling the surging power between my thighs, doing my utmost to hold the bike on line and all the time the wind tearing at my face and eyes.

We passed RAF Dishforth on the right and tore on as RAF chaps and civilians, out for a quiet Sunday stroll, stood and stared as our noisy machine shattered the tranquillity of the countryside; birds took to the air and animals ran for cover.

Geordie was head-butting me now to gain attention. He obviously wasn't going to risk letting go the vice-like grip round my waist to gain attention with his hands and his shouting had done no good.

Suddenly a car came into view around the bend. The bike was closing the gap on the slow-moving car so quickly I knew we weren't going to make it. Geordie was clinging on for dear life as I pressed with all my weight on the footbrake. My heart was thumping like a steamhammer as I fought to control the bike that was snaking in all directions.

What must have lasted for seconds seemed like hours. Just before we were about to ram the back of the car I swung the front wheel towards the ditch. The machine dropped into the ditch at an angle and the speed drove it up the other bank and we took off, machine and bodies crashing through a hedge halfway up its height and leaving a ragged gap.

I lay on my back gasping for breath and looking up at a clear blue sky. Everything was peaceful and quiet. It was a beautiful summer's afternoon. The 'caw' of a crow brought me back to reality and I sat up, covered in bits of hedge, and noticed a few scratches and blood on my hands. My face felt sore too. There was Geordie, sitting up looking at me not ten feet away.

'You mad bastard, Fizz, you really are crackers. I must have been barmy to suggest riding pillion with you driving,' he said, pulling bits of hedgerow from his clothes.

'Wasn't that just fantastic, though, Geordie, the biggest thrill of my life,' I grinned at him.

'Well, you won't be getting another by the look of it,' he said, 'Your bike's on fire.'

For the first time I looked towards the bike, which had careered on for a further twenty feet after we had deserted it. A cloud of grey black smoke was engulfing most of the frame. I got to my feet with a few aches and pains and rushed over to my most precious possession. Geordie joined me.

'The rear wheel brake drum is glowing red,' said Geordie, whipping out his pride and joy and peeing on it. I joined in. Steam and sizzling joined the smoke as we stood there in the edge of the corn stubble and emptied our bladders. Suddenly we saw the funny side of the situation and went into fits of uncontrollable laughter.

'Are you all right, you chaps?' asked a stranger, who suddenly appeared at our side. A woman was standing a few paces behind him.

We quickly withdrew our tackle and did up the buttons as our faces burnt with embarrassment.

'Yes, we're fine, thanks very much,' I said, hoping he would go away.

'Brakes seized up, I see,' he said, 'Thought something went wrong. Well, if you're sure you're both all right.'

'Yes, fine, thanks,' I said and he wandered off back to his Austin Seven, the slow car that had got in the way in the first place.

We got the bike back on the road with some effort but minus the headlamp chromium ring and glass, which stayed hidden in the corn stubble. Only the tractor's blade would find that because we couldn't.

Our unique cooling system had freed the back brake and we were pleasantly surprised when the engine started. Geordie would only get on the pillion if I promised to drive at a funeral pace, and we drove back the three miles or so, much to the surprise of the Sunday afternoon walkers, at a very sedate pace, waving and smiling at everybody.

'You must think you're doing a bloody lap of honour, you mad bastard, Fizz,' said Geordie, laughing his head off.

So my first motorbike experience was chalked up and word spread throughout the hangar, 'Don't ride with bloody Fizz, he's as mad as arseholes.'

I was really happy at Topcliffe. I loved my work on the old Hastings, I had a good understanding boss, a goodhearted and happy gang of technicians and two good friends in Spud and Geordie. Our work and social life ran to a steady pattern and life went along swimmingly. I'd been at Topcliffe five months and I was accepted, popular and happy. I could stay there for the rest of my service and I wouldn't complain.

'Fizz, Chiefy wants you in his office,' shouted Ted as I lay in the Hastings belly struggling with a hydraulic pipe I was trying to renew.

'OK, Ted, be there in a minute,' I shouted back.

Chiefy was always wanting us for something. I had no fear of seeing him these days as I was confident in the standard of my work and had been praised a few times for my thoroughness and neatness.

'You wanted me, Chief,' I said, smiling at his familiar, trustworthy face.

'Yes, sit down, Fizz,' he replied, looking serious for a change.

Signals started to flash in my head, my smile disappeared. I felt that what he had to say wasn't about work, something else was wrong.

'I don't know how you're going to take this, but you have been posted,' he said, gravefaced.

I was stunned and couldn't take it in at first. I'd only been at Topcliffe five months and it never occurred to me that I would be moved, that is, not for a few years anyway.

'But Chief, I've only been here a few months, why should they want to move me? I like it here, Chief, can't you do something about it?' I pleaded.

'Wish I could, Fizz, I don't want to lose you, you're a valuable member of the team now, but orders are orders, ours is not to reason why and all that,' he said, smiling weakly.

'Oh Christ, Chief, I'm fed up with starting at new places; where have I got to go to?' I asked, only half interested.

'RAF North Luffenham in Rutland. You've got to report in by next Monday morning, 0800 hours. Here's your official orders, ticket and so on,' he said, handing me a package. 'It's a lot nearer your home than here, that's one advantage, Fizz.'

I didn't know what to say, there was nothing I could say, I just sat there taking it in as Chiefy gave me a fag and tried to get me to look on the bright side. He was a terrific chap and he'd given me a good start in my career. I was always thankful for the time spent with Flight Sergeant Richardson, my first Chiefy.

CHAPTER 13

Love in a Graveyard

The train drew into Stamford railway station and once again I struggled with my webbing harness as the amused faces of travellers looked on.

I 'phoned the camp from outside the station and then waited an hour on a dull, overcast, September day for the transport to arrive. The miserable blowy day was a perfect match for my mood. I had no enthusiasm or excitement whatsoever in this posting and could see no rhyme or reason for it, nor was I ever told of one.

An RAF car arrived and I bundled my gear in the back as the chatty driver asked a million nosey questions.

We drove the eight miles or so from Stamford in Lincolnshire to RAF North Luffenham in Rutland and I took little notice of the route or scenery as it passed.

We passed through the usual guardroom barrier and into the neat little camp. All RAF camps were build and laid out to a similar pattern and there were no shocks. The usual oblong square of grass surrounded by one storey, brickbuilt, flat-roofed billets greeted my bored gaze.

'End billet, mate, room four,' said the driver who had been given instructions what to do with me. 'Report to Corporal Beaumont, he's got all the gen – he's your billet corporal.'

'Thanks, mate, see you around and I'll buy you a beer sometime,' I said, as I made my way to my new home.

'I'll keep you to that,' he shouted back as he drove away.

The billet was exactly the same as Topcliffe, twenty steel-framed beds, ten down each side, a tall wooden and plywood locker by each bed, the usual two tables and forms and that bloody awful, shiny, brown linoleum floor.

Only one chap was in the room as I entered that Sunday afternoon and he lay on his bed writing a letter.

'Just arrived, mate?' he asked stupidly as I hoisted my kitbag and backpack through the door.

'Yes,' I said, rather politely, 'Any spare beds?'

'Take your choice, mate, seven empty at the moment,' he replied, indicating the beds in question.

'Where is everybody?' I asked.

'Most are on long weekends, the rest are at the football match,' he replied.

'What's your name?'

'Bob Freeman, but my mates call me Fizz,' I said.

'Funny moniker, but welcome, Fizz, my name's Jim,' he said, still lying on his bed, his chin propped on his elbow.

I unpacked as the conversation continued, and stowed all my possessions neatly on the locker shelves, after which I went for a lovely warm bath and soaked away some of the anxiety that was always present when I first arrived in a strange camp.

The billet was filling up when I returned and they seemed a friendly bunch of guys. Acceptance of a new face was easy when you were all level, all the same.

The fact that I'd come from an operational 'drome and not straight from a training camp made acceptance that much easier. My long black wavy hair and my well-worn battle dress put me in the old sweats class, quite undeserved, I might add. When, in answer to questions, they found out I'd been working on Hastings during the Berlin Airlift, which none of them had experienced, I was placed higher in their esteem and was immediately accepted as one of them.

'We're all off to the NAAFI, you coming, Fizz?' asked Jim as I lay there writing a letter home. I knew Mother would be worried until she heard from me, as I told her in my last letter I was being moved.

'Yeah, I'll be right with you,' I said, jumping up and fiddling with my collar studs, trying to get them through the hole over my clean over-starched collar.

The NAAFI was super, better furniture than any I'd seen before and there was a little kiosk that sold gifts. I remember that later on I bought a pure silk scarf for Mum with the RAF crest on it.

I ordered my favourite snack, double beans on toast and a mug of steaming hot tea.

The NAAFI was full with the returning airmen, some playing cards, some boozing, others chatting up the NAAFI girls. The piano was tinkling away and the pianist's friends were standing around him watching, with frothy pints in their hands. The hubbub of conversation was interrupted now and again as someone dropped a plate or mug on the stone floor, which was always followed by a big cheer. This was the life I'd come to know and enjoy, the security of a crowd and friends, a fairly easy life where nearly everything was organised for you, you were told what to do, where to go and how to behave, and provided you conformed, everything was okay.

I was sitting with Jim and a crowd from our billet swopping stories, all trying to impress one another, when someone passed the table. Out of the corner of my eye I saw this unruly red hair sticking out in all directions and a long sharp pointed nose. I couldn't believe it was true, there he was, my benefactor for tea and wads at Locking.

'Carrots!' I shouted. He turned and recognised me straight away. His face lit up as he came towards me.

'Fizz, where'd you come from?' he asked in his Brummy twang.

I quickly drew up another empty table to the two we already had and Carrots and his mates joined us. It was just great finding a familiar face in a strange world and we sat and talked and drank tea until the NAAFI closed.

Carrots had passed out with the next entry and this was his first posting. As luck would have it, when I reported in the next morning I was assigned to the same hangar as Carrots. As we were both the same trade we worked together and became firm friends.

The aircraft at North Luffenham were Dakotas, Valettas and two Vikings. The principles of your trade were the same whatever aircraft you worked on; only the hydraulic and pneumatic systems and layout of the aircraft varied. Inspection schedules, Form 700, inspection systems and procedures were the same. All one had to do was to learn where everything was; and possibly a few different technicalities.

With Carrot's help and a good Chiefy again, I soon settled into my new surroundings and things weren't so bad after all.

Jim, the guy I met the first night, turned out to be a fitness fanatic and would put on a tracksuit most evenings and go for a run. I couldn't resist the temptation so I joined him in my shorts and pullover. He was quite surprised that I could easily keep up with him and the third time we went out we finished up in the camp gymnasium. Jim was in the camp boxing team and two nights a week plus Wednesday afternoon the team had training sessions. I watched them train that first night with a friendly muscled sergeant who was the team coach. Nobody knew of my past and I was determined that no one should, I had no desire to start boxing again. I left them at it, trotted back to the billet for a shower and sauntered over to my favourite place to have my beans on toast and to find Carrots.

Within a couple of weeks you'd have thought I'd been there years. One soon settles into a RAF camp after the first one, they're all the same. It's just the airmen you have to get to know and that comes easy as your service gets longer. I began to feel quite at home.

On the first Saturday night at North Luffenham, Carrots, Jim and I had taken the 'garry' to Stamford. Jim had been going to the dance hall regularly and persuaded Carrots and me to join him. Stamford in 1949 was bisected by the A1 trunk road; the road took a couple of sharp right angle bends and went right through the centre of the town. The centre market area was cobbled on both sides of the main road. The dance hall, as I recall, was outside a graveyard with its church on the other side.

That first night, we entered the dancehall as the dance was just getting underway. It was like going into a big shed. The room was about fifty feet long plus the stage at the far end which stood three feet high. The middle-aged band of piano, drums, saxophone, trumpet and accordion were discordantly playing a waltz. No one was dancing.

The room was thirty feet wide, and down both long sides was a row of tin, bum-chilling chairs hugging the wall. The row on the left-hand side was already half-full of young girls with various bored expressions, a few of them talking to their neighbours.

The right-hand row of chairs boasted only two budding Romeos, hair slicked back with brilliantine and loud Arthur English ties. Their eyes were slitted like Chinese against the curling smoke drifting across their faces from the casually hung Players Weights cigarettes, as they eyed and sized up the possibilities on offer, thirty feet across the room.

Sixteen individual bulbs hung from wires high in the air, and hardly lit the large hall, casting shadows in corners and edges and dulling any light-heartedness one might have had before entering. No tables to put down your tea or soft drink, which could be purchased through the refreshment hatch down the stage end of the hall. The floor was the table and ash tray. A large football of one inch square mirrors hung expectantly and motionless, waiting the call to 'spot' the lovers in an hour's time.

The grey-haired band leader, squeezing his accordion, stood midstage, grinning inanely at the empty floor. Saturday night, dance night, October 1949.

Jim's date turned up half an hour later, just as the first brave couple ventured onto the virgin floor for a quickstep, to the great delight and relief of the band leader. We had drunk two cups of tea by then and smoked four cigarettes each. More prospective dancers were drifting in, mostly females. The males arrived in gangs an hour later when they had purchased sufficient liquid courage to cross the thirty foot wide dance floor with careless abandon, never considering for a moment the embarrassment that a refusal would bring – thirty feet back to your seat with all eyes watching.

Jim's date was called Brenda, a plain-looking girl with a perfectly round face, straight black hair parted in the middle, and black-rimmed spectacles – Keyhole Kate's twin sister, I thought. She spoke nicely in spite of her plain looks, but I could imagine, by her well-washed and faded polka-dot dress, that she came from a big family or poor parents or both. She said she had come on a special coach from Peterborough. Apparently a coachload of girls came every Saturday, the RAF's eligible bachelors being the attraction, I suppose. Her bright red new shoes made her feet look huge and her dress look old.

I wondered if it was true what they said about red shoes? I tried to catch the reflection on her shoes and grew excited. As though Jim was reading my thoughts, he took his darling Brenda onto the floor and they twirled away like two professionals. I could see that they both loved their dancing and they spent most of the night on the floor.

Carrots and I sat smoking, watching the couples drift by as the hall filled up to bursting. The band became more adventurous as the night went on and tangos and sambas gave an opportunity to the good dancers to show off their skills. My feet were itching to dance but there was no way I was going to risk crossing that thirty foot void and possible getting a 'No, thank you'.

'I'll come with you for the next quick-step,' said Carrots for the umpteenth time, indicating one or two possibles.

'Not tonight, Carrots, I don't feel like it,' I lied.

I'd been taking everything in. As soon as the MC bandleader announced a dance the fellas would stampede across the wooden floor like a charge of elephants. Two-thirds would get their choice and the cream of the beauties were gone. The unlucky third would then ask their second choice and then there were two or three disappointed Romeos left standing, having had two refusals. Maybe two of the three would wisely give up and drift embarrassingly back to their seats, but there was always one thick enough to continue down the row of rejects, not considering that the odds were lengthening with every refusal. Even a reject didn't want to be third, fourth, or fifth choice.

Between dancing I had studied the goods in the shop window opposite. I put them into two classes: firstly the smart, well-dressed ones that I liked but were obviously, to my way of thinking, too good for me, above my station as a lowly ACII. The second, and by far the bigger group, were scruffy, always talking and smoking, which I didn't fancy at all. So we sat there, watching, smoking and alternately getting cups of tea.

I still hadn't progressed any further with my education into the female world from Jill Murphy's brown, dirty and holey knickers, soldiers in the woods at Warley Barracks and lastly Mrs Bell and her bathroom.

My friends at Locking didn't have girlfriends, or money to find them, and my five months' outings at Topcliffe had been singing in the pub. I had never thought seriously about having a girlfriend, and working in the close proximity of WAAFs like Splitpin and Laurel and Hardy didn't exactly encourage in me any desire in that particular direction.

Of course barrackroom jokes and braggards' stories had added to my knowledge a little, or at least I thought it had, but I sat there, the innocent and naïve virgin, content to look and listen.

'Would you like to dance?'

I looked up . . . and fell madly in love.

Vera was a redhead with sparkling lively blue eyes. She was one of the 'posh' ones I had spotted earlier. I'd dismissed her as too good for me because she was so smart and neat and clean looking. Her beautiful red hair had waves to both sides of her head which were held there by two matching, mother of pearl hairslides. At five foot eight inches she was above the average height of most of the other girls in the hall, and I could just see a hint of brown freckles on her lovely smiling face, as she bent forward. Her eyes were perfectly set, I did hate close or sunken eyes – and a well-proportioned nose set off her face admirably. An expensive white blouse fitted high to her neck with lace trimming to neck and long sleeves. The lovely long pleated grey skirt two inches past her knees, reminded me of a slim kilt, and her shiny, grey patent shoes just set her off in a class of her own. Carrots and I had been in such deep conversation and the hubbub of noise was so great, that we hadn't heard the MC announce a 'Ladies invitation'.

I stared up at this beautiful vision and my face caught fire as my heart pounded and tried to get out of my chest. Was it me or Carrots she was asking? – it was me! – she was smiling at me, and oh! she had perfect white teeth, I was in a dream – surely I was dreaming.

'Well then – shall we dance?' she asked again with a mischievous smile in her twinkling eyes.

I followed her to a space on the dance floor and drank intoxicatingly on the waves of sweet perfume left in her wake. She turned and put her arms out to me and through the dimmed lights I could see that enchanting smile, the smile, just for me. The bank was playing the 'Anniversary Waltz'; how appropriate, how memorable, how lovely the band sounded now.

The football was rotating, sending its silver stars dancing across her face and clothes. We touched and a tremble of excitement went up my arms, down my back, down my thighs and my toes flicked. Heaven, I was in Heaven. We glided round in a dream, hands held high a few inches apart.

My god . . . it touched me, only lightly but it touched me; we went into a complete turn and her breast touched me; my head was definitely hot and banging. No handkerchiefs now, our hands were touching and her skin did feel soft. My right hand rested gently on her back, I could feel her brassière strap. I had such excited feelings; Mrs Jenkins certainly would not approve of her pupil acting like this. Vera waltzed beautifully, as light as a feather. We were well matched at five foot eight and six foot respectively, both slim and light on the feet. Oh, how good life was all of a sudden.

'I haven't seen you here before,' she said, smiling sweetly. What lovely thin sensuous lips she's got, what a lovely smile, if only the waltz could go on forever, but alas, the music had stopped.

'This is my first time, actually,' I said, putting on my best impressive voice, 'Could I buy you a lemonade?' I didn't want to let her go because I knew I wouldn't make it across that floor in the stampede.

'Thank you, I'd like a soda cream please,' she said sweetly.

We talked and we danced and we talked. Vera was from Peterborough, she came on the coach, it was only her third visit. She worked in a bank and was an only child. Her parents were not happy at her travelling to Stamford on Saturday but her girl friends had convinced them everything would be all right. Her father was a solicitor and had a car. This confirmed my assessment, rich and posh, not really my station, but she seemed to like me a lot and showed no signs of wanting to return to her friends. As for me, I was in my seventh heaven. Both Jim and Carrots gave me huge grins and knowing winks as we glided by on 'A Slow Boat to China.'

The last waltz struck up: 'Who's taking you home tonight.' We waltzed into dreamland, I was up in the clouds. Mrs Jenkins' eight inches was forgotten as our bodies touched and moved as one. What pleasure, what delight, as the warmth of our bodies fanned the furnace of love. I was gone, totally oblivious to anyone else in the dance hall, touching, swaying, gently gliding, as the music poured over us and the new experience, the first experience of dormant, pent up and innocent love was unchained and set free.

The music stopped, I came to and open my eyes. The floor was more than half empty and the band were packing up.

'Shall we get our coats?' asked Vera.

We stepped out into the cold night air. I looked up at the clear night sky, stars twinkling, just like Vera's eyes, and the half moon smiling down on me to set the seal on a perfect night.

The drystone churchyard wall across the cobbled road propped up embracing couples under the street lights. A coach, with more couples surrounding the back, stood twenty feet along the road.

'It won't go for ten minutes,' she said, smiling up at me. Taking all the courage I could summon, and drunk on love, I said:

'Let's walk then,' as I took her elbow and steered her through the lychgate into the graveyard. She didn't resist or say anything, which gave me encouragement.

We stood under a small tree surrounded by graves and headstones where we could easily see the coach and wall lovers. We were in the dark of the tree and couldn't be seen. Now I was nervous, what to do? I desperately wanted to kiss those lovely lips, but how should I go about it? What would her reaction be? Would I upset her? I was lost.

'Are you coming next week?' I asked, really for something to say, really to break the silence, to give me time to think, to work out a plan.

'Yes, are you, shall we make it a date?'

My head decided to go down . . . our lips met . . . I shuddered all over. Her arm went round my neck ... her lips pressed harder on mine. Feelings I had never felt before engulfed me, my first kiss, my first girl, my first love.

As the lorry made its way back to camp I sat in the gloom of the canvas looking up with renewed interest at my friend the moon and its family of twinkling stars.

'Come on, Fizz, get out, you're in a bloody dream, you haven't spoken a word all the way back,' said Carrots.

CHAPTER 14

Fireworks and the Field Marshal

We'd met three Saturdays in a row; the weeks seemed to be long now waiting for Saturdays to come. It was the last week in October, a Sunday morning, and the billet was practically empty as all but four of us had gone home for a long weekend pass.

A quiet lad called Robin slid down the polished lino on his pads and handed me his mug of tea he'd brought back from breakfast. The other two room-mates were deep in their slumbers.

'Thanks, Robin,' I said, sitting up in bed and sipping my tea.

'You were in late again last night; did you have a good time?' asked Robin, who rarely went out. He was a real studious fella, always reading or making model aircraft.

'Yeah, smashing, thanks, met my girl again and had a lovely time.'

I hadn't told Mother yet that I had a girlfriend; she had often asked me when I went home if I'd met anybody and it always embarrassed me. 'Waiting for the right one to come along, aren't you, love?' she used to say, and then laugh.

I'd just received a letter asking when I was coming home again. I intended writing to her, and I had a little surprise up my sleeve. Mother had said in her letter that it was hard to get fireworks and she didn't think there would be much of a show for the three young ones on November 5th. This morsel of news had set my brain going and a challenge had presented itself. What if I could arrive home with some fireworks? Rockets and things, that would surprise them.

On Friday I had been working on a Valetta; we called it the 'Pig' because of its big, fat, pig-like fuselage or belly. In the cockpit of the Valetta, just behind the co-pilot's seat and above the back of his head, were stored on an open rack four large distress cartridges and a pistol. The cartridges were three inches long and about one inch in diameter, and they came in four different colours. They were used to signal distress if the aircraft ditched or got into trouble. It was the airframe mechanic's job to check these and replace where necessary. I had 'acquired' two of these cartridges, a red and green, and they were now hidden among my clean underclothes awaiting my pleasure.

I got up and took a leisurely bath and returned to the billet. Robin was sitting at the end of the table working on his Ajax balsa wood model. All his wood, plans, balsawood cement, razor blade and tissue paper were spread out on the table. His fourteen-inch-long fuselage structure, which was three inches square at the front and tapered off to a half inch square at the tail, was now covered in white tissue paper and he was applying the dope to tauten it. The two-foot wingspan had already been 'doped' and the tissue had stretched smooth and taut.

'Looks good, Robin,' I said, as I slid by on my pads, 'When's the test flight due, today?'

'No, won't be finished today, Fizz, I've got the tailplane and undercarriage to do yet.'

The smell of peardrops filled the room as the dope fumes rose and ensured the two sleepers had sweeter dreams.

It was nearly ten o'clock, over two hours to go to lunch, so I decided to have a go at making my fireworks. I placed the two cartridges on the end of the table on their thick brass compression cap ends. Robin looked up.

'Christ, Fizz, what you gonna do?' he asked, concerned.

'Just experimenting, Robin, I only want the powder out of 'em.'

He returned his concentration to the delicate task of cutting out his intricate tail section and probably thought I was mad anyway. He kept himself to himself.

I sat at the very end of the table, and with my dinner knife prized round the thick crinkled end of the red cartridge. I took my time and with the help of my dinner fork I eventually succeeded in having the one inch diameter collar pointing upwards.

The sleepers slept on, Robin continued to concentrated on his labour of love and all was peace and quiet.

I removed the thick cardboard disc from the top of the cartridge and peered in at the grey powder. Now what? I thought. I had no specific plans and was waiting for inspiration. I fetched my Cherry Blossom tin, took off the lid and poured a little pyramid of the mysterious powder from the cartridge case into the middle of the tin lid. I sat back and admired my work. Now what? – See what happens, came back the answer. I carefully lit a cigarette and then, gingerly, with outstretched arm, presented the red end slowly towards the powder ... NOTHING. I pushed the cigarette end right into the pyramid ... NOTHING. I withdrew the fag, dragged on it, blew on the red end to make sure it was red hot and quickly put it back in the powder ... NOTHING. Sod me, must be a 'dud', probably been on its rack for years.

I prized round the rim of Mr Green cartridge and removed the thick cardboard disc. I looked in: the powder looked the same, it smelt the same.

I got the tin lid of my Duraglit. Everything was quiet. Robin was deep in concentration, so was I, but I was getting impatient. I poured a small pyramid of identical powder from Mr Green cartridge into the centre of my new tin lid. I lit a new cigarette, arms length again, slowly, gently, the red tip advanced on the new pyramid, it touched it ... NOTHING. I penetrated it ... NOTHING.

Sod me. I sat back and took a drag on my fag as my tense body started to relax. Surely not two duds, I thought, what a waste of an hour.

I sat there smoking, wondering what to do next. Impetuously I struck a match and presented it straight to Mr Green's pyramid.

A great blinding flash hit my eyes. Panic, sheer panic gripped me.

I instinctively grabbed, through the green haze and thickening white smoke towards the offending Duraglit lid, thinking, I supposed, that I could throw it out of the first floor window, but the lid was red hot. As I grabbed it, dropped it, and pulled my painful hand away, I must have knocked over Mr Red cartridge but I didn't know this as only a second had passed.

Bright red flashed into the green cloud and became a fierce jet three or four inches in diameter.

As I sat there spellbound, shocked and burnt, I could see through the thinner smoke at table level Mr Red cartridge lying on his side, brass percussion cap pointing up the length of the table. His innards were alight and the low roar of noise was heightening in pitch as he spewed out a three inch long widening jet of red fire. The table end was burning nicely as the brass percussion cap started to glow red. Two, three seconds, I don't know how long it took, but the sight of it gripped me motionless in panic. I grabbed at Mr Red in sheer desperation as his roar reached fever pitch, but he saw me coming. He took off up the centre of the table straight through Robin's beautiful fuselage and mainplane.

By now Mr Green had decided to join in the fun. He had been blown onto his side by Mr Red as he passed by and had been ignited by Mr Red's jet but I only had eyes for Mr Red who cleared the end of the table and landed a further six feet up the billet on the lino floor.

There were voices shouting and screaming somewhere in the smoke-filled room and I did catch a glimpse of a naked body flashing across a bed like an Olympic hurdler but I was fiercely concentrating on Mr Red's antics and was determined to have him out of the window.

Unfortunately, these distress flares are designed to hang in the sky and light the area for up to two minutes and Mr Red had only been going for about fifteen seconds, so he had a lot of life in him yet.

Shell-shocked, eyeballs scorched, and right-hand fingers burnt, I was on all fours, just below cloud level, making for the other end of the table which I'd just seen Mr Red leap off. There he was, catching his breath after his six foot leap.

As I approached, he noticeably sank lower in the lino as his red-hot brass end glowed and his roar, which had lulled perceptively, revved up as more innards caught fire.

I had him in my sights and made a demented, suicidal lunge, both hands to the fore but alas, he was quicker. He took off like a jet-propelled mole, with a roaring, lino-burning ferocious, red-flamed arse.

He shot around the floor, ricocheting off bed legs, lockers, skirting boards and even visiting someone's Sunday best boots. His speed of travel was quick and fascinating as I charged around on all fours trying to catch him. I supposed I was hoping to get out of a very serious situation. If I could only get the two cartridges out of the window and clean up the billet I might get away with it. It was a forlorn hope.

The wonderful pattern he was burning in the lino fascinated me as he criss-crossed, bumped, and changed direction without even a sign of slowing down or running out of energy. He must have had kind feelings towards me, maybe because I'd released him from the small dark shelf in the pilot's cabin or maybe because I'd given him a chance in life to shine, to show what he could do after years of gathering dust. Whatever the reason, he kept well clear of me and made no threat to my person.

What's that? Mr Green just flashed by. Well, not by, he came straight at me. I had to move quickly or he would have had me. Obviously Mr Green didn't like me. 'Whizz', there he went again, he hit me on the wrist that time; God, it did hurt.

My eyes were hurting, my hand was burnt and also my wrist; it was getting dangerous. I had to get out. I got up and stumbled up the billet through dense smoke and red and green haze.

I staggered out onto the landing to look for the fire buckets, coughing my heart out. My room mates were nowhere in sight.

I grabbed a bucket of sand, ignoring the pain in my right hand and arm, and re-entered the pyrotechnic arena with the avowed intent of burying both Mr Red and Mr Green. I saw through the dense smoke a red mist cloud towards the end of the room. When I got there I found Mr Red boring an escape hole in the bottom of a wooden locker. His glowing red brass cap was already a half inch into the soft wood. I let him have it; the full bucket of sand soon put paid to his antics. Now for Mr Green. I retreated to the landing, blackened, burnt and coughing as the camp fire-brigade came running up the stairs.

I was taken off to the ambulance, and left Mr Green in the fireman's capable hands.

Standing to attention, a snowdrop either side of me, in front of the Wing Commander's desk, I felt sure that twenty-eight days would be the minimum sentence I would get.

My right hand and wrist were one massive blister, like a huge spider's back. The dry dressing made it look worse as my hand hung out of the white sling around my neck.

The adjutant was reading the list of charges and it was the first time I'd heard them. Stealing government property, wilful damage, it went on and on.

The medical officer's report was read out also: severe burning to right hand, wrist and arm, scorched eyeballs. Finally came the damage report:

'In all my days, Freeman, I've never seen a case like this. What on earth happened, man?' asked the kindly old Wingco.

It was then that I had a revelation: help, from above. Up to then no official had asked what happened and nobody really knew except Robin. To my knowledge he hadn't been questioned; in fact nobody thought about anyone else being in the billet other than myself as it was the monthly weekend off.

'Well, Sir,' I began, thinking on my feet and with the most innocent expression I could muster. 'I was cleaning my battledress jacket with petrol outside the back of the billet. I brought the jacket into my room and stupidly attempted to light a cigarette, Sir. The match end broke off as I struck it on the box and it ignited and dropped onto the jacket which I had put on the radiator to dry.' I looked at the Wing Commander with baleful eyes.

'Well,' he said, 'that doesn't explain the distress cartridges being in your room.'

'They were in the jacket, Sir. I'd serviced a Valetta on Friday and changed two old grubby cartridges during its normal service, Sir. I put the two old cartridges in the inside pocket of my battledress jacket when I was in the cockpit and meant to hand them into stores for disposal, Sir, but I forgot.'

'Didn't you feel them when you were cleaning the jacket, man, surely they're big enough?' he asked.

'No, Sir, we only dunk it in the bucket, holding the collar, to get most of the grease off,' I replied.

This was in fact standard practice as often we didn't wear overalls and our work uniforms got grease patches all over them. A bucket of aircraft fuel or sometimes a carbon monoxide fire extinguisher were standard cleaning materials, both methods giving off toxic fumes but acceptable by the erks in all innocence as a cheap way of cleaning.

The Wing Commander was very patient and somewhat intrigued by this unusual case, as I'm sure were the two snowdrops, who had to listen and no doubt to pass on the unwinding tale. The Wingco then whispered to the adjutant. The adjutant left the room.

'So the jacket caught fire – what happened next?'

'Well, I attempted to get the jacket out of the room, Sir, but it was blazing madly. I think I got halfway up the room when I had to let it go as my hand was burning. Then, Sir, the cartridges went off,' I said with a most painful expression, glancing quickly at my injuries.

'I see, I see,' he said, concerned, as the horrific picture dawned on him.

The adjutant returned and handed a note to the Wing Commander.

'Well,' said the Wing Commander, reading the note, 'We can confirm you did service the Valetta last Friday.'

He picked up the Fire Chief's report and read it slowly. 'I gather from this account you acted responsibly in returning to the scene with a fire bucket. Commendable action in the circumstances. Wait outside, will you.'

I was marched back into the room five minutes later.

'Well, Freeman, you were negligent in not returning the cartridges to the stores and no doubt your chief will have something to say about that, but your subsequent action was very commendable. I think you have suffered and will suffer with your injuries and that should teach you a valuable lesson. Case dismissed.'

I couldn't believe it, nor could any of my room-mates. It was the talk of the camp. I remained nervous for some days, thinking there might be problems if the powers-that-be decided to question Robin or the other two who were in the room at the time. After a few days of not hearing any more, I settled down and thanked my guardian angel for looking after me.

Two visits a day to the medical centre and 'light duties' in the hangar for a while and my injuries soon healed. Chiefy was sympathetic and the whole episode was soon forgotten.

'You'd better go on "circuits and bumps" for a few nights, Fizz; that won't strain your bad hand,' said Chiefy.

'Circuits and bumps' was the term given to training new pilots at landing and taking off procedures.

The first night I sat at the end of the runway, huddled up next to my 'trolleyacc'. The trolleyacc was a bank of huge accumulators in a small two-wheeled cart. The batteries were plugged into the aircraft to re-start it if the engines stalled.

I was well wrapped-up against the cold winter night and could hear the Dakota droning on its way round. The trainee pilot would do thirty or forty landings and take-offs that night. My job was to signal with my two special torches for the aircraft to stop at the end of the runway. I would then nip underneath and mark a crayon line on each of the two tyres, check the undercarriage, then re-appear, keeping well clear of the rotating propellers, and signal the pilot to continue. I would then go back to the comparative comfort of my trolleyacc.

This procedure was an airframe mechanic's job and quite enjoyable once you got used to it. After making four crayon lines, the fifth was scored through the existing four. Within a few hours the outside of the tyre wall was a mass of crayon marks. These marks would be assessed by the servicing mechanic the next day and the tyre changed if the required landings had been recorded.

As I sat under a clear starlit sky listening to the wind, I was wrapped in thought. Life wasn't bad at all, I liked my job and I had good mates. I was getting plenty of sport, as every Wednesday afternoon was for recreation, there was football on Sunday and I had one or two runs a week, ending up in the gym for an hour. Yes, I was fit and healthy, but above all I had Vera – who had become the centre of my world and was never out of my thoughts.

As I sat there dreaming, the cocoa wagon arrived and rabbits were running in front of the headlamps. The Hillman Runabout pulled up on the grass and I was then the proud possessor of a mug of hot cocoa and doorstep beef sandwiches. It was three o'clock on a cold winter morning, and I left the icy wind outside and sat in the cab with the driver.

The runway lights stretched into the distance and threw their brightness over tarmac and grass alike, an obvious attraction for the many rabbits and hares playing under the stars.

The driver returned to his duties as the Dakota taxied up and I nipped under the wing, crayon and torches in hand to do my checks.

'OK, Skip,' I shouted to the wind as I signalled the pilot. The 'kite' rolled away as I hunkered down, blanket around me, and resumed my thoughts with trolleyacc, rabbits and icy wind for company.

For some unknown reason my eldest brother Victor came into my mind. Maybe it was the rabbits – we used to catch them together when we lived near Worcester. Vic had been promoted to corporal and was getting on really well. The last time our paths had crossed was in the summer when we were on leave together. I never forgot that weekend, when I learnt a valuable lesson.

Vic and I went out together on the Saturday night, both in uniform. We had a few drinks here and there and, at ten-thirty, we were waiting at a bus stop in Brentwood High Street for the last bus home. Vic was a boxing champion by now and Mum and Dad were very proud of him.

As we stood at the kerb edge talking, a singing drunk came up to Vic, took one look at his uniformed chest and started to abuse him.

'Call yourself a bloody soldier,' he said, bringing his sneering face right close to us. 'Bloody Civvy Street soldier, no ribbons, never seen service, 'ave you sonny? he sneered.

'Go home, mate, you're drunk,' Vic said, smiling.

I was completely taken aback. All my instincts said, 'Give him a right hook,' but not Vic. He stayed calm and smiled at the fella.

'Drunk, am I?' repeated the abuser, 'I'll show you if I'm drunk, I'll give you a lesson, soldier boy, you'll never forget.' He slurred, as he drew out of his flapping mackintosh pocket a pair of yellow kid gloves.

The drunk swayed as he pulled on one of the gloves and continued to abuse Vic all the time. Vic continued to smile as I held myself back from popping the bloke one.

The drunk stood sideways on to Vic as he pulled on his second kid glove. He was mumbling away to himself, 'Soft as shit civvy soldiers', and craftily threw a looping right hand from his concealed side, but Vic saw it coming. He easily moved away from the punch, caught the drunk's fist in one swift movement and twisted the arm up the drunk's back. The drunk let out a shriek and his feet momentarily came off the ground. Vic marched him up the street, protesting every inch of the way, and presented him to a patrolling policeman.

'Hold on to this fella until I catch my bus, Constable,' he said, 'He wants to fight but I've got better things to do.'

I never forgot that weekend. It seemed to me if you have the skill and the power you don't need to fight. Vic could have beaten him with one hand but he chose not to. I never forgot that lesson.

The nights on circuits and bumps passed off without incident and I returned to my hangar and continued my work, learning more and more each day. Life settled into a regular pattern of work, sport and Saturday nights dancing with Vera.

It was during this period that the Chief sent for me.

'Fizz,' he said, 'we are expecting Field Marshal Montgomery's personal Dakota tomorrow. It will be here for two weeks and a special maintenance team will be assigned to it. You will be the airframe mech. The aircraft will be under strict security in its own hangar. Report there tomorrow morning.'

'Yes, Chief,' I said, elated at the thought of working on Monty's personal kite.

That night in the billet I was having my leg pulled by my mates, some of them envious, I suppose, at not being selected.

'Why do you think they selected you, Fizz?' asked Jed, the billet loudmouth. 'I suppose they'd rather have you in their sights all the time else Monty's kite might go up in flames if they didn't.' He laughed and others joined in.

They still didn't know the whole story of the fire in the room and they couldn't imagine how I'd got off scot free.

'Nothing to do with that,' I said when the laughter had subsided. 'Probably Monty made a special request for me, seeing as he hasn't seen me since we last met in June 1946,' I said smiling.

The room was in uproar as everybody laughed at this ridiculous statement. I'd previously told them that Monty had inspected me at Trooping of the Colour in the Dukies but no one really believed it.

Monty's Dakota arrived the next day with his personal crew, but no Monty. We, the maintenance gang, couldn't wait to get on board. Our eyes goggled with surprise as we scrambled up the special steps into the fuselage. Instead of the great open mass of ribbed interior we were used to on our own Dakotas, Monty's kite was divided into compartments.

To the right of the entrance was a special 'posh' toilet. The next section of the fuselage held a single bed bolted firmly to the floor. A door opened from the bedroom into the main part of the fuselage and what a sight that was. The fuselage was lined throughout, with not an inch of bare metal to be seen anywhere. There were eight plush and comfortable seats each side of the fuselage, grouped in pairs facing one another, with an eighteen-inch polished table between each pair. Oak panelling to the sides of the fuselage extended to just above table height. There was individual subdued lighting above each table. The floor was carpeted. The whole aircraft: mainplane, fuselage and tailplane, was highly polished, as though coated in silver – not the dull grey we were used to.

For two weeks I serviced and polished that aeroplane. Daily flights took it off to I know not where and it returned at all hours of the day and night, but not once did the keen maintenance crew see the famous General. At the time Monty was deputy Supreme Allied Commander Europe (Eisenhower was the Chief). After two weeks the flight crew said their farewell to us and the faithful old Dakota took off into the blue.

This famous aeroplane is now part of a superb collection of World War Two aircraft and vehicles housed in the aerospace museum, RAF Cosford, near Wolverhampton. (Minus its bed I'm afraid.) It has now been re-painted in the wartime livery of Dakota KG.374, in memory of Flight Lieutenant David Lord, DFC, who was awarded a posthumous VC for his part in the drop zone drama that took place north of Arnhem on 19 September 1944.

CHAPTER 15

False Teeth

Christmas 1949 was spent with my family at their 'new' council house at Larchwood Gardens, Brentwood, but I just could not wait to get back to camp and my girlfriend Vera.

That first Saturday of the new year found us in our favourite haunt – the dancehall at Stamford – swapping stories about our family Christmases, and doubly enjoying each other's company. The time flew by as we talked and danced and we were surprised and disappointed to hear the last waltz being announced.

We strolled into the churchyard and made for our usual spot from where we could see the coach. I was holding her in my arms when she looked up at me and said,

'We should see each other more than just Saturday nights.'

I hadn't thought about seeing her more often. It had never occurred to me. Saturday night was the accepted thing and anyway, with Vera living in Peterborough and me south of Stamford, with no transport and little money, it seemed impossible, but the thought was exciting.

'OK, I'll see you tomorrow,' I said, without giving it any thought other than the fact of having Vera to myself, away from the dancehall crowds.

'Oh, that's good, where shall we meet?' she said excitedly.

'Outside the swimming baths at two o'clock,' I replied.

I saw her onto the coach and we were both full of excitement. 'Till tomorrow, sweetheart,' I whispered.

'Tomorrow,' she repeated, her eyes sparkling like moist diamonds, as I stood outside the open coach window. I waved like mad as the coach disappeared into the dark night.

'What are you looking so excited about?' asked Jim as we boarded the lorry. 'I'm seeing Vera tomorrow afternoon outside the baths,' I said proudly, 'And it was her idea too.'

'Lucky bugger,' said Jim. 'Wish Brenda would come over on a Sunday; Vera must think a lot of you.'

Sunday morning started off somewhat overcast and I said a little prayer for the sun to come out. God must have been busy, being Sunday, and a gentle rain started at lunchtime.

The only means of transport, other than the Saturday night garry, was the 'sit up and beg' RAF issue bicycles. These were painted in RAF blue and had white stencilled identification numbers on them. They were assigned strictly to certain personnel whose duties necessitated considerable movement around the camp, such as Military Police and certain senior NCOs. These bikes were for use on the camp only, but it had been a habit of a few of us to 'borrow' a bike now and again to visit the odd village pub. There was an art in knowing whose bike was whose and when he would normally use it.

I decided to borrow the hangar bike as it wouldn't be needed until Monday morning. The tricky bit was getting off camp with it in broad daylight; getting back in the dark would be a doddle.

My mates in the billet offered their advice in friendly banter although deep down, most of them already considered me crackers for the things I'd been getting up to.

I set off in the drizzle, picked up the bike and pedalled to the back of the airfield. The weather was a godsend as visibility was poor and the MPs wouldn't be patrolling in the rain. God was on my side after all.

I arrived at the open-air swimming pool just outside Stamford in plenty of time. The pool was closed during winter and I was the only human being in sight. The icy rain was being whipped into my face by the wind as the weather deteriorated, so I sheltered under a large tree thinking it wasn't such a good idea after all. What on earth could we possibly do in such weather?

Two o'clock came and I grew excited, looking left and right for her father's car. Perhaps, I thought, her mother would be in the car with them. Maybe they'd drive us somewhere for tea.

Two fifteen came and went. Maybe they were delayed, I thought. Two thirty, still no car but hope reigns eternal. Two forty-five and I was beginning to believe she wouldn't come. At ten past three, wet, bedraggled and fed up, I mounted my borrowed transport and head down, into the wind and rain, I pedalled for camp.

God wasn't on my side after all. Halfway back, sweating with exertion but soaked to the skin with rain, a vehicle overtook me and stopped. I looked up to see an RAF fifteen hundredweight truck. The passenger cab door opened and out stepped a snowdrop.

Seven days detention in the guardhouse came hard after a year of good conduct. The military police were the same inhuman beings that I'd encountered at training camp and they gloated that they'd got me at last. It appeared that they were set on having my company after the cartridge affair and, being disappointed that time, they had made up for it with their ridiculous orders and punishments, but I took it in my stride with a renewed hardening of my feelings towards the imbecile breed of RAF policemen.

Vera ignored me and I ignored her for most of the first Saturday night I was back in circulation. Plenty of people wanted to dance with her as I sat there with Carrots, miserably pretending not to notice her. I was at the tea counter when she came back from the toilets and she had to pass me in the queue. I had to say something.

'Thanks for not coming to the baths,' I said sarcastically as she passed. She turned on me with fire in her eyes.

'It's you that didn't come, I waited an hour, you RAF chaps are all the same,' she said and stalked on.

As I sat down I noticed she was with another chap but I was determined to have it out with her, but the last waltz was called and she was dancing in someone else's arms. I went back to camp miserable and confused.

I had often joined Jim in his boxing training sessions and the following week, after the sharp exchange with Vera, I was in the gym one evening. The sergeant instructor had been trying to persuade me for weeks to join his team but I didn't want to.

'You get extra time off for training before a championship and special food,' he would say.

I liked my trade and didn't want time off, but that didn't stop me going down the gym for a workout now and again in the evenings.

'Have a couple of rounds with Bomber,' said the sergeant that Wednesday night. 'Only a friendly, Bomber will take it easy, won't you Bomb? Just like to see how you shape up,' pleaded the sergeant.

Jim and my keep-fit mates were standing round in a half circle, silent, waiting for my reply. Bomber, a bullying lad, stood there gloved up and banging his gloved fists together as he grinned threateningly at me. He seemed to be daring me to fight him. The pregnant pause, as everybody waited for my answer, put me in an awful spot. I didn't want to box the fella but I didn't want to be thought a coward either.

'Bomb'ul take it easy on you, Fizz,' said the sergeant. Christ, I wished he wouldn't keep saying that.

'All right,' I said, feeling press-ganged into the situation.

When Dusty Miller had last seen me I had been five foot four inches and seven stone two pounds. He would have been amazed to see me now at six feet and half an inch and weighing eleven stone twelve pounds but I still remembered what Dusty taught me and I was thinking of this as I gloved up.

As my mates stood around the ring watching, the sergeant struck the bell and we were off. It took some time for me to relax to the task and sure enough Bomber just blocked my punches and threw out gentle lefts and rights, sometimes catching me, sometimes not. The first round seemed a long one but I was getting in my stride as the bell sounded.

Round two and I was getting through his guard a bit now. Bomber responded by catching me with a couple of crisp but gentle combinations to head and stomach. Things were hotting up apace.

I noticed that when I threw a left jab he parried with his right and let his left glove drop at the same time. I tried two more lefts and each time he did the same. I moved around on my toes, biding my time and then poked out a straight left, his guard went down and I threw a hard right. He saw it coming and moved his head sufficiently for me to miss his chin but the blow was enough to make him stagger back into the ropes. The onlookers chorused their approval and were shouting encouragement, mostly to me, as Bomber threw caution to the wind.

In his temper he let his boxing skills go as he came at me. I danced away from his repeated charges, flicking my left in his face as I did so. I was really enjoying myself as my footwork was far superior to Bomber's flat-footed approach.

His face was growing redder as I danced out of reach. I kept catching him with straight lefts which only made him more determined to nail me. The shouting continued as I puffed my way round the ring waiting for the bell.

Then he got me, a haymaker. I saw it coming but too late to do anything. It hit me full in the mouth, blood everywhere. The sergeant appeared in between us holding us back. We hadn't heard the bell. My mouth must have been open when the blow hit me because Bomber had snapped off the front two upper teeth at gum level. Stupidly, neither of us were wearing gumshields.

The RAF dentist removed the rest of the two teeth and no amount of pleading could persuade him to let me have false teeth for at least three months.

'The gums have got to harden, Freeman, the holes have got to fill up. Be a good chap and stop worrying me, come back in three months.'

I cursed that pilot officer dentist. What young man wants to have a huge gap every time he opens his mouth? They could have put teeth in the holes in the gums. They could have given me a temporary denture and renewed it when the gums had hardened, but no, come back in three months. It virtually meant confined to camp for three months as I wasn't going to let anybody see me like that.

To add to my misery, Jim came back from his Saturday night dancing to say that Vera wanted to see me. Apparently she had kept the date outside the baths at Peterborough while I stood outside the baths at Stamford. I had assumed that as her father had a car he would bring her over. How Vera had expected me to get to Peterborough on a Sunday of all days I just couldn't fathom. Anyway, it was all academic now; my confidence had gone with my teeth so I told Jim to say I'd been posted and left it at that.

I then spent a miserable three months absorbing wisecracks and feeling sorry for myself. I ventured to the local village pub a few times and braved going home to see my parents.

The long three months came to an end and the gap was filled by two badly fitting RAF teeth. My mouth felt twice as big and I looked like George Formby. I tried playing my cornet but it was hopeless. I vowed to get some private teeth at the first opportunity.

I had been getting good reports sent in by my Chiefy as to my competence in carrying out my trade duties. Chiefy had put me in the hydraulic bay, repairing and testing components, a sign of recognition that I was a good tradesman, so I was pleased the day he sent for me to say I was posted to RAF St. Athans, South Wales. His recommendation that I should be trained to Fitter IIA standard from the present Mechanic status had been accepted.

I said my farewells to Carrots, Jim, and many more mates and with kitbag, webbing, and new teeth, I set off for rainy South Wales.

CHAPTER 16

Singing a Song

There were always eyes in a guardroom. Cruel eyes, vicious eyes, superior eyes, sneering eyes. Eyes attached to small undeveloped brains. Eyes you couldn't always see. Eyes searching endlessly to satisfy the appetite of those small tramline brains. Eyes waiting to feed the impatient mouth, the sneering mouth, the mouth so used to uttering the small repertoire of insults sure in the knowledge that they were the power, they were impregnable, they were the masters of the minions that passed before them.

'Airman, yes you, come here!' screamed one of a pair of snowdrops.

I was stunned, I thought I'd left that bawling stupid world behind. I'd come on a technical training course to learn more about my trade. I was keen to learn, happy to get the opportunity and it had never occurred to me that it would be anything other than learning. Flashes of Father being shouted at when I was a boy came back into my mind. I strolled across to the belligerent-looking corporal who stood with his partner, surveying their little domain of road entrance, enjoying their normal day's 'essential to the Air Force' work. I was just AC1 bottom of the pile material and they knew it.

'Stand to attention, airman,' said the corporal as I stood there relaxed in front of him. I gently brought my feet together.

'Name and number,' he said.

I imagined he wanted to know them but he didn't ask; still, don't be awkward.

'1920683 AC1 Freeman, Corporal,' I drawled.

'You're a scruffy sod, Freeman. Report to the barber's shop, get your hair cut, then smarten yourself up and report to me here tomorrow morning.'

I couldn't argue with that as my hair was very long and thick, and hung over my collar. Life had been pretty easy at North Luffenham.

RAF St. Athans was two units on the same site: a maintenance unit that undertook major repairs for other aerodromes and a training camp for various trades. I was posted to the training unit.

St. Athan was memorable for the amount of rain that could fall, day after day, and still life carried on. The other difference was the main road to Barry and Barry Island some five miles away. This road came through the camp and divided the living accommodation for trainees from the work areas: lecture rooms, hangar and parade ground. This division was very important in my case because it meant passing in front of the guardroom each day as we went to and from work. It also gave more power and control to the 'wet behind the ears' young military police corporals who stood in pairs at the road barrier, outside the guardroom, and lorded their power over anyone entering or leaving the base.

It came as a great shock to the laidback style of life that I'd become accustomed to. The stroll to the hangar in the morning to start work. The good relations with senior NCOs in the hangar. The life in the billet had been clean and tidy with no excess of bullshit. People had talked, they didn't scream or shout. No personal insults and degrading scenes. Suddenly my whole world had changed.

I went to the barber's in the lunch period and had a quick trim and the next morning, somewhat smarter, having pressed my working clothes, I reported to big-mouth at the gate. He walked round me slowly, his fierce eyes boring into me. His mate stood in front of me oozing superiority. Loud-mouth appeared again before me.

'I ordered you to get a haircut, why haven't you been?' he shouted. Bugger me, I thought, as I stood relaxed in front of him, here we go again, same bloody games.

'I had it cut yesterday, Corporal,' I said quietly.

'You call that a haircut?' he shouted, 'Report back to the barber and tell him to give you a regulation haircut, then report back to me again tomorrow morning.'

'Christ, Corporal, I came here for a training course, not a bullshit course,' I said angrily.

They could see I was a regular and that I'd got some service in and this influenced their stupid mentality. They couldn't go as far with regulars and get away with it as they could with new entrants but they did try it on. It was often a battle of wits and nerve.

'Less of your bloody lip, Freeman, regulation haircut and report to me in the morning ... that's an order, now go.'

Two more mornings of insults and controlled, ego-shattering replies found me being marched to the barber's, under escort, and receiving my regulation short back and sides. And so my card was marked, the bastards had me plumb in their sights and were just waiting to nail me with something substantial.

It wasn't just me, of course, that the snowdrops picked on. Sandy, my new pal, also got pulled up, but he was quite a bit smarter than me and his sandy hair was shorter and had natural little tight curls. He only needed one haircut to his already short hair to satisfy the little Hitlers, but I was the attraction. It was as though I had painted in large letters on my forehead: 'awkward sod – I hate snowdrops'. Somehow they knew I was their meat, my eyes surely gave me away.

I met Sandy getting off the train the night we arrived. We were both joining the same course for Fitter IIA training. He was nearly twenty, a handsome fella with a totally extrovert personality. We soon clicked and became real buddies, spending our work and leisure time together.

The training programme was all absorbing and we soon settled down into a regular routine. The instructors were superb and I was lapping up every minute. I fell into the routine that Weedy and I had used and re-wrote my notes every night. The practical sessions on the workbench, on sections of aircraft and in the various service bays, allowed me to shine. I was in my element and the weeks quickly flew by.

Saturday night was dance night. Saturday night wasn't Saturday night unless you went to a dance, that's where the life was, that's where the excitement was, that's where the girls were.

Gwyn was a quiet one, timid, even a bit shy. She didn't smile much either – that's why I fell for her.

Nobody asked her to dance; they asked her big-bosomed friend with postbox-red lips but not Gwyn. She was flat-chested. Her plain oblong face and square chin looked scrubbed white but she had a high cheek colour; natural it was, no make-up, she was from a religious family. Her straight up and down dress, buttoned high to her thin neck, had been washed a few times. A belt round the middle would have helped, at least it would have broken up the straight line of five foot seven inch frame, but no, straight up and down she stood, in her faded blue best dress.

I didn't mind crossing the dance floor to ask her. I'd classified her as my station in life, definitely not posh and certainly not rich. I knew I could feel comfortable with her.

The dancehall at Barry was a great improvement on the plain hall at Stamford. A balcony overlooked the purpose-built oak block dance floor. A full band was on stage and averaged a hundred years younger than the ancient musicians of Stamford. Beautiful lighting, chairs and tables and full refreshments including alcohol, were all available in this palace of love.

'I'm off for a dance, Sandy,' I said and, taking a deep breath, crossed the great divide as the few likely prospects left on the other bank preened themselves, watching through the sides of their eyes as I approached.

'May I have the pleasure?' I asked with a smile, bowing from the waist and proferring a bent arm. Mrs Jenkins would be proud of her protegée now, I thought.

'Yes,' came the weak, surprised voice.

The other rejects glared in annoyance and surprise. 'How could he ask her?' I could hear them say. Comparisons in life are funny things, talk about the eye of the beholder!

'You don't talk much,' she said quietly as we waltzed.

'Sorry, I was miles away,' I replied, which wasn't much of a compliment.

'You're a nice dancer,' she stated.

'Thanks, so are you, did you take lessons?'

I liked her true sincere blue eyes, they looked straight at you when she spoke and I was taken to stare at them a few times during the dance. There was a sadness deep in her eyes, which smiled warmly, but they'd been hurt or seen sadness somewhere. It was partly her eyes but mostly her genuine, sincere and naïve self that made me want to see her more and more.

Gwyn returned my affection a hundredfold and within three weeks she asked me home to Sunday tea.

'Mam would love to see you, I've told her all about you. You will come won't you?' she pleaded.

Sunday was a pretty useless day so, like a lamb to the slaughter, I walked up the hill on the outskirts of Barry that bright but cold October Sunday afternoon. Usually I walked up in the dark after our night's dancing, but now I saw the area clearly for the first time.

As I breasted the hill, the row of grey, daunting houses came into view, smoke curling from the chimney pots. The terrace was quite long, at least twenty houses, I guessed, and set forty feet back off the road. Most front gardens were dug for winter but patches of cabbages and knobbly sprouts were greatly in evidence. Opposite the row of council houses and across the narrow road was a row of magnificent oak trees with fields beyond. It was under the oak trees where I stole my goodnight kiss.

There she was, my Gwyn, standing on the front stone step of number eight in a small frilly pinny, waving excitedly as though I didn't know where to go.

I marched up the path, inspecting the ranks of brussels sprouts that stood to attention either side of me. Eyes peeped round curtains, and neighbours conjectured on the likely outcome of my visit.

'Mam' was a darling, welcoming me as though I was a long-lost son. Gwyn's father, collar- and tie-less, rose from his old arm chair and extended his hairy arm in genuine greeting, his deep Welsh voice calm and controlled as his sharp eyes took in every detail of my six foot frame. Gwyn's younger sister and brother gazed in admiration at me and never left my side.

'Come in, Bob, sit yourself down; it's a long walk up that hill,' Mam stated, pointing to the sofa which had surplice-white antimacassars neatly placed in position. The cosy feeling of the low-ceilinged livingroom, fire roaring in the large zebo black grate, the pictures on the walls, the crammed mantelpiece and cared-for furniture, was much like being at home.

Gwyn was beaming at me as the questions came thick and fast.

'How long have you been in the Air Force then, Bob?' asked Gwyn's father as he removed and refitted his pipe in his clenched teeth, all the while looking in the fire, not at me.

'Are you a pilot? do you fly planes?' asked Gwyn's younger brother before I had had time to reply to the first question.

'Three years this month, Mr Davies,' I replied. 'No, I don't fly aeroplanes, I mend them, I'm a fitter,' I said, promoting myself – it sounded more impressive than 'mechanic'.

'Regular then, are you? not national service then?' stated Gwyn's father.

'That's right, Mr Davies, eight years I signed on for.'

'H'm' was his only reply. I guess he was summing up my prospects as he stared into the flames with his secret thoughts.

'Let's have you all up at the table; Bob can sit here, now,' said Mam, appearing from the kitchen with a mountain of thinly cut bread and butter.

We sat before a groaning table of delicious food. It was obvious that extra efforts had been made. Tongue and ham, salad, jelly and blancmange, fairy cakes and small sausage rolls, all plated out neatly on the white tablecloth; it was a meal fit for a king. Gwyn sat next to me with our backs to the window, her brother and sister opposite and her mother at one end of the oblong.

I was nervous sitting there with my hands on my lap. It was like being in a shop window, constantly under the gaze of so many eyes. Only Mr Davies was acting normally, I thought, as he got up last from the fire in his collarless shirt and thick hairy trousers held up with canvas braces. He unhurriedly took his place at the head of the table. As his bum hit the seat his deep voice boomed out:

'We thank thee Lord for this food and for our work and play. We are ever mindful of thy love and generosity, Amen.'

Somewhat startled at the unexpected outburst of prayers, it was Mam's voice that brought me back to life.

'Look after Bob, then, Gwyn, see he gets plenty to eat,' she smiled.

And so my first of many Sunday teas commenced, usually followed by all the family going to chapel in the early evening.

Gwyn was reluctantly excused from accompanying them on the occasion of my visits as I delicately explained that my church was different; but I'm sure Gwyn's father didn't approve.

As the months and visits went by, Mr Davies became warmer to this foreigner in uniform and invited me to join him for a drink at his Railwaymen's Club in Barry. There were no pubs open on a Sunday but one could get a drink in the Working Men's Clubs. He soon found he had a new snooker partner and poor Gwyn was left at home with a long face. It became quite difficult to please them both so Sunday teas became rarer and rarer.

Sandy was quite an athlete, his speciality being the three miles. Wednesday afternoon was sports afternoon, all studies stopped. Sport was plentiful in the services and every encouragement was given to take part in a variety of games and competitions. As Sandy was my mate I joined him in the cross-country runs; we also went for a run one or two evenings a week.

When I was on leave in June I ventured out one Saturday night to a dance at St. Thomas's church hall in Brentwood. It was the Brentwood Athletic Club dance. A friendly crowd of healthy-looking people were sitting around enjoying themselves and I felt completely out of it. I wished I'd come in civvies instead of uniform as I stood out clearly as not one of them. I had no interest in athletics as such; to me this was just a dance, a night out at the beginning of a fortnight's leave. As I sat there sipping my tea, a bald-headed chap crossed the floor towards me. He had a pleasant, smiling face and pulled up a chair to my table.

'Hello,' he said, proferring his hand, 'I'm Des Pond, secretary of the Club. I haven't seen you at any of our dances before?'

'No, I haven't been before, saw it advertised in the Gazette, didn't know Brentwood had an athletic club.'

'You must be a high jumper or hurdler with those long legs,' he said, 'What's your speciality?'

'Haven't got one really, do a lot of running though.'

'Seems a pity to me, talent going to waste, how long are you on leave for?'

'Two weeks from yesterday,' I said, carrying on a conversation that seemed to be getting nowhere; I wasn't particularly interested in it anyway. I was more interested in getting a dance; there were some lovely girls around.

'Why don't you join us on Monday night? you might find it interesting and we'll see what you can do,' he asked sincerely.

'Where at?' I asked, for politeness' sake.

'Just down Hartswood Road, on the opposite side of the road to the War Memorial, the school playing fields. Six o'clock we start. I'm sure you'll enjoy it, will you come? he asked.

'Yes, all right then, six o'clock, thanks.'

That ten minutes with Des Pond was a turning point in my sporting career. Through Des's encouragement and regular letters I took up sprinting, hurdling and high-jumping. He would enter me for events throughout Essex and plead with me to come home some weekends to compete. As the years went on, and through Des's help I became RAF 2nd Tactical Airforce (Germany) high hurdles champion (1954) and the record stood for four years. I repaid Des in part for all his help and encouragement when, in 1956, at the brand new Hornchurch Stadium, I took the gold in the final of the 120 yard hurdles for Brentwood Athletic Club. But all this was in the future. At that period of time I was cross country running with Sandy and, following the run, I would complete the exercises listed in Des's letter and training schedule.

One of the exercises of a good hurdler is the ability to dislodge a matchbox from the top of a three foot six inch high hurdle with the inside knuckle bone of the ankle. The theory is: the longer one's in the air, the longer the race will take. It's imperative then to flatten out over the hurdle and get the feet on the ground as quickly as possible. A quick snap through with the 'trailing' leg is essential.

I was demonstrating this technique to Sandy and some of my mates as we traversed the camp roads between lecture rooms. We were laughing and enjoying ourselves and doing no one any harm when the air was shattered.

'Airmen, come here, that silly bugger doing the goose step.'

The five of us came to a momentary halt as we gazed twenty yards to the right where two snowdrops were standing in the shadows, between the huts.

'Ignore the bastards, come on,' I said, as I continued to walk on. My mates hesitated, except Sandy, who joined me.

'What did you say? What did you say?' screamed a snowdrop, now running full belt towards us.

Why is it that when everything is perfectly happy and tranquil my whole world is shattered by these bastards? Christ, we were only enjoying ourselves.

'Airmen, halt!' he screamed, out of breath, as he came in front of us.

We stopped and gazed at the red, bloated face.

'What did you say back there, come, what did you say?'

'I said, Corporal, that I didn't think you were shouting at us, we're only walking to our next lecture, it couldn't be us, we've done nothing wrong.'

'That's not what you said, Freeman,' said the second snowdrop (my haircut tormentor) as he joined us.

'Corporal, we are supposed to be in the lecture room G by now, can we go?' I asked.

'You'll go no bloody where 'till I tell you,' he sneered, 'who do you think you are, God Almighty?'

'If I were Corporal, I'd make a few changes around here.'

'You cheeky bastard, you've too much lip for your own good, put your hat on straight and stand up, man,' he commanded.

Sandy stood beside me, with the rest of the gang a few yards behind. I felt nothing but annoyance with these two national service conscripts in front of me. They were probably both a year younger than me and they didn't have to earn their stripes either, those came with the job. Their service couldn't be more than six months, if that.

'I resent being called a bastard, especially by you,' I said. 'Now can we go?'

'You're improperly dressed, Freeman, consider yourself on a charge,' said my haircut MP, flipping my undone breast-pocket flap.

'Christ, you must be hard up for something to do,' I sneered at them.

'Insubordination – two charges, that'll do fine,' smiled my tormentor.

'Go fuck yourself,' I said sharply. That wiped the smile off his face.

'You're under arrest!' he bellowed, totally out of control. And so I was.

Fourteen days in yet another guardroom. Fourteen days of misery. Another sergeant, right out of Heckner's mould, lorded it over his wet-behind-the-ears corporals and the prisoners. Sergeant Garrett was a fearful sight – where did they get them from? He shouted and bawled at me on that first day. His two eyes were at different heights and sunk into the middle of his face which gave him a massive forehead. His nose was bent at right angles. One eye looked sideways as the other looked forward. I wasn't sure which eye to look at when he was speaking. His long thin face had the skin stretched on it like a skeleton and when he started raving I waited for the skin to break.

I didn't like him and he certainly didn't like me. I didn't like the corporals and they didn't like me. I didn't like the world and the world didn't like me. I now started to slide down that slippery hill of 'sod the whole world'.

No longer would I jump when they said jump, no longer would I co-operate. I became hard and disruptive and made their arteries harden as they bawled their orders helplessly into my deaf or mute ears.

I refused to double everywhere. I took my time with all my fatigues and jobs. I gently trotted in the exercise yard and walked when I felt like it. They bawled and they shouted, and they shouted and they bawled. They threatened and re-threatened. I marched to meals and just wouldn't double.

Sergeant Garrett put me on another charge. He chose insubordination. Seven more days were added on to my sentence.

'Now, you awkward bastard,' he raved, as we returned from the admin. office. 'Seven more days to add to the ten you've got left to do, seventeen days. If you know what's good for you you'll obey orders in future. Now double march!' he screamed not two inches from my left ear. I marched off at a steady pace.

'I said double!' he screamed.

I continued my steady pace, a snowdrop 'doubling' each side of me but with short paces so they didn't get in front.

Garrett was at a complete loss. For the first time in his career his bawling and shouting were having no effect. He was also being shown up in front of his own corporals.

'I'll break you, you bastard, if it's the last thing I do, I'll break you,' and he cursed me all the way back to the exercise yard.

A new plan was devised by Garrett. During the day I was given fatigues in different messes, mountains of potatoes to peel, mountains of washing up, scrubbing, on hands and knees, miles of floor, all supervised by a snowdrop, and taken back periodically for kit inspections and the two sessions daily in the punishment oblong. From six o'clock to ten every day I was kept fully occupied.

Locked in my cell at ten o'clock I soon fell into an exhausted sleep. I was woken up every hour or so, no doubt to the orders laid down by Garrett.

'Wake up prisoner, do you want to go to the toilet?' smiled the night corporal.

'What? no, sod off,' and they laughed as they slammed the door.

All through the night this procedure went on and by morning I was shattered.

'Now, prisoner, are we going to co-operate?' said Garrett, rather softly for him. 'Light duties and a good night's sleep, not to be sneezed at,' he said.

The effect of this harassment was twofold. One, I was so tired I couldn't move fast if I wanted to, but more to the point, it made me more obstinate and determined to continue with my non-co-operation.

'Come on, Freeman, I'm giving you a chance, I don't normally give anybody a chance . . .'

'I can't believe that,' I said, without calling him Sergeant.

'All right, prisoner, if you want it the hard way, you'll fuckin' well get it – get him down to the cookhouse and work his arse off,' barked Garrett at the attendant corporal.

Too tired to march, I now strolled; what the hell, I couldn't get in any deeper. I was missing out on my training but I wasn't really bothered now, I was so fed up with my lot I hardly thought about it. I longed to see Gwyn but even she wasn't in my thoughts much. My battle with authority had taken over my complete mind. My biggest worry was that they might send me somewhere else, maybe a RAF corrective prison somewhere.

The corporal tried to persuade me to 'double' march – 'Go on, mate – for your own good,' but no, a walk was all I would give them.

'Keep at it, Fizz, you'll soon be out,' shouted a hidden voice from the bowels of a hut. I waved and the corporal looked towards the row of lecture huts but no one was in sight. That call made my spirits rise, at least for a while.

After three nights of being woken up by a not so happy corporal, the pendulum swung, words of whispered sympathy were now coming my way and my nights became undisturbed again.

Threat upon threat from Garrett produced no changes in his prisoner, and after twenty-one days, with a final regulation haircut on the last day, I'm sure they were all glad to see the back of me. I'd done them out of so much job satisfaction that the whole guardroom breathed a sigh of relief as I strolled into the sunshine in full battledress order, kitbag on shoulder and hummed my way through their red and white barrier.

Back to Sandy, Gwyn, dancing Saturdays and singing on Fridays.

They called it the longroom for obvious reasons but a more appropriate name would have been the singing room, or entertainment room. I never saw this room unless it was bursting to overflowing with people. It must have been the most popular pub in Llantwit Major or even the Welsh valleys, in January 1951.

The miners and their wives came down from the mining villages by coach on Friday nights. Full of life and laughter, their musical conversations and determined sense of humour filled the room. They threw off the frustrations of their mole-like existence, and left their cares behind in the coaldust bathwater, emptied out in their cobblestone backyards.

A few pints, a few laughs, a good sing-song and the enjoyment of each other's company made it all worthwhile, the highlight of the week. Sing and drink your cares away.

The Welsh mining families were warm friendly people and soon took you into their circle. For five months Sandy and I spent our Friday nights in the longroom, and it was like being with a big family.

The piano player was one of the family and, as I watched his magic fingers fly over the keys, another pint was placed on top of the piano for him by an appreciative 'brother'.

'What you going to give us tonight then?' Glynis shouted in my ear.

Singing was like a religion to these lovely people and the longroom echoed to beautiful Welsh tenors and baritones every Friday and Saturday night.

Glynis was the MC, the organiser, and wife of one of the regular contributors to this glorious feast of amateur talent.

At eight o'clock the 'tray' went round the longroom. Every family threw sixpence onto the tray. Glynis divided it up to three prizes and anyone could sing, recite or tell jokes. The audience were very appreciative of all the acts and gave their whole attention to them. It made for a wonderful evening.

'I've a new tear-jerker tonight, Glynis, but put me on later, will you?' I shouted above the noise.

'What's it called then?' she asked, pencil poised over her sheet of paper.

'An Airman's Lullaby,' I replied.

'Never heard of that, love, not rude is it?' she laughed, with a twinkle in her eyes.

Eight thirty and most of the miners had downed three pints or more to clear their dusty throats and Glynis was on her feet, banging a tray for 'quiet'. The evening entertainment was about to begin.

Sandy and I were sharing a table with two mining families to whom we had become attached. We had first become friendly some months previously and now, after many nights of conversation, knew intimately about each other's families. If only we had had transport, they dearly wanted us to visit them. I smiled across the table.

'Before I call on our first singer tonight,' said Glynis. 'I've an announcement to make, see. It's a surprise really,' she said, dragging out the last syllables of 'really' with a flick of the tongue. 'There's one amongst us we've all come to love and it's his birthday you see, not today, mind you, but Sunday.'

At this point Glynis produced a large square iced birthday cake from the back of the room and placed it in front of her. White and pink icing, stars and candles, and in the centre of the square top was a figure of a singer, mouth open, arms outstretched.

Glynis and her husband lit all the candles and I sat watching and shivering with emotion.

'Right now, let's all sing Happy Birthday to one who always sings so lovely to us. Happy Birthday, Bob – come and blow out the candles, love.'

As I rose, full of emotion and tears welling up in my eyes, the piano struck up 'Happy Birthday' and half the miners of Wales lifted the roof off the pub as their voices joined as one.

'Mum, I've got a girlfriend,' I announced, a few weeks after the first Sunday tea.

I was home for the weekend and there was only my mother and me in the kitchen. I'd never told her about Vera, it all happened and finished so quickly.

'Oh that's lovely, Bob, what's she like? Have you got a photo?' she beamed.

Mother found out all about Gwyn that weekend; she wouldn't leave the subject alone.

Before I returned to camp on the Sunday afternoon I had promised to bring Gwyn home for a weekend. Mother was so excited about seeing her I couldn't refuse.

The following weekend Gwyn and I went roller-skating at Barry Island. There was a good pleasure park there and we took to spending our Saturday afternoons together, then home for a quick tea before going dancing.

'Did you tell your Mum about us?' Gwyn asked rather nervously, as we boarded the bus for Barry Island.

'Yes I did, she was that excited, wanted to see a picture of you straight away,' I said, watching her face break out in smiles.

'Oh, lovely,' she said, clutching my forearm excitedly. 'What did she say when she saw the photo?'

'What a lovely girl.'

'She didn't . . .'

'She did, honest.'

'You're not making it up now, are you?' she said mischievously bringing her face close to mine.

'No, I'm not making it up. She wants you to come home with me for the weekend; I said I'd ask you.'

'Oh, fancy,' she said, nearly squeezing my forearm dry of blood in her excitement as her face took on an excited radiance. 'I don't think my father would let me do that, not go to London, not on my own. We've never been out of Wales, see.'

'You wouldn't be on your own, you'd be with me,' I said, smiling at her innocence.

'I know that,' she said, jiffling in her seat and pulling herself closer to me. 'But it's still on my own, like,' and she giggled at her secret thoughts and fantasies.

'We'll ask him, that's the only way.'

'Oh no, don't do that, leave it to me and Mam. Mam has a way of getting round him, that's it, we'll leave it to Mam.'

The following Saturday the decision was made. What went on, how Mr Davies was persuaded to let his daughter visit the mysterious and often, according to the newspapers, the 'Terrible Capital' remained a secret. A private chat and counselling from Mr Davies left me in no doubt that I would be held responsible for his treasure. And so, two weeks later, we went home to Brentwood.

Gwyn received a rapturous welcome from Mother and a polite and friendly welcome from Dad. Her eyes sparkled and shone all weekend as we took in the sights of London: Buckingham Palace, The Tower, Madame Tussaud's, Regent's Park Zoo. We did them all and dear Gwyn was breathless with excitement most of the time. Mother fussed over Gwyn and the whole weekend was a tremendous success, except for the broad hints Mother kept dropping every time she got me alone.

'She'll make you a lovely wife, Bob,' she would say.

'Mum! – we're not thinking of that, we haven't known one another long,' I said, exasperated.

'You may not be thinking of it, but Gwyn is, take my word for it, son.'

On another occasion:
'Where would you live if you did marry, Brentwood or St. Athans?'
'Mum – not again!'
'Just if, son, just if.'

The months had sped by, the studying, the sport, the singing, the dancing, the courting and the guardroom all played a part in the speeding of days, weeks and months, until the five months training course was completed.

'Congratulations, Fizz, we're now fully qualified fitter IIAs,' laughed Sandy as we crowded round the noticeboard, jostling for position, as the pinner of the notice board tried to extract himself from the eager and excited crowd. Sure enough we'd both passed with high marks and were now at the pinnacle of our trade.

'Think of all the extra money, Fizz; what are you going to spent it on?' he asked jokingly as we made our way to the NAAFI with a crowd of our successful mates.

'I'm going to save like mad for a motorbike,' I said, 'Had one once but it was a bit of a banger. The next one's going to be a super job.'

Within days it was farewell time again, always a sad time. It takes weeks to get a really good mate and the bond between you thickens with each setback, each sharing of the last fag before payday, each punishment, each hour swotting together, each night out. It all adds up and thickens the bond, each confidence, each hardship, each sharing. When you're like brothers never were, it's time to say goodbye, not *au revoir*, goodbye. Time to start again.

CHAPTER 17

Gwyn, Soco and Freddie

Jerry was an irrepressible character. Jerry Chilcott to be correct, a right Cockney sparrow. The lads called him 'Spiv'. Jerry would sell you anything – on tick – from a packet of fags to a french letter. Always quick with an answer, always smiling and cheerful, he was a character never to be forgotten.

'Can I nip out for a haircut, chief?' he cheekily asked one morning at ten o'clock tea break. We normally went in our own time to the camp barber.

'What? In the King's time?' asked Chiefy.

'Well, it grew in the King's time,' came the quick reply.

'Not all of it,' said Chiefy, thinking he'd got him.

'I don't wan' it all 'orf,' chirped the incorrigible Cockney.

Yes, Jerry was quite a character. He was wirey, thin, with a face like a ferret. His eyes never stopped moving and his grin never left his sharp thin face. About five foot nine with brown straight hair, big eyes for his thin head and a Pinocchio sharp nose like a swordfish. He was amusing to look at and fun to be with.

I was fortunate to be put in the same billet as Jerry, and I took to him straight away.

Hemswell in Lincolnshire was a typical RAF camp, standard layout, but the living accommodation and NAAFI oblong was to the right of the main entrance. The main entrance was an eighty yard straight road from the public road to the inevitable guardroom. The admin. block was opposite the main entrance guardroom barrier. Behind the living accommodation was a medical block and workshops and behind that the hangars and runways.

With Spiv's help I soon found my way round and he was a great help in the hangar where we both worked. He was an engine fitter (Fitter IIE).

Hemswell was part of Bomber Command with the impersonal Lincoln bombers, huge ugly-looking planes that had served so well during the war; and the beautiful and graceful Mosquito, the balsawood and wire-cabled fighter bomber which was also a low level reconnaissance aircraft. I came to love the Mosquito as my favourite aeroplane.

'Well, Fizz,' said Chiefy Blackmore, 'Now you've got a week under your belt, how do you think you're going to get on with Lincolns?'

'They're big buggers, Chief, take some getting used to, but the other mechanics have been a great help.'

'Good, I think you should work on your own now, come, I'll show you what I want you to do.'

We left Chiefy's office and crossed the hangar floor to one of the two Lincolns in for servicing. We went up the mobile scaffold tower and onto the frightening height of a Lincoln mainplane.

'Skin damage, Fizz; your records show you're good at these repairs,' he said, indicating the damaged area on the top of the leading edge. 'Have a go at that and I'll check later.'

'Chief,' I said excitedly, 'Is that Rudy down there?'

I couldn't believe my eyes as I pointed to a figure swaggering across the far end of the hangar. His beret was on the back of his head, his hands in his overall pockets, as he whistled his way to the stores counter.

'Jim Moore, a good tradesman, do you know him, then?'

'Sure, Chief, we joined up together. Haven't seen him since we left Locking, over two years now.'

What a bonus to meet up with my good friend Rudy again. We celebrated that night and within a week Rudy fiddled a swop and joined me in the same billet.

Rudy had just come back from leave and was already a fitter, and had attended the course at St. Athans six months before me. He was handsomer than ever and was courting a girl in Scunthorpe, the steel town about seventeen miles away.

I wrote to Gwyn telling her all the news. She knew I was saving up madly to buy a new motorbike; I'd promised to visit her as soon as possible. We were then getting considerably more pay than I had as a mechanic and every payday lunchtime I chanced passing the guardroom, then went up the eighty yard entrance road, across the public road, to the local post office.

'Another seven pounds,' said the old postmistress, looking at me with soft smiling eyes through her crystal clear glasses. 'You must be saving hard for something special.' The soft eyes became mischievous.

It was true, six weeks, as regular as clockwork, I deposited my seven pounds in post office book Warley Common 10869. But I hadn't bargained on Spiv starting a poker school.

The school started off reasonably well controlled in the first few weeks. Spiv was very choosy about whom he would let play. Six players were the maximum, six who had money, six who could take losses without fuss, six regulars who were known and passed Spiv's unspoken test. Rudy wasn't a card player, he liked the 'gee gees' and placed a daily cross-double with the camp bookie's runner. So, with Spiv and me, plus Spiv's four selections, the poker school was born.

With the rules agreed: a player could only double the last bet, five shillings was the maximum bet, no playing blind, threepence in the kitty for starters – the school got under way.

Poker became a compelling disease for all of us, winners and losers alike. Some players fell by the wayside, promising never to gamble again. Others took their place and the school settled down to a way of life on pay night and Sundays, from five p.m. until midnight.

The first few weeks I paid dearly for my lessons and experience but I watched, I noted, I learnt. The dear old lady at the post office was quickly giving up on me as my visits to her increased. Not to put seven in, but to draw three out. Of course, while all this was going on, my motorbike was getting further away.

Gwyn's letters stopped after four months – no explanation. I wrote continually but – no reply. I could only think her parents had got to her, and it's true to say that if I'd really made the effort I could have gone to see her earlier. I was so tied up in my own selfish little world of sport: I was doing a lot of running and hurdle training on the excellent sports field; Saturday night dancing with Rudy at Scunthorpe; poker; and a little group of musicians I'd formed on Thursday nights in the NAAFI, that I'd given no priority to dear Gwyn. I used the lack of a motorbike as an excuse.

'Get yer sel' doon there,' said Rudy when I talked over my problem with him.

I was due home on a week's leave and filled up a form to withdraw all my money from the post office. The first day I got home I put down the deposit on a secondhand Triumph motorbike, maroon with girder-fork suspension.

The following day I set off for St. Athans, to surprise them as usual. It was five months and two weeks since I last saw my darling Gwyn.

'Give my love to her, Bob, and say you're sorry.'

As Mum's words were spoken, I kick-started the bike and excitedly drove out of Larchwood Gardens, disturbing the early morning peace and the Sunday lyers-in.

I got lost a few times on the way there; my leather helmet was hot in the August sunshine and my goggles were sticking to my face. I'd stopped three times for a break and to let the bike cool down but now, full of pride at my achievement of making the long journey and tense with excitement, I breasted the familiar little hill and saw the dull grey terrace of houses.

I pulled the hot bike onto its stand, switched off the petrol and pushed my goggles onto my forehead. I glanced at my watch, three thirty, just in time for tea, I thought, as I smilingly surveyed the row of curtained windows. Not a soul in sight, not a movement.

I walked up the garden path looking for sprouts, but lettuces were growing in their place. I knocked on the door, seething with happiness. Five months is a long time, should I take her in my arms and kiss her? or just kiss her or what? Would she dash into my arms and cry with relief?

Steps were coming up the corridor, they were Gwyn's – or were they? Maybe Mam's? I didn't know, I'd never listened to her steps before.

The door opened. It was Gwyn. I beamed my smile at her lovely face.

'Surprise, surprise, Gwyn, it's me,' I said taking a step forward, ready for the embrace.

She stepped back. Her face went candle white – no smile, her eyes opened like saucers as her bottom jaw dropped.

I stopped, one foot forward over the threshold, poised like a frozen statue. We seemed to stand facing one another for years. What was wrong? I couldn't take my eyes off her face, she couldn't speak. We stood and stared at one another.

Her head turned sideways as she glanced down the darkened corridor.

'Who is it, Gwyneth?' came Mam's voice up the hall.

Gwyn's head returned to me but her eyes made a quick nervous flick down and up. My eyes followed.

No, no – I couldn't believe it – look again – I looked, but it wouldn't sink in. Gwyn's little frilly pinny was balanced on the bulge, hardly covering the top.

I stared, open mouthed.

She screamed.

Mam ran up the narrow darkened hall and cried out, 'Oh my God.'

Mam pulled Gwyn in and slammed the door. I floated away into a nightmare – shattered.

I got home somehow without a crash, having slept half the night in a field. I made excuses to Mother and went back off leave early.

The baby wasn't mine, I'd not so much as touched her bare breast. I sank into a period of depression. No more letters to write each evening, no more day dreaming of my girl before I fell asleep at night. Listening to my mates talking about their girls, or, the braggards – 'had me end away again last night' – only pushed me further into the abyss of torment and self-pity.

'What are you walking like that for, Fizz?' asked Chiefy Blackmore that first week back from Wales.

'It's me big toenails, chief, giving me hell they are.'

Years of walking, marching and running in ill-fitting boots and shoes had taken their toll and I now had double-decker toenails growing on top of one another. They were quite painful and not nice to look at.

'Get yourself off to the medical centre then and get them sorted out,' said Chiefy.

I was still in a 'couldn't care less' frame of mind and performing daily tasks like a man in a dream. I felt there was nothing to look forward to now I'd lost Gwyn, nothing to plan for. Each day was a drag and I was feeling sorry for myself. Chiefy had tried to pull me out of the depression with his homespun philosophy but alas, to no avail. Rudy, Spiv and my mates kept their distance after the first few attempts to cheer me up met with abuse.

'OK, Chief, I'll go now, maybe the MO will see me,' I replied.

I'd never reported sick in over three years of service. I'd had my 'jabs' when I was with Transport Command at Topcliffe and boosters every six months since, but apart from the burns problem and my new teeth, I'd kept clear of medical centres. The sick parade regulars repeated stories of being accused by the MOs of 'lead swinging'. It was said that the bottle of horrible-tasting 'white mixture' was the common treatment given to all those who reported sick. I'd steered clear of all this nonsense so far, treating the common cold myself.

In my self-pitying, depressed mood, I shuffled from the hanger to the medical centre. With my head down, and fully engrossed in considering the pain involved in having my big toes operated on, I trundled on. I was awakened from my reverie as I pushed through the front entrance swing doors.

'Airman – come here – yes, you.'

I looked back, still holding the door half open. The voice was a few yards behind me. My toes were aching as I turned my head to see who was shouting at whom.

'Yes, you, come here and look smart about it,' commanded a stationary pilot officer.

He looked no older than eighteen and his new uniform shouted out 'I've only just joined the RAF'. His baby face had never seen a razor. I let the door go and stumbled towards the officer.

'Yes, Sir,' I said, standing loosely to attention.

'Can you read?' he asked sarcastically.

'Yes sir.'

'Well, read that notice and read it out loud.'

I looked to where he pointed. A stencilled painted notice about a foot high stood on two uprights in the grass verge entrance.

'Entrance for Officers and NCOs only. Other ranks enter at rear of building,' I said aloud.

'Well, you can read? what excuse have you got for disobeying an order?'

My thoughts flew back to childhood in India. I was my father. The pilot officer was a subaltern. I could hear the horses in the stables, smell them. I could see Mum holding our hands as she stood waiting while the subaltern degraded Father. My toes ached like hell.

'Well – what have you got to say for yourself?' he sneered.

'It's a bloody stupid order – Sir' I said, in one surging outburst.

His face drained to white and his baby eyes opened wide as he stared at me in disbelief. My toes hurt more when I stood still and the pain increased my anger towards this posh-voiced officer.

'You swore at the King's uniform,' he shouted, 'I'll have you charged for that, name and number,' he screamed.

'Oh – fuck off, I'm fed up with the lot of you.'

Twenty-eight days, no arguments, no excuses, twenty-eight days detention, bad toes and all.

A month later I wrote a letter to the commanding officer. I set down in great detail the inequalities of service life. The bullshit, the pomposity of officers, the stupid and unreasonable regulations – like the discrimination of entering the medical centre. I used terms such as 'educated mohicans' to describe the regulation haircut and explained the uselessness of monthly kit inspections, telling him we kept a spare set of most things 'just for his officers to look at'. I asked questions: 'What does a highly polished floor contribute to the skills of a first class tradesman?'

I don't know what I expected from this written outburst but I just had to do it.

'Don't be a stupid sod, tear it up,' said Rudy and Spiv, 'You'll only get yourself deeper in the shit.'

I wouldn't listen. I felt better for writing it down and I posted it in the admin. block.

I never received a reply. I don't even know whether the CO ever received it.

Another month rolled by, the eighth since I'd arrived at Hemswell. I was getting on well in the hangar despite my indiscipline outside work and Chiefy seemed to treat me as an equal. My expertise on problem areas of the Mosquito was gaining me a reputation. Flying problems that could not always be corrected on the ground had to be experienced in the air.

'Fizz,' said Chiefy, one bright sunny morning, 'I want you to go up with Mr Sockerlosky and see if you can sort out his left wing low and yawing. We tried twice to trim it out from his verbal reports but it's still the same. You need to go up to see how the kite's reacting.'

Flight Sergeant Pilot Sockerlosky was a Polish pilot who had stayed on after the war. Chiefy called him Mister for some unknown reason. Soco, as he liked me to call him, was a happy-go-lucky guy, full of good humour and fun.

That first of many flights with Soco was pure business and carried out in a serious vein. He had port aileron droop and a badly-trimmed rudder and after three lots of adjustments and three test flights the kite flew hands off. I was delighted with the result, as were Soco and Chiefy.

From that beginning I was now deemed the expert on trimming 'Mosies' and as Soco was the test pilot and trainer we often worked together. I'm positive that Soco invented problems later on, just to get me up there with him.

Soco had a lady friend of long standing who lived in Scunthorpe, some seventeen miles from the 'drome. Rudy and I also did our dancing in Scunthorpe, usually at the 'Baths' dancehall, which was converted from swimming in the summer to dancing in the winter. This huge Victorian building entertained the big bands of the day and attracted crowds in their hundreds.

I'd met a tall girl called Rosa and we had been seeing each other for some weeks. She had mentioned that Stan Kenton and his Big Brass Sound was appearing at the Baths so we booked tickets for the following Saturday. It was during that evening that I met up with Soco and his lady and a very pleasant evening was enjoyed in his cheerful and extrovert company.

On the Wednesday of the following week Soco came in with a flying problem and we took off.

'Where does your girlfriend work?' asked Soco as we flew over the patchwork fields and farms below.

It was a clear frosty winter's day as I gazed down on the neat world below. It was a different world up there, a world without care. All the troubles were left on the ground. Soco was a terrific pilot but he did like to show off. He would bank and roll, climb and dive, knowing full well that I was on the verge of being sick many a time, but he would just laugh. The unwritten, but widely accepted, hangar rules were that anyone who was sick in an aircraft had to pay half a crown into the hangar 'booze-up' kitty and clean the mess up themselves.

'At Hydroprest Concrete, Ashbyville, why do you ask?'

He grinned mischievously. 'That's off the Brigg Road, isn't it?'

'Yeah, I think so.'

'Good, let's pay her a visit' he said grinning.

I looked down and could see we were passing over Kirton Lindsey. We were soon over the Scunthorpe-Brigg road. Soco banked left and shadowed the road the mile or so to Ashbyville.

'There,' he said pointing, 'that must be it.'

I looked down at what looked like a goods yard, stacked with all manner of concrete products. Two wooden huts, not unlike the RAF billets at Locking, stood in the middle of the stacked concrete products. I could see a bike shed and people standing at hut doorways as Soco took us in low. He then pulled back on the stick and set the 'Mosy' on its haunches as we climbed near vertical. Thank God that was over, I thought as we shot away from the ground. He must have flown well below regulation height limits as I could see faces clearly as we skimmed the compound and huts, but Rosa's face wasn't there.

'Did you see her?' shouted Soco above the engine noise.

I had a job to speak as I tried to keep my stomach from erupting through my throat.

'No she's not there,' I mumbled. That was my mistake.

'Have another look then,' he said laughingly as he threw the stick forward and we dive bombed straight at the wooden huts.

My mouth gushed like Niagara Falls as I went into an uncontrollable bout of sickness. I was covered; my clothes, the cabin floor and controls, all took a pasting. Poor Soco realized too late that he'd gone too far.

We returned to base and I paid my half-crown, scrubbed out my cockpit and had my leg pulled by the entire hangar. The true story of why I was in such a state was never told. That was Soco's and my secret.

A tousle haired, rugged and thickset chap appeared behind the counter in the sports hut. He was a new face and one of a batch of newly arrived conscripts.

'Gisa bat, ball and three stumps mate,' said Rudy as Spiv and our roommates stood outside the wooden sports hut. Often on a summer's evening we'd have a go at cricket, six a side, one set of wickets only and one man batting at a time. It was good fun and passed an hour or two until NAAFI time.

'You cricketers, then?' asked the dark wavy-haired counter assistant.

''Course we are, the best in the RAF,' said Rudy grinning.

'I'll join you at five when I'm finished, if you like,' said the friendly fella.

'All right, can if you want,' said Rudy, signing for the gear.

We set up the stumps at the end of the coconut matting which covered the concrete cricket slab. The concrete slab was on the edge of the sports field opposite the guardroom. We'd been playing half an hour when the friendly counter-assistant arrived.

'You can join Fizz's team,' said Rudy, 'They're nearly all out, anyway; it's twenty-three for five wickets.'

My team were all out for fifty-five with our seventh man from the stores getting a sprightly thirty-one. He was quite a nifty batsman.

'Right, Rudy, fifty-six to win, or the beer's on your team,' I said provocatively.

'Dinna fear, we'll knock them off for two wickets,' grinned Rudy.

I took the first over, bowling against the wildly swinging Rudy. He scored ten runs; we were definitely in trouble.

'Can I have a go?' asked our high-scoring batsman.

'Can you bowl, then?' I asked.

'A bit,' he grinned.

'OK, try one over,' I said, throwing him the ball.

He set off away from the pitch, pacing out his run. Ten, twenty, thirty paces and still he strode on.

'Come orf it, mate, it's not bleedin' Lords,' said chirpy Spiv as a few others joined in with ribald comments. Rudy stood there relaxed and grinning, bat held a foot above the ground and feet planted a yard apart.

The bowler started his long run as the quiff of jet-black hair bounced on his forehead. He came thundering on at a tremendous pace and I stood wondering if he was playacting, joking, having a bit of fun?

Whoosh, he released the ball. I didn't see it travel, but I looked at the wicket spreadeagled, with one stump five yards back behind the others.

'Bloody hell, what was yon un?' said the bewildered Rudy, staring at his splattered wickets.

Rudy's team were all out for fifteen and as we made our way back to the NAAFI for our free beer, congratulating our demon bowler on taking all six wickets, Spiv asked:

'And what's your moniker then, not Larwood, is it?'

'No, Trueman, Freddie Trueman,' he replied.

I hadn't heard of Freddie Trueman until that day but the cricket world had. Freddie was just coming into his own and I believe he was picked that year for the tour of India, his first overseas tour.

Yardley, the England selector, visited the camp within the first two weeks of Freddie's service at Hemswell and was aghast to find him bowling on a concrete wicket. A grass cricket square was quickly laid out for England's number one fast bowler after Yardley had spoken with the CO. Grass cutting and sports equipment issue and maintenance were to be his only duties during his national service. His 'service' was often interrupted by long absences on 'England duty'.

Freddie mixed well and was very popular amongst the erks. His celebrity status didn't affect his earthy, wisecracking manner. He could quaff three pints to my one any time.

The media made a great fuss of Fred and he would laugh as he posed in the cookhouse with his plate of sausage and mash. Sundays he would purchase all the newspapers and we would all crowd round having a good laugh at the inventiveness of the press. At various times they had Freddie courting a publican's daughter in Gainsborough or some other poor wench in Crowl. Fred did visit these places in his 'Beetle', the name he painted on his three-wheeled car, but most of the stories were pure fiction.

We had many good times together but sadly he wasn't the Freddie Trueman I met in a pub outside Doncaster some ten years later.

'Trout, James, you know how I like them, grilled on both sides,' he said to the waiter in his attempted 'posh' accent. I didn't enjoy talking to him that night about his London contacts and his life. I prefer to remember him as ACII Trueman, an earthy friendly character.

CHAPTER 18

Mablethorpe Floods

Saturday the thirty-first of January nineteen hundred and fifty-three.

A tragic day. A day to be forgotten but often remembered, especially on gusty January nights, especially in coastal towns and villages, especially when the wind howls and the rain lashes down. A nightmare. A nightmare that lasted two nights and two days.

The rain was almost stopping the windscreen wipers on the high-wheeled three-ton Bedford lorry and the wind was catching the lorry sideways-on, shifting it bodily across the road as each gust caught us. The headlight beams cut through the sheets of darkened rain as we tried to keep the tail-lights of the RAF bus in view. 'Make all speed to police control centre in Mablethorpe,' the officer had said and that's just what we were trying to do.

An hour earlier, about one a.m. on that fateful Saturday, we arrived back from a night out at Scunthorpe and were met at the guardroom barrier by the duty officer and MPs. The rain was lashing their faces as the officer ordered us all into the guardroom.

Tim the driver and I got out of the cab as the four other airmen jumped over the tailboard and we gathered in the guardroom totally mystified as to what was going on.

'Right, chaps,' said the officer, 'We have an emergency on our hands. The police in Mablethorpe have informed us that the sea wall has been breached, quite a big slice actually. The town is flooded and it's expected to get worse at the next high tide. They have requested all the help we can muster but, as you know, nearly everybody's away on long weekend pass, sod's law I suppose. I have twelve men outside in the camp bus plus you six. Who's the senior man?'

'I am Sir, LAC Freeman,' I said.

With over five years service plus my elevation to leading aircraftsman, I was by far the senior, which now gave me the privilege of riding in the cab with the driver on Saturday nights.

'Right, Freeman, nip off to the stores; there's a clerk waiting. Load your lorry with anything that might be useful in rescuing people from their flooded houses and get back here as quick as you can. You'd better change into uniform too.'

We soon arrived at the lighted stores block and the other four airmen, who were also courting girls in Scunthorpe, joined me at the stores counter.

'What you got for us, mate?' I asked the bespectacled, half-asleep stores clerk.

'Nuffin',' he said, all dopey, 'I was just told to open up and stand by.'

'Oh Christ, come on fellas,' I said, leaping over the low wooden counter.

''Ere, mate, you can't – '

'Oh sod off, mate, we're in a hurry,' I said as my eyes darted down the racks and around the storage areas.

'Blankets!' I shouted as I spotted shelves of them at the far end of the row. 'Tom, you and George load some of them on the lorry.'

'But you'll have to sign and where's your order?' whined the clerk.

'Piss off, mate,' said Tom, grabbing an armful of blankets. I continued my search and unearthed two cardboard cartons of torches and five aircraft dinghys.

'You can't take them,' said our by now hysterical stores clerk. 'You've got to have special permission.'

'Look, mate,' I said, fixing him a glare, 'People are dying out there, or didn't you know? If you write down what I've got, by the time it's loaded in the lorry, I'll sign for it, all right, but keep your bloody red tape and moaning to yourself!'

He shot off for his pencil and pad as I lifted a deflated dinghy and made for the lorry.

We arrived back at the guardroom after stopping by the billet for a quick change. Two more volunteers had been unearthed from somewhere and joined our lorry.

'Now, Freeman, make straight for the police control point at Mablethorpe; there's sure to be someone to direct you when you get to the outskirts of town. Of you go, and good luck, chaps,' said the officer, with obvious relief that he'd done his duty and could then put his feet up.

We were nearing the town after a hairy and frightening race through the darkened wet country lanes. Without warning the lorry went into a sideways skid. Great cries of anguish rose above the high wind and lashing rain as the six bodies in the back travelled from tailboard to cab and sideways. The side of the canvas-covered lorry hit the back of the bus forming a T.

'What's that mad bastard up to, stopping dead like that?' asked Tim angrily and 'Are you all right, Fizz?' as an afterthought.

'Yeah, just about,' I said, shaking my head to clear the buzzing, having nearly cracked open the windscreen. 'I'd better check the others.'

Only a few bruises and sore heads in the lorry but a steaming, leaking radiator on the bus had put paid to its travels for a day or two. We stood in the rain shining our torches on the poor donkey that had stopped the bus's progress.

'Didn't see it,' said the bus driver, 'What the hell's it doing in the middle of the road at this time of night?' he asked himself, baffled. The donkey was hee-hawing and trying to get to its feet.

'Come on, you fellas, let's see if it can stand,' I said.

We lifted the donkey upright and it hobbled across the road.

'It seems all right, nothing broken anyway. Let's move the bus now so Tim can get through with the lorry. We'll send a message back to camp about the bus and the breakdown gang should be here in the morning.'

Everyone disembarked and pushed the useless bus into the side of the lane.

'You guys might just as well get your heads down on the bus; it's no good me taking any more of you on the lorry as we won't have enough room for transporting the rescued. See you,' I said as I strode back to Tim, who had straightened up our lorry.

We entered Mablethorpe without encountering any police or control points. Only two lorries going in the opposite direction flashed their lights. We stopped the next lorry coming up the hill.

'Where's the police control?' Tim shouted at the driver into the wind.

'Dunno, mate, we've only been here an hour, this is my first load of women and kids. Make for the seafront and you'll see the rescue centre; it's in two foot of water so take it easy,' and off he went.

We followed the road he'd come up and as we reached the bottom of the gradient the wheels of the lorry entered a foot of water.

As we slowly proceeded we spotted two stationary lorries parked in the gloom of a large building just off the road to the right. Water was lapping in and out of the building entrance as people carrying children and possessions were loading the lorries. A maroon Salvation Army caravan stood in water; the Sally Army women, oblivious to the water lapping round their ankles, were dispensing hot tea or Oxo to rescuers and rescued alike.

'Who's in charge, mate?' I asked a soldier who was lifting families into his lorry.

'Dunno, mate, there's a police launch down on the front shouting orders through a loudhailer but it's six to eight foot deep down there. The rescuers are bringing all the residents here and we're shipping them to rest centres on higher ground at Sutton.'

'Thanks, mate, see ya.'

I went back to the lorry. My mates looked over the tailboard waiting for the gen.

'Get a torch each, blow up the dinghys and let's get cracking,' I said at the six sombre faces peering down at me. I went round to Tim in the cab.

'Tim, we're going in with the dinghys. You stay here. Find out where the rescue centres at Sutton are. We'll be back to fill you up as soon as we can. If they need you for others, that's OK by me. Do what we can, eh? See you, Tim.'

We climbed in our five brand new dinghys, each man holding the rope of another dinghy, and our camel train set off paddling towards the sea front.

The rain had stopped and the sky was just losing its darkness as we paddled along in the gloom. What struck me was the lack of activity as we paddled on. The water was now halfway up the front doors of the houses leading down to the front. We saw faces at upstairs windows but no panic, no calls for help. I was in the lead dinghy with Tom. One man was in each of the other dinghys. We passed one rowing boat full of people heading the other way. A loudspeaker was blasting out messages in the next road warning people that they should leave their homes. Suddenly an amphibian 'duck' appeared out of the gloom and came alongside us making huge waves as it did so. It was packed with families and had an American crew.

'Say, buddy, it's good to see ya, we need all the help we can get,' said the Yankee voice. A uniformed policeman appeared from the other side of the boat.

'I suggest you start checking in the High Street, get all the shopkeepers out. Don't take no for an answer as it's going to get worse at high tide. Good luck,' he shouted, as the engine roared and the 'duck' swung away from us, creating such large waves that we sat there bobbing up and down like corks in a waterfall. We turned the corner into the High Street as daylight crept over the lapping water and we got our first sight of the devastation.

The ten-foot-high white paling fence that had boarded in an amusement park and a caravan site was completely uprooted and floated in various lengths everywhere. Two caravans that had previously been on a site somewhere were now lying on their sides in the main road, protruding a foot above the lapping water. To the right of the High Street some twenty or thirty caravans were crushed together, some on top of others. Bits of brightly painted funfair boards and fixtures floated along in line abreast. Fairground apparatus protruded at crazy angles from the dirty water.

The row of shops to the left, which ran at right-angles to the sea wall, had taken a sideways pasting! Doors were burst open, some hanging on one hinge. Display windows were broken, goods were floating against sharp glass edges and were rocked by the moving water.

There was little noise anywhere, no shouting, no people, no rescuers. Occasionally I heard the megaphone and later I saw two rescue boats. Where was all the activity?

An empty rowing boat came bobbing along with its oars stowed inside.

'Tom,' I said, looking back at him padding whilst gazing at the destruction. 'Let's get that rowing boat – it will be better than this dinghy.'

We transferred to the rowing boat and George captured another one.

'What shall we do with the dinghys?' asked George.

'Find another boat for the other guys and then trail the dinghys to street corners and tie one to each lamp post. Some poor bugger might be pleased to find one. We'll start at this end of the street and check every house and shop. The boats can work together, checking a building each and leap-frogging each other. We must keep together. Hurry up back, George, we won't be far away.'

Tom and I started for the end shop but a shout from further up the street attracted our attention. We rowed towards a man hanging halfway out an upstairs window.

'I've convinced the missus to go now, she wouldn't go before.'

'Right, come on down and we'll take you to safety.'

'She won't come on her own, she's nervous, you'll have to help me.'

'All right, I'm coming up.'

We rowed to the open front door of a sweet and tobacconist's shop only to find the rowing boat was too wide to pass through the door.

'I'll go and get her, Tom, hang on.' I let myself over the side into the debris-strewn ice-cold seawater.

The water came up to my chin as I pushed my way into the murky water of the gloomy shop. Sweet bottles were floating amidst papers and toys. A teddy bear floated by on its back surrounded by a football, boxes and coloured rubber balls. I forced my way to a door at the back of the shop and found the stairs. The man's face appeared at the top of the stairs and he was holding a lighted candle in a brass candleholder.

'God bless you, son, God bless the RAF. She's in here,' said the scrawny-looking man.

'Come on, darling, we're off for a boat ride,' I said cheerfully as the water cascaded off my uniform all over her carpeted lounge.

'Is it very deep?' she asked in a nervous voice. 'I think we ought to hang on a bit, it's the shop, you see.'

'Not as deep as it is going to be at high tide and you must come now, you might not get another chance,' I said, bending over her chair and picking her up. She was only a lightweight. I carried her across the lounge but she started to struggle.

'Wait a minute, I need my things. Let's pack some things, Fred, and my coat and handbag.'

'No time for packing, love, but your husband can bring your coat and handbag. There's a lot of people waiting to be rescued, you know,' I said, holding tight to her writhing body.

I descended the steps and entered the water as she let out a terrifying scream and started to struggle. Her husband shouted it was too deep for him and he stayed on the stairs. I carried the screaming and crying woman through her shop, lips pressed tight to keep out the raging water she was churning up with her kicking legs. I unceremoniously dumped her in the rowing boat and returned for her five-foot husband who was praising the RAF and God, all the way through the shop.

'OK, Tom, let's get them back to the centre,' and I crawled aboard like a drowning rat.

We saw the other two rowing boats at the end of the street and waved. Tom rowed like a champion and we found Tim and the lorry.

'Wrap a blanket round 'em both, Tim, they're soaking wet. The others will be back with people shortly. Do you know the way to Sutton?'

'Yes,' said Tim, 'Do you want a blanket – you look awful already, have you been swimming?'

We returned to the High Street, passing George's boat with two adults and two children in it. The other boat was halfway along the High Street when we got there. Daylight had crept upon us without our noticing it.

'Have you checked all the shops up to here?' I asked Harry in the third boat.

'Yes, most people have gone already, probably when it first happened. I had a job convincing that last lot to move, though.'

The next few shops were empty except for a few chickens that had amazingly made their way to the upstairs lounge of a butcher's shop. I was inspecting a camera shop and doing my usual shouting.

'Anybody in? Hello, anybody there?' and as usual, no reply. I poked my head above the top stairs and looked over a familiar lounge scene. The place was dead. I was descending the stairs when I heard a 'bump' as though something had been dropped on the floor in the flat above.

Retracing my steps I crossed the lounge and tried a door but it was locked.

'Anyone there? Hello, is there anyone there?' I shouted. Not a sound. I put my shoulder to the door and pushed but the door held firm so I lashed out with my booted foot and kicked the door panel at lock-high level.

'All right, I'll open it, don't break it down,' shouted a voice as a second voice shouted, 'Open it, Jim, quick!'

The door opened to reveal a huge lady lying fully clothed on top of her bedclothes. She had irons down both stockinged legs to her special boots. Her husband stood by the open bedroom door, pale and trembling.

'We're moving everybody out,' I said, 'you'll have to come, police orders.'

'No, we're staying put, we'll be safe here,' said the lady on the bed.

'Madam, high tide's expected soon, you could have four foot of water over your bed in no time,' I said impatiently.

'I told you, Mildred, we should have gone to start with; he's right you know.'

'Can you walk?' I asked.

'I'm not going anywhere,' she replied sharply.

'Then we'll carry you,' I said sternly.

'You certainly will not.'

'Oh, Mildred, what he says is right, come on, love, we must go – he's doing it for us.'

'Get her ready, I'll go and get some help,' I said, making the decision for them.

I went down the stairs and called Tom. Tom was three inches shorter than me but broader and compact. His weight-training might come in handy after all. Tom's face appeared in the lapping water. His arms were doing the breast stroke to keep his head above water but he still managed to smile.

We dripped all the way back to the bedroom as I explained the situation to Tom. She was still lying on the bed with a stern resolute face.

'I'm not going, so you can forget it,' she said shuffling herself lower on the banked up pillows behind her back.

'One each side, Tom, and we'll cradle her,' I said.

'Can I help?' asked her lightweight bespectacled husband.

'We'll manage, thanks, bring her things.'

We lifted the protesting fourteen stone body to a chorus of abuse.

'I can walk – watch where you are putting your hands – mind my dress,' as she struggled in our cradle. We made the top of the stairs which were too narrow to allow us to descend.

'Put her down gently.'

'We can't carry her like this,' said Tom 'I'll be under water and so will you.'

'I'll have to piggyback her to the boat,' I said, 'Means holding my breath across the shop, you can push from behind using her shoulders and kicking your feet. Come on, let's give it a go, we've wasted enough time.'

Tom held the protesting woman in position. Her husband was pleading with her to co-operate. I stepped down two steps and backed into her huge thighs, lifting her frock up a bit to get her well onto my back. She screamed, Tom pushed and I grabbed. We rocked on the top of the stairs as my body took the strain.

With Tom holding and steadying we descended, one jolting step at a time, resting on each step. We entered the cold lapping water to hysterical outbursts of 'Jim, I shall drown, don't drop me, Jim, where are you?'

The water rose slowly up my already soaked and cold body and still we descended the stairs. When we reached the floor the water came over the bridge of my nose but the lapping waves splashed over my eyes. God help us, this was it. With lips firmly pressed together I attempted to walk through the shop to the bobbing boat thirty feet away.

I could feel Tom pushing behind me and I started to panic. My mouth opened and I gulped in salt water and started to splutter. I pushed up on my toes to try to get air. Her wet thighs were slipping from my cold hands. The boat was in front of me sideways on. A last panic-stricken effort to summon strength as I leaned her top half against the boat side. Tom was shouting at her as he pushed her shoulders into the boat. I came up for air and we struggled and pushed her massive backside as she cried out in terror. The boat was almost sideways to the heavens and rapidly filling with water. The last steel-lined leg was pushed into the boat and the boat righted itself. We hung on the sides gasping for breath.

We both went back for the frightened husband and we were soon loaded. We sat in a foot of water as Tom rowed us back to the lorry.

With our two, Tim now had fourteen on board his lorry and, as the first ones had been there over an hour, he decided to drive them over to the rest centre at Sutton.

'I should get a hot drink and a breather if I were you,' said Tim, handing us a couple of blankets. 'The others are over by the Sally Army,' he said.

'Fair enough, Tim, will do, we feel knackered already.'

'Excuse me,' came a voice from the lorry.

I walked over to the tailboard to see what the problem was. Three men were leaning over the tailboard looking down at me.

'Take this, son, and share it amongst you, you're real heroes you are and we'll never forget what you've done for us,' said the man from the camera shop, proferring a great roll of pound notes. I was astonished and embarrassed at the gesture.

'No, thank you, it's good of you, but we're only doing what we have to do, thanks all the same,' I said, turning away.

'Take anything from our shops, anything,' he shouted, but nothing could have been further from our minds. Later that day though, with half a lorry of young kids, we remembered the man's words and retrieved two large jars of boiled wrapped sweets which Tim dispersed to the crying kids as they were loaded aboard.

After a couple of hot drinks and a sandwich, all given out free by the lovely Salvation Army volunteers, we returned to the fray and cleared the High Street. There still didn't seem to be a surfeit of rescue craft although the American 'duck' was regularly seen loaded-up and making giant waves. An Army unit was working somewhere but we only saw them when we returned to the pick-up point. No doubt there were other pick-up points elsewhere.

The police launch came alongside and we reported the High Street cleared. We were then directed to check a side street off the front, but to return within one hour to the pick-up point and await orders, as high tide was expected.

The side street seemed to be empty. We shouted, called and inspected three-quarters of the street without contacting a soul, and then Tom spotted a face peering from behind a net curtain of an upstairs window.

We rowed towards the front door of a small post office. The front door was hanging open into a passage, with stairs to the right.

I climbed the stairs and tried the door at the top but it was locked.

'Madam, rescue services, open the door!' I shouted into the hollow quietness of the house.

'Go away, I'm staying,' said a high-pitched voice.

'Madam, open the door or we will have to break it down.'

'Go away, go away,' she shouted.

I set to kicking the door lock area. It was difficult balancing on one leg on the small square landing.

'Stop that. Wait a minute,' she said as bolts were drawn and the key was turned.

I entered a Victorian parlour with cluttered up oak display cabinets, horsehair armchairs and sofa, large aspidistras in china bowls, brass fender around the fire place, and brass coal scuttle. Rugs were laid on top of carpets and a musty smell of mothballs pervaded the air.

A withered but proud grey-haired woman stood defiantly in front of me. Her hair was neatly and tightly combed back over her head and a grey bun was netted to her neck. Her black lace shawl covered her shoulders and her pinafore dress. Her small feet were clad in sidebutton boots. She looked over her pince-nez spectacles and fixed me with a fierce, determined stare.

'Thank you, young man, but I not going anywhere. I am perfectly safe up here. You had best be on your way,' she said, not unkindly.

'Madam, I . . .'

'Miss, if you don't mind, I am not married.'

'Yes, um, Miss, I have orders from the police to insist that everybody moves out before the high tide in an hour's time. It could get a lot worse now that the sea wall is down.'

'Young man, this is a post office. I have money, postal orders, stamps and valuable documents all in my safe. I am not leaving them unattended.'

'Mad – Miss, I cannot take no for an answer, we are wasting time. I don't want to force you but you've got to go. We'll take your money with you.'

'I see, and where will you take me?' she asked, defiantly.

'To the rest centre, Miss – now, where's your safe, upstairs, or downstairs?'

'Here, of course, it would be no good downstairs, would it? I always bring the money and postal orders up here every night; it's the safest way, you see.'

'Show me the safe then, we'll empty it into your shopping bag.'

Her beady eyes peered at me above her spectacles as she struggled with a lifetime's distrust of strangers. I could almost hear her mind asking, 'Can I trust this scruffy man standing here with his long black hair stuck all over the front of his face and with water pouring off his sodden smelly clothes all over my carpets?'

My temper was rising. I was wet through, cold, tired and hungry.

'Miss, we're wasting time. You're either going to go with or without the contents of your safe. What's is to be?'

She walked across the room and pulled an armchair forward to reveal an old-fashioned safe next to the chimney breast. She extracted a large key from her clothing, unlocked the safe door and pulled it open.

'Good God. It's stacked high.'

'Of course,' she said, 'All those large bags are coins, I don't bank coins much so there's quite a lot.'

'Well, we can leave those and just take the notes, they will be perfectly safe until you return.'

'Certainly not,' she fired at me, 'every last penny will go with me,' she commanded.

We loaded two full shopping bags with coins and still there were more small blue sacks of them.

'I'll take these two down to the boat, they're very heavy,' I said, lifting the two bags.

'You will do no such thing young man, they will not leave my sight.'

I was totally exasperated with this finicky old spinster who seemed to have no sense of urgency or appreciation of the danger she was in. Her total thoughts were directed solely toward her post office and her money. I crossed the lounge, went down a few stairs and called for Tom, who must have been getting worried at my non-appearance.

We cleared the rest of the safe into a pillowcase and were ready to go.

'You'll have to watch us from your stairs as we put the money in the boat. We can't carry you and the money together,' I said.

'Carry me, you will do no such thing, young man. You bring your boat to the bottom of my stairs,' she said disgustedly.

'Miss, the boat won't even come through the front door, now do come on and stop this arguing.'

'You'll wait until I've got my hat and coat on,' she stated forcibly.

We eventually got her down the stairs to water level, black hat, coat and all. Tom swam off and got into the boat, the old lady crouched low watching proceedings.

'Ready, Tom?' I asked.

With a shopping bag full of blue sacks of coins on each shoulder I entered the water, hopping up and down and taking a breath of air on every hop up above water level. The passage was only fifteen feet long and I soon deposited my load under the critical gaze of the lady in black. The pillowslip was easier and I returned for the reluctant spinster.

'Do you want a piggyback or shall I carry you?'

'Piggyback is out of the question; as for carrying, it seems I have no choice,' she said in a most disgusted voice. For the first time I felt sorry for her as she stood trembling on the stairs.

'Put your arms around my neck,' I said, as I bent forward and placed my arms under her thighs, 'and no kissing.'

'Such a thing to say, young man – oh – oh – it's cold, my lovely coat, be careful, don't drop me.'

I could hear her easily enough but I was eye-level to the water with my lips tightly sealed. Tom lifted her lightweight body in as I clung to the side of the boat catching my breath.

Tom extended his arm and gave me a pull into the boat as the old lady arranged her wet clothing over her knees and squeezed water from handfuls of her dress and coat, clucking with her lips all the time.

'Shall we carry on checking or take her back?' asked Tom.

'You will do neither, young man, I'm not leaving here without Walter; I would have thought that was obvious.'

Tom looked at me and I looked at Tom. She's going crackers, I thought, must be the cold water.

'Who's Walter, Miss?' I asked mystified.

'Walter, my budgie Walter of course, I should have thought that was obvious. Off you go now and don't get him wet.'

If I hadn't been so cold and wretched I would have laughed. Tom looked at me in amazement.

I went over the side and fetched the bloody twittering budgie, cage and all. As I advanced, eye level to the water, and Walter chirping away above my head, I couldn't believe it was really happening. The spinster only had eyes for Walter. Tom was grinning from ear to ear as the top of my head advanced towards the boat, crowned with a golden budgie cage.

Tom pulled me aboard gasping for breath as the spinster said, 'Don't get back in yet, I need his stand and his packet of seed.'

I flopped in the bottom of the boat almost under her knees, trying to catch my breath. I looked up at her unfeeling eyes.

'Miss – If you want anything else you can bloody swim for it. Come on, Tom, let's get back to the centre.'

We were released by the police after high tide on the Sunday evening; all of us were shattered. We made camp, hot baths and bed and expected to be called for on the Monday morning. We were not called for, we were never called for. No thanks, no 'well done'; in fact it passed off as though we hadn't been there.

We weren't looking for medals, or praise even, just recognition by the powers that be that we had taken part, done our bit.

The salt that was rubbed into our disappointment came with a Monday morning tabloid headline and picture: 'Hero saves woman from floods on Canvey Island.'

The six of us had brought out thirty-one men, women and children – and of course, one budgie.

CHAPTER 19

Tripoli and Nero

For some reason the RAF left me at Hemswell a very long time, over three years in fact. I had started off my first year with one long visit and two short visits to the 'Snowdrop's Hotel'. But the second year I took a lot more breaks with them. I was known at Hemswell as the 'jailbird', and the conversation often turned on what I would go down for next.

Things could have been different I supposed, but, as Heckner had said, 'Leopards don't change their spots', and so it was with me. Silly things, stupid things, but that was it. I wanted reason, understanding, dialogue if you like. I wanted commonsense to prevail but no, it never worked out like that.

The night before the annual athletics match I was out on the sports field training with a few of my mates. The one hundred and twenty yard hurdles had been positioned in front of the VIP enclosure. The hurdles race was always first in any athletics match.

When I measured between each hurdle I found distances varying from nine foot seven inches to ten foot two inches. They were not the weighted hurdles we used in later years; these were pinned into the turf with steel hooks. The correct layout should have been fifteen feet to the first hurdle, then exactly ten yards between each hurdle and a fifteen yard finish. To obtain three paces between hurdles and keep one's rhythm the hurdles must be exactly ten yards apart. I'd been running in hurdle races for over two years now, both for Des Pond throughout Essex and for the RAF at various meetings. The Warrant Officer in charge of the sports day was supervising his minions marking out the various tracks.

'Excuse me, Warrant Officer,' I said, approaching him in my tracksuit. 'The hurdles are all different distances apart, can they be placed at ten yard intervals, please?'

'Might have known it would be you complaining, Freeman,' he said with a scowl.

I guessed he wasn't used to working in the evening and was in a bad mood.

'They're perfectly all right, now bugger off – I'm busy.'

'But sir, you can't run a hurdles race with hurdles at different distances, it's impossible to get your paces in.'

'I said bugger off, now go,' he growled.

'Can I alter them, Sir? I don't mind.'

He turned on me glaring with temper.

'If I tell you again, Freeman, you'll be back in the guardroom where you belong. When you get to the White City call on me and I'll personally measure your hurdles, until then, fuck off!' he bawled.

'And fuck you, too,' jumped out of my mouth.

Self inflicted? Yes, I suppose so.

After this latest visit to the Snowdrop Hotel I returned to Chiefy, the hangar and my mates. We sat in the crewroom at ten o'clock with our chipped enamel mugs, sipping tea and eating our Banbury cakes. Rudy, Spiv and the gang were all there pulling my leg and exaggerating my misdemeanours.

'How many days have you done now, Fizz?' asked Spiv, 'Must be a bleedin' record, whatever it is.'

'How many different guardrooms have you been in?' asked Ginger.

'Which was the worst?'

'Bugger jankers and snowdrops; for christsake change the subject,' I said, getting humpy.

The crewroom door opened and Chiefy's face appeared.

'Pop in the office when you've finished your tea, Fizz, I want a few words.'

'Rightho Chief,' I said as the door closed.

'Another bleedin' heart-to-heart, Fizz, I reckon Chiefy's wasting his time with you, you're a lost cause,' said the laughing Spiv.

I walked into the familiar office with its one wide desk covered in paperwork, the walls papers with charts, servicing schedules and notices. Chiefy sat behind his desk with his back to the large, steel-framed picture window which gave a panoramic view of the airfield.

'Take a seat, Fizz,' he said, looking intently at me.

Not another fatherly talk, I hoped; I braced myself.

'How would you like to go to Tripoli?' he asked.

His question, out of the blue, left me speechless. I gathered my thoughts as he sat smiling at me.

'A posting, Chief? Where's Tripoli?'

'Tripoli is in Libya and it's not a posting. I have to pick a team to go out there for six weeks to maintain two Lincolns and a Mosquito. It's to do with the spring Naval exercises.'

'Well, yes, Chief, it sounds terrific – I'd love to go,' I replied, excited at the prospect of going abroad.

'There's a condition, a promise, before I make my decision. You're the best airframe fitter I've got and you will need all your skills out there to keep the kits flying. Ingenuity might be called for because you'll have no backup. The aerodrome is called RAF Idris, over fifteen miles into the desert. It's only a stopover for transport going to the Far East. You'll have to take everything with you that you might possible need. You can do the job if you can KEEP OUT OF TROUBLE. That's where the promise comes in. If you let me down I'll wash my hands of you,' he said sternly.

I could see this was a plum job and I knew that a number of my mates could do it, but Chiefy had picked me, the troublemaker.

'I'll keep out of trouble, Chief, honest I will,' I said pleadingly. Chiefy ignored my reply.

'You go away now and think about it. I'll see you again in a day or two, then I'll let you know my final decision.'

We flew out a week later in March 1953, five different tradesmen and a corporal, all sitting between the radar scanner and the Elsan toilet in the fuselage of a Lincoln. Our mates, somewhat enviously, had seen us climb aboard clutching our cardboard boxed meal: an apple, and a carton of orange juice. The aircraft trundled down the runway and ponderously climbed into the clear blue sky on that crisp March morning.

It was difficult to talk above the engine noise and vibration and after a while we settled down with our own thoughts.

Nervous excitement sparked the eyes of the maintenance team as the Lincoln landed and taxied along to its parking area. The sun's rays reflecting off the sand hurt our eyes as we disembarked and made our way, in pools of sweat, from the 'parking pan' towards the wooden-hutted camp.

'Only the flight crews can be accommodated in the camp,' said the receiving NCO as we followed him round the hangar. 'You maintenance guys will live in the compound.'

The compound was fifty yards outside the main gate and across a large flat vineyard with not a tree in sight. We saw the high wire-netting with its barbed wire top as we trundled on in our thick serge uniforms.

'In here, get washed up and change into your tropical gear,' he said. 'This is Ali, he'll guard and clean your billet. You can trust him and he speaks English. I'll come back later to brief you,' and off he went.

We all felt a little awkward and embarrassed as we surveyed each other in our shorts, cotton shirts and cloth caps. Our legs and arms were snow-white as opposed to Ali who stood there, shiny chocolate-coloured, smiling at his new charges.

'Where did you get that dagger from?' asked Bill, our corporal who was in charge of the maintenance team.

'That's me boy scout knife,' I said, smiling at Bill, 'No airframe fitter worth his salt would be without one.'

We went out into the glaring sun to inspect our sandy compound. The twenty metal half-round Nissen huts were circled by palmtrees and high wire-netting.

An Arab, slouched on a ragged camel, moved slowly past the outside of the wire fence. We could see across the vineyard to the main camp and guardroom entrance.

'Right, let's go and find the cookhouse – I'm starving,' said Bill.

We left our compound and hot Nissen hut and ate dust as we crossed the vineyard and came up to the guardroom and entrance barrier.

'What's that bloody big cage for?' asked Spike, the engine fitter.

'Buggered if I know, wait here and I'll find out where to go,' said Bill as he passed between huge yukka plants and palmtrees fringing the path into the guardroom.

We soon found the cookhouse and arrangements were made between the friendly duty cook and Bill for a meal. It was only a small camp with possibly a hundred bodies all told. They had no aircraft of their own, just the odd flight stopping over for refuelling. Our visit was therefore something of an occasion, something to break up the monotony of a fairly dull existence.

We got the full story of the camp from the cook. Although the runway and camp was now called RAF Idris, its previous name, throughout the war years, was Castle Benito. It was in fact Rommel's headquarters during the Desert Campaign. The iron-framed dome cage, about eight feet high and six feet in diameter, a little larger than a telephone box, was where Rommel had kept his famous pet ape.

It seemed to me I was destined to keep bumping into the path of the great Field Marshal Montgomery as the cook mentioned his name. It appears that he over-ran the camp during his famous Desert Campaign. The compound where we were billeted was originally the prison compound – was somebody trying to tell me something?

We settled down to servicing our three aircraft daily. They went out on irregular sorties, their main task being to drop tons of 'glitter', shiny lengths of long tinsel streamers, to jam the 'enemy' radar during attacking exercises. Three weeks went by before we hit our first airframe problem.

I'd had quite a few burst tyres, more than expected and possibly due to the tremendous heat, when the 'Mosy' came in with another flat tyre.

'I've used up the spare tyres I brought out with us, skipper,' I said to the pilot as we surveyed the damage.

'Well, can't you repair it?' he said. 'I've got to take her up at 0650 come rain or shine.'

'I didn't bring any rubber or an annealing iron; the new tyres should have seen us through.'

'Well, they didn't,' he said, becoming annoyed, 'See what you can do and let me know how you get on. I'll be in the mess.' He strode away irritably.

It was six o'clock at night, pitch dark and I'd only come back to give directions with my lantern torches for parking the 'Mosy' overnight. The fellas were expecting me to join them in the NAAFI soon – some hope of that. I made my way to the darkened hangar.

The hangar was a dead place. A huge great barn with offices and workshops running the full length down the inside and they must have been padlocked up for years judging by the thick cobwebs and dust everywhere.

At home our hangars were alive with people and noise. Every area was occupied and lived in.

RAF Idris was a tomb. It had taken the authorities some hours to find a key to let us in to the hangar when we first arrived. We used only the workbenches at one end and had to repair most of the antiquated machinery necessary for our needs, including the air compressor.

I found some light switches and flicked them all to 'on'. One in every eight bulbs worked, throwing an eerie glow through their dust and cobweb skins.

I selected two doors that might possible be tyre bays or workshops. Huge cobwebs, layer upon layer, hung over the doors and walls. The silence, the cobwebs and the eerie light had me in a nervous state. Should I go and fetch my mates? I decided not yet. I must find an iron and some rubber sheeting.

The doors were padlocked.

My footsteps echoed and bounced off walls as I hurriedly strode the length of the hangar back to my toolkit in determined mood to retrieve my largest hammer. Back down the silent hanger to the selected door. I placed the padlock on its side in the hasp, getting my hands covered in thick furry cobwebs in the process. One mighty blow was enough to spring the lock. With the sound ringing in my ears I removed the lock and pushed the door open. A shower of dust engulfed me.

I found a switch and two bulbs came back from the dead. Three tin tables, tin chairs in various angles, two mugs crawling in green fungi, a crumbled newspaper on a table, cobwebs, dust, it was like the *Marie Celeste*.

My hammer and I tried two more rooms, to discover an office and a hydraulic bay. We were starting to lose patience.

My hammer was now pounding a very obstinate lock and my hundred-percent concentration was shattered by running feet. I stopped and turned, expecting to see ghosts.

'Bloody hell, Fizz, what the hell are you doing?' said the surprised Bill, surveying the three broken padlocks and hasps. 'We heard the noise across the camp as we came to look for you. We thought you were knocking the bloody hangar down. What's up, what's going on?' he asked, baffled.

'Probably missing his girl, Bill, taking it out on the hangar instead,' and they all laughed, except Bill who was quite concerned at my extraordinary behaviour.

'Keep your hair on, Bill, the Mosy's come in with a flat and it's due up to 0650. I've no spares so I'm looking for an annealing iron and some rubber to repair it.'

'That may be, but you should have told me first, not go berserk. How are we going to explain all this?' he said, pointing to the broken padlocks on the open doors.

'Bugger all that, nobody ever comes in 'ere, it's getting the Mosy up that's important.'

'Yeah, that's right, Bill, let's get at it,' chorused the others.

Bill couldn't argue with the five of us, who had become quite close in the three weeks we'd been together. Bill was usually very quiet, not bolshy or commanding, just a bloody good engine fitter who had been promoted. He didn't revel in his stripes or being in charge, preferring the quiet life; this was the first time I'd seen him riled.

'It will take three of you to jack up the Mosy in the dark and get the wheel off, that leaves one to help me search,' I said to my mates.

'All right, I'll give the orders if you don't mind,' said Bill, still feeling shirty.

Bill went to the Mosy to supervise, or maybe just to be out of the hangar whilst Air Force property was being destroyed.

Spike and I continued the search and were rewarded an hour later when he found a sack containing an annealing iron and contour plates, but no chains or rubber.

The others returned to the hangar with the punctured tyre.

'You might as well go to the NAAFI now Jim's got the iron to work,' I said. 'In about two hours I'll need some help again though.'

'How are you going to manage without rubber – never mind chains?' asked Bill as we all stood at the benches at the end of the hangar. My mates had stripped the tyre from the hub and now I was ready to start work.

'I'm using an old inner tube, may have to cook it a bit longer to ensure a good bond; as for chains, I'll use this length of hemp and a toggle for tightening it,' I said.

'I'll stay and help Fizz and you lazy buggers can send us over some tea and wads,' said Spike laughingly.

A great crowd of fellas, we all mucked in and helped one another whatever the problem, whatever the time of night or day.

We passed the vineyard between the guardroom and our compound daily. The Arab farmer's face could hardly be seen for his robes which just left his eyes and nose peering out. His two acres of vineyard, no walls, fences or anything to denote the extent of his land, were just heaped-up rows of earth, much like rows of earthed-up potatoes in England.

Sometimes the farmer was working near our path to the camp, sometimes he was four hundred yards away, poking with his hoe at the enemy weeds. His village, which I'd visited and where I'd frightened all the inhabitants into their huts rather than face my camera, was about a mile away. Each day he came to work on his donkey, a little pathetic bony creature. We could see him through the Nissen hut windows as we sat up in bed drinking our tea, courtesy of the faithful Ali.

The donkey trudged past the window at two miles an hour with the farmer perched astride his backbone, carrying his hoe pointing past the donkey's head.

A slow motion charge at an invisible tent peg. The farmer's feet scuffed on the ground each side of the donkey and his robed figure brought to mind a biblical scene found on Sunday school stamps.

The donkey, whom we'd named Nero, moved slowly because he knew what was in store for him. Once he'd passed our hut and come to the vineyard the farmer dismounted. He then crossed the donkey's front legs and tied them with a leather thong. The donkey stood all day, with no shade, no drink, in the blazing sun. We all felt for that poor donkey.

'Don't keep moaning, Fizz, do something about it,' said Spike as I fed a few tit-bits to the poor beast.

'What the hell can I do? I've tried talking to the farmer but he doesn't understand a word I say.'

The day came when the farmer wasn't in sight. We had planned taking each other's pictures sitting astride the donkey. Jim had the camera. Spike, for some reason, was steadying the donkey's backside with a hand on each of the two round hip bones sticking up through its skin, as I prepared to go first.

'Get his legs straight, Fizz, or it'll look funny,' said Jim.

I drew my boy scout knife from its leather sheath attached to my belt and cut the leather thong.

Nero straightened his own legs and looked at me as much as to say thanks. I cocked my right leg over his bony body and rib cage and as my right foot hit the ground Nero took off.

Two miles an hour nothing, he was supercharged. What decided him to propel me through the desert I don't know; maybe he was thanking me for a month of tit-bits. Hoots of laughter and shouting followed my dust trail as Nero made straight for the camp entrance. My legs were trailing each side and, as he galloped, his backbone attempted to split my crutch in two as I bumped up and down crying out in excruciating pain.

A 'white' snowdrop must have been watching from the guardroom window, and, seeing what had happened, he came rushing down the path to the road barrier to join the 'brown' Arab snowdrop who was always on duty at the barrier.

'The 'white' snowdrop was now astride the road in front of the barrier and raised both arms for Nero to stop. Nero didn't understand the gesture and increased speed as he lined up on the snowdrop.

The ensuing and enthusiastic entourage were shouting encouragement somewhere in the dustcloud to the rear and, as the pain reached my chest, my middle was numb by that time, I glimpsed the 'brown' snowdrop convulsed in laughter at the side of the barrier.

'Halt – stop,' squealed the 'white' snowdrop as we came up within twenty feet of the barrier. Nero was deaf, dumb or happy, whatever; he thundered on as the 'white' snowdrop did a kamikaze dive to the left, almost being stabbed by Nero's pointed ears. The barrier, the red and white barrier, was about to cut me in half.

I had no control on Nero; he had no harness or halter. I was completely in his hands, or rather on his back, truly at this whim, his mercy, as we bumpily freewheeled towards the slicing machine. I glanced to the right, my head nodding fifteen to the dozen, and didn't know whether to laugh or cry as the pounding on my crutch continued.

The 'brown' snowdrop was crying with laughter as he laid his body across the counter-weight. I instinctively lay flat along Nero's neck, just like a good cavalry man would. The barrier started to raise as I skimmed under, catching the back of my head.

Nero charged on as the entourage increased by two, one white, one brown. Past Rommel's ape cage, along the main road and through the centre of the camp. A small canvas-covered truck took avoiding action, mounted a kerb and hit a palm tree. Still Nero ploughed on.

Past the big black hangar, body racked with pain, I unceremoniously fell off onto the tarmac.

Nero stopped – turned around slowly – bent his head as he looked me straight in the eye, and then let out a great hee-haw, which was donkey language for 'I did enjoy that – didn't you?'

There was a confrontation with my white and dusty breathless snowdrop. The entourage surrounded us on the tarmac and had grown to over thirty grinning onlookers. Bill appeared from the crowd; he'd missed most of the spectacle as he had left the Nissen hut early to meet up with the pilots for his daily orders.

'Let's not talk here,' said the wise Bill above the noise and laughter, 'We'll go back to the guardroom and sort it out – can you walk, Fizz?' he asked as I sat recovering on the ground.

Bill was aware of my promise to Chiefy, also that I was his only airframe mechanic. A half hour of Bill's persuasive quiet talk, corporal to corporal, and the fact that the truck wasn't damaged, got me off the hook. In fact the snowdrop was different to those in the UK, more laid back and a bit older. A whipround and a crate of beer later we became good friends and even got a wave as we passed in and out of camp.

The six-week tour soon passed and we were keen to get back to Hemswell and familiar faces. We'd stowed cartons of cigarettes in wingtip inspection panels and 'doped' over them. Watches and jewellery were in knotted french letters secreted in the toilet fluid. We had even stitched up a gold necklace in the first-aid kit. Customs, who always met incoming RAF aircraft, weren't going to get anything off us, or so we thought.

The flight home was uneventful until we were circling Hemswell. Bill tapped me on the shoulder and pointed to the oxygen mask which also held the intercom. He already had his mask on. I put on the mask which was dangling from the side of the fuselage. Bill's voice came over the intercom.

'Skipper wants a word with you – he's on now, Skip,' said Bill as he eyed me across the radar scanner.

'Fizz – d'ya read me?'

'Loud and clear, Skipper.'

'I'm in next, the undercarriage is down but the brake pressure gauge shows 80 psi, is the gauge U/S?'

'Shouldn't think so, Skipper, everything was in perfect order before we left.'

'Come forward, then.'

I unplugged my intercom, made my way to the cockpit and plugged in again. Skipper pointed to the gauge.

'Can I try the brake lever, Skipper?'

'Yes, go ahead,' he said, removing his left hand from the joystick.

The lever was 'floppy', not doing any work. The brake control to the actuator on a Lincoln bomber was through a lever and bowden cable attached to the joystick. The bowden cable was almost identical to the cable used for the brakes on bicycles. The brake cable on the Lincoln ran down the front of the joystick with other cables and was usually clipped in position. I traced the cable with my hand and found it was bulging out free of the retaining clips about shin high to the pilot's legs.

'Can I borrow your map torch, Skipper?' I said over the intercom, although I was only a foot from his face.

He passed me his torch as the engines roared in my ears. I heard him tell the tower he was going to do another circuit as I turned on my back and wriggled under his legs.

'Sorry about this, Skipper,' I said over the intercom.

I inspected the black-covered bowden cable and found a kink in the steel-sprung outer casing. It must have caught somewhere and the kink was jamming the inner control wire to the electro-hydraulic actuator. I withdrew from between the skipper's legs.

'Sorry, Skipper, but there's a kink in the outer casing of the cable; it's trapping the inner control wire. There's nothing I can do about it up here, it needs a new cable,' I said, looking at him over my mask.

'That's the reason why I had to jerk the stick back when we took off. Can you release the brake pressure?'

'Could do, Skipper, but then you'd have no brakes.'

'All right, Fizz, thanks, go back to the others and stand by.'

I then heard the pilot informing the tower of our problem and I looked at my nervous mates who were all listening to the skipper over the intercom.

'Foxtrot to control, do you read – over,' said the calm, almost lazy voice of our pilot.

'Loud and clear, Foxtrot one – over.'

'Our brakes are U/S, tower. I'm going to do another circuit to jettison the fuel. It will be a bellyflop – no undercarriage for this one. I shall put her down on the grass left of two-six runway. Have all emergency services ready – repeat please – over.'

'The tower confirmed the message received. Skipper's voice confirmed undercarriage up and we roared on round another circuit.

'George,' said the pilot to his navigator.

'Yes, Skip.'

'Take charge of the rear, see the maintenance team know the drill,' and he continued his dispassionate discourse.

'Piece of cake chaps, don't get excited. I'm going to sit her down on the nice lush grass at the side of the runway. All emergency services are standing by and they will follow us in. Once we come to rest, exit through the escape hatch quickly, but don't panic. The crew will use the cockpit emergency hatch, maintenance team the astrodome hatch. When you get out, clear right away from the aircraft as quickly as possible. Good luck.'

'Don't panic,' he said, so matter of factly. I looked at my mates as my heart pumped at my chest. Nervous eyes flicked from one person to another and Spike's eyes were popping out of his terror-stricken face.

George arrived and stood on top of the radar scanner casing.

'Right, chaps,' he shouted above the engine's roar, 'We go out in reverse order of seniority. I want the junior man to sit under the escape hatch, legs wide apart. The second junior man to sit between the first man's legs. The rest of you will do the same the other side of the bulkhead. Now let's all move up to the escape hatch behind the astrodome. No rush, and don't panic when we hit *terra firma*.'

Only seconds had passed since the skipper had ordered 'Emergency Stations'. The roar of the engines heightened the panic of the situation. Death was a distinct possibility and we all knew it. None of us had been involved in a crash landing before but because of our job we had witnessed many other crashes and often the old high-octane aircraft went up in flames. The first out would obviously have the best chance. We stumbled up the fuselage, over the bulkheads towards the allotted emergency exit.

'Jim will never get his fat arse through the exit, George,' shouted Spike, 'He should go last.'

Sweat was dripping off Spike's nose-end. We were now all standing in the radio op.'s section of the fuselage, Jim at the front, right under the escape hatch. Strained faces were all staring upwards at the twelve-inch by thirty-inch escape hatch.

'What if it's stuck and doesn't open?' shrieked Jim, who was on the verge of total panic.

Jim's hand reached upwards.

'Hands off that bloody panel, don't you dare touch it,' George bellowed.

Jim's flat face was contorted with fear and tears were in his eyes.

'What difference does it make now? We're all going to be killed,' he screamed.

'Don't talk stupid, man, and get a hold on yourself. Get in position – all of you – now,' commanded George.

I was fifth in line for exit. Bill, our corporal, sat between my legs – number six, George was last.

The noise of the engines was deafening and we could feel the kite losing height. We were all braced against one another like a coxless seven, tensed in every muscle, no restraining or safety belts, just free bodies praying, promising, and trembling, as the kite sank lower and lower.

Down and down we went for what seemed years; we crushed each other as we leaned backwards and the engine's laboured noise added to the tension.

We waited and prayed, we prayed and we sweated. My whole life went before me. I could see my mother's face, her soft loving eyes. 'How are you, darling?' she was saying – then we hit.

Tearing, wrenching, screaming, banging, buffeting – all at once – noise everywhere, the aircraft slewed to port and we all shot to starboard. We rocked on, bouncing and banging and then – silence.

'First man – come on, hurry, for Christsake,' shouted George as we fumbled around, dazed, rubbing bumps and bruises and scattered along the fuselage.

We all knew the fuel tanks were full of high octane fumes, and we didn't need much encouragement to move. We quickly crowded beneath the escape hatch as George released the catch and pushed the panel outwards. The sirens and bells of the emergency trucks screamed in. The first three quickly negotiated the hole.

'Get a move on,' I shouted as Jim, the fourth man, struggled in the hole.

Too bloody fat, his bottom half dangled inside the fuselage, legs flaying the air.

'That will do,' said George sternly, 'You'll get your turn. I'll grab his legs, you two push his arse.'

Bill and I jumped forward and, with superhuman effort, heaved the fat arse through the hole.

'You're next, Fizz,' said George.

I went through the hatch like a bullet from a barrel. Christ, we were high up. I'd never thought about that. The fire-engines and emergency vehicles were drawn up or just arriving, and airmen were running in all directions. Jim was still standing on top of the fuselage, five feet away, clasping and unclasping his hands, mouth agape and staring into the distance.

'Jump,' I screamed.

He looked at me, lips trembling and his face gaunt.

'No. They're bringing a ladder.'

I took a step towards him and gave him a push. We slid from fuselage to mainplane and to the ground. He lay in a heap, moaning. I got up but my ankle and arm were hurting. Two fireman grabbed hold of Jim's arms and legs and carried him away. I hobbled after them as fast as I could go.

We all lay on the grass fifty yards away. Someone gave me a fag. I looked at the Lincoln resting on her belly, props bent, and being coated in white foam. Everyone had got out safely and the kite hadn't gone up in flames, which could easily have happened. I thanked God for our imperturbable skipper.

CHAPTER 20

Hospitalized

'Good to have you back, Fizz,' said Chiefy a week later. We'd all been given a week's leave following our Middle East detachment. 'You had a lucky escape from the "prang".'
'Sure did, Chief; I thought it was curtains for sure.'
'Did you keep clear of trouble while you were out there?' he asked, smiling at me.
Bill was taking two weeks' leave but he'd promised to keep mum about the donkey episode.
'Sure, Chief, all plain sailing, no problems at all,' I lied.
'Good man, now keep it up; you can if you really try, you know,' he said encouragingly.
And so I picked up the threads of UK life again, courting Rosa at Scunthorpe, training hard at athletics and running my Thursday dance band.
Two months later Chiefy sent for me again. He took an interest in my development and sent me on a training course for Canberra bombers at English Electronic at Blackpool. I passed the course and became qualified to instruct on Martin Baker ejection seats. The Canberra, sad to say, was destined to replace my graceful Mosquito.
On my return from Blackpool I was keen to get out and see my girlfriend Rosa, and couldn't wait to see my Triumph, which my mates were doing up for me in my absence.
That first night back I set off for Scunthorpe, some seventeen miles distant, and the motorbike engine's throaty roar shattered the stillness of the dark night as I gave it full throttle. While I'd been away from camp my mates had stripped

the Triumph and re-sprayed and rewired it for me. I was proudly putting it through its paces on the 'B' class road between Hemswell and Kirton.

I knew the road well, straight and undulating, the only sign of life being a rabbit or pheasant darting through my headlight beam.

I was on the downslope of the approach road to Kirton village, which runs alongside Kirton Lindsey aerodrome and was prepared for the sharp bend to the right, into the built-up area. The road split to both left and right at this point and a huge oak tree grew where the road split and acted as a roundabout.

As I approached the bend at speed, so excited to be going to see my girl after a long absence, I flicked the switch on my handlebars to dim the headlights, flew in panic through the pitch-black darkness and attempted to demolish the two hundred year old oak.

It was daylight. There was a hazy picture of two faces, one fat and round, and one thin and beautiful. They had white hats on. Their lips were moving as they stared at me. They kept coming and going but wouldn't come into focus. There was a buzz of talk and a clank of metal pans. There was a strong smell of disinfectant. The beautiful face was talking, she came into focus, she was holding my fingers. Her thin lips were inches from my face. Kiss me, I thought.

'He's coming round, Sister – can you hear me? Just nod gently if you can hear me,' said the beautiful lips.

I seemed to be strapped in a strait-jacket. My face, head and neck were covered in tight bandages. My wrists and lower arms were in plaster. I could only feel one leg. Panic set in.

'You're lucky to be alive,' said beautiful lips. 'You're in Scunthorpe War Memorial Hospital. You've had a very nasty motorcycle accident, but you will be all right, so don't worry.' Don't worry, she said, and there I was with probably only one leg.

I couldn't move my jaw to ask questions; indeed, I couldn't move anything. I just lay there, flat on my back and could see as far as my eyes could rotate.

The cream shining ceiling and walls, the frame and curtains around my bed were my world for some days. Beautiful lips explained my injuries.

'Don't try and talk,' she said that first day. 'Your jaw is broken and has been pinned in position. You have a bridge plate in your mouth to hold your teeth apart and your lower jaw is strapped to your head. We will be able to feed you with liquid nourishment,' she smiled.

I was dying to ask her about my leg but I could only lie there like a mummified corpse as she continued:

'You've broken both wrists and they're in plaster casts but they will mend all right. If that's not enough, you have shattered one knee and had sixteen stitches in your leg, so both legs are strapped together as one. My, you have been in the wars, but you'll mend if you stay quiet for a few weeks,' she said encouragingly.

The sheer relief of knowing I had two legs brought a brief smile to my face beneath the bandages and a grunt of agony erupted from my bandaged mouth as hot sharp pains shot from my broken jaw through my head.

'Now you must keep still and calm, else that jaw will never knit together,' said my lovely nurse reproachfully, not knowing the reason for my agonizing grunt.

My first food came at lunchtime in the form of creamy soup poured gently, a little at a time, from the long spout of a small white teapot. My caring nurse smiled and chatted away as she administered her duty with loving care.

'We don't know who you are and don't know what you look like,' she said, 'but I've a feeling you're going to be a good patient.'

How I wish I could have talked to this lovely nurse, even write, but that was out with broken wrists. I could only stare through my bandages at her lovely face and hoped that she could read the gratitude in my eyes.

'The police are coming this afternoon to try and find out who you are, but how they are going to do that, I have no idea,' she said. 'Sister has given them ten minutes only until you get stronger, and remember, you have to stay still.'

At two o'clock two uniformed policemen appeared at the side of my bed with my nurse.

'Ten minutes, Sergeant, else Sister will be most upset,' she said as she left.

'We know you can't speak or write,' said the sergeant by way of introduction. 'But we have to try and find out who you are and who are your next of kin. Someone will be worried about you somewhere,' he said gently, fixing me eye to eye. 'We can deal with the circumstances of the accident when you're better, nobody else was involved. When you were brought in to the casualty department last night your clothes only contained money. No wallet or any identification was found so I'm going to ask you a few questions. A small nod for yes, and a little sideways movement for no is all I want you to do. Can you manage that, do you think?'

I gave a small nod from my supine position and felt a little pain below the ears.

'Good man,' he said, 'Do you live in Scunthorpe?'

I tried to move my head but was scared of the reaction I might get, and only my eyes rolled.

'That was a 'no', Sergeant,' said the constable.

'Do you live in Kirton Lindsey?'

Again my eyes went sideways to the right and back to the left.

'Do you live in Lincolnshire?'

I stared at the questioner. That was a difficult one to answer. I lay thinking what was the best thing to do without confusing them. If only I'd been in RAF uniform instead of civvies they would have soon found out who I was. If I answered no, how could they possible find Brentwood as my home, yet if I said yes, they would still think I was a civilian and probably never think of me being in the RAF.

'You've hit on something here, Sarge; he probably works here and lives in another county,' said the constable.

'Do you work in Scunthorpe steelworks?' asked the sergeant. Eyes left and right. 'Do you work in Scunthorpe, then?' Eyes left and right.

'Sorry, Sergeant, you'll have to leave him today, he's still heavily drugged; try again tomorrow,' said the round-faced sister.

'He's a right mystery man, Sister, we'll have to think about it. We will come back tomorrow.'

I lay in bed full of confused thoughts. I had been on my way to Rosa's house when the accident happened. She was expecting me and would be at a loss from my non-appearance. My motorbike; I wondered where it was and what state it was in. Jim had re-wired it and I could only guess that he had incorrectly wired the headlamp dipper-switch but I wouldn't blame him. I should have checked all the lights before I started out, and anyway, I was riding like Geoff Duke on the Isle of Man circuit.

Then there were my mates at camp: Rudy, Spiv, Jim. They would all be wondering why I'd gone AWOL. Now the police and their daft questions.

I lay there getting more uncomfortable by the hour as my back sweated and my whole body cried out for a good scratching.

The police appeared again the next day and had a prepared list of questions. We were getting absolutely nowhere. After much flicking of fingers the constable got my message.

'I think he wants us to put a pencil in his fingers, Sarge.'

Only half of three fingers protruded through the plastercast and it took a little while for them to get the pencil where I could hold it. I was laid out flat without a pillow and could not see my fingers.

'Right, you've got the pencil, we will put the tip of the pencil on the pad and you try and write something,' said the sergeant.

I lay there picturing the pencil point and attempted to write RAF. It took three goes and two dropped pencils before the constable excitedly spoke the magic words:

'RAF, Sarge, he's in the RAF.'

My body relaxed into the mattress. At last we were getting somewhere.

Within minutes they established that I was from Hemswell and the inquirers departed to inform those that had to be informed.

A week passed by as my lovely nurse cared for the patient who now had a name, but no face. The original bandages were still in place, and the white, long-spouted teapot continued to dispense its mysterious liquids between the slit in the bandages of the mummified patient.

'Sister says we can prop you up today; that will be nice, won't it?'

Two nurses propped me in a half-upright position and I saw the ward and fellow patients for the first time. The feeding table that straddled my bed was tilted towards me and nurse laid a daily newspaper on it for me to read.

'We'll pop along now and again and turn pages for you; now you just relax and read,' she said as she left.

I gazed around the large, clean ward. The high-ceilinged old-fashioned ward contained thirty-four tall iron beds, all set on shiny linoleum. Tables covered with vases of beautiful flowers were standing in the middle of the ward. Patients were moving about in various coloured dressing gowns, while others were lying in or on their beds, either reading or listening to the wireless over their headphones. My nurse and her colleague were making someone's bed further down the ward towards Sister's office. Sister was looking through her window at the activity in her domain. I lay there, two-thirds of the way up the ward, taking in the new and unfamiliar sights.

'Thar's alive then, Mr Mummy,' said the large cherub-faced man in the bed opposite me and across the ward.

I looked across at this jovial happy face who was grinning a million smiles towards me.

'He carn't talk to thee Sef, his jaw's broke!' said the fat man in the bed next to Sef.

Now I recognised the two voices that I'd only heard for the last week. Two happier voices I'd never heard in a hospital ward before or since. All day they entertained one another with stories, jokes or readings from papers or books.

These two heavy men, both nearing sixty years of age, had a childlike spirit of devilment and humour. Neither had reason to be happy and cheerful, as each was paralysed from the waist downwards. They were waiting for a bed in a specialist hospital in Leeds, but their misfortune did not dampen their zest for living.

'I naw it's broke,' said Sef, 'but we ought to cheer poor bugger up. Lets tae 'im a joke Wilf, go'n lad, thar first.'

I forced my eyes away from them both and attempted to concentrate on my newspaper. I wasn't a great one for reading newspapers but tried my hardest to concentrate on the first page of boring reading. At least this kept my eyes away from the smiling devilish pair, but I couldn't stop my ears hearing him.

The jokes came thick and fast, all in the Lincolnshire dialect and my newspaper was forgotten as I peered through my bandages across the bottom of my bed, at this marvellous happy double act. I knew that if I laughed it would be tremendously painful. My jaw was aching as I gripped it tight onto the wooden spacer in my mouth to suppress the bubbling laughter in my stomach. I could feel my eyes were moist as I tried to slip down my bed out of sight. If only I could block out their voices, I thought, as my jaw ached more and more.

'Now what's happening here?' said Sister, appearing between the bottoms of our beds. 'You're not annoying Mr Freeman, are you, Sef, you know he's got a broken jaw.'

'Nay Sister, cheering im a might is all we're doing, Wilf and me.'

'Well, he can't talk and you mustn't make him laugh. My nurses have told me about you two and your jokes. Just leave him alone or you might make his injuries worse.'

With that mild ticking off Sister departed, stopping down the ward to speak to her nurses. She pointed back towards us and we knew that we were the subject of discussion. I slunk down behind my newspaper, out of Sef's and Wilf's line of vision, but my ears were finely tuned to their lovely dialect.

'He's in t'RAF tha' knows,' said Wilf's voice, 'Probably one of them piolots.'

'I was in t'army,' replied Sef. 'Joined in nineteen fifteen, talt'em I was elder than sixteen. Them silly buggers at Lincoln barracks believed I too,' he said with a chuckle.

I was listening intently to this natural conversation between these two friends who seemed like brothers, but had only met through adversity. Their chemistry obviously clicked for they chatted endlessly all day, each trying to top the other's story.

'What were it like?' asked Wilf.

'Fist six weeks, confined to barracks, all that bloody marching and drill, it were bloody agony,' said Sef, 'but when six weeks were up we went arrt in our new uniform, reet smart were we.'

'What did tha do first, get drunk I'll wager,' said Wilf.

'Nay lad,' said the chuckling Sef, 'It were a lass I wanted, a lass I could gis a good thumping to,' he laughed. 'I got one an all, fell for the uniform see, and me handsome face.'

By then I was listening intently, trying to imagine him in his First World War uniform, just sixteen and full of life.

'Took her along river bank I did, picked her some buttercups,' he said, remembering with pleasure. 'We sat in lonely spot and I helt buttercup under her chin to see if she liked butter. By, she did giggle, right giggler she were.'

'Did thaa thump her?' asked the impatient Wilf.

'I'm coming to that, wait on lad,' said the churtling Sef. 'I tried kissin' first but she turn't her head away giggling.

'"Thar can't kiss me 'till tha no me name," said she.

'"Well what is it?" ses I.

'"You got to guess," said she, giggling again.

'I was getting 'ot by now, I just wanted to get on with the thumping, not play't bloody games. "Brenda", ses I.

'"No", she ses, "keep guessing."

'I were bloody fed up with this game, I just wanted to have 'old of her. Helen, Mabel, Mary, May, Louie, Margaret ses I, reeling off every name I could think of.'

"No", she said in fits of laughter.

'I didn't think it were funny, I were fud up wasting time.

"Gee us a clue", I said in desperation.

"right", she ses, thinking, – "it clings to churchyard wall."

"SHIT", I said, quick as a lark, laughing as I said it.

'She burst into tears and ran up the riverbank shouting "No, it's IVY!"'

On the word 'shit' I let out a tremendous roar of bottled-up laughter followed immediately by a scream of pain. I had been so totally absorbed in the story I'd forgotten where I was and what was wrong with me. Sister and nurses crowded round my bed as I writhed in agony. I was carted off to the operating theatre to have my jaw re-set. The laughter had put me back to square one and after the jaw was re-set I was placed in another ward and never saw my jovial friends again.

CHAPTER 21

Wing Commander Elliott

Spiv's poker school had become well established and now was part of our regular weekly routine. The rules had gone by the board and there was no longer a maximum bet; the sky was the limit. We had all been 'inside' for gambling and now took extra precautions. We played in the drying room on the first floor, with the door handle removed, blankets over the windows and a paid lookout by the front entrance to the block. The drying room was about sixteen foot long and eight wide. Radiators ran along the walls, and steel tubes, about six feet high, across the width. Washing or, more often, our uniforms were hung from the tubes to dry.

We felt safe now in our new venue.

I could hardly see through the smoke haze that hung low over the table as the six card players looked at their cards through slitted eyes. The one bulb in its coolie-hat shade hung by its homemade extension lead four feet above the table. All was quiet. Two thermos flasks, filled in the NAAFI earlier, stood with a half-eaten Eccles cake on the floor nearby. It was eleven thirty on a Sunday evening in August 1953.

'Someone's short in the kitty,' said Spiv, breaking the silence.

'Dealer's privilege,' said Jed, tossing in his two-bob bit.

'How many?' asked Jed, looking at Spiv.

Spiv pushed three cards towards him, not speaking. Nobody spoke much at poker. It was hoped that other players would be so intent on their own cards that they wouldn't notice how many you discarded, and you certainly didn't say it out loud for all to hear. I hadn't picked my cards up, as I preferred to see what the others did first. I thought Spiv had probably got a pair. He picked up his three cards as I scanned his face for reactions, but not a twitch. A pair, maybe a prile.

Jed moved to the next man. I watched again, he took two. He could have nothing or possibly a prile, but he was a reckless gambler and likely as not he would have nothing.

The next guy was a safe gambler; he never flannelled, he only bet if he had something. He took one, probably going for a flush or a run. I bet he'd fold on the first bet.

I watched them all and only then lifted my cards. I took three to a pair of queens. I drew a pair of kings and a seven.

The betting commenced as Spiv threw in a ten-bob note.

'You're ten and up ten,' said the second man.

'I'll go the pound,' said the third.

'Your pound and up two,' said the fourth.

Christ, there's some hot stuff here, I thought.

Two of them were always reckless, however, and the conservative gambler always had one bet if he had a pair. Another factor was that they mostly lost their judgement as we approached finishing time at midnight. The losers tried to recover their losses by bigger bets; the winners were happy to win more.

'You're three pound and up five,' I said, throwing in a white tissue paper fiver and three one-pound notes.

'Too hot for me,' said Jed and stacked.

'Me too,' said the next.

There was a long silence while the conservative gambler struggled with his thoughts, looked at his cards again, checked his money. Relooked at his cards again. We sat patiently watching.

'You bastards will never learn, will you?' said a quiet voice outside the smoke and ring of light.

Our chairs scraped on the concrete floor as we turned to peer into the gloom at the other end of the room.

The sergeant of the guard stepped into our light in his stocking feet, grinning all over his face, with a large pencil held up for us all to see.

'Makes an excellent door handle you know, a pencil. You buggers never learn, do ya. You shouldn't mix with bloody Freeman, he's the Pied Piper of trouble.'

Sergeant Strivens and I knew each other well; we'd spent a lot of time together and hated each other's guts. He had a personal vendetta against me and had failed to break my spirit as he had vowed to do. I knew how it felt to be hounded like a criminal. I'd seen a film where the prisoner had been released and vowed to his wife he'd go straight, no more crime. He got a job and worked hard, refusing all the offers and temptations of his criminal friends but, whenever there was a hold up or robbery in the district, the police would always pick him up and grill him for two days or more. He was always a suspect, they wouldn't leave him alone.

Sergeant Strivens had the same mentality. If something went missing in a billet miles away Strivens would have me turn out my locker and put me through questioning. He would stop me at the entrance barrier on my motorbike, undo the petrol cap, take a sniff and say, 'That's high octane, Freeman, aircraft fuel, right, lad?' as though expecting me to admit it.

'No, Sergeant, never – very difficult to prove anyway.'

'I'll catch you putting it in one of these days, then we'll see who's smiling – sod off.'

I'd enjoyed the cut and thrust with Strivens but of late I was thinking of what the old Wingco had said the last time I was on a fizzer.

'This will be your last chance, Freeman. If you come before me again I shall have to consider sending you away to a corrective establishment. You're a bad influence and a bad example to the young national servicemen.'

I turned back to the table and started to pick up the pot from the middle. My nice white fiver, the other notes and coins. I thought I would return the bets later.

'Take your filthy hands off that, Freeman, that's confiscated, that's evidence.'

'It's our money, Sergeant, and we're having it,' I said resignedly.

'Leave it, Fizz, don't get in deeper,' said Spiv.

'Good advice there, Freeman, but you wouldn't recognise good advice if it was stuffed up your arse,' said Strivens sarcastically.

'Why are MPs so coarse, Sergeant? Is it their training or lack of education d'ya think?' I asked, throwing caution to the wind and entering the fray as was predictable.

Gasps of surprise from some of my poker friends who were witnessing, for the first time, a confrontation between Strivens and me. Not Spiv though, he'd seen it all before.

'Can't you let this one go, Sarge, if we promise to pack in cards for good?' asked Spiv pleadingly.

'Let it go, Chilcott, let Freeman off, that would be a dereliction of duty. You're all on a charge, and Freeman's on two. Insubordination, that should cook your goose this time, Freeman; we'll get rid of you for good,' he said, smiling viciously.

'It 'ull be a fuckin' holiday to get away from a bastard like you. I hate your guts.'

'Corporal,' he screamed, 'you're a witness to those swear words. Take Freeman to his cell, tomorrow we'll throw the book at him. The rest of you be in the admin. office at nine fifty sharp – now get to bed.'

As I lay in my cell I felt sure that this was the end of the road. I contemplated, for the first time ever, running away; it wouldn't be difficult. Surely the next day would see me sent to a military corrective establishment and that would mark me for life, set me on a criminal path, no turning back. If I absconded it would be court-martial when they eventually caught me, as they surely would. There was no way out, I'd reached rock bottom. I am what I am but I know not why, I thought.

I was lying on my hard mahogany mattress trying to find answers. Where had I gone wrong? Where did it all start? And why?

I used to blame the Army and their treatment of my Dad, but that was an excuse. It hadn't affected Vic or my other brothers. No, it was God, he made me different, he put in that rebellious streak, the anti-authority bolshy streak. I lay there blaming God, blaming anybody but myself, and asking myself why? Where did it all start?

I remembered Mr Cotton beating the baby monkey in India and my reaction in attacking him, which led to the first feel of Dad's leather belt. After that belting I hated Father, but that didn't stop me throwing the inkpot at Mrs Marks, my teacher, and getting another leathering. Even Mother's pleading not to go to 'that smelly bazaar' fell on deaf ears. It was no good feeling sorry for myself; I was obviously born a tyrant and my destiny was set from the beginning. Each beating or hardship had grown another anti-authority skin on me. The terrifying memory of the birching had cemented my resolve and determination never to kow-tow to anybody, whatever they did. Well, if that was so, I thought, as I lay there, hands behind head, this would be the big test, the make or break of Robert Bruce Freeman.

'The day of reckoning for you,' said the gloating Strivens as I marched between my escorts the short distance to the admin. block.

Spiv and the other four gamblers were already in the corridor when we arrived. They were all charged as one, on the same single charge. Five minutes later they were marched out of the chargeroom, straight down the corridor and disappeared round the bend without the opportunity of a signal, smile, or anything.

I was then marched in by the happy Strivens and resigned to the fate that awaited me.

'Prisoner, halt, right turn. Prisoner 1920683 Freeman, Sah,' said Strivens.

I stared straight ahead, capless, at a picture of Spitfires flying in formation on the office wall opposite. It would be bloody Spitfires, they got me into the RAF therefore it seemed appropriate that they should be there at the finish.

There was a long silence with just the noise of my unfit escorts' breathing. I could feel the eyes of the Wingco boring into me. Why doesn't he get on with it? I thought. If he's going to chop my head off, chop the bugger off, I don't care, but for Christsake don't hang it out.

'Wait outside, Sergeant, with your escorts,' said the calm quiet voice of the Wingco.

An eternity of silence ensued. I was as surprised as Strivens. This had never happened before, this was not according to plan, this wasn't in the text book.

'Sergeant – outside with your escorts,' quietly repeated the Wingco.

'Sah,' said Strivens, coming back to life and marching his two snowdrops outside.

I stood still, upright, staring forward, wondering what was coming next.

'Stand at ease, Freeman,' he said.

I relaxed, mystified at the change from normal procedure and wondering what was coming next. Usually it was a pompous and superior lecture on my misdemeanour, then something derogatory on my character, then a prophecy of where I was going to end up. After this ear-bashing came the quick question,

'Have you anything to say for yourself?' spoken with a discouraging inference which meant 'Don't bother – I wouldn't believe you anyway.' Then the sentence that was arrived at before you even entered the room.

'You're aware, I'm sure, of what Wing Commander Woodward said to you when you appeared before him on your last charge?'

'Yes, Sir,' I said, coming to attention.

'Stay at ease, Freeman, stay at ease,' he repeated quietly. 'Well, doesn't it frighten you, then? The prospect of being sent to a corrective establishment, it's really the end of the road, you know.'

'Yes, Sir, it does frighten me,' I said, in all truthfulness.

There was then a long thoughtful silence while he flicked through the brown cardboard file in front of him, stopping every now and again to read a few lines. I stood waiting and wondering.

'Freeman, you fascinate me. It's now nearly six years since you joined as a boy entrant. Have you any idea how many days detention you've done in that time?'

'Quite a lot, Sir,' I replied, starting to feel guilty.

'One hundred and four days, Freeman. That *is* "quite a lot", isn't it?'

'Yes, Sir,' I said.

'Unauthorized driving of the camp water bowser, turning it over on the perimeter track, six hundred pounds worth of damage and all for a bet,' he read out from my file.

'Refusing to use the back entrance of the medical centre. Swearing at the warrant officer physical training. Drunk and disorderly three times. Stealing a RAF bicycle, cap badge upside down, gambling, swearing at an NCO, resisting arrest; refusing orders and so it goes on and most charges had a second charge of insubordination.' He paused for breath and looked up at me from behind his desk, almost with fatherly interest.

A long silent pause filled the room.

'Last week you ran against the famous Macdonald Bailey and Brian Shenton at Lincoln, didn't you?' he asked, out of the blue.

I was amazed that he knew. I'd represented the RAF in the one hundred yards sprint against England's number one and number two sprinters. In fact, Macdonald Bailey was one of the fastest men in the world at that time.

'Yes, Sir, but I came in last.'

'I know, I was in the stands with my wife watching. We also saw you at the RAF annual championships. You were first in both the high hurdles and four-forty hurdles weren't you?'

'Yes, Sir, and I set a new high jump record,' I said, getting carried away.

'Exactly, Freeman, that's why I find your case fascinating.'

I was completely lost by then. Where was all this leading, what about Strivens standing outside probably trying to catch the quiet conversation going on inside? This new Wingco Elliott was certainly different from Wingco Woodward who had been posted six weeks previously. I'd come in front of quite a few different officers in my time but they were always the same. No chat, no reasoning, no discussion, they were all the same until now, until Wing Commander Elliott arrived on the scene.

'I spoke to Flight Sergeant Blackmore, your Chief, this morning and he has nothing but praise for your work. He tells me you went on detachment for the Mediterranean Fleet exercises and did a splendid job. He can't understand, no more than I can, why you can be a top tradesman, a fine athlete, run the camp dance band, be popular and liked by everyone and yet have the most atrocious disciplinary record I've ever come across in my twenty years' service. There must be an answer somewhere, what do you think it is?' he said with concern, looking up at me.

By then I was feeling decidedly lost, punch drunk. I had come in prepared for a quick sentence; my body and mind were set for that. I would have taken it as I'd taken many sentences before. I would have been calm, resentful, and obstinate. As the sentence was pronounced I would have said to myself, 'and sod you too, do ya bloody worst.' I could cope with that, the expected – but now – this.

I stood there feeling my body quiver; my stomach was churning. I bit my upper lip to keep my emotions in check. I didn't want to break down. This was agony, I'd rather have three rounds with Rocky Marciano than this totally new treatment. Funny though, I'd always criticised my superiors for not discussing my offence, not reasoning, not trying to find out why I did what I did. And now an officer was genuinely and sincerely discussing and trying to fathom my peculiar behaviour. I couldn't handle it.

'I don't know, Sir,' was all I could get out of my trembling lips.

'You and me alike, Freeman; surely you've thought about it sometimes, when you've been in your cell. What really makes you resent authority so much that you swear at your seniors and disregard standing orders and regulations? You must have some idea, man?' he said, a little sharper.

'Sometimes it's unfair, Sir; sometimes it's because I am being sneered at and degraded,' I blurted out.

'That's better – now we're getting somewhere,' he said with a slight smile and a happier voice. 'Now think of this – if it's unfair, as you call it, isn't it unfair for the other three hundred airmen? Why don't they refuse to co-operate? Why aren't they all on charges? As for sneering and degrading, if you obeyed orders there would be nothing to sneer at you about, am I right?'

'Yes, Sir.'

'Tell me this, Freeman – have your protests achieved anything?'

'No, Sir,' I said, now completely lost and putty in his hands. All my barriers were down. I was a quivering jelly.

'When you joined the RAF you swore on oath to obey your superior officers and NCOs, did you not?'

'Yes, Sir.'

'There is a good reason for laying down orders and regulations. It's all to do with discipline, obedience. Where would we be in a battle situation if the

Commander said "charge" and you refused? What effect would that have on the others? Discipline, Freeman, is of paramount importance in the services, surely you can see that, man?'

'Yes, Sir,' I said, just stopping myself from saying 'Sorry' which nearly slipped out.

I was by then absorbed in the Wingco's reasoning and was ready to do anything he said. All resistance had left my body. I was vulnerable to anything.

'So – what we have here is a top tradesman, a fine athlete, a musician, a popular airman and a man with the worst disciplinary record it has ever been my duty to witness. Freeman,' he said, looking me straight in the eye. 'You know what you are don't you? You're a rebel – a rebel without a cause – wouldn't you agree?'

I looked at this understanding man, this man who had laid bare my career to date, this man who had taken the time to reason with me, this man who seemed to be sincerely interested in me and my behaviour. I felt weak, ashamed even. At last someone had asked 'Why?' and I truly didn't have a plausible or genuine reason to counter his arguments. I was a rebel and I hadn't a cause.

'Yes, Sir,' I said, softly and sincerely, feeling for the first time ashamed, lost, repentant.

Wing Commander Elliott read for a few moments, or at least appeared to be reading. I stood at ease but felt I had been standing there a lifetime. I was wet with nervous sweat and tension. Maybe he wouldn't send me away, maybe I would get another chance, possibly fourteen days' detention. If I did, I promised God I'd behave, co-operate, do anything to make amends to this man who seemed to care genuinely about ME.

'Freeman,' he said looking up at me, 'Would I be wasting my time trying to change you? Would you ever be able to keep clear of trouble? Think man – think hard on what I say. I don't want your quick answer. I'm asking you, for the first time, if you can change your ways, start again, become a model of good behaviour?'

'Yes, Sir, I'm sure I could, Sir,' I said as convincingly as I could.

'I don't think you realise what I am asking. It's one thing to stand there on yet another serious charge and promise to change to what you've never been, and quite a different matter when in a week's time you're being ordered to do something you think is "unfair" or even being shouted at. Think, man – I'm asking you for a firm promise, a promise to scrub the parade ground if you're told to, to obey without question, to conform like everybody else. Well, can you do all these things and become what you've never been before?'

'I'll really try, Sir, I really will.'

'Well, Freeman, trying might not be enough but I am going to give you the chance. Flight Sergeant Blackmore thinks you deserve this chance and I agree with him. If you prove us both wrong it will be the end of the road. Do you understand that?'

'Yes, Sir, thank you, Sir, I won't let you down,' I said, not knowing what the sentence was going to be.

'Well Freeman, you will be as surprised as I nearly am. I'm going to take a chance with you and dismiss these two charges, but on your solemn promise that you will keep well clear of trouble, keep your temper under control and obey orders without question. You're not to discuss with anyone what has been said in this room today and I shall send for you in eight weeks' time to see how you're getting on. IS THAT ABSOLUTELY CLEAR?'

'Yes, Sir, I understand clearly,' I said, but I couldn't believe what I'd heard. Dismiss the charges, let me go. No corrective establishment, not even detention – I must have dreamt it.

The Wingco crossed the room and opened the door.

'You can come in now, Sergeant,' he said casually.

Strivens marched in for the kill. His two corporals took up their position either side of me.

'Bring them to attention, Sergeant,' said the re-seated Wingco.

'Prisoner and escorts ah-ten-tion!' commanded the revitalized, confident and expectant Strivens.

'Thank you, Sergeant. Now, remember what we've discussed, Freeman. Case dismissed,' he said, closing the cardboard files on his desk and stacking them in one pile.

We stood in silence. Obviously Strivens was trying to understand the Wingco's last order. His brain was struggling to comprehend but he couldn't take it in; he couldn't believe he had heard correctly.

'I said case dismissed, Sergeant,' calmly repeated the Wingco. A further pregnant pause before Strivens came to life.

'SAH!' he shouted in a dream.

We marched into the corridor. The baffled Strivens was shell-shocked.

'What went on in there, Freeman, why did he let you off?' he asked in somewhat of a daze.

'I don't know, Sergeant,' I said, which was really the truth.

'You said something, lad, you must of said something, you must be the jammiest bugger in the Air Force but you'll be back, mark my words you'll be back, now DISMISS.'

I walked in a dream back to the hangar. I went over, time and again, what the Wingco had said, what I had said. I was determined to be faithful to the Wingco and keep my promise.

My mates were baffled. Surprise, laughter, disbelief and questions greeted my return. 'You must have shot a bloody good line, come on, Fizz, tell us the truth, what did you really say?' asked Rudy, as my mates crowded round me, amazed at my unexpected return to the hangar.

'What's this – a union meeting?' asked the smiling Chiefy, who had come out of his office to investigate the hubbub and noise that had greeted my return.

'You can give Fizz the third degree at lunchtime, back to work now,' and the crowd dispersed.

I went with Chiefy to his office and thanked him for his kind words to the Wingco which had undoubtedly helped me get off a serious charge and possibly a corrective centre punishment. I didn't tell him what the Wingco had said and he didn't ask, he just told me to calm down and take life more easily instead of always being the centre of attention.

'Keep your nose clean, Fizz, you haven't got to prove anything to your mates, just to yourself, and remember you may never get another chance if you balls this one up.'

'Right, Chief,' I said, fully determined to stay well clear of trouble.

Six weeks had crept by since my promise to Wing Commander Elliott. Six weeks in which I'd concentrated so hard to keep out of trouble.

Strivens and his cohorts had stopped me on a number of occasions as I journeyed to and from the post office. I had answered their cries of 'Airman, come here,' as smartly and quickly as a new recruit but oh! how it hurt to conform like an inferior animal. They had been baffled, of course, by my obedience and indeed mystified at my calm and polite replies. I was actually starting to enjoy this role reversal. Their baffled looks and mystified expressions when they failed to provoke me gave me an inward warmth of satisfaction. I was still beating the buggers at their own game.

I had to watch my mates, though. They'd cost me five days 'inside' by just reversing my cap badge. That was last year but I still checked my badge daily.

Spiv was put out twice over. First because I'd got off and he and the other four had had a fortnight confined to barracks, and secondly because I'd given up cards. His new school now played in an outhouse behind the billets.

'Come on, Fizz,' he would say, 'It's not the same without you. We've got a padlock and chain on the inside, the windows permanently blacked out and we pay two lookouts now.'

Poor Spiv couldn't persuade me from the straight and narrow and had to give up trying.

Battle of Britain celebrations, September 1953. I stand with the crowd surrounding the hangars and airfield. We have Canberra bombers on show for the first time and I am on duty, telling the public all about the new 'plane, its Martin Baker ejection seats and explosive bolt canopy. I've been trained well at the English Electric Factory outside Blackpool and am now showing off my knowledge to the public.

The crowds are spellbound by the daring flying display now taking place. Thousands of heads turn skyward, millions of eyes focus on one little 'plane as 'Ahs' and 'Ohs' erupt as though orchestrated by an invisible hand. The camp Tiger Moth is being thrown around the sky in unbelievable manoeuvres, then a steep dive off the airfield and the crowds lose sight of the biplane for a few seconds. Gasps as fingers and arms point and all eyes move to the right. The Tiger Moth hops the boundary hedge and zooms across in front of the crowd not twenty feet above the ground. The crowd roar their approval, the applause drowned by the engine, as I look up at my friend Soco. Clad in his leather helmet and goggles, his scarf flying from his neck, he waves to the crowd like my hero Biggles. I grin with pride and delight as my friend flies by, born to be a pilot, born an extrovert, he is now doing what he loves to do best, showing his unquestionable skills and devil may care spirit to his audience.

Back with the joystick and he shoots into a climb. Up and up he goes, then levels out, the engine cuts out, he goes into the 'falling leaf' routine. The plane rocks gracefully from side to side as the now quiet audience are held spellbound, eyes firmly fixed on the romantic craft. He floats nearer and nearer the ground. The crowd are hushed, I tighten up. Although I've watched him many times I've never seen him leave it this late. Still it floats downwards, rocking gently from side to side like a falling leaf. Christ, only about two hundred feet left. I take a deep breath to shout as the engine revs and he loops up into safety. The crowd go mad, shouting, cheering, and clapping. I stand still, gently trembling.

'Christ,' says Ginger, my other half on public duty, 'That was too close for comfort, he must be off his nut.'

Soco makes another low level pass in front of the crowd, waving and taking his applause. He pulls back on the joystick and the little biplane responds by climbing for the heavens. What next, the crowd wonder, as Soco levels out and prepares for his finale. The Tannoy announces the Tiger Moth's final manoeuvre, the 'rolling barrel'. Soco's *pièce de résistance* now has the crowd captured, all eyes are riveted on the daredevil Tiger Moth as Soco cuts the engine again. The kite goes into a slow, lazy spiral towards the centre of the aerodrome and about a hundred yards in front of the roped-off crowd.

Down – down – she gracefully floats, turning in a gently spiral, as the crowd stand transfixed. Complete silence as a million people hold their breath. Still she spirals forward.

'Now,' I say under my breath – but no – Soco continues down.

'NOW, NOW, you stupid bugger, NOW.' The crowd is getting restless. Ginger grabs my arm.

'NOW!' I shout, 'Soco, NOW!'

The Tiger Moth stands straight upright, its nose embedded in the green turf, its tail pointing to the heavens. Sirens scream as fire tenders speed across grass towards the plane. I am running too. A motorbike overtakes me. The plane is still balanced on its nose. I can see Soco struggling with his harness but his forward body weight makes it difficult to release the catch. The motorbike rider is nearly there. The plane starts to fall. It topples forward on its back. The motorcyclist jumps from his machine whilst it is still travelling and runs towards the plane. I am half way there when the explosion and blinding flash throws the motorcyclist backwards. The plane is a ball of fire, a massive inferno. Neither I nor anyone else can do anything to save my friend, Soco; he didn't stand a chance.

It took a long time to get over Soco's death. It was so dramatic, so awful and such a waste of a good life. I tried in vain to find the address of his lady friend but to no avail. I've no idea how she found out in the end. I never will forget my friend Soco.

The following Monday I sat in the hangar crewroom at morning tea-break. Soco's death was still on my mind. None of my mates were close to him as I had been. They were gibbering away about the football results, with Rudy centre stage, extolling the qualities of Rangers, the only football team worth talking about, according to him.

'Fizz,' said Chiefy, whose face appeared around the open crewroom door. 'Report to the Wingco right away, will you?'

'I'm on my way, Chief.'

'Eh, what you bin up to now?' queried Spiv.

'Wingco changed his mind, back on that fizzer again, I reckon,' said Jim, laughing.

Rudy came across the room looking concerned and said softly,

'D'ya know what it's about, Fizz, ha'ya been in some trouble?' he asked with genuine concern.

'Don't know, Rudy; I'd better get over and find out.'

'Aye, but keep calm, Fizz, it canny be much.'

I strode out of the hangar wondering why the Wingco had sent for me so soon. It was barely seven weeks since my last charge and he did say eight weeks. I racked my brains for the answer. I'd done nothing wrong, why did he want to see me so soon? I'd half expected eight weeks to pass, then nine and ten. It wouldn't surprise me if he never sent for me. I didn't really believe or trust anybody in authority; I had no reason to.

'The Wingco's sent for me,' I said to his clerk.

'Wait here, then,' he said, getting up to go and check. He didn't have to ask my name; everybody on camp knew Fizz Freeman after over three years' residence.

'Right, knock on the door and go in,' said the clerk, on his return.

My heart was thumping as I entered the Wingco's office.

'Ah, there you are, Freeman,' he said as I took up the 'at ease' position in front of his desk.

'How have you been getting on?' he asked with a smile.

'Fine, Sir,' I said nervously.

'No trouble, no problems?' he queried.

'No, Sir, no problems at all.'

'That's good; I knew you could do it, but seven weeks isn't long, is it? The question is, can you keep it up, I mean all the time?'

'Oh yes, Sir, I'm sure I can.'

'I believe you, Freeman. It may surprise you to know that I witnessed a short confrontation between you and Sergeant Strivens last Thursday lunchtime. I was entering this building when he called you back off the entrance road. You handled yourself well that day, although I realized it wasn't easy for you. Have you had many such skirmishes with the military police in the last seven weeks?'

'Yes, Sir, four or five times,' I replied.

'Good, that shows you can master your emotions if you really try. I'm very pleased and so will Chiefy Blackmore be when I tell him. He seems to take a particular interest in you, doesn't he?'

'Yes, Sir, we get on well; I really like my work and he appreciates it,' I replied, feeling quite relaxed.

'Well, Freeman, both Chiefy Blackmore and I agree that you would make an excellent NCO. Poacher turned gamekeeper, if you know what I mean. Here is a stores order. Report straight to the stores, draw your corporal's stripes, and have them sewn on your uniforms by tomorrow morning. Off you go,' he said, handing me the stores order and smiling broadly at my amazement and hesitation.

'But, Sir, I don't want to be a corporal,' I pleaded. 'I'd lose my mates and I can't give orders.'

His smile left his face as he stood up from his chair.

'I didn't ask you if you wanted to be promoted. You *are* promoted. You're now a corporal. As for mates, as you call them, you'll find new mates when you arrive at your new posting. You're moving to Oldenburg, West Germany next week. Chiefy will fill you in. Don't you see what you're getting, man, a new start, a fully fledged corporal in a new camp where nobody knows you, a new life. Now get off to the stores and get your stripes.'

I wandered in a dream, forgetting to thank the Wingco. The stores assistant thought it was a joke but, getting no reaction from me, produced the goods. I floated back to the billet and started sewing and preparing myself for the reaction of my mates when they returned from work.

I took a few days' leave to say farewells to Rosa at Scunthorpe and my parents at Brentwood. It saved me from the barracking of my mates but Rudy and Spiv were really pleased for me.

I returned to Hemswell for a final check-out, and was sad to leave my faithful Chiefy Blackmore. When we shook hands for the last time I felt the emotion in my chest and quickly strode away from the hangar.

Rudy, Spiv and Jim saw me off, none of us knowing whether we would ever meet again. Three years at Hemswell, three eventful years of sport, guardhouse, music, work, friendships, fun and drama.

I looked at the guardroom as the lorry drew under the raised red and white steel boom. The snowdrop corporal stood there; our eyes met. My arm started to come up to give him the vee-sign. I thought of Wingco Elliott just in time. Ah, what the hell, I thought, as I tucked my hand down by my side. I just smiled. (Yet my fingers were open in a vee as I did so.)

CHAPTER 22

The Verge Inn

Bicycles, thick thighs, funny hats, rubber knickers, cleanliness, sausages, cobblestones, and courtesy, that was Oldenburg, West Germany, in 1953.

Everyone seemed to have a bike, a new bike. The special cycle tracks that ran parallel to the roads carried the population around the town in animated safety. The thighs, the thick powerful thighs were on the bikes; the rubber knickers were on the thighs.

The well-built farmer type fräuleins stood astride their bicycles, lifted their dresses to waist level and plonked their ample, rubber-covered bums on their bicycle seats. Quite a different approach to life than the conservative, feminine, prim and proper English girl undertaking the same feat. As for the rubber knickers, there were various theories for their existence; sufficient to say they were extras covering the garment underneath.

The town always seemed to be free of litter and a distinct first impression of cleanliness and tidiness surrounded the new visitor. Courtesy towards the occupying forces seemed strange and unexpected. Somehow I expected resentment but all I found was courtesy, smiles and helpfulness from shopkeeper, restaurateur and public alike.

The strange, tight, crown-covering hat worn by most German men struck me as odd and military. The mile-long sausages – *Bratwürste* – dangling between a thumbful of bread were delicious to eat and guaranteed burping and indigestion for the next four hours.

Old gaunt and dismal buildings did not blend with the new, nor did the occasional cobblestoned road with its vicious camber.

Oldenburg, with the river Die Hunter running through it was a pleasant town, so unlike any I'd experienced before. Its modern stores and picturesque oldfashioned shops and side streets offered a new experience, and exciting change from all that had gone before. The shops were full of goods but certain foodstuffs were still in short supply and English cheese, tinned fish, coffee and English cigarettes were prized possessions and excellent bargaining tools.

In the centre of Oldenburg was a British Forces leisure building. The RAF and Army mixed in their free time and at weekends in the mammoth bingo sessions for large prizes, at cinema shows, eating and drinking, plus shopping in the tax-free British goods stores which sold everything from food and clothes to hardware.

The Oldenburg Athletic Club, the VFB, had wonderful facilities including a floodlit cinder track and various trainers for different events. I was accepted as a member without hesitation and joined a band of dedicated German athletes every Thursday for a vigorous, non-stop three-hour training session. Two tracksuits, one worn on top of the other, was a compulsory gimmick of the club and were worn for the full three-hour sessions. I improved my running times tremendously under the strict eye of the trainer and went on to represent the RAF throughout Germany, winning the hundred and ten-metre hurdles and high jump in the Second Tactical Air Force Championships in the following year.

Oldenburg became our main centre of leisure and relaxation although the RAF camp provided plenty of leisure pursuits, including dances and sport. The camp boasted its own cinder track which was right outside the billet I was put in charge of.

Oldenburg offered me that new life, that new start, and I was hungry for it. Happiness, contentment, freedom, even respect had come my way since I had arrived only seven short weeks before, with two stripes on my arm.

Wingco Elliott had been correct. No one did know my background, except my CO, of course. I was accepted as an established corporal with six years service. The odd nosey question in the first week: 'How long have you been made up, mate?' received the regular answer: 'Eight years mate,' – 'Lying sod, you haven't been in that long.'

The corporals' club had something going on most nights from bingo to weekly dances and I soon became accepted after a few ballads and the odd rude recitation.

The lifestyle suited me just fine and I had everything a guy could ask for.

The new challenge to my trade skills was Sabre jets, fantastic aircraft and exciting to work on. I was now with the Second Tactical Airforce (AI Wing)

HQ Fighter Command, and had a good chiefy once again and a great gang of tradesmen; life at work couldn't have been better.

My charges outside work hours consisted of seventy-two airmen, most of whom were national servicemen. Our billet was the usual flat-topped oblong, two rooms of eighteen on the ground floor and two rooms on the first floor. Ablutions and drying rooms were in the centre of the oblong as were the entrance doors and stairs. My private bedroom with table, chair, wardrobe and cupboard was on the first floor next to the stairs. No other corporals were in residence so I had all four rooms to administer.

The airmen had come to accept me as a friendly sort of guy and no incidents occurred in the first few weeks, but familiarity and friendliness can often be misconstrued as weakness. By my nature and background I was determined not to bawl, shout or degrade anyone, nor was I going to put anyone on a two-five-two. My feelings must have shown themselves to some of my charges.

It was well past eleven o'clock at night as I wove my way uncertainly towards my billet, a little worse for wear after a night in the club. It was only a distance of three hundred yards as my billet was second in a row of ten from the club, canteens, and NAAFI.

As I approached the front entrance, yells, shouts, laughter erupted from the building and the lights were blazing in the downstairs corridor. I pushed open the fully glazed swing door to witness a fire extinguisher fight in full swing.

I was probably half an hour earlier than usual as I looked in at the warring factions. The movement of the door attracted the attention of the nearest erks and they started to run down both corridors.

'It's not good fucking off!' I shouted, 'I've seen your faces; report to my room in five minutes.'

The corridors were painted gloss green from floor to four-foot level, and gloss cream to ceiling, but now walls and ceilings were covered in foam. The floor was awash and sand was everywhere. It had been a good fight.

I retired to my room, smiling. For the first time since I'd been promoted I wished I was one of them. What better than a good battle to let off steam, have a laugh. Something to talk about for days, something to recount, relive, laugh about. Now I was a corporal, now I was in charge, now I was past all that? – was I hell, I wished I'd been part of it. A knock on my door as I pulled on my pyjama bottoms.

'Come in,' I said, sitting down on my bed.

The door opened and the first sheepish faces appeared. They were pushing from the back, all trying to get in and look at the new corporal's room.

'Hold it there,' I shouted, standing up and looking over the heads of the five in the room, to the sea of faces in the corridor outside.

'OK, Stevens, you seem to have the guts to come in first; what's it all about?'

'Just a friendly challenge between rooms one and two, Corp, but others joined in, sort of,' he said seriously, wondering what this new corporal would do.

'I suppose it started with a bet, did it?'

'Yes, Corp, that's right, Corp,' he said brightly and then wished he hadn't as his face dulled.

'Right, I don't want to know any more; this time I'm not even interested who started it. I'm just going to bed. When I get up in the morning I will inspect every inch of the corridors, ceilings and floor. I shall also check that all extinguishers and fire buckets are full. If I find things to my liking I shall forget the matter; if not we will all meet again. Now I'm going to bed.'

They woke me from a deep sleep at three thirty. I peered at my alarm clock as Stevens, accompanied by a back-up party, was saying:

'All finished, Corp, ready for your inspection.'

I looked up at his serious concerned face, was he getting at me? Was he doing a Freeman? No, I decided, he was genuine.

'Sod off, Stevens, and put my bloody light out,' I grumbled as I turned over in bed.

'Yes, Corp, thanks, Corp,' I heard as I dropped off to sleep.

Letter-writing now took on a greater significance. Everybody wrote home, some daily, some like me, once a week. Besides receiving a letter the highlight of the week was listening to Two-way Family Favourites at Sunday lunchtime. Most airmen lay on their beds listening to the Tannoy, hoping against hope that their request would be played, dreaming of their loved ones, counting the days to demob. The national servicemen were a pain in the arse to the regulars. 'Three hundred and twenty-one days to go,' said the conscript as he crossed off another day from the large chart pinned inside his locker. This daily recital of 'days to go' was the source of much bad feeling between the career men and the passers-through, but now I was removed from all this aggro, cocooned in my own room, writing to my Rosa. Rosa and I planned to marry but her widowed Mother was against the match, as were the 'Aunties' who brought Rosa up. We decided to wait until she was twenty-one in March and go ahead anyway, and were now saving like mad for the great day.

Christmas was soon upon us but having only been at Oldenburg two months I wasn't entitled to leave, so I had the job, with others, of arranging the Christmas festivities for those left behind.

The Commanding Officer put up two crates of beer for the best bar constructed in any billet and agreed to judge the entries. By now, after showing my men one or two shortcuts in their kit inspections and correcting two incidents that would normally attract official charges, they had been knitted into a proud team and showed me respect and enthusiasm. We entered the competition with Stevens, the rascal and undisputed leader of the men, suggesting the design and material.

'Let's build a bar right across the width of the room with saplings,' suggested Stevens as all those left behind for Christmas congregated in room two. 'Nobody else will think of that. We could make the furniture out of saplings too, a real rustic pub bar and lounge,' he enthused.

'Where are we going to get the wood, pinch it, I suppose?' quipped Saggers. 'We've only a week to do it in.'

'That's the problem, Corp, it'll be a bit risky but there's plenty in the copse just over the hedge. What do you think?'

The excited faces waited for my response.

The fellas were now looking up to me with renewed respect, having got the message that I had perfected all the tricks they tried to get away with. I could nearly always second-guess their motives. I didn't want to dampen their enthusiasm but I could see the obvious risks to me and my stripes. This passing thought was outweighed by the exciting challenge and a sense of being one of them, togetherness. If I said no they would go off the boil and I would lose them.

'It will have to be well-planned and no one must breathe a word of what we're doing.'

A collective sigh of relief, followed by a babble of excited voices filled the room following my agreement. Plans were agreed and I was in it up to the neck. The saplings were in a wood that bordered the camp, easily accessible from our billet and on the other side of the camp away from the guardroom and other prying eyes.

We worked at night in two gangs of four. Tracksuits, dark clothing and plimsolls ensured some quietness and ease of movement. Saplings were cut low to the ground and leaves and brushwood camouflaged the stump; no two saplings were taken close to one another. Two worked while two look-outs patrolled the immediate area.

Three nights of three hours each saw the camaraderie of the group of rogues grow. Their enthusiasm to win the competition heightened as we began installing the bar during the day. After each of the three night sorties I lay in my bed thinking what a stupid sod I was. Why hadn't I said no to start with? I liked the privileges and status of my rank so why was I risking it? I lay there thinking of the consequences if it came to light that not only did I know what my men were up to, I was actually involved in it.

I had three restless nights and a week of worry and inner turmoil. There was no way back, I just had to go through with it.

The RAF station employed quite a lot of local labour and I had become friendly with Oover in the paint stores and Herman in the carpentry shop. I asked Herman if he could purchase for me some five-inch round stakes for making tables and chairs and also to slice up on the lathe to manufacture wooden ashtrays. He was only too delighted to help and the small amount of timber arrived on site the next day. We could have cut larger diameter timber from the woods but it would show up too easily and was harder to carry, so we stuck to cutting two-inch saplings only. With Herman's assistance I now had half an answer as to where we got the timber for the bar.

The day for judging arrived and our bar stretched right across the width of the room with a trellis divider between the lounge bar and the public bar. The benches and tables looked a real treat and very professional. The wooden scooped out ashtrays gave it a finishing touch. My friend Oover had made the requisite signs for lounge, public bar and pub name.

We stood around smoking and waiting for the judging party to arrive. My chaps were talking excitedly and were very proud of their achievement. Not a flicker of nervousness or even a mention of what might happen if we were found out. Why should they worry, I thought, looking round at their excited faces, Corporal Freeman will look after us.

The CO's eyes opened wide with surprise and astonishment as I conducted him down the corridor and opened the door to the pub.

'That's more like it, by God, you have gone to town,' he beamed as he surveyed our handiwork. My followers were standing behind the bar grinning with pride at the CO's words.

'What do you say, Doubleday, first-rate job, what?' asked the CO of the pilot officer in the entourage of four judges.

'First rate, Sir, leaves the boxes and tables we have seen so far way down the field. Where on earth did you get all the wood from, Corporal?'

I fet my men stiffen. Trust a bloody junior officer to come up with that question, I thought, as I looked him in the eye and quickly replied:

'A German civilian arranged it, Sir, through the carpentry shop.'

'Marvellous,' said the CO strutting around the lounge, 'We have one more bar to inspect but from what I've seen so far I think it's academic. Gentlemen, I believe this standard of entry deserves more than two crates of beer; what say we go to four crates, then they can entertain their rivals.'

A chorus of 'Absolutely Sir', 'Here, here', answered the CO's remarks as I stood there thinking of my lie. What if the pilot officer checks, what if word gets out from somewhere else.

'Excellent show, excellent show, only thing that lets you down is your sign. Someone can't spell, it should be VERGE you know, you'll have to have a word with your sign maker,' remarked the serious CO.

I looked at the judges, two junior officers and two flight sergeants. Their faces took on various grimaces as they looked at my pub sign and suppressed their giggles. The VIRG-INN hung proudly between the two bars.

Christmas morning. The crisp and cold air helped dispel the heads full of beer fumes, and clear the glazed bloodshot eyes, as we prepared for the perimeter track race.

The organisers were shouting through megaphones as the still half-drunk participants loaded up their vehicles at the various points around the aerodrome perimeter.

Motorcycles were the back markers and had the full four and half miles to do. Each bike had to have four bodies onboard. Cars got a half mile start but had to carry twelve bodies inside the vehicle.

Bicycles carried two people for the one and a half miles to the finish. Runners had one mile to run to the tape. All teams had to be in fancy dress.

The whole camp had turned out for the race, married families as well. The crowd of onlookers took up various vantage points round the perimeter but the majority congregated near the three 'Beer Stops' in the last mile. Each vehicle or runner had to stop three times in the last mile and all participants had to drink a pint of beer at each stop. This would be my downfall.

My newly purchased seven hundred and forty cc., shaft driven, BMW motorbike stood gleaming in the weak winter sunshine. I sat there, arms at full stretch around one of my men who was perched on the petrol tank. Two more, including Stevens, who wouldn't be left out, clung on behind. I was revving the engine and trying to see forward as final checks were made by the starters on the sixteen motorcyclists.

We could see the other groups of cars, bicycles and runners stretched around the perimeter track, everyone waiting on the starter's gun. The noise of engines ripped the crisp December air as the impatient starter shouted at a team of French mademoiselles who couldn't stay on their motorbikes for laughing. As each one lifted her colourful dress to reveal garters on stockinged legs and frilly knickers, the crowd roared their approval. These 'drag' artists had really entered into the spirit of the fancy dress. My team were Arabs, in long white sheets for robes and towels for head dress.

There was excitement in the air as the starter looked for the green flag from the other starting points.

Bang went the gun as I wound up the throttle.

'Give her the lot, Corp!' screamed Stevens in my ear as his arms crushed the breath out of me.

The bike leapt forward. I attempted to see where I was going but my face was covered in the flapping head-dress towel of the man on the petrol tank.

Stevens was shouting something as the bike bounced over rough ground but I was too intent on finding my eyesight to hear. The man on the tank was also shouting instructions as I struggled with blindness, trying to keep the bike upright.

My eyesight returned after some one-handed driving and pulling the offending towel from the head in front of me. I now had a full sight of nothing. Where was the race? We were bounding across the grass towards the hangars.

I swung the bike round and saw bodies and motorbikes in various stages of remounting at the start point. Stevens was laughing his head off as I came up to the start point again. Someone stood in our way, waving like mad. It was an Arab; what the hell was Saggers doing there, I thought. He should have been clutching on to Stevens.

I stopped to pick him up.

'You brought most of 'em down as you went straight across them,' laughed Saggers as he remounted. 'Never seen nothing like it in me life.'

We set off again with the back markers to great cheers from the crowd. My seven hundred and forty cc. German bike far outstripped most of the poor machines in the race as we zoomed past bike after bike to the shouts and vee signs of the teams.

We gained rapidly on the loaded cars that were zig-zagging along in drunken fashion. It became an obstacle race of dodging vehicles.

'Mad bastards,' rang in our ears as we approached the first beer stop.

Four foaming pints. The adjudicator stood watching as the crowd shouted their encouragement. I looked round the track as cars and motorbikes skidded to a stop around us and beer was everywhere. There was a crowd four hundred yards ahead, including a car, at the next beer stop.

'Come on, Corp, get it down,' shouted Stevens who had downed his pint in one breath. Saggers and myself still had half a glass full and were both struggling already. I took a deep breath and had another go, ensuring plenty spilled around my face and not too much down my throat.

We set off in pursuit of half a dozen cars, two motorbikes and all the bicycles and runners.

By the time we left the second beer stop the race seemed to take second place to hilarity and gamesmanship. The participants were half-drunk when they started. Now, with two pints inside them and in full party spirit, the buggeration factor came to the fore. Vehicles' speeds were now down to five or ten miles an hour as cars and bikes weaved in front of anyone trying to overtake. Choruses of rude songs vibrated from the cars as they stretched out, line abreast, bodies hanging out of windows with arms outstretched, to form a barrier.

We were approaching the line of cars, looking for a gap to get through, when a car swerved to miss a wobbling cyclist. The car hit its neighbour, the neighbour swerved into its neighbour and, in a flash, cars, motorcycles and bodies met in a great slow-motion heap of squealing brakes, scraping metal, shouts and screams and then silence. It seemed all over before it started but fortunately no serious injury occurred.

The race was abandoned but nobody cared, it had been a great laugh and put everyone in party spirit for Christmas Day.

Drinking continued in the Club and NAAFI and eventually spilled into the billets. The air was filled at lunchtime with Tannoys blaring out 'Two-way Family Favourites'.

When the programme finished, the homesick airmen lay on their beds in a stupor feeling sorry for themselves. This was the time to strike, I thought.

I climbed out of my bedroom window, my B flat cornet tied round my neck, and pulled myself up onto the flat roof of the billet. The camp was quiet as the revellers lay around in drunken stupors, some dozing, some writing to loved ones, and all taking a breather and a rest before the night's entertainment began.

I sat cross-legged, like an Indian bazaar trader, put the unmuted cornet to my lips and blasted out on the still air choruses of 'There's no place like home'. The sound of the cornet carried clear across the silent camp.

Within seconds shouts started, and a few minutes later men were erupting from billets with the intention of putting a stop to this intrusion into their melancholy reverie.

'There he is!' shouted the first arrival, pointing at me.

'Must be bloody drunk. Knock it off, Corp.'

A crowd gathered below as I played away, grinning at their amused faces.

'We're trying to get some kip, mate,' a voice shouted as a clod of earth whistled by. I continued, changing my tune to 'The Quartermaster's Stores'.

The crowd grew as the missiles increased. The whole camp came alive and gathered below. I was now on my feet, marching up and down the flat roof, dodging turf, lumps of mud and a tin mug. The crowd below were now in high spirits. Laughter, rude remarks and requests for tunes were all coming from below as I started to play 'Colonel Bogey'.

They started to sing the chorus and 'Bollocks to all the NCOs' wafted across the 'drome. There were still a few in the crowd that were set on shutting me up and, as I soaked up the attention and cheerful spirit of the majority, the water hit me.

Some bright sparks had run a hosepipe from the mains and hit me fair and square with the first onslaught. I put down my cornet, stood on the edge of the roof and raised my hands in surrender as the water jet cascaded off my chest. A great cheer, clapping and laughter ended another episode of that Christmas in 1953.

'Fizz, how would you like a fortnight on the Isle of Sylt?' asked Chiefy Adkin in the new year.

'Where's that, Chief, and what would I be doing?' I asked, only half interested.

My mind was going back to the previous day's conversation with my Chief. He had had a few words with me, probably prompted by others, about my behaviour as a corporal. It appeared I was too friendly with the other ranks and the arguments that had been going on for some time in the Corporals' Club had now reached higher ears.

Possibly it was to do with the fact that the last heated row in the Club had ended when I got hold of an off-duty snowdrop and threatened to stuff his white-topped cap down his throat.

A few corporals, mostly snowdrops and rock-apes (the name given to the newly formed RAF Regiment, whose only job was to defend the aerodrome against the invisible enemy) didn't like my preference of eating my meals with the erks instead of using the special screened-off area of the canteen set aside for corporals. 'Bad for discipline,' they said. 'Balls,' said I.

'Are you trying to get rid of me, Chief?'

'No, lad, it's good experience, you'll have a team with you. Sylt is just off the northern coast of Germany. We go there every year to train new pilots at target and gunnery practice over the sea. You'll enjoy it I'm sure; after all, you've been involved in rescue on the last two crashes here, so you know the drill.'

True enough, but it wasn't a very pleasant task being the first on the scene when a fighter aircraft ploughed into the deck. I felt ill for days after the last accident when the pilot was almost unrecognisable yet the mouth kept talking calmly. That gave me nightmares for weeks.

Sylt wasn't a true island as it was joined to the mainland by a single-track railway line set higher than sea level. As our train made for the island on that Sunday afternoon, the sea surrounded us, not five feet below the track, and it was very unsettling.

The small island had a single airstrip, a servicing hangar, living accommodation in wooden huts and a canteen. No NAAFI or other means of entertainment. The officer in charge addressed us as we disembarked:

'Your duties will be to service the squadron and provide crash recovery should you be needed, which I hope you won't. We have mostly new pilots under training and four pilot instructors. You will be confined to a one mile radius of this base. The nudist colony on the beachline is strictly out of bounds.'

The nudist colony, he said. My eyes lit up. I'd never seen a nudist colony.

We commenced work on the Monday morning as the Sabre jets and Meteor trainers flew in from Oldenburg. There wasn't much to do as we sat in the cab of our fifteen-hundredweight crash recovery truck. We were excited at the new environment, the sand-dune type scenery, the great number of small birds and the isolation of it all. The second Sabre taxied past our truck as the third turned off the end of the runway. A training Meteor was just touching down; all the usual routine, I thought, as I lit another Woodbine.

'What are we going to do at nights, Fizz, with no NAAFI to go to? We'll have to amuse our . . .'

'Christ, she's retracted,' shouted the driver as he revved the engine and pulled away.

We all saw it happen but the driver reacted first. The Meteor had approached the runway correctly with its undercarriage down but, just before the wheels touched the tarmac, the undercarriage retracted.

As we bumped across the grass following the siren-screaming ambulance, the trainer skidded down the runway streaming off a river of sparks and pieces of metal underbelly. It then ploughed off the runway into the virgin grass and came to a halt.

The convoy of rescue vehicles drew alongside as the pilot drew back the canopy and clambered out of his cockpit. The trainee pilot sat motionless, staring in disbelief at his controls. We released his harness and dragged the dead weight clear of the aircraft. He turned his head to us with an inquisitive expression on his face as though he was asking, 'What the hell do you think you're doing?'

'Come on, Jamie, wake up,' said the pilot, giving him a shake as the ambulance crew put him on a stretcher.

Foam was splashing all around us as the fire engine blanketed the aircraft. Helpers were everywhere but dear Jamie was in a world of his own.

A crash already, the first hour of our fortnight. I couldn't believe it; was this going to be the norm for the next two weeks?

We got the airbags under the wings and lifted the crumpled jet high enough to get the slings around and three hours later the useless fighter was parked near the hangar. There was nothing we could do to repair her: major surgery was required, so she was left for the experts.

For the next few days we stayed alert and expectant as the planes took off for gunnery practice over the sea, firing at targets placed in the heaving waters or targets towed by other aircraft. We watched them every second throughout their landing and breathed with relief when they taxied off the runway.

When Friday arrived and no further incidents had occurred we were back to our complacent selves, hardly noticing the activity on the runway.

'What are we going to do tomorrow?' asked Ken, a national serviceman driver of our vehicle. 'There's sod all to do round here, we'll have to kip all day, or play cards or something.'

'There's the nudist camp,' said Pinky jokingly. 'We could take our clothes off and join 'em.'

'Yeah, that would be a laugh, right enough,' replied Ken.

Flying finished at midday on Saturday and we retired, after an ample lunch and bottle of beer, to our huts.

'Who's for football?' shouted the energetic Ken but received little response. Most of the guys were set for a sleep or writing a letter. I listened to their muted conversation as I lazed on my bed in my private room.

'You going to join us, Fizz?' I heard Ken shout outside my bedroom door.

'No thanks, Ken, thinking of going for a run later.'

'I'll join you if you like,' he replied.

'Fine, give a knock in about an hour's time.'

We set off at a steady trot, not too fast, I thought, as Ken didn't look like a runner, anything but with his big belly, fat thighs and kipper feet.

'I bet you're heading for the nudist camp,' he said with a twinkle in his eye.

It had crossed my mind, just out of curiosity of course, but I hadn't planned such a move. My runs at night had been round the airstrip as it had been too dark to venture far afield. This was the first run in daylight.

'Shouldn't think there'd be anybody there in February, probably closed down for the winter,' I replied, as we puffed along through the rough sandy soil.

It was a nice crisp afternoon with pale sunshine in a bright hazy sky, ideal weather for a good healthy run.

'That officer wouldn't have warned us if it were closed,' puffed the thinking Ken.

That's true, I thought, but I can't imagine people leaping about in the nude in this weather.

'I'm game if you are,' gasped Ken.

'I should give over talking if I were you, you'll be knackered soon.' Poor Ken was gasping after the first mile so we settled to walk a spell.

It was very quiet, just the noise of the sea and the screech of the seagulls, not a soul in sight, as we topped a grass-covered sand-dune and made for the general direction of the beach.

'Look, there's some log cabins and smoke coming from the chimneys. I wonder if that's it?' said Ken, pointing far to the left.

The sea was racing up the beach a half mile in front of us.

'Doesn't look like a nudist camp to me,' I said, having no idea what a nudist camp would look like. 'Let's go on to the beach and make our way along the water's edge towards the cabins, can't do any harm.'

We trotted along the beach eyeing suspiciously the cosy-looking log cabins from a distance. We were running at the water's edge and about four hundred yards from the encampment which lay well back off the beach.

As we drew nearer, voices wafted across to us in gutteral German cries; something seemed to be going on behind the row of cabins. We trotted on nervously and were in line with the first cabin in the row, but thirty yards of beach separated us.

'Guten Tag, meine Herren. Sie sind Engländer, nicht?'

Two great hairy Germans, wearing only sandals, appeared from between the cabins and beckoned us towards them. Mesmerized by the power of nudity and their large smiling faces, we approached at the jog.

'Bluff it out, leave the talking to me,' I said out the side of my mouth as we approached the grinning nudes.

'Bier? Ja?' asked the bearded one, gesturing with his hand and arms.

'Danke schön,' I replied in my pidgin German as we came to a stop in front of them, keeping our eyes pinned to their faces.

'Gustav,' said Hairy, pushing his hand out.

'Bob,' I said, 'this is Ken,' as we shook hands.

'Velcome, velcome, Bop and Ken, this is Fritz.'

'Kommen Sie hier, bitte,' he beckoned as they both turned to lead the way between the huts.

We followed the big bums, one totally covered in black hair, the other hairless but hanging like a hammock. As Ken and I looked at one another, his cheeks puffed out and his eyebrows raised ready to burst with laughter. My God, what have we got here? I was thinking as I winked at Ken.

We walked towards the hilarity and shouting. Rounding the hut corner we looked from our shaded position on a mass of agitated human flesh cavorting with careless abandonment. Each side of a high net, long elongated breasts flopped up and down like collies' ears. Fat bums, big bellies and various shapes and sizes of German *Bratwürste*, dangled, wobbled, heaved, and flapped, as the ageing volleyball players gave their all in an attempt to recapture their youth.

Gustav's words brought the game to a halt and the sweating players surrounded the two clothed runners. As hands were shaken and greetings exchanged by the leather-skinned, ageing population, who showed not a flicker of embarrassment, an angel appeared from one of the log cabins.

As I shook her pure white hand my eyes took in the stark beauty of her twenty-year-old body. Her sharp featured face and high forehead was crowned with the longest blonde hair I'd ever seen. It cascaded down her back over her beautiful small bottom. Her pert, beautifully matched breasts curved proudly upwards and her slim waist, against wide, child-bearing hips, gave her six-foot frame a classical touch.

Beauty I'd never seen or dreamed of before stood before me and I was breathless. A mermaid, that's what I thought she was.

'Beer,' she said again, bringing me out of my coma and trying to release her hand from mine. Her pale blue eyes told me she knew what I was thinking.

'Danke, danke,' I said, releasing her hand, but not her body from my eyes.

I glanced at Ken as we both walked uncomfortably amid the nudist throng to one of the cabins. Some of them spoke good English and as they assumed we were pilots, we let them continue to assume so.

They relaxed in front of a glorious log fire in the large open hearth as steins of beer were handed round. My mermaid had disappeared into the kitchen and only the grotesque and obese surrounded us.

Their little colony or club were mostly retired people who came over from the mainland at weekends during winter, but who lived there during the summer months. They were very happy people and I envied their contentment and child-like happiness.

We were entertained to a few rousing German songs and they seemed genuinely pleased to have visitors; in fact it was difficult to get away. Only after we'd promised to come back again did they let us go. Half-drunk and still in a dream, we shook a million hands, and devoured a multitude of ageing flesh. A memorable ten seconds of the beautiful, desirable mermaid and we were returned to reality as we staggered through the dusk back to whence we had come.

'Christ, Fizz, I'd crawl over broken glass for that blonde girl, wouldn't you? When are we going again?'

'Yeah, she was the most beautiful thing I've ever seen. Christ, what a cracker.'

'The guys will never believe our story, they'll say we're swinging the lamp,' said Ken.

'They won't, Ken, 'cause you aren't going to tell them. Not a bloody word to anybody and I mean it.'

'Oh hell – still I suppose you're right. Shall we go again, though?'

'I'm not, Ken. I don't push my luck nowadays. You do what you like, but don't implicate me. When we get in just say we got lost and that's why we've been out so long.'

'Fair enough,' said Ken, realizing by my tone of voice that I meant business. In the event, Ken was too shattered to talk and when we eventually arrived back he flopped on his bed in a heap. I lay on my bed sweating, thinking of my mermaid and reliving those glorious seconds together.

The following week passed slowly and boringly as we did our serving checks and stood by on crash recovery. By Friday we were becoming excited at the prospect of returning to Oldenburg and taking up our normal pursuits.

'Bloody boring detachment this is, shan't volunteer again,' said Pinky the armourer, as we sat in the truck playing crib.

'The only good thing is that we haven't spent any money,' said Ken, winking at me and bringing back memories of my mermaid.

'Funny though,' said Alec, the fourth member of the crib team. 'We get a prang in the first hour here and nothing since. I thought it would be prangs every day the way it started.'

'Bloody good job it . . .'

Screaming sirens interrupted Bill's reply as we looked towards the runway. A jet trainer was skidding on its steel trellised cockpit down the runway.

'Christ, she flipped over,' screamed Pinky as Ken struggled to find his gear-lever between Alec's legs.

We shot across the grass, four in the cab, bumping our heads on the roof as the truck was thrown around on the uneven ground.

Ken was driving like a madman as we overtook the fire-tender and ambulance. He screeched to a halt and we all shot against the windscreen. Bill was out first and I followed, as we sprinted for the cockpit. The other crash vehicles arrived and as their engines were switched off we heard the terrifying screaming. It was coming from the front cockpit. We must have both looked at the same time and a stream of vomit cascaded from Bill's mouth as we knelt on the tarmac looking in at the trainee pilot hanging upside down in his harness.

His legs had been smashed below the knee and were hanging downwards. Blood was running down his neck and upside-down face. His eyes were full of blood as he blinked madly to maintain vision. His head was turned towards us as his mouth screamed amongst the streaming blood. His eyes were pleading for help. He hung there, screaming, terrified and helpless.

'Can you break that side panel, Fizz? I've got to get at him to give him morphine,' said the first aid Chief beside me.

I smashed the thick perspex canopy panel with a hatchet as foam rained down on us. The medic broke off the end of two glass phials and unceremoniously jabbed them into the neck of the screaming, dangling trainee pilot. Within seconds the screaming was transformed into moans. The pilot in the rear cockpit seemed to be uninjured and fully conscious.

'Get her raised up as quick as you can, Corporal,' ordered an officer, as though I didn't already know that.

My men were putting the airbags under the inverted mainplanes as I redirected the crane gang to place one of the slings further forward of the cockpit. Better to have belt and braces, I thought, as I didn't want the aircraft to pivot on its nose.

The CO and most of the men were now congregated around the foam-covered aircraft as she started to rise from the ground.

'Not too far, hold it there,' shouted the officer in charge.

Many willing hands prised back the canopies and the medics went to work. They lay on their backs supporting the weight of the still moaning trainee pilot, his harness was released, and his body lowered to the grass.

The pilot was next. He stayed calm and talkative as he was gently released and taken off in the ambulance with his colleague. The whole operation had taken only forty minutes. The intensity and seriousness of the situation had forced us to carry out our duties while controlling our emotions, but when the ambulance had left I started to shake all over. Nobody wanted to talk as I stood there trying to control my limbs. I sank to the floor by the side of the truck.

'Have a fag, Fizz,' said Ken, handing me a lighted cigarette. He hadn't been involved other than in driving. 'Shall I nip to the cookhouse for a brew?'

'Yes, Ken, good idea, get plenty.'

We worked like robots getting the crashed aircraft moved to a safer refuge so that the airstrip could be used again. Then each man retired into his private thoughts as the last day at Sylt drew to a close.

I went off my food for a week. I could not get the picture of that trainee pilot's blood-covered eyes and mouth out of my mind. We were informed later that he had recovered from his injuries but whether his legs were saved we had no idea.

We settled back into the routine of Oldenburg and I was writing letters planning my wedding to Rosa. We would have been married before but for the opposition. I remember a visit to her grandmother's house when we first announced our intention to marry. Rosa always visited her Gran on a Sunday and often during the week. One of Gran's unmarried daughters, Auntie Louie, lived with her and cared for the ninety-year-old lady.

Sunday tea was a family ritual. As well as the resident spinster Auntie Louie, her two sisters, Auntie Emily and Auntie Nelly were always there with their husbands, both married couples being childless. They thought the world of Rosa and helped finance her upbringing as her widowed Mother didn't work and had little income. Dainty sandwiches, seed cake and queen buns were the standard bill of fare and the excitement of the evening came after tea was cleared away. Two hours of cards, played for a halfpenny a hand with such vigour and excitement, one could be forgiven for thinking it was Monte Carlo, with a thousand-pound pot.

The Sunday we announced the good news a cold shadow descended on the throng. After some furtive glances and whispering behind hands, Nellie's husband Uncle Jim ushered me, with a cold-eyed smile, into the sanctuary of the holier than holies, the front room. Given a glass of sherry, I sat alone on the high-backed horsehair sofa and was watched over by two porcelain dogs, one each side of the brass fender round the hearth. The door was firmly closed and the meeting at the high altar commenced. I strained my ears to catch the conversation as poor Rosa was bombarded from all directions.

'You're too young, Rosa, wait another couple of years, there's plenty of time yet,' pleaded Auntie Nellie.

'You want to find a nice local boy, these RAF people are never at home, you'd see nothing of him, love,' said the caring Louie.

'He'll never make anything of himself, those RAF types never do, anyway, he's not even in a union,' slipped in Uncle Jim, the shop convener at Lysaght's Steel Works.

And so it went on for over half an hour. Rosa could not be persuaded to change her mind and misery descended on the household. We ate our tea almost in silence. After tea we went for a walk rather than suffer the card game. Not one word of congratulations came my way that night.

After eight happy months at Oldenburg I went home to marry Rosa. The ceremony took place on 23 June 1954 at St. Hugh's Church in Ashby, Scunthorpe. We spent a memorable ten day's honeymoon in Scarborough, then Rosa went to live with my parents at Brentwood, Essex.

I arrived back at Oldenburg feeling on top of the world. Within two weeks I took part in the Second Tactical Air Force's Annual Athletics Championships and set a new record for the one hundred and twenty yard hurdles. So much for married life, I thought. I was fit, I was happy and enjoying my service life. My corporal's pay was now supplemented by a married allowance for Rosa. She had a good job as a cashier at the Co-op in Billericay. I had passed my Technical Sergeant's exam but had to wait a further year for my service qualification before becoming a sergeant.

How life had changed, I thought, as I sat writing to Rosa. I often thought of Wingco Elliott and silently thanked him for giving me this new start in life. My old life seemed far away now. I no longer looked over my shoulder waiting and expecting trouble. I seemed to have a different outlook on life altogether. In a year's time I could be a sergeant and Rosa could be living with me in married quarters. I was even thinking seriously of signing on if all my dreams came true.

Life in the RAF could be a good life, I decided. I had a lot to thank my favourite, understanding Wingco for, if I ever met him again. Where might I have been without him? I shuddered at the thought.

Life settled down into the routine of enjoying the work and camaraderie of the hangar, with plenty of sport and social life in the club. The weeks flew by as Rosa's regular letters piled up in my special tin box, each letter having been read a dozen times. I just could not wait for my next leave, which seemed a long way off. We only got our entitlement every six months, so I was due again at Christmas, four months to go.

One day, out of the blue, at ten o'clock on the Tuesday morning I was sent for by the Wing Commander.

'Corporal,' he said, as I stood in bewilderment in his office, 'You're wanted back at Hemswell, some sort of inquiry, I know no more than that. There's an escort outside that will accompany you. You leave today. I hope we see you back here soon,' and he called in the military escort.

I looked at the two snowdrops in total disbelief and fear.

'Am I under arrest, Sir?' I asked.

'Technically, yes, these men have been sent out to escort you back but I'm sure it won't be a formal affair,' he said, looking at the two snowdrops. I was shattered.

CHAPTER 23

The Inquiry

We travelled by train to the Hook of Holland. My mind searched every avenue of my past life at Hemswell for the reason for my arrest but to no avail. Frightening pictures of my past life flashed before me. The terrifying fears returned a hundredfold. If my two escorts knew the reason for my arrest or the nature of the inquiry they weren't saying. Three corporals together, they tried to chat and be friendly.

'Let's have a hand of cards to pass the time,' said one, producing a well-soiled pack.

'No, thanks.'

Maybe it wasn't to do with Hemswell. Maybe that's just where the inquiry was. I started to think of St. Athans, no, nothing there. North Luffenham then, only the red and green cartridges, no, it couldn't be that. Topcliffe, couldn't be Topcliffe, only place I had a clean sheet. It had to be Hemswell.

We caught the night sailing to Harwich and I spent a restless night tossing and turning in my canvas hammock-type bed, fourth up from the floor and next to the throbbing engines in the bowels of the ship.

Two trains later we arrived at Gainsborough railway station and a car was sent to pick us up.

As the car entered the long drive from the main road to the guardroom my heart sank to a new low. The fear of not knowing what was about to happen, what I'd done, why I was wanted, left me desolate. I was weaker in resolve at that moment than I'd ever been. I didn't know what I was up against so I couldn't prepare. Maybe I'd gone soft after nearly a year as a corporal. I knew one thing, I was scared and totally vulnerable.

'You'd better kip down in here for the night,' said the duty snowdrop as the three of us entered the familiar guardroom.

I looked into cell one, a familiar home that I'd stayed in often. It was now dark and too late to expect any action until morning. Another night of not knowing, I thought.

'Get washed up and we'll go find a meal,' said my still friendly snowdrop companions. The duty snowdrop, whose face was new to me, continued to read his newspaper. No one seemed the slightest bit interested in my arrival and although it calmed me down it didn't stop the gnawing worry in my guts.

They gave me extra bedding that night, the privilege of rank again. My door was left open, so I wasn't classed as a prisoner, or so I thought. Sleep wouldn't come. I lay there fully dressed, digging over the same ground but, try as I might, I could not think of anything that I hadn't already paid my debt for.

I thought of Rosa sleeping at home in Brentwood. At least she didn't know what was happening and that was a blessing. The more I thought the more despondent I got. Just when everything had been going well, just when life looked grand, fate had to deal this card. I could feel another change in my life was about to happen, but what would that be?

'Want a brew, mate?' said the snowdrop, handing me a mug of tea. 'Can't sleep, eh?'

'Thanks, mate, no, nor would you if you'd been dragged back from Germany without a word of explanation. Come on, mate, what's it all about? You must know, I won't let on you told me,' I pleaded.

It was well past midnight as he sat on the end of my mahogany plank bed sipping his tea. No other prisoners were in custody; we had the guardroom to ourselves.

'Sorry, mate, orders, you know. They'd have my balls off if I said anything.'

'You do know, then?'

'Sorry, mate, drink your tea and try to get some rest,' and he got up and left the cell.

I must have dozed off eventually out of sheer exhaustion. I hadn't slept the previous night on the boat and had been using up nervous energy since I left the Wingco's office at Oldenburg.

'Wake up, mate, better get washed if I were you. You're due in the admin. block at nine.'

I was sitting on one side of an eight by two foot table at the end of the conference room. It was five minutes to nine. One snowdrop escort stood at ease inside the room with his back to the door. We waited in silence.

There was a small desk and chair to the right of my table and two chairs over by the door. The large room, which in my day had contained a long centre table and twenty chairs, plus other smaller tables and display boards, looked empty and felt cold and depressing. Many a happy hour had been spent in the same room during my three years at Hemswell organizing camp concerts and gala days. This time I sat waiting my fate.

Footsteps were the first thing that set my nerves tingling; quick jumbled-up footsteps came up the passage from the front entrance rattling on the wooden linoed floor. The door burst open as the snowdrop guard jumped out of the way. A busy sergeant, hair slicked down on his small head and rimless clear glasses, strode into the room clutching a cardboard file. A corporal followed the sergeant and he made straight for one of the two chairs by the door and sat down. A WAAF LAC brought up the rear. She was carrying a briefcase and took her seat at the small desk, opened her briefcase and arranged the files and note pads.

'Corporal Freeman, 1920683 Corporal Freeman, to be precise. We have got the right man I hope,' said the beaming five-foot four-inch sergeant, glancing at his open file.

'That's correct, Sergeant,' I said, rising.

'Stay seated, Corporal,' he beamed. 'Important to establish the correct identity for the records, of course,' he said, standing with his cardboard file open in his hands. 'Be silly to ask the wrong man the wrong questions wouldn't it?'

I sat there, unimpressed. I never did trust short arses; in my experience, they always had a chip on their shoulder.

'Now, this shouldn't take long, a few questions, a few answers, a signature and you can be on your way back to Germany tonight.' More huge grins.

'What's the inquiry about, Sergeant? No one's told me anything so far.'

'All in good time, Corporal, all in good time. Pure routine and tidying up details. You're the last of dozens. Now, where were we? Ah, yes. Corporal Carol over there is a witness to our conversation, and to see fair play of course. LAC Wooley is recording our conversation.'

I didn't like this man, I could feel he was putting on an act, baiting a trap. Within minutes I had him taped as a devious bastard. I'd need all my wits about me with this fella. If only he would say what it was all about I might stand a chance of preparing some sort of defence, but no, he held all the aces.

'How long were you at Hemswell, Corporal?'

He had his files, he knew how long I'd been stationed there, why ask?

'Three years, Sergeant.'

'Yes, three years. Quite a bit of it spent in detention by the look of it. You seemed to attract trouble, Corporal, or were you just unlucky?'

A big sarcastic smile spread over his mean shifty face. No answer was my reply as I stared back at the calm and confident inquisitor.

'No, I don't think you were unlucky, Corporal; I mean, racing a water tanker around the aerodrome perimeter track for a bet, that's nothing to do with luck – more like stupidity. Now this one's different,' he said, staring at his notes, 'Using the front entrance of the medical centre, now that was unlucky that you got caught, wasn't it?'

I still stared at him, trying to fathom his approach. Was this the softening-up session? Whatever it was, it was getting on my nerves, tension was rising and I was becoming increasingly frustrated.

'What's the point of these stupid questions, Sergeant? They're in the past, I paid for them.'

'Now don't get lippy, Corporal, I'm conducting this inquiry. You'll do yourself no good by getting shirty. I'm establishing your background, that's all. Now, where were we?' he said, turning over pages in his file.

I stared out of the window behind him and could see clearly across the road to the sports field. The bright August sun was shining down on two chaps kicking a football to one another. I could see the coconut matting cricket strip where Freddie Trueman had fired down his bouncers and shattered Rudy's wicket. Happy days with Spiv and the gang.

'Ah yes, gambling, a regular gambler, weren't you? Poker, I think, yes, that's it, it's here. Twice inside for gambling and plenty of insubordination by the look of it. Did you like being the centre of attraction? Did you crave to be popular amongst the ranks? Were you a hero to the national servicemen, a hard man, eh? I can see your type now. How you ever got your stripes is beyond me.'

His smile had now left his face and his close piggy eyes bored into me. The crunch was coming, I could feel it, but I just stared back at him defiantly. Do your worst, you bastard, I thought. His face broke into his slimy smile again.

'How long have you had your best blue?'

This unexpected change of tack had me rattled. Why ask about my uniform, for Christsake? Was this a diversionary tactic to get me off balance, to catch me out? I couldn't connect the question anywhere.

'About eighteen months or so.'

'Eighteen months, I see. Your shirt looks new, how old is that?'

'I haven't a clue. I'm always buying shirts.'

'Always buying shirts, like to keep smart, do you? How many pairs of boots and shoes have you got?'

'Two pairs of each. What's all this about, Sergeant, a bloody verbal kit inspection by the sound of it?' I said, as I lost my temper at the stupidity of the proceedings.

'Just remember where you are, Corporal. This is an official inquiry and I will conduct it any way I see fit. You're doing yourself no good at all with these outbursts. Just answer the questions and mind your language.'

'Inquiry into what, Sergeant? You haven't told me yet,' I spat at him sharply.

'You'll know soon enough. In the meantime we will continue, if you don't mind. Now, were you a good gambler – I mean – a winner or a loser?' And that greasy smile again. What was this guy aiming at? I could not even guess where all this was leading.

'Sometimes I won, sometimes I lost. Where's all this leading, Sergeant?'

'Just answer the questions, Corporal,' he said, growing impatient with my continual interruption to his flow.

'Over all, over the whole time you were gambling, would you say you ended up a winner or a loser?'

Nosey bastard, what had that got to do with anything?

'I don't see what that's got to do with the RAF, Sergeant; that's my business,' I said defiantly.

'You'll answer the question, Corporal or take the consequences, now, winner or loser, which were you?'

'Private life, Sergeant. Nothing to do with the RAF. I've paid the price so you can ask all you like.'

'Stand up, Corporal,' he shouted, totally losing his temper.

The other corporal witness jumped up at this unexpected turn of events. The WAAF note taker looked up at me with a nervous twitch to her cheeks. The snowdrop was also on his feet.

I towered nine inches above the bespectacled runt and glared down at him as he glared up at me. He was no doubt wishing he hadn't ordered me to stand now that he had to strain his neck to look up at me. I stretched myself to my full six-foot one-inch height. Now, you bugger, what's next?

'I'll ask you the question once more. Think carefully before you answer. Refusing to answer a question can be a serious offence. I will wipe from the records what's gone before. Now – in your three years of gambling, did you end up a winner or loser?' he asked, quietly and breathlessly.

You could hear a fly rubbing its back legs, it was so quiet. Four sets of eyes were staring at me, as breath was held back. I looked straight down into his cold goldfish eyes, defiant in every sinew of my body. At last I had something to grasp hold of after two days of misery lost in a fog.

'Private life, Sergeant. My business, nothing to do with the RAF,' I whispered.

His face turned to beetroot as his piggy eyes tried to widen. Impasse. He was lost. The unexpected had turned the tables. A shower of spit erupted from his mean thin lips.

'Inquiry adjourned,' he spat out as he turned and rapidly left the room. His two aides followed at the scramble.

Back in the guardroom I literally sweated it out in the oppressive heat of the summer day. No word as to when the inquiry would continue, no word as to whether I'd be required again, no word of what to do with me.

Whether the inquiry team were seeing other people I doubted, unless they were kept somewhere else, and that seemed unlikely.

'Any news, Sergeant?' I asked the sergeant of the guard who'd just walked in from his lunch.

'What sort of news? – shot at dawn is the rumour,' he grinned as he checked the duty roster chart. This new sergeant was a definite improvement on his predecessor, or was it that I was a corporal and only technically a 'visitor'.

I lay around all afternoon waiting for the call that never came. The evening meal was as embarrassing as lunch, seeing a lot of faces that knew me, answering embarrassing questions.

'Couldn't stay away, eh, Fizz? Come back for a holiday?' asked Wagger, an old sweat of a corporal and well respected as a wisehead.

'Something like that, Wagger; how goes it with you, getting plenty?'

'Bet your sweet life. Everything is fine, Fizz.'

I couldn't talk freely with the snowdrop escort hanging on every word but I dearly wanted to ask two questions.

'Is Wingco Elliott still here, Wagger?' I asked nonchalantly, sure in the knowledge of getting the affirmative.

'No, retired three months ago, same time that Chiefy Blackmore went to Odiham, bad day for the flight that was; still the new Wingco and Chiefy are good sorts.'

Depression, shock. Wagger had answered my two questions at one go. I'd lost both my benefactors. In my rambling thoughts I was clinging to the hope of assistance or help if things got tough. Fate had dealt another card, a black ace.

That night I went over every word of the inquiry. Previous charges seemed to interest the Sergeant. Then it was my uniform, shirts and shoes. Then it was gambling. 'Was I a loser or a winner?' Why that question? It had to be something to do with money, yes, that's it, money. Maybe the cashier's safe had been broken into. I thought about that. No, couldn't be. I'd been left nearly a year, it wouldn't take a year to investigate that.

The post office, why not a break-in at the post office?

Long investigation, tracing all the regular users, questioning, statements, yeah, that could be it and it fitted. I was a regular user so I'd been put on the list of suspects. Ah, but hang on, that would be a civilian police investigation or at least a joint effort. No, it couldn't be the post office.

Midnight again as I looked at my watch.

'Any tea, mate, I'm sweating cobs,' I said, looking round my cell door.

'Two heads, one thought, I'm just off to make some, mate, don't bugger off, will you?' he said with a laugh.

I was either growing older or my stripes and service changed the jailers, because these snowdrops were almost human. Mind you, many of them had only served a few months of their eighteen-months conscription period. When they came up against over six years' service and two stripes some respect was shown. No doubt they could change like the chameleon bastards they all were when they had the upper hand.

Suicide, one of the regular card school had committed suicide. Yeah, that could be it. Lost a lot of money at cards, pinched some maybe, could see no way out and did himself in.

I went through the card players I could remember. There had been so many of them over the years. My mind stopped at one particular game. King George VI's official birthday. We always had a parade and march-past in the morning, then the rest of the day off. I'll never forget that day. The card school was well into its stride when all six players decided to stay in and bet. I was 'blind' with one other chap. The other four had to double our stake. We stayed blind as the kitty got bigger and bigger. They were betting like idiots. Over seventy pounds was in the pot before two players folded. The other blind bloke looked and stacked. The pot rose to one hundred and eleven pounds. A hell of a lot of money to a ranker. One sighted player and I were left. I nonchalantly glanced at my cards. A running flush, Christ, my lucky day. I pushed for the sky and threw in twenty. He had to see me. His prile of kings hadn't a chance. I picked up one hundred and fifty-one quid, the biggest pot we'd ever had. Peter was his name. Peter Bingley, stores GD. He never played again. No, it couldn't be suicide, that would be civilian police again, surely. I seemed to spend all night going over my past life as I tossed and turned in my mahogany bed.

'Wake up, mate, get washed up and we'll go to breakfast.'
'What time does the inquiry start?'
'No idea, mate, I'm off duty at nine anyway.'

I hung around the guardroom all morning. Maybe this is their way of breaking down my resistance. Keep him on tenterhooks, get him depressed, play him along like a fish. He'll be glad to do or say anything to get back to his mates in Germany, if we can get him depressed enough.

I intended to show a calm exterior although I was boiling inside. I felt sure the snowdrops were reporting back to the midget sergeant so I put on a calm, confident air, and stopped asking questions. All I wanted was my good life, back in Oldenburg.

At ten to two I was marched over to the inquiry team again. I felt relieved that something was happening but also apprehensive at what the outcome might be. I sat there waiting, trying to control my mixed emotions and thoughts, trying to make my face look confident and untroubled.

The footsteps came scrambling up the corridor. Whoosh, the Brylcreemed midget stood grinning in front of me. He'd had a few drinks I reckoned. His two lieutenants took up their usual positions.

'Well, Corporal, I've had time to talk to one or two people who know you well. It seems you're a real Jekyll and Hyde character: a good athlete I understand, ran the dance band as well, quite a character by all accounts. In view of this I'm prepared to forget what happened yesterday if you agree to co-operate for the rest of the inquiry. I'm anxious to get back to headquarters for more urgent work. We can tie this up this afternoon with your help. What do you say?'

'That suits me fine, Sergeant.'

'Good, good, let's get at it, then. I'm going to come straight to the point – that's what you wanted, wasn't it? – although you've no doubt guessed what it's all about as you were involved in it.' He looked at me with a knowing sly smile, judging my reaction to his words.

'I haven't a clue what you're referring to, Sergeant.'

The smile disappeared from his face.

'In February the external auditors made a spot check on Hemswell stores and found large quantities of stock missing. Naturally I was informed and immediately commenced an investigation. That investigation has led to you.' He paused for effect, stabbing me with the intensity of his eyes, looking for signs of guilt, watching my every reaction.

'I still don't know what you're on about, I've had nothing to do with the stores, ever.' I glared back at him.

My mind was in turmoil. I'd hardly ever been in the stores, never mind swiping anything. Surely they weren't going to pin robbery on me.

'You might not have actually stolen the goods yourself but you received them, which is the same thing. I have signed statements to that effect. You see, we have the culprits, friends of yours from your card school. They have been dealt with and are under lock and key. I just need your signed statement that you received certain items from them and you can go,' he smiled hopefully.

I was more than amazed, I was staggered. Firstly, I knew absolutely nothing about a stores fiddle at Hemswell or anywhere else. I'd never had free clothing or illegally purchased clothing from anyone. Only one Stores GD ever joined our card school and that was Peter Bingley. Bingley was a regular career man and even if he'd been involved I felt sure he wouldn't implicate others, he wasn't that sort of guy. No, I calculated that his measly sergeant was clutching at straws.

'There's no way I'm signing for something I didn't do, Sergeant. This is all news to me. Can I see the statements involving me, please?'

'Don't make it hard on yourself, Corporal, I have proof. All statements are confidential to the inquiry. Your best bet is to sign and get it over with.'

'I've never had so much as a bootlace from stores without paying for it so I'm sure I'm not signing for something I've never had.'

He strode across the room to the notetaker's desk and looked through a few files stacked neatly in front of her. Taking a sheet of paper from one of the files he retraced his steps and placed it in front of me. My eyes caught the WAAF notetaker's eyes and they held mine for a fleeting second. They were sympathetic, trying to tell me something, believing my story, I'm sure of that.

'Read that, Corporal. You can change a word here and there if you want. It lists what we know you've had from the stores, not much I might add, some have had a lot more. You can alter the words a bit and after you've signed it we can close the chapter on the whole episode.' He was staying calm and trying to be persuasive.

I glanced down at the paper. I felt all eyes were on me. How I wished I could talk privately to the WAAF; she knew what was going on. A Mosquito swooped low over the admin. block; I'd recognise those Merlin engines anywhere. I thought of Soco and his death. What a bloody horrible world.

I glanced at the sheet of paper again, my mind full of other things. My eyes were attracted to an inset paragraph which was a list of items I had supposedly received. One best blue uniform, four pairs of trousers, two pairs of shoes, four shirts, two ties, one pair of plimsolls, two cap badges.

'Lies, Sergeant, it's all lies. If I'd had anything I would admit it, but that's all lies,' I said, pushing the statement across the desk towards him. He glared at me, showing his annoyance and impatience. The statement was ignored.

'I've heard it all before, Corporal, a million times before. So you want to be difficult, do you?' and he strode across the room again and selected another file from the WAAF's desk. He returned and stood in front of me.

'You joined up as a boy entrant in October 1947. I make that six years and nine months ago. In that period your record of purchases from the stores, payable through deductions from your pay, have amounted to, one pair of trousers, two shirts, one pair of boots and two berets. Now, are you telling me that just about all your kit has lasted over six and a half years? By your own admission, only yesterday, you stated, and we recorded, that the best blue uniform you're now wearing is only eighteen months old. Need I go on, Corporal? Just sign that paper and be done with it,' he said triumphantly.

I sat there trying to absorb what he'd just said. I never realized I had purchased so little and it never dawned on me that such records were kept. It certainly looked bad from their suspicious eyes but the facts were different. Ever since my time in the Locking guardhouse when I met Gibbons, I'd taken his advice and bought my uniforms and kit from an Army Surplus store in Romford, just seven miles from Brentwood. Some of the prices were cheaper than the RAF charged and you always had a good selection and personal service.

'Sergeant, I repeat that I have never received any kit from anybody other than through normal channels. I have purchased most of my uniforms and kit from an Army Surplus store. That's why my records don't show much, and I'm not signing for something I haven't done.'

'I was warned you'd be difficult, Freeman,' he sneered, dropping the 'Corporal', as venom came out of his eyes. 'I've been easy on you so far but I can play awkward if that's how you want it. You're only making it worse for yourself. You'll stay in custody until this matter is finished to my satisfaction. I've heard all these excuses before, Freeman; they're rubbish, lies, unless of course you can produce the receipts.' He raised his eyebrows enquiringly as his eyes sneered down his pencil-thin nose.

He had me there. What guy keeps receipts? What reason would I have to hang on to bits of paper? I could never have guessed that I'd be asked to account for where I got my kit.

'No, Sergeant. Why would I want to keep receipts? I didn't know this was going to happen, but it doesn't alter the facts, that's where I got my kit.'

He looked at me with an attempt at a fatherly smile. 'Got you', it said. In a quiet restrained voice he said:

'No, Corporal, I didn't think you'd have receipts. Your word against my evidence. Accept it lad, you've lost. Sign the paper and let's forget all about it, eh?'

All eyes focused back on me. I went weak. I was tempted to get it over with. It would be goodbye stripes for sure, back in the ranks, LAC Freeman again. Probably another posting. What would Rosa think?

I looked past my inquisitor and out of the window. Some lively erks were setting up three cricket stumps at the end of the coconut matting. A chap was chipping golf balls at the far edge of the sports field, an officer I suppose; it was a 'posh' sport for the rich. The officers had a squash court near this mess. I'd played on it a couple of times. The flight lieutenant in charge of the athletics team had given me permission. I didn't know how to play squash so I'd just hit the ball and chased it, good training for sprinters and I'd enjoyed it. An officer had come along one day as I was playing.

'Aren't you an airman?' he said, annoyed, as he looked down from the balcony.

'Yes, Sir.'

'Well, what do you think you are doing; this court is for officers only?'

'Flight Lieutenant Jones gave me permission, Sir.'

'Did he now? We'll see about that. Off you go.'

I never did play squash again at Hemswell. The thought of that incident raised my blood pressure again. Unfairness everywhere you turn. Sod the RAF.

'Come on, Corporal, just sign at the bottom and I'll get your travel warrant and you can be away,' he said, picking up his pen that had been lying in front of me, and holding it out.

'I'll not sign for what I haven't done, Sergeant; I don't care what you do to me, I won't sign,' I said quickly, with heaving chest.

'Then I'll throw the bloody book at you, that's what I'll do,' he spat out. 'I've run out of patience with you, Corporal. I've given you a chance, I've tried to make it easy. The evidence is staring you in the face and your defence is nil.'

He paused for breath as he paced up and down in front of my table. He stopped and stood motionless. Silence filled the long room as he looked out of the window, trying to control his temper. He turned quickly, indicated for his corporal to join him and went out into the passage. I was left with the snowdrop and the WAAF. I looked at her as she leaned forward over her notepad, pen in hand. Her eyes came up to mine and a wisp of a smile touched her cheeks. My tense jaw relaxed as I tried to interpret her thoughts.

The door opened and the connivers returned.

'Against my better judgement, Corporal, I've decided to let you sleep on it. Think of the evidence against you. Think of the consequences if you continue to refuse to sign. I'm sure when you have thought it through you'll realise it's in your best interest to sign the statement and clear this matter up. We'll resume again tomorrow.'

As I went back to the guardroom with my escort I felt completely drained. How happy I'd been just a week ago. I had even been thinking of signing on. Now, a week later, my whole world had changed. The past, that I thought I'd buried, had now been dug up in full measure. The rebellious and awkward attitudes that had been my way of life for so many years had been converted into a responsible and fairly disciplined outlook, thanks to the perception and faith of Wing Commander Elliott. Now all this good work had been negated in one monstrously unjust, trumped-up charge. I was shattered. If they had got me for something I'd actually done then I could accept it, but all I'd been accused of these last two days was totally unjustified. I had no idea how I could prove my innocence. If he had got a signed statement naming me as a receiver of stolen goods then there was no way out, but I couldn't believe he had such a document. I reasoned that the regulars from the card school had been implicated in some way, including Bingley. Bingley had been 'inside' with Spike and me for gambling. It doesn't take Sherlock Holmes to link Bingley's extra financial income from missing stores goods with the card school players. Yes, that was it, I'd bet a year's pay that all my card-playing mates had been subjected to an inquiry grilling. They would all be as surprised and nonplussed as I was, but they'd all have a stronger case than me. Not one of them purchased their kit from an Army Surplus store to my knowledge. They should have full records of purchasing through the RAF. That surely made the shortarse sergeant's job nearly impossible, but it also made my case look worse. If the inquisitor sergeant couldn't pin anything on them, and I'm sure he couldn't, he'd try all the harder to pin it on me.

I tossed and turned throughout the night and was roused as usual by the duty snowdrop.

'Come on, mate, take a swig of this. Friday today and I'm off on weekend pass,' he said cheerily, handing me a brew.

Friday – four days since the Wingco had sent for me, it seemed like four years. I felt numb in the head, my body was tired, how much longer would this nightmare go on? I asked myself.

We started again at nine o'clock. The relaxed, smiling, piggy face beamed down on me.

'Friday, Corporal, the weekend before us to enjoy ourselves. The sooner we're done the sooner we're off, eh?' he said, unscrewing the top of his fountain pen.

'Now you've thought about it I'm sure you realize it's in your interest to clear this matter up, close the chapter, get back to work, eh?' and he pushed the typed statement towards me and proferred his pen.

She was looking at me again, I could feel her eyes; so were the two corporals. Eight eyes focused on my face. An expectant hush held the room. I took a deep breath and tried to control my thumping heart, as I slowly and quietly replied,

'No, Sergeant, I've said it before. I didn't receive these listed items and I'm not signing to say I did.'

Silence in the room. His teeth clenched, his lips pursed and his jaw muscles vibrated as he stood there staring straight into my eyes. My face muscles tightened as I held his gaze. It seemed ages before he let out his breath.

'Right, Corporal, enough of this, I've been patient long enough. I have evidence of you receiving stolen goods. I have official records showing that you haven't purchased hardly anything through official channels. I have your signature for goods to the value of one hundred and thirty-one pounds, twelve shillings, that were never returned to stores. Enough evidence to remove your stripes, put you inside for three months and then drum you out of the service. You'll wish you'd bloody signed when I've finished with you. I've been too lenient, too soft, that's because I've been listening to your friends out there, but no more. When I leave Hemswell today you'll stay in detention for weeks until your case comes up. Hear me – weeks,' he shouted, totally out of control.

Ranting NCOs I'd been used to for years, their shouting had little effect on me. I could wrap myself up like a hedgehog, switch off, day dream, look but not hear. But my signature for one hundred and thirty-one pounds, twelve shillings. What on earth was he on about? He stopped for breath, so I jumped in.

'What signature, Sergeant?' I nervously asked.

A grin spread over his face. His dart had hit the target. He detected my nervousness. He strode to the files on the WAAF's desk, selected one, opened it and picked out a piece of paper. He returned to my table smiling, scenting success.

'Deny that's your signature, then, Corporal.' He thrust the paper at me. I couldn't believe my eyes. It was an official stores-book counterfoil. There was my unmistakable signature at the bottom. I read the words above. TO GOODS – FIVE DINGHYS, ONE HUNDRED BLANKETS (GREY) – TWO CARTONS OF TORCHES (20 per carton).

'Christ, Sergeant, they were taken to the Mablethorpe floods. That was nearly two years ago. You must know that.'

'That's your story, Corporal. If they did go there, you were responsible and didn't return them. They are missing from stores and I have your signature. Did you get a good price for the dinghys?' he leered.

I was fuming and had to control a strong desire to knock the smile off his leering face. He had my back to the wall and he knew it. The memory of those two days saving people rushed through my mind and the injustice of this last accusation cut deep into my senses. I felt like fighting and crying at the same time.

'The dinghys were tied to lamp posts in eight foot of water. We used rowboats for rescuing people. The grown-ups and children were soaked through by the time we got them to the lorry on the edge of the floods so we wrapped blankets around them. They were then driven off to rest centres. We didn't see the blankets again. We used some torches ourselves, eight of us. I don't know what happened to the rest. You've only got to ask the chaps who were with me, they'll tell you it's true. We were there for two days you know.'

'A pretty sight I'm sure, dinghys tied to lamp posts. That really is a new one to me, I thought I'd heard it all. Ask your friends you say – they were all probably in it with you.'

He had the upper hand and he was enjoying it. What else could he possible dig up? I was empty, sick to the stomach.

'The statement's still there. Do yourself a favour, you can't possible go against all this evidence.' He pushed the pen nearer. I pushed it away.

'No,' I said, 'Never.'

'You're an exasperating sod, you've had your chance – now I'll throw the book at you. Take him away – and make sure he's kept under lock and key,' he barked.

Back in the guardroom, hot, sweaty, depressed and dejected I overheard the snowdrop who had been present at the morning session recounting the story to his sergeant. I stood looking out of the barred window in the main office. The duty corporal sat at his desk by the door. It was another lovely summer day as I watched a cyclist pass in front of the admin. block. Airmen were coming and going in and out of the main entrance. I could hear the throaty roar of the Lincoln bomber engine being revved-up over by the hangars. If only Chiefy Blackmore had been there, he'd sort something out, I was sure.

There was nothing I could do. All the talking had been done. The wait would be long. Would it be weeks or months before my case came up? Where would they put me, surely I wouldn't be kept at Hemswell all that time? What about Rosa, I'd have to write and tell her as she'd be looking for a letter. If I didn't tell her where I was she'd notice the English postmark and wonder what was going on.

'Corporal – sorry about this but you're confined to your cell until I get some clarification on your case and status,' said the sergeant of the guard.

I didn't argue. I walked into cell one, lay full-length on the bed and the door clanged to. The key turned. Sod the world, sod everybody.

They took me to lunch under double escort. I had changed back to my old self of a year ago. I was ready to fight the world, authority or anybody who upset me. I neither wanted to talk to nor to look at anyone. I was in between nowhere, not knowing what the present or the future held. A victim of life maybe but ready to fight anything that they could dream up for me.

I ate little and talked not at all. My young escorts wisely left me to my thoughts. Back in my cell I stared hard at the lightbulb, trying to think, but my brain had given up, it was blank. I lay in a void.

The key grated in the door. I looked at my watch. Three o'clock. I must have lain there for over an hour with not a single thought.

'This way, Corporal, you're wanted,' said the duty snowdrop.

I got up off the bed. Like a faithful dog I followed the MP without question. We passed through the outer office and stepped into the raised entrance porch.

'In there, Corp,' he said, pointing at the door of the sergeant of the guard's office, I entered.

'Sit down, Corporal, sit down.'

I couldn't believe it. Slimy face himself, I thought I'd seen the last of him.

The office was ten feet by eight feet with a small desk, a filing cabinet, and four chairs. There was a family portrait on the wall of the sergeant of the guard, in uniform, with his arms round a woman, and a beautiful blonde-headed girl of about ten years old. My shortarse inquisitor sat behind the desk. He beckoned to me to be seated in front of him. We were the only two present.

'You disturb me, Corporal, you really do,' he said softly. 'Don't think I enjoy my job, I don't, but someone has to do it. I don't like ruining people's lives, it gives me no satisfaction. I was about to leave but I thought – why not a quiet chat, off the record? No note-taking, no witnesses, just you and me. You see, all I want to do is clear this case up. Now, if I can do that with the minimum effect to your career, then we both end up winners – don't you agree?' he said, turning on the best smile he could muster.

I could feel a glimmer of hope coming through my depression. The snake-charmer sergeant had a doped cobra swaying in front of him. Was he going to throw me a lifeline? Was there a way back? The charmer held the snake with his eyes.

'Yes, Sergeant.' Sway, sway.

'Gooood, good. When I put in my report I also put forward my recommendations. They always take note of my recommendations. Now,' he said, eyes gleaming not two feet from my nose, 'I can recommend that you keep your stripes. I can give good grounds for leniency, such as your activities in helping keep up the morale at Hemswell, the running a dance band, organizing camp galas, representing the RAF at athletics. All these things will help if I put them in my report. I can almost guarantee a reprimand will be all that will happen. You'll keep your rank and life will go on as before. Now, I can't be fairer than that, can I?'

We sat there like two conspirators, not two feet apart, the sergeant leaning across the desk with his piggy eyes looking up at me, oozing me to agree.

'That's very good of you, Sergeant, thank you very much,' I said, not believing my own ears.

'Good man, that's settled then; sign here and I'll be off,' he said, as he drew the paper quickly from his pocket and unscrewed his pen.

'Oh Christ, not that again; I'm not signing and that's it.'

He stood up slowly and leaned across the desk. I could feel hatred burning his body. His nose was nearly touching mine, and his face was twisted into a grotesque mask of detestation.

'You bastard, Freeman – you pigheaded bastard,' and he knocked the desk aside with his thighs as he scrambled for the door.

'Corporal of the guard – he's all yours.'

Back in my cell I lay trembling. That was it, he wouldn't be back. I'd have to wait until Monday at the earliest to find out my fate.

I was totally and utterly disillusioned with the RAF. They had changed my whole world, turned it upside down. The injustice of it all was beyond belief. Sure, I'd brought a lot of it on myself in the early years, but why? Because I was sticking up for myself, refusing to be treated like shit, a second-class, brainless piece of shit with no opinions.

Sure the forces needed discipline, but where does whitewashing coal and 'anything else that doesn't move' come in? The AOC's inspection may be important but gallons of whitewash on everything. He knows, the CO knows, authority knows the soul-destroying bullshit that goes on everywhere, but do they care? Of course not. Got to get the OBE, you know.

The CO must have known about the separate entrances in the medical centre: 'Bloody good idea, Forbe-Jones,' I expect he said.

Airmen play squash? – never, old chap, put 'em in the boxing ring, that's all they're good for.

Regulation haircut for rankers, make them look like convicts, that will put them in their place.

Now, being dragged in for something I knew nothing about, an inquiry where you can't ask questions, a trial where you're denied a defence. What happens next time something goes wrong – would they drag me in again?

As long as I was in the RAF I was vulnerable, a marked man. As long as I was in the RAF I wasn't entitled to an opinion. As long as I was in the RAF I would never be respected as an intelligent human being. Sod it then – I'd get out of the RAF.

I spent another depressing night in cell one. Next morning, Saturday, I was escorted to breakfast and totally resigned to my fate. My shell was moving like a zombie, all my emotions drawn within myself. The world seemed distant, everything an echo, I was functioning on automatic pilot.

Back in my cell after breakfast I was cleaning my shoes in a dream; it was almost nine o'clock.

'You're wanted in admin., duty officer's just rung,' said the snowdrop.

I was escorted to the admin. block and straight into an office. The duty officer looked up at me standing there to attention with a snowdrop at the side of me.

'Ah, Corporal Freeman,' he said, looking up with a boyish fresh-faced smile. 'They've finished with you now, you can be on your way, here's your travel warrants. Report back to your unit immediately.'

I stood looking at his hand proffering the documents. Had I heard right? Was it a trick? Was I dreaming?

'Your documents, Corporal,' he repeated, jabbing his hand forward again.

I took hold of the papers while still in shock.

'Back to Oldenburg, Sir?'

'Yes, that's what I said, man.'

'What about the inquiry, Sir?'

'Oh that's buttoned up. Sergeant Bullock left a memo with me for the CO. He saw me last night, just before he left with his team. He said he wouldn't require you any more but I thought well, you couldn't go off last night, what's one more night anyway, so I left it until this morning to tell you.'

I stared at the young pilot officer with fire in my eyes. What's one more night? he'd said. What's one more night?

'Are you all right, Corporal?' he asked uncomfortably. I came out of my stare.

'Yes, Sir. Will I hear any more, Sir, will there be any charges?'

He looked at me, shuffled through some papers on his desk and found the memo he was looking for.

'No, Corporal, you're in the clear – according to this, you shouldn't hear any more about it. Now, on your way and good luck.'

'Thank you, Sir, thank you for ...' I bit my tongue, saluted and left.

CHAPTER 24

'Up Yours'

I arrived back at Oldenburg on the Sunday night, almost one week, one weeklong nightmare behind me. I was too dispirited to think of going to Brentwood for a quick visit and I didn't want to explain my presence in the UK in this frame of mind. Far better to write to Rosa when I'd sorted my thoughts out.

There was plenty of time to think on the long journey back to Oldenburg and my plan of action was formed well before I got back to camp.

Before reporting to work on the Monday morning I went to the admin. centre and obtained and completed the necessary forms applying for a 'discharge by purchase'.

A discharge by purchase scheme had been brought in the previous year, 1953. One could apply for discharge, at a price, subject to certain criteria, such as overmanning in your rank or trade, changes in technology requirements for certain trades and occupations. It was purely a gamble and I believe it rested also on the recommendations from the unit. The forms I'd completed had sections for my wing commander and my CO to compete their remarks and recommendations.

The cost of discharge was worked out on the individual's remaining service, his trade, his rank and the cost of any special training he'd received.

Having completed the requisite forms I felt much better and returned to work hoping and praying I'd be successful. I wrote to Rosa and told her I was trying to buy myself out but I didn't explain why.

My Wingco sent for me on the Wednesday. He was a very understanding man but quite surprised to receive my application. I explained as fully as I could what had happened at the Hemswell inquiry and he listened intently.

'Nasty experience, I can see that,' he said sympathetically. 'But I think you're a little hasty. Why don't you put it all behind you? Forget it. Continue with your career. You'll be a technical sergeant next year.'

'I can't, Sir. I've thought it through and made up my mind.'

The Wingco spent time trying to get me to withdraw my application but eventually accepted that I intended to go through with it.

'Well, Corporal, if that's what you want I'll do my best to help, but you'll find authority and unfairness out there on Civvy Street. It's life, you know. What will you do if you do get released, and where do you think you'll end up?'

'I don't know, Sir, but if I ever get to a position where I can change a few things in the world I surely will.'

Three long weeks passed before I was given the news. Subject to payment of one hundred and fifty-six pounds, a lot of money in 1954, my application for discharge would be accepted. I was deliriously happy.

I received my orders to report to RAF Innsworth, Release Discharge Section, in Gloucestershire, where I was to hand in my kit and receive my discharge papers. I looked through the orders that the admin. sergeant handed me.

'Where's the travel warrants, Sarge?' I asked, as I stood happily in the admin. centre.

'Didn't they tell you? If you're discharged by purchase you have to find you own fare home from your unit to the release section. Just thank your lucky stars you're not in the Far East.'

I was shattered. The last indignity. I only had a few pounds between me and starvation, having sold my motorbike to raise my discharge money. I went back to my men who had put on a party for me the previous night and sold the only thing of value I had, my B flat cornet. The cornet my Father had brought for me a lifetime ago in Charing Cross Road. I was very sad about that.

I arrived at RAF Innsworth at midday on a cold and wet September day but the weather had no effect on my high spirits. This was the big day, the last day in the RAF.

'You can keep one complete set of clothing if you like, uniform, shirt, shoes and so on,' said the stores receiver. 'Some chaps like to go home in them. A fixed charge of six pounds, nineteen shillings is all it costs.'

'Not me, mate, I don't want any of it.'

I stripped off in the corner of the stores to the amazement of two other dischargees and handed in all my kit.

'Right, mate, here's your clearance papers; take them to the discharge officer in the admin. block.'

In the gathering gloom, and as a last frustration, the officer told the three of us to wait in the corridor. He eventually deigned to see us and, for the last time, I stood in front of a seated officer, this time in civvies, as he slowly checked my papers.

'Discharge by purchase, eh? Couldn't you stand the pace?'

Keep calm, keep calm, don't let him get up your nose.

'Well?' he said, waiting for an answer.

What the hell's it got to do with you? I thought, clenching my fists.

'Just got married, Sir,' I managed to say.

'Hm,' he sneered.

I stood there waiting while he read the papers and fiddled uninterestedly.

'This is your service certificate and discharge book. Your discharge is effective from 0800 hours tomorrow. There's a hut kept specially for people like you to sleep in. Hut sixteen, send the next one in.'

Another night in the RAF – that was the last thing I expected. I found hut sixteen and my two colleagues soon joined me.

'Never mind, mate, one more night's sod all, let's go and have a few jars in the NAAFI.'

We sat chatting and joking for a couple of hours and although they seemed content to play the thing out to its full course my feet were itching to get on the move. My mind was excited and active, I knew I couldn't stay there another night. I had been expecting to go that day and I bloody well would.

'I'm off, fellas,' I said, standing up.

'Give over, mate, there's more than half an hour of good drinking time left yet.'

'Off home, mate, not one more bloody minute in the RAF for me. Good luck in Civvy Street.'

I left them with gaping mouths and I strode out of the NAAFI, picked up my suitcase from the hut and made my way round the camp roads towards the entrance.

Feeling lightheaded with booze and the excitement of the moment, I had the urge to walk on the white line down the middle of the road, the white line to freedom. Pale moonlight threw à grey, unearthly glow over the buildings on either side of the road as I turned the bend. There was the guardroom, lights blazing, forty yards ahead, forty yards to freedom.

My pace quickened as I followed the white line, chest heaving with excitement. As I came nearer the dreaded red and white barrier I noticed the sergeant of the guard standing on the plinth of the guardroom entrance, light above his head, taking the night air. He was standing at ease, hands behind his back and, as I approached, I noticed he raised his weight onto his toes drawing in his breath. Then his heels came down again as he exhaled. The shiny black peak of his cap was moulded to his forehead and half an eye gleamed out either side of it. He relaxed there, surveying the still night; how many times have I seen that picture, I thought.

I strode out of the gloom, firmly stuck on my white line. I could feel his eyes latch on to me in bewilderment. Straight by him I went, not ten feet away, while his brain wrestled with the puzzle. I lifted the barrier pole with my left hand, suitcase in my right, and went under.

'Who told you to lift that barrier?' His voice cracked the still night air like a rifle shot.

I paused, barrier at the slant, held by my left hand that formed an arch. I turned my head and looked back through the arch. He'd stepped off the plinth and was glaring towards me. Two faces appeared at the barred window looking out at me.

'Oles, Sergeant,' I replied quietly, with a nervous, frightened inflection in my voice as my chest pained with excitement.

'Oles who?' came back the quick reply.

I let the barrier go and it clanged down on its metal support.

'ARSE OLES SERGEANT, ARSEHOLES,' and my body erupted into uncontrollable laughter.

I turned my back to the barrier, threw my head back and shouted for all the stars to hear: 'Arseholes, Arseholes,' as I laughed my way into Civvy Street.